FLAME
OF
SEVENWATERS

FLAME
OF
SEVENWATERS

JULIET MARILLIER

A ROC BOOK

ROC
Published by New American Library, a division of
Penguin Group (USA) Inc., 375 Hudson Street,
New York, New York 10014, USA
Penguin Group (Canada), 90 Eglinton Avenue East, Suite 700, Toronto,
Ontario M4P 2Y3, Canada (a division of Pearson Penguin Canada Inc.)
Penguin Books Ltd., 80 Strand, London WC2R 0RL, England
Penguin Ireland, 25 St. Stephen's Green, Dublin 2,
Ireland (a division of Penguin Books Ltd.)
Penguin Group (Australia), 250 Camberwell Road, Camberwell, Victoria 3124,
Australia (a division of Pearson Australia Group Pty. Ltd.)
Penguin Books India Pvt. Ltd., 11 Community Centre, Panchsheel Park,
New Delhi - 110 017, India
Penguin Group (NZ), 67 Apollo Drive, Rosedale, Auckland 0632,
New Zealand (a division of Pearson New Zealand Ltd.)
Penguin Books (South Africa) (Pty.) Ltd., 24 Sturdee Avenue,
Rosebank, Johannesburg 2196, South Africa

Penguin Books Ltd., Registered Offices:
80 Strand, London WC2R 0RL, England

Published by Roc, an imprint of New American Library, a division of
Penguin Group (USA) Inc. Previously published in a Pan Macmillan Australia edition.

First Roc Printing, November 2012
10 9 8 7 6 5 4 3 2 1

RoC REGISTERED TRADEMARK—MARCA REGISTRADA

LIBRARY OF CONGRESS CATALOGING-IN-PUBLICATION DATA:
Marillier, Juliet.
Flame of Sevenwaters/Juliet Marillier.
p.   cm.
ISBN 978-0-451-46480-4
I. Title.
PR9619.3.M26755F57   2012
823'.912—dc23   2012021394

Set in Palatino

Printed in the United States of America

PUBLISHER'S NOTE

This is a work of fiction. Names, characters, places, and incidents either are the product of the
author's imagination or are used fictitiously, and any resemblance to actual persons, living or
dead, business establishments, events, or locales is entirely coincidental.

The publisher does not have any control over and does not assume any responsibility for
author or third-party Web sites or their content.

For my sister, Jennifer,
who opens hearth and heart to dogs in trouble

ACKNOWLEDGMENTS

Thanks to my daughter, Elly, for invaluable help with plot wrangling. Fiona Leonard answered my equine questions and Glyn Marillier my maritime questions, though any errors are mine. The canine parts of the book are largely based on personal experience. A special thank-you to rescue dog Harry, who worked his way through three levels of obedience training while I was writing this book.

My editors, Brianne Tunnicliffe at Pan Macmillan and Anne Sowards at Roc, were at every turn both professional and supportive, as were Libby Turner, Claire Craig, and Julia Stiles. My agent, Russell Galen, is an ongoing source of wise advice.

CHARACTER LIST

Sean		chieftain of Sevenwaters in Ulster
Aisling	(*ash*-ling)	his wife
Liadan	(*lee*-a-dan)	Sean's sister, lady of Harrowfield in Cumbria
Bran		Liadan's husband, master of Harrowfield
Deirdre	(*dair*-dreh)	second daughter of Sean and Aisling, Clodagh's twin
Illann		Deirdre's husband, chieftain of a territory bordering Sean's (southern Uí Néill)
Emer and Oisin	(*eh*-ver and u-sheen)	children of Deirdre and Illann
Maeve	(mehv)	fourth daughter of Sean and Aisling, foster daughter to Bran and Liadan
Finbar		son of Sean and Aisling
Clodagh	(*klo*-da)	third daughter of Sean and Aisling, Deirdre's twin
Cathal	(ko-hal)	son of Mac Dara; married to Clodagh
Firinne and Ronan	(*feer*-in-yeh and *roh*-nan)	twin children of Clodagh and Cathal

Conor		chief druid; uncle to Sean and Liadan
Ciarán	(*keer*-aun)	senior druid; half uncle to Sean and Liadan
Luachan	(*loo*-a-khan)	a young druid; Finbar's tutor
Rhian	(*ree*-an)	Maeve's personal maid
Garalt		stable master at Harrowfield
Emrys	(*em*-riss)	head groom at Harrowfield
Donal		groom at Harrowfield
Doran		Sean's senior man-at-arms
Nuala	(*noo*-a-la)	his wife—cook at Sevenwaters
Eithne	(*eh*-nyeh)	Aisling's personal maid
Orlagh	(*or*-la)	serving woman at Sevenwaters
Cerball	(*car*-ull)	man-at-arms
Rhodri		man-at-arms
Duald		stable master at Sevenwaters
Cruinn		chieftain of Tirconnell (northern Ui Neill)
Tiernan	(*teer*-nan)	his elder son
Artagan	(*art*-a-gan)	his younger son
Daigh	(rhymes with *sky*)	Tiernan's friend
Niall		man-at-arms
Mac Dara		prince of the Fair Folk at Sevenwaters; Cathal's father
Caisin	(ka-*sheen*)	a lady of the Fair Folk (called "Caisin Silverhair")
Fiamain	(fia-vin)	sister of Caisin
Dioman	(*dee*-maun)	brother of Caisin
Breasal	(bras-al)	Caisin's councilor
Fraochan	(*freh*-khan)	Mac Dara's councilor
Labhraidh	(*low*-ri)	a man of the Fair Folk
Sleibhin	(*sle*-vin)	a man of the Fair Folk
Mochta	(*mukh*-ta)	a very big man of the Fair Folk
Bounder		Maeve's beloved dog from childhood, now deceased

Swift		a fine yearling
Blaze		Luachan's mare
Broccan and Teafa		Sean's wolfhounds
Bear and Badger		two black dogs
Cú Chulainn	(koo *hoo*-lan)	a legendary hero
Maelan	(*meh*-laun)	character in Ciarán's story
Baine	(*baw*-nyeh)	character in Ciarán's story
Tuatha Dé Danann	(*too*-a-ha deh *donn*-an) or (*too*-a-ha deh)	The Fair Folk, legendary dwellers in Erin. "People of the goddess Danu"
Uí Néill	(ee *nay*-ill)	an influential clan in Irish history (O'Neill)

Note: the fada or Irish accent has been omitted from some of the names, both on this list and in the text of the book, for purposes of simplicity.

FLAME
OF
SEVENWATERS

CHAPTER 1

My aunt taught me to hold my head high, even when people stared. My uncle taught me to defend myself. Between them they made sure I learned courage. But I could not be brave about going home.

I was ten when the accident happened: young to be sent away from home and family. My parents must have believed Aunt Liadan could achieve the impossible. True, if any healer could have cured me, she was probably the one to do it. But my hands were beyond fixing. Although she never said so, I think my aunt expected to keep me at Harrowfield only until I had learned to live with my injuries. But days grew into seasons, and seasons into years, and whenever the suggestion was made that perhaps I might return to Erin, I found a reason for saying no.

At Harrowfield the household knew me as I was, not as I had been before. They had learned quickly that I hated fuss. People let me do what I could for myself. Nobody rushed to snatch things away when I was clumsy. Nobody treated me as if I had lost my wits along with the use of my fingers. They did not stare when I chose to walk about with the scar on my head uncovered. All the

1

same, I did not need to travel far from the safe haven of my uncle's estate to know that in the eyes of the outside world I was a freak.

Back home at Sevenwaters, the world changed without me. A little brother was born. My sisters married, had children, moved away. Family joys and tragedies unfolded. I would hear about them many moons later, in the occasional letters that reached us in Britain. I could not write back. I sent words of love, penned for me by the Harrowfield scribe.

If I could have slipped back into my childhood home without a ripple, I would have done it long ago. When I'd been under her care two years, Aunt Liadan had spoken to me frankly about my situation. My hands had healed as well as they ever would—there could be no further improvement. I'd always need someone to help me. I'd never hold a knife or spoon with my fingers. I'd never use a spinning wheel or a needle. I'd never be able to comb my own hair or fasten the back of my gown. Swaddling a baby, holding a child's hand, those simple things would be forever beyond me. My aunt set it out with kindness and honesty. She did not insult me by couching the hard truth in gentle half-lies. In her embrace, I allowed myself to weep. When I was done, I dried my tears and vowed not to weep again. I was twelve years old.

The next morning I made two lists in my mind. First, the things I might as well forget about. Marriage. Children. Plying a craft of some kind. Managing a household, whether that of a chieftain like my father or a more modest establishment. The list was long.

Next, the things that were possible in my future. I struggled with this, wishing I were a different kind of girl. It was a shame my sister Sibeal was the one with a spiritual vocation, for if ever there was a future suited to a person in my circumstances, it surely lay among the sisters of a Christian nunnery such as St. Margaret's, situated less than a morning's walk from Harrowfield. I considered this for some time, liking the notion of a sanctuary where folk could not turn that special look on me, the look that mingled pity, horror and fascination. I saw that look on the faces of strangers passing on the road. I saw it in the eyes of visitors to my uncle's hall, though they concealed it quickly when they learned who I was. And I did like quiet. But try as I might, I could not find much of a contemplative streak in myself, nor a wish to spend my days in prayer to a deity I was not quite sure I believed in. Besides, nuns worked hard. The sisters at St. Margaret's were up at dawn gardening or cooking or performing the hundred and one tasks that kept their establishment going. What use would I be with that?

I could read. We sisters had been fortunate to have parents who saw the value of such a skill for girls, and when I came to Harrowfield, Uncle Bran's scribe continued my lessons. But I could not write—I would never perform a scribe's duties myself. I could sing, but did not like to do so in public. I knew plenty about herbs and healing, since I spent a great deal of my time watching Aunt Liadan at work in her garden and stillroom, or observing as she patched up various injuries. But my knowledge was all theory, no practice. Where Liadan's fingers were deft and strong, apt for chopping and grinding, for gentle laying on of poultices or decisive cutting away of diseased flesh, mine were the claws of a dead thing, stiff and immobile.

My lists had not been encouraging. It was hard to think of any life I might have in which I would not be a burden to someone. Father was chieftain of Sevenwaters, a leader with a broad domain to oversee and a number of powerful and volatile neighbors to deal with. Our family lands were located in a particularly strategic spot, right between the holdings of rival branches of the Uí Néill clan. My uncle and foster father, Bran, was always prepared to discuss such matters with me. Since I could not exercise my hands in spinning, weaving and sewing, or in baking and brewing, I made sure I exercised my mind instead.

I had seen at the age of twelve that my presence back home would be of little value to my parents. Nothing had occurred since then to change my opinion. Mother would be managing the household perfectly, as she always had. A daughter who could contribute only advice, not practical help, would hardly be an asset. I could not be offered as wife to a chieftain Father wanted as an ally. Who would want me? I would not even be able to eat at the family table when visitors were present. I would be a hindrance, an embarrassment.

I had known this ever since I learned my hands would get no better. But, where my return home was concerned, it was more convenient excuse than valid reason. The fact was, I was afraid to go back. Deep down inside Courageous Maeve, the young woman convinced by her loving aunt and uncle that she was as strong as any warrior, there cowered another Maeve, a child of long ago. Ten years old, stumbling into the smoky darkness of the fire that had broken out in an annex at Sevenwaters. Bounder was inside; I could hear him whining, frightened, wanting me. Half-blinded by the smoke, I tripped, reached out to steady myself and laid my hands on an iron door bolt, hot from the fire. Everything went dark for a while. They told me, later, that my father had saved my life, risking the flames to find me and carry me out to the open air. When I came to, the flesh of my palms was burned to angry blisters. My face was marred. And my beloved dog was dead. Back in Erin, the ghosts of that night were waiting for me.

When I made my lists, I was a child. I hardly thought of the one skill I had that might shape the future for me. It came as naturally as breathing, and it was perhaps for that reason that I considered it nothing special. Years later, when the day finally came for me to face my fears, it was this skill that drew me home to Sevenwaters.

"Maeve, may I speak with you?"

Uncle Bran had come to stand by me at the dry-stone wall surrounding the horse yard. In the yard, Emrys was training Swift to a halter. Stable master Garalt was on the opposite side, eyes watchful. Emrys ran; the yearling moved with him, a vision of power and grace, like clouds before an easterly breeze or summer waves on the shore. His pale coat shimmered in the light; his feet were a dancer's. That we'd bred such a remarkable creature here at Harrowfield was a source of immense pride for Garalt and for every groom trusted to work with Swift. And for me. I was the one who had gentled Swift's dam through a difficult foaling, and it was I who had been called in, time after time, to calm and settle this magnificent young creature as he grew toward maturity. For Swift had his mother's temperament, all fire and pride, and that made him difficult to train. Sometimes it seemed to us that he would sooner die than submit to authority, however kindly that authority was imposed. Hence my presence today while Garalt and Emrys worked to convince Swift the halter was not an enemy to be fought off with all his considerable strength.

"Of course," I said with a smile, wondering what made Bran sound so serious. My uncle and I were friends; we did not stand on ceremony.

He was not quick to enlighten me, but stood by me watching as Swift tested Emrys's control, now seeming almost compliant, now fiercely resistant. There was a long way to go with him. Not that he'd ever be a riding horse; he'd be too valuable as a breeding stallion. But he must be trained to tolerate human touch, to submit to being haltered and led, to being rubbed down and checked for injuries, to having draughts administered, and all the other handling needed to keep him in robust health. Garalt and I had already discussed which mare Swift would be put to first, when he was mature enough, and what the chances were that he'd sire a foal that was his own equal.

"I'm sending him away," Bran said. "First as far as Sevenwaters, then on to Tirconnell, at your father's request. A gift for one of the Uí Néill chieftains. It will be partial restitution for an event that occurred on Sean's territory last spring, something they're calling the Disappearance. That"—he indicated the horse with a movement of his head—"is the kind of gift that would placate the most difficult of men."

I felt as if I had been dropped from a great height. For a while I had nothing to say. Bran's dogs had come with him and were jostling around my skirts, nosing into my hands, seeking attention I did not have in me to give right now. I cleared my throat, wondering whether what I felt was the onset of tears. "Have you told Garalt?" I managed.

"Not yet. I will when he and Emrys are done here. This decision will upset a lot of folk, Maeve. I didn't make it in haste. I received the message from your father some time ago. While I was considering it, further information came in through my own sources. This is necessary."

"When?" I asked. Garalt's seamed features were all concentration as he watched the yearling. I wasn't sure I could bear to witness the moment when he was told his pride and joy was being packed off across the sea, so far we would likely never hear whether Swift had sired any foals at all, let alone a charmer with quicksilver in its steps.

"Before the autumn gales set in." Bran turned his gaze from Swift to me. I thought he was about to express regret or sympathy, for both were in his steady gray eyes, but what he said was, "There's something further I want to put to you."

"Oh?" I could not imagine what was coming, unless he was about to ask me to break the bad news to Garalt for him.

"The most even-tempered of horses hates the motion of a boat. I don't need an expert to tell me what a risk it is to transport this particular creature over to Erin. Swift is going to need more than the attentions of a groom or two, even if they're as capable as Emrys. Liadan tells me Garalt's injured foot won't heal in time for him to travel with the horse. Would you be prepared to go?"

My jaw dropped.

"Only as far as Sevenwaters, of course. You'd take your maidservant with you. Your father can arrange for Swift to be safely conveyed on to Tirconnell."

When I did not answer—I was still trying to put the pieces together in my mind—my uncle added, "It's a great deal to ask; I know that. You have your reasons for not wanting to go back and I respect them. But this isn't a request that you return to live with your parents. I'm asking you to do a highly skilled job; a job nobody else can do. It's not so much for my sake as for your father's. He's in a difficult position, and this will help him. It's for the horse's sake, too. I know you're attached to the creature. With you there, we can be reasonably sure Swift will survive the trip without doing himself serious damage."

Emrys had brought the yearling to a halt. Garalt had limped over to speak to him and was standing beside Swift, one hand resting on the animal's neck. Swift stood still for now, but he was trembling. They'd lead him into the stables for a rub-down, and then, I supposed, Bran would break the news. What if I told my uncle the truth: that the thought of going home awoke the frightened child inside me? What if I refused to do it? Then Garalt would not even have the reassurance that Swift would travel safely. He would be as quick as I was to imagine the possibilities if a highly strung creature, taken away from everything familiar, were to be loaded into a boat and sent off across an expanse of unpredictable ocean.

"I have some questions," I told Bran. What sort of insult or injury required restitution beyond the means of a prominent Irish chieftain? What in the name of the gods was the Disappearance? "But you should tell Garalt now. I can't pretend to him that nothing's happened. Can we speak about this later?"

"Of course. So you will consider it?"

Through the gathering clouds of misgiving in my mind, I recognized his courtesy in making this a request, not an order. Bran and Liadan were my foster parents; they had authority over me. Bran could simply have told me I was going home. Instead he had shown respect, and I honored him for it even as I shrank from the task itself.

"I'll consider it, Uncle. You should tell Garalt that you've asked me to go with Swift; that will soften the blow." I drew a deep breath. "I'll come with you when you tell him," I made myself say.

My foster father offered me his heavily tattooed arm and I hooked mine through it. "Thank you, Maeve," Bran said. "You have a gift for imparting fortitude, and not only to creatures. Come then, let's do this."

After supper, I sat with my uncle and aunt in a little private chamber, and Bran gave me Father's letter to read. Much of it concerned matters my uncle had already discussed with me, and all of it was couched in careful language, for such missives, even when borne by the most trusted of messengers, could still fall into the wrong hands. In a time of unrest this might lead to the destruction of alliances and the breaking of treaties. My father wrote in part:

Of recent times there has been a marked increase in the activity of which we advised you some time ago: unexplained acts of violence against both people and property, instances of malevolent meddling, the circulation of strange rumors and tales. We have been plagued by events of this kind since before the time of Finbar's misadventure; it is easy enough to guess their source. You understand, as I do, that there is a possible solution to this difficulty, involving the return of a certain family member. This would involve immense risk. It seems a monstrous thing to ask of anyone. I seek your honest advice on the matter.

There have been accusations from all sides regarding the events to which I refer, and many of those are directed at me and mine. In the past it has generally been possible to make peace with the offended folk, in some cases through restitution in goods or silver.

However, an event has occurred that dwarfs the previous occurrences. It is a deeply troubling development. The offended party is Cruinn of Tirconnell. If he were able to prove the fault was mine—the circumstances suggests that it was—this could become a matter for the High King. I am, therefore, now reassessing my approach in consultation with my druid uncles.

You may already have heard what occurred through other sources, but in summary it was this: a troop of Cruinn's warriors, led by his two sons, was riding southward on the track that skirts the western margin of the Sevenwaters forest. We know they passed our northwestern guard tower about two hours after dawn, and that there were sixteen of them, all well-armed. My sentries reported this, and it tallies with what Cruinn told me later. Their purpose was to visit a chieftain of the southern Uí Néill, whose daughter was betrothed to Cruinn's elder son. My sentries commented that the riders seemed to be in high spirits.

What happened next, nobody knows. The sixteen men never arrived at their destination. They did not pass our southwestern guard tower or Illann's watch posts south of our border. They did not come home. Mes-

sengers were sent. A search was carried out. Once I was informed of their disappearance I set my own search in place, since outsiders do not easily find their way in the Sevenwaters forest. Nothing. No trace. It was as if those sixteen men had vanished into another world.

Long after, when all possibilities had been considered and discounted and Cruinn's accusations were becoming personal, the lost men began to reappear. One was found squeezed into a hollow tree, his knees against his chest, arms curled over his head as if to shield him from attack. Stone dead. A man taking pigs out to forage discovered another on the ground beneath a bees' nest, his body reddened and swollen by stings, his face smeared with honey. His body was still warm; he had lived for close to two moons from the day of the disappearance. The third man was discovered sprawled at the foot of a cliff with his neck broken. The clothes he had been wearing when he rode out were gone; instead, he was clad in strange garments made from feathers.

As time passed, twelve men were discovered within the Sevenwaters forest, each in a different place, each killed in a different way. None had been dead long. Someone was playing with us. Cruinn was beside himself with fury. This was happening on my land, under my watch. And his sons were still missing.

The last four have not yet been found. Perhaps our adversary has tired of his game. In any event, he has made his point. In doing so he has divided me most emphatically from those I had considered allies, both to the north and the south, for the chieftain whose daughter was to wed one of these men clamors against me as loudly as Cruinn does. What occurred has already become legend in these parts. Folk refer to it as the Disappearance.

Brother-in-law, I would welcome your counsel on this matter, and that of my sister. I will offer compensation to Cruinn, of course. Although this was not my doing, the bodies of these men were found on my land, and I must bear some responsibility. But what can compensate for the loss of a son? Of two sons? I understand Cruinn's grief more closely than he can ever realize. I will provide gifts; a fine stallion, perhaps, though I doubt there is any animal in my stable that would match Cruinn's standards—horses are his passion and he breeds the best in Tirconnell. That is one issue. The other is tackling the cause of this disaster, and that task is beyond you or me, I believe.

Let me know your opinions as soon as you can. Meanwhile, my re-
gards to Liadan and to my daughter. I hope Maeve is thriving. We miss
her.

Well, I missed them, too. But not so much that I wanted to go home.

"Does Father mean Mac Dara is responsible for what happened?" I asked. The letter lay on the table before me; the candle cast its flickering light across my father's strong black script. He had chosen not to have a scribe write this for him. I could understand his reasons for that. "Has Cathal's father continued to stir up trouble ever since he failed to get his son back?"

"That's what Sean means," Aunt Liadan said, "though he won't say so directly in writing. He's implying that Cathal could return to Sevenwaters and attempt to confront his father. That would be perilous. Mac Dara is a creature of the Otherworld, powerful and without scruples. If Cathal put himself in his father's path he'd be risking everything. When Mac Dara abducted your little brother and used him as bait to lure Cathal back under his influence, he cared nothing for who might be hurt along the way. And now Cathal and Clodagh have the children . . . It's surely too high a risk, even at this extreme." My aunt's neat features were grave, her lovely green eyes full of disquiet.

"Sean must take some action," Bran said. "If he allows this to continue he will lose all his allies. The whole of the north could be plunged into conflict once more. Sevenwaters has long been a stable domain amid the Uí Néill disputes, and its chieftain a peacemaker, despite the natural misgivings of other leaders concerning the Sevenwaters forest. Folk sense it is a haven for the uncanny, even if they have no proof of it. They know the tales of your family's past. But even in the most confronting of those, the Fair Folk have not taken this sort of malicious action toward humankind. Mac Dara's on a quest. A quest to bring his heir back to his own realm, if necessary by waging a campaign of fear throughout the entire region until Cathal feels obliged to return and challenge him. Sean's right; this must be stopped."

"Wouldn't my father disapprove of your sending me home at this particular time?"

Bran opened his mouth to reply, but Liadan answered for him. "He would be concerned for your safety, as indeed are we. I expect Sean is relieved that your sisters have left Sevenwaters now, since anyone in the family could be the target of Mac Dara's malice."

"Would Mac Dara attempt another abduction?" Bran asked.

"Perhaps what happened with little Finbar taught him how powerful the bonds of love can be as a means to manipulate humankind," said Liadan. "In the end that attempt failed, of course, but it did draw Cathal into the Otherworld for some time." She and Bran exchanged a glance. If there were anything to make me regret the married life I would never have, it was the little looks and touches and soft words between these two. Master and mistress of a grand estate they might be, but in private they often reminded me of a pair of young lovers, constantly surprised and delighted by each other.

"We don't underestimate the danger you'll be facing if you choose to undertake this journey, Maeve," Bran said. "It is real enough. But there are dangers everywhere in the world, even here at Harrowfield."

"And there are opportunities everywhere," put in my aunt. "This would certainly be challenging for you, and not only because of Mac Dara. The decision is entirely yours. But if you plan to face this particular difficulty at some point, now seems a good time to do so. Swift must travel; you're the only one who can keep him safe on the journey."

I cleared my throat. "Once I reach Sevenwaters they will expect me to stay there," I said. "Mother and Father. When they sent me here, it wasn't meant to be forever."

Bran regarded me levelly. "True, Maeve. And once you reach home, it will be Sean and Aisling who make the decisions about your future."

"But don't forget," Liadan said, "that your father has seen several of his daughters follow paths of their own choosing. It's fortunate that Deirdre made such a strategic marriage; she made up for the rest of you girls." Her smile was wry. "We would send a letter with you, letting your parents know that you were welcome to return to us and make your permanent home here, if that was what you preferred. Whether Sean chose to overrule your wishes would be up to him, of course. But, Maeve"—my aunt's tone softened—"I am sure he and your mother really miss you. Aisling must be quite lonely with all your sisters gone, even Eilis. She would be happy to have you back home."

Briefly, I imagined myself as the unwed daughter of Sevenwaters, growing gradually older and sourer as I played the role of companion to my aging parents, while remaining incapable of setting a hand to any useful work around the house. I did not much care for that picture. *Who's that?* a visitor to the house would ask, seeing my drooping figure on the stairs. *Her? That's the fourth daughter, the one who never married. A cripple; terribly burned. Can't do a thing for herself.* I wondered whether Father would let me help in the stables.

"I can't refuse to go," I said, feeling a sensation like a cold stone in my belly. "It's enough of a blow for Garalt that Swift's being sent away."

There was a little silence. I watched the candlelight playing across the curiously patterned features of my uncle and the vivid, watchful ones of my aunt.

"But I know that's not a good enough reason to say yes," I said, talking more to myself than to them. "I will tell you the truth. This scares me more than anything has done since . . . since those days after I was hurt, before I came to Harrowfield. The moment I step inside the borders of Sevenwaters it will all come back, not just for me, but for everyone who knew me then. And I hate that. I hate pity. I hate people being sorry for me. I hate them saying what happened wasn't fair and calling me 'that poor girl.' This is the life I've got; there's no changing it. I'd rather just get on with it. Going home feels like going backward." And when neither of them said a word, I added, "It sounds selfish, I suppose. They are my parents. I imagine they do miss me. And I would like to meet little Finbar."

Liadan smiled. "Not so little anymore. He'll be seven years old by now. Close to the same age Sibeal was when you last saw her. And now she's married and living far away in the south. It is a long time, my dear."

"Ask yourself," said Bran quietly, "which is the braver choice."

There were no excuses left. I drew in a deep breath and let it out again. "I know what I have to do, Uncle Bran. And I will do it. After tonight, I'll set my feet forward and hold my head high the way I always do. You've taught me well. You've been good examples to me, the two of you. I can't imagine you ever being afraid of anything."

Bran gave a crooked smile. "Everyone is afraid of something. Know your fears and you're a step further away from letting them rule you. But you're right—on the field of battle a brave face will help you stand strong. If you put on the semblance of courage, courage itself is easier to find."

Rhian was packing for our journey. She had already set out what she thought I would need, and now held up each garment in turn for my approval before placing it on the length of linen she had spread on my bedchamber floor, ready to make a bundle. The quick turning of her head, the look of bright inquiry in her eyes reminded me of a little bird of some kind, perhaps a sparrow. Her slight stature and cloud of wispy brown hair emphasized the likeness. Her hands were deft and sure.

It was fortunate that my maid and helper spoke fluent Irish—it would make the journey easier for her. Rhian's mother had been an Ulster girl. When Rhian's father, a crewman on a trading vessel, had chosen to leave the sea and work the land, the family had settled in his home region of Cumbria, in the village that lay close to Harrowfield. This would be Rhian's first visit to her mother's homeland. She was somewhat nervous about the voyage, as the daughter of a seafaring man might well be after years of witnessing her mother's anxiety. Concerning Sevenwaters itself she had no fears, only endless questions.

"What are druids like?" she asked me as she spread out a gown for folding. It was hard to know how much to pack, since I had no idea how long I would be staying at Sevenwaters. A turning of the moon—just long enough, I judged, not to seem an insult to my parents—or the rest of my life? "Didn't you say some of your kinsmen belong to that brotherhood?" Rhian went on. "Do they have magical powers?"

"Not that blue gown, Rhian. I don't suppose I'll be attending any grand banquets or suchlike. Keep it to plain, practical clothes. One good outfit for company, a reasonable supply of shifts and stockings, a couple of comfortable skirts and tunics for outdoors— that should be all I'll need. I daresay my sisters will have left a few things behind that I can borrow if I must. We don't want to be weighed down with bags." She would be the one carrying them, and she was a tiny little thing.

"Isn't one of your sisters a druid?" she asked, not waiting for a reply to her earlier questions. In private, with just the two of us, she did not use "my lady" but called me by my name. Rhian was my hands, and had been since soon after I first came to Harrowfield. Brows had been raised at the time, I was later told. There was I, ten years old and severely injured, and the maid Aunt Liadan chose for me was less than a year my senior, a little girl herself. My aunt had been wise. Rhian and I had finished our growing up together. My handmaid had helped me in more ways than anyone understood. She was closer to me than the sisters I had not seen for so long. They felt like characters in a story, and never more so than when Rhian asked me about them.

"Sibeal, yes. We all thought she was destined for a spiritual life, and she has one, but not at Sevenwaters. She lives in the south now, and she's married, which was a big surprise. The druids there are of a different kind. They work hard out in the community, teaching and healing. They don't sound much like the druids of Sevenwaters, whom I remember as quite solemn and mysterious. You may meet my father's uncles when we get there. Uncle Conor's very old now. He is chief druid. I don't know much about Uncle Ciarán. We saw far less of him. They live in the forest. They come out to perform the seasonal rituals, as well as handfastings and burial rites."

"It sounds very different," Rhian said, rolling up a pair of stockings.

It was; quite how much so, I could not adequately convey to her. While my father's household might on first acquaintance seem like that of any regional chieftain, the forest around it was no ordinary forest, and many parts of the family story were hard for outsiders to come to terms with. Some of it Rhian already knew, for the two of us were in the habit of telling tales before we went to sleep. But I had no way of conveying to her how vastly different Sevenwaters was from the nominally Christian household of Harrowfield. It was different even from the rest of Erin. In my homeland the old faith was dwindling, with few chieftains sanctioning the open practice of its rites.

"In some ways, druids are like Christian monks or nuns," I said, wondering how much of the Sevenwaters I remembered from my childhood was still there. It might all be changed now. The family would certainly be different, with my sisters away and only young Finbar left. "But their church is out of doors, under the trees. The rituals mark the turning points of the year. I remember . . ." I fell silent, an image in my mind of my cousin Fainne with a lighted torch, helping Uncle Conor rekindle the hearth fires. "It doesn't matter," I said.

Rhian gave me a swift glance but held her silence. She could read me better than anyone.

"Druids are remarkable storytellers," I said, banishing the fire image. "Sibeal always had a talent for that, even as a small child, and she seemed to know what people were thinking without being told. There are skilled healers among them. Generally they're quiet and wise and perhaps a bit remote. Uncle Conor is rather different. He used to visit us quite often, to advise Father."

There was a silence; then Rhian said, "Maeve?"

"Mm?"

"Mother has tales about the Fair Folk, but she makes them sound like something from ancient times, not quite real. When you talk about the Fair Folk and those other strange beings, it sounds as if they're right out there in the forest, only a short walk from your parents' home."

I had not told her what I knew about the Disappearance. Now did not seem a good time for that. "I've never seen any of the Fair Folk," I said. "But Sibeal used to see them when she was little. And you know the story about my baby brother being abducted. Cathal, who married my sister Clodagh, is the son of a fey prince. Clodagh and Cathal have both been to the Otherworld. You remember what I told you about their rescuing Finbar and taking the little twig and leaf baby back to its mother."

"So that really is true, all of it?" Rhian's hands had stilled halfway through folding a kerchief.

"Did you think I was making it up?"

A blush suffused her cheeks. "I thought you might be adding parts to it to make a better story."

"There was no need to add anything; it's a startling enough tale as it is. As for how much is true, I believe it all is, but I can't be sure, since it happened after I left Sevenwaters and I heard it secondhand. My family has many stories of that kind. You asked about magic. We could encounter it, I suppose, but it's far more likely that we won't. A lot of the time Sevenwaters is an ordinary household like this one. There may be uncanny folk out in the forest, but people still do all the ordinary things: raising stock and growing crops, cooking and washing and tending to children." I couldn't tell her about Father's letter and Mac Dara and the Disappearance. She might refuse to come then, and how would I manage without her?

As soon as this thought occurred to me, I felt how selfish it was. Rhian should not have to come with me if she didn't want to. She wasn't just my maid, she was my friend. I owed her the truth.

"The Fair Folk aren't always benign," I said. "One or two of them are dangerous—like Mac Dara, the one who stole my brother. They say he's still there, in the Otherworld part of Sevenwaters. And . . . well, it seems as if he's still making mischief." Mischief was a most inadequate word for the apparent slaughter of twelve innocent men, some of them in the cruelest fashion. "Stirring up trouble for my father, because Mac Dara failed to lure Cathal back to the Otherworld. Some men were killed; not my father's, but the sons of another chieftain and their party of men-at-arms." Rhian was listening with such fascination that she had completely forgotten the packing. She knelt stock-still watching me. "That was only a few moons ago, Rhian. I thought I should tell you, in case you decide you don't want to come with me."

"Not come?" The rapt expression was replaced by one of horror. "Not go to Sevenwaters? Of course I want to come!" After a moment she added, "Besides, how would you manage without me?"

I grimaced. "Someday you'll want to marry and have a family of your own. I can't expect to have you with me forever. It's not much of a life for you, being my shadow day and night."

Rhian grinned. "If the fellows around here are the best I get to meet, I might be still unwed when the two of us are old women," she said. "Now, should I pack another pair of shoes?"

CHAPTER 2

e set sail from a sheltered bay half a day's ride from Harrowfield. The boat was a sturdy cargo vessel, not large, but fitted out for the transport of horses; the crew did not seem unduly alarmed by Swift's rolling eyes and twitching tail. We'd stayed a few nights at a local farm, waiting for the right conditions, for the boat's master wanted to make the trip across to Erin in a single day. That could only be done with calm seas and a favorable wind, and the day would be a long one indeed, but nobody wanted to unload and reload our precious cargo on an island mid-voyage, nor was the master prepared to lengthen the trip by trailing a sea anchor overnight.

The boat was beached and a ramp laid from the pebbly shore up and over the side. The vessel had raised deck areas fore and aft, with long oars to maneuver her in and out from her mooring. In the open hold between these decks was a pair of horse stalls, solid timber with a system of ropes to secure the animals.

We blindfolded Swift; we'd never have gotten him up the ramp otherwise. Emrys led him; I walked beside him, my hand on his neck. I talked him up step by step, feeling like a liar as I reassured him with visions of green fields. When he trembled and froze half-way up the ramp, I whispered in his ear, stroking him gently, until he took another step forward and another.

The crew were patient; they knew horses. Eventually we had Swift in the hold and in a stall, with a contraption of canvas and ropes holding him securely in place. Emrys had bandaged his legs, fearing he might otherwise hurt himself by kicking out in the close confines of the stall. Once he was settled, the crew launched the boat with an efficiency born of long practice, and we were on our way.

We were at sea from soon after dawn until close to nightfall. Rhian was sick. I was so busy with Swift that I had no time to consider how dizzy and wretched I felt. I hadn't a spare moment to think about Sevenwaters or being afraid or how small Uncle Bran and Aunt Liadan and my cousins had looked on the shore, waving good-bye. Emrys and Donal shoveled dung and brought water and hay. The crew did their job, fastening and unfastening ropes, adjusting the sail, from time to time exchanging unintelligible shouts. I stood by Swift's head, soothing him, talking to him, singing him through the long, nightmare journey as he traveled farther and farther away from everything familiar. "Green meadow. Clear water. Kind hands and quiet."

We reached the shore of Erin in fast-fading light. I had hoped that Swift's exhaustion might mean we would get him off the boat more easily, but he was beyond frightened. Still blindfolded, he made a wild surge for freedom the moment we got him out of the stall. The grooms managed to hold him.

At the top of the ramp he shied, whickering, and almost knocked me over. It took some time to get him down. When his feet finally touched solid ground I felt myself let out a long sigh, as if I had been holding my breath all the way from the far shore.

While the crew unloaded our baggage, Emrys walked Swift on the shore to calm him. Two of Uncle Bran's men-at-arms had come with us as an escort. There was a settlement nearby with an inn where we could be accommodated for the night. We reached the place to find several of Father's men-at-arms waiting for us, along with one of the Sevenwaters grooms. This was unsurprising. Father's special bond with Aunt Liadan, his twin, allowed them to communicate mind to mind over distance: she had let him know we were coming.

The men from Sevenwaters did not look askance at me; they had been warned, I supposed. Their leader introduced himself as Cerball. "Lord Sean said to tell you, my lady, that he regrets not being here in person to welcome you. There's been a death in the family, and there were various arrangements to make."

"A death?"

"Lord Sean's uncle, Master Conor, the chief druid. Passed away only yesterday. A sad loss."

"Yes, it is." I meant it. I remembered Uncle Conor as a wise, kindly old man, always ready to spend time talking to us children. He had told very fine stories. I was sad that I would not see him again.

"Lord Sean suggested you might wish to spend two nights at the inn, since you'll be weary from the trip over the water," Cerball said.

It would give Swift time to settle before we rode on. And it would mean I did not have to face my family quite so soon. I opened my mouth to say yes, and heard Uncle Bran's voice in my mind: *Best face your fears straightaway; putting things off only makes them harder.* I'd had ten years of putting this off. "If Swift is calm in the morning, we may as well go straight on," I said.

Thanks to the presence of Irish grooms at Harrowfield over the years, Emrys knew enough of the language to make himself understood. He offered to sleep in Swift's temporary stable; the yearling was too valuable to be left unguarded in such a place overnight. I helped settle Swift, stroking him in the way he was accustomed to and whispering in his ear. "I want to run away, too. I want to cast off the ropes and run wild in the woods, leap into the sea and swim away, anything so I need not go home tomorrow."

I stayed in the stables so long that Rhian came out to look for me. When we walked through the communal dining chamber people peered at me and spoke behind their hands. I was too

21

weary to stare them down. I asked Rhian to fetch some food and retreated to the sleeping quarters we'd been given. My status as a chieftain's daughter had earned us a small chamber to ourselves. We ate and slept. We woke next day to find our escort preparing for departure. Emrys had judged Swift none the worse for wear, and well able to move on without further rest. The men from Sevenwaters had brought riding horses for us, along with a pack animal for our bags, such as they were. After a hasty breakfast we were on our way.

Riding, for me, meant sitting on a horse behind Rhian with my arms around her waist. I could maintain a reasonable purchase this way provided the road held no sudden surprises. We'd had plenty of practice over the years, mostly on an amiable old mare that had once been Aunt Liadan's riding horse. A broad-backed, quiet gelding was led forward now for my maid and me to ride. Emrys chose a steady-looking mare for himself, and took Swift on a short leading rein, riding at the back of the line in the hope that this would keep the yearling calmer. I'd have liked to go directly in front of them, but Cerball insisted Rhian and I ride with men-at-arms before and behind us. With my mind on the Disappearance, I did not argue.

I had wondered when I might start to feel a sense of homecoming. This was the land of my birth, after all; the land of strange tales, warrior queens, wise druids and peerless heroes. After we had ridden some way I saw wooded hills in the distance, and folds of land that had a certain shadowy charm. We passed a chain of little lakes that shone under the cloudless sky. Some way farther on we began to pass through stands of beech and birch. I did not know how far away Sevenwaters was, and I wasn't prepared to ask. I could remember almost nothing of my earlier journey, leaving home as a hurt and frightened little girl. Only Aunt Liadan's kind voice and the poultices she put on my hands and face, cool and soothing. And her telling me I had beautiful green eyes just like my mother's. I remembered that.

"This is so exciting!" Rhian said over her shoulder as we headed down a track under arching trees. The sunlight through the high canopy cast a dappled light onto the ground; it transformed our horses into fey creatures spangled with gold and silver. "We're nearly at Sevenwaters—just think of it!"

"I'm thinking about not falling off," I told her. "And wondering whether I'll be able to walk when we get there."

"But just think," my handmaid went on, undeterred, "in these woods all sorts of creatures might be lurking, leprechauns and clurichauns and little fey people, the ones that creep into the barn and drink the cows' milk!"

"There might be, I suppose. From what I remember, they don't show themselves to passersby."

She was about to reply when a flock of little birds arose suddenly from the foliage all around us, twittering in chorus. From behind us came Swift's unmistakable whinny of alarm.

"Lady Maeve!" I could hear the urgency beneath the careful calm of Emrys's tone.

"Stop," I said. Rhian reined in our mount. The men-at-arms around us halted theirs. I slid off the gelding's back to the ground—I could get off a horse quite well, if clumsily; it was getting on that was the problem—and walked back down the line. Emrys had dismounted. He still had hold of the leading rein, but Swift stood shivering, quarters bunched and ready for flight. The yearling was strong; if he really put his mind to the task of escaping us he could do so with little difficulty. Then he would indeed run wild. In this unknown place, we'd likely never find him.

Emrys moved in quietly until he could put a hand on the halter. I walked with practiced slowness to Swift's other side, where I touched the backs of my hands to his neck and murmured reassuring words to him. We stayed like that awhile, not rushing our nervous charge, and eventually he was calm again. But when I met Emrys's eye, I knew we shared the same misgiving. The quick movement of birds was not enough to scare a horse to the point of breaking loose, not even a touchy creature like Swift. Had he seen something else?

I returned to the gelding and Cerball dismounted to give me a lift up. "Well done, my lady," he said. "I see you know your horses."

"Thank you, all of you, for having the good sense to stay back and let us do that. Swift isn't the calmest creature even at home in his own stable. Cerball, how far do we have to go from here?"

"When we come over the next rise we'll be able to see the edge of the Sevenwaters forest and the nearest guard tower. Ready to move on, my lady?"

I turned my head and saw that Emrys was back on his horse, with Swift under good control. "Yes," I said, wondering if I'd ever be ready for Sevenwaters and knowing there was no point in such speculation since I would be there soon, whether I wanted it or not.

"Forward!" Cerball called to his men. I wrapped my arms around Rhian's waist and we rode on.

The forest was a massive dark blanket, smothering the hills, obscuring any landmarks. I did not know how far into that seemingly impenetrable wood we would have to ride. As we drew closer to the edge of it, I made out a guard tower—a walled platform atop great poles, as high as the old oaks that grew behind it. A shout of challenge rang out from up there. Shortly afterward, five armed guards emerged from under the trees to stand in a purposeful line, blocking our path.

"Cerball," I began, "what—"

"No cause for alarm, my lady." Cerball raised his voice. "Oak and shield!"

"Birch and blade!" came the response. Weapons were slid into sheaths, grins appeared on weathered faces, and one of the guards strode forward to stand by the gelding that bore Rhian and me.

"Lady Maeve," the fellow said. "Welcome home."

"Thank you." I held my head high as Aunt Liadan had taught me and tried not to notice the flicker of uneasiness in the man's eyes; where Cerball and his companions had been well prepared for our first meeting, this guard failed to school his reaction on seeing me close up. Folk tended to find my appearance pleasing enough on first glance, especially if I wore a veil over my hair, for much of my face was not burned. Aunt Liadan had told me I looked very much as my mother had when young. If I dispensed with the veil, people saw the mark that disfigured my brow and temple on the left side, and the patch where my hair would not grow. On second glance they noticed my hands. Then their expressions would turn to pity or, in the case of some folk, disgust. After that, they generally looked away.

"My name is Rhodri, my lady. Cerball will have explained about the sad loss of Lord Sean's uncle. If not for that, your father would have been here to welcome you."

"I understand. Do we ride straight on to the keep, Rhodri?"

"It's a long way, as you may recall, my lady. We'll provide some refreshments here before you go on, and something for the horses."

I could not remember how far it was; when I had lived here as a child, I had rarely traveled beyond the borders of the forest. But, as before, I did not feel I could ask the question. "Thank you."

"We're to provide two more for the escort," Rhodri went on, glancing at Cerball. "Lord Sean's orders."

Cerball nodded, and we rode on to the watchtower, where more armed men were waiting near a shelter at the foot of the poles. I did wonder about the escort; it seemed to me Cerball's five men-at-arms and the two who had come with us from Harrowfield, along with three grooms, was surely more than sufficient. But then, there was the tale of the Disappearance, and in particular the way those men had turned up dead, one after another, within this very forest. That must weigh heavily on the whole household. I held my tongue on the matter. I had been away a long time; perhaps long enough to forget what a deeply unusual place the forest of Sevenwaters was.

Bread, cheese and ale were brought out from the shelter at the foot of the tower. I refused the food but drank the ale, holding the cup between my wrists. The horses were tended to. Rhian wrapped a portion of the food in a cloth and put it in her pouch. Then we mounted again and rode into the forest.

I had not thought it would be so far. As children, my sisters and I used to go up on the roof sometimes, though Mother frowned on it as unsafe. From our perilous perch the forest resembled a magical garment of every shade of green. It wrapped itself around the keep and shawled the shining expanse of the lake and stretched as far as the eye could see. Today, riding along a shadowy track that seemed all too ready to lose itself under the oaks, I could understand why outsiders found the place unsettling. It was said that the pathways through this forest had a habit of suddenly changing. A way that not long ago had led a traveler directly to the keep might now take him on a twisting, tangling route to nowhere. This odd phenomenon did not apply to the Sevenwaters family; for us, the paths led where they should. At least, that was the story.

Rhian knew this tale from me, but it did nothing to dampen her excitement. She looked one way, then the other, her eyes shining, her cheeks flushed pink. Plainly she was hoping to spot a clurichaun under the trees or a sylph up in the branches. My sister Sibeal used to say that you saw such beings only when you weren't looking for them. I did not know whether that was true, for I had never seen clurichaun or sylph, Fair Folk or Old Ones myself. Only, sometimes, I'd thought I glimpsed a gossamer creature darting through a sunbeam, or heard the shuffle of odd little feet in the ferns. No more than that.

It took the rest of the day to reach the keep. We stopped by a stream to rest, and while the men were watering the horses Rhian broke the food she had brought into small pieces and wedged each in turn between the inflexible first and second fingers of my right hand so I could feed myself. Long practice had made us efficient at this, and I was done by the time the men returned. I'd have eaten quite happily in front of our grooms and men-at-arms, but doing so before my father's guards was another matter.

As we rode I considered what lay ahead. I pictured the stone walls of the keep, tall and grim. There had always been men-at-arms by the gateway, their tunics bearing the family emblem, two torcs interlinked, in blue on a white background. Within the gateway lay the courtyard, with stables and other outbuildings at the far side. My mind took me through the main door of the keep and into the living quarters. The grand dining hall housed several tables where family, guests and other members of the household all sat together to eat and be entertained in the evenings. There were musicians, storytellers, druids. Such visitors were often accommodated in the annex set within the walls but apart from the main building. To reach it, you went out the door from the kitchens and across the courtyard. But perhaps the annex wasn't there anymore. Hadn't someone told me, back when I was too sick to listen properly, that Father was having that whole building taken down? That, after the fire, he could not bear to look at it?

"Are you still comfortable?" Rhian asked me as we rode down a steep track with a gushing stream to one side. The ferns that hugged its course were spangled with tiny droplets. It was the sort of place where my sisters and I had often played in the old days, floating leaf boats, building dams, picking herbs.

"Comfortable, no," I said. "I'm coping. How about you?"

"I'm fine." She shifted a little in the saddle. "But tired. I'll be glad to get there."

"If they were expecting us to spend two nights at the inn, they may be surprised to see us today."

There was a silence; then Rhian said, "Your family will be delighted to see you, even though this must be a sad time for them." This remark showed her uncanny ability to guess what I was thinking.

"I hope so. And I hope they don't assume I'm back for good."

She waited again before answering. "They'll want that," she said. "Didn't you say all your sisters have moved away now, even Eilis?"

"So I heard, though the news about Eilis sounded odd. She went to Galicia. That's a long way."

"There will be lots of stories to tell," Rhian said, and then, in quite a different voice, "Maeve?"

"What?"

"You'll think I'm being silly."

"Tell me what it is and I can make up my own mind whether it's silly."

"I keep seeing things. Or half-seeing them. Figures moving about under the trees, only when I look again they're only shadows. And things flying that aren't bats or birds."

I considered the stories my handmaid so loved to hear, full of quests and spells and beasts that changed into human folk. If anyone was going to turn a trick of the light into a dragon or a flying horse, it was Rhian.

"Don't you remember what I told you?" I kept my tone light. "The Sevenwaters family and those who travel with them are always safe in this forest. So even if you do see something, you need not worry about it. We must be nearly there by now; it's almost dusk. Besides, you were the one who wanted to see clurichauns."

"This was much too big for a clurichaun." Rhian's voice was a whisper.

"We'll be fine." I turned my head to look back at Swift. The yearling had his head down. Even he was tired. "How much farther?" I asked the man closest to us.

"We're almost there, my lady."

This was indeed so, for as we crested a little rise, the waters of the Sevenwaters lake appeared before us, pale and mysterious in the fading light. And there, across the broad and glimmering expanse, was the keep, its stone walls rising above a softening stand of trees. A banner flew atop the tower: the torcs of Sevenwaters. Many torches flared, and a sound of singing reached us across the water. On the far shore, where the sward ran down from the stone walls to the lakeside, I could just make out the figures of men and women standing in a great circle.

Conor's burial rite. We still had to ride a certain way around the shore, but it looked as if we were going to arrive right in the middle of it.

We moved on. My stomach felt tight, my skin prickly with nervous sweat. Most likely my family were not expecting me to arrive until tomorrow. With no time to school their features, how would they look at me? Would I see their true feelings in their eyes? Was that what I feared? It came to me that it was possible to be afraid of your own fear, and that such a phenomenon was utterly ridiculous. I would think about Swift, and how good it was that he was close to a warm stable, a hearty feed and a rest. I wished he was not being sent on from Sevenwaters, to live among strangers.

The track followed the lakeshore for a distance, then went back up under the trees. We emerged on level ground not far from the keep gates and were immediately halted by guards. As the men from the watchtower made their explanations, I saw that one face was familiar, even after so long.

"Doran!" I exclaimed.

"Lady Maeve!" Father's chief man-at-arms came over to help me down, smiling. "Welcome home!" He eyed Swift with some curiosity.

"I'm sorry if we have arrived at an inconvenient time," I said. "The yearling needs to go straight to the stables." That was the one priority there was no arguing with. "And either Emrys or Donal here—they are Uncle Bran's grooms—must stay with him until Father knows the situation. Could you arrange that for us?"

Doran took control with the ease of long practice; he was a trusted member of my father's household, one of many loyal and capable retainers. When I was a child I had not thought the seamless running of my family home anything unusual. We'd all known our mother could be content only when her domain was perfectly ordered. I remembered the way she drilled us in sewing a faultless hem, in the intricacies of fine embroidery, in the baking of a perfect pie. In my case, that training had been wasted effort, since I would never perform any of those tasks now, even imperfectly.

With remarkable swiftness grooms, guards and horses were despatched toward the keep. Rhian and I stood beside Doran, looking down the sward to the place where flaming torches illuminated the great circle of folk. A white-robed figure stood in the center, chanting in a clear voice.

"I won't go in until I've spoken to my father and mother," I said quietly. "It doesn't seem right. But I can't march down there in the middle of a burial rite, if that's what it is."

"It's hard to believe Master Conor is gone," murmured Doran. "I think we all imagined he'd be here forever. He was buried earlier, Lady Maeve, out in the nemetons. This is more of a celebration. That's what Master Ciarán said. Prayers for safe passing through the gateway, recognition of Conor's life and his good deeds. That man was a great friend to folk, and a wise adviser to your father. He'll be missed." He fell silent, perhaps wondering whether he'd spoken out of turn.

"I'll wait here until they come back to the house," I said. "Rhian, you must be exhausted. I'm sure Doran can find someone to take you in if you'd prefer that."

"I'll wait with you, my lady."

Doran favored my handmaid with a smile. "Are you back for good, Lady Maeve?" he asked me.

The tightness moved up to my chest. I could explain about Swift, of course, and why I'd finally come back after so long, but that was not a real answer to this question. I had better prepare one, since it would be asked over and over. "I'm not sure yet," I told him.

We waited, and while we did so I played a game: picking out anyone I could recognize, or half-recognize, in the circle down the hill. The torchlight added to the challenge, painting each face with a moving pattern of gold and shadow. I looked for my little brother first, as there were only a few children there. Finbar was seven; he'd be bigger than my cousin Fintan's children back at Harrowfield, and his hair would either be red like my mother's and mine, or dark like Father's. Was he that lad putting up a hand to cover a yawn? Or the one bending to tie up a shoe that had come loose? The others were all girls, or too small . . . But wait. A boy was standing very still beside a figure in a long robe, perhaps a druid. Indeed, the child was unnaturally still, like a rabbit frozen in the fox's stare. A white face; a mop of dark curls. Shoulders very straight. Hands behind his back. I could not see his features clearly, but that stance was all unease. Perhaps this was the first death

Finbar had experienced. I felt a jolt of recognition, unexpected and not entirely welcome. My brother. My little brother.

The druid who was conducting the ritual stretched out his arms and intoned a prayer. Fragments were carried to us on the evening breeze: "Fly with the west wind . . . Swim with the mysterious beasts of the ocean . . . Rise with the flame of renewal . . ." *Ciarán*, I thought, my skin prickling with the power of the words. Even if I had not recognized my other uncle, Conor's half brother, by his dark red hair and his imposing height, I would have remembered that voice, full of dignity, deep and sure.

"They say Ciarán will be chief druid now Conor's gone," Doran murmured. "He's very much respected, both within the brotherhood and elsewhere."

"Maeve," whispered Rhian, who was staring in fascination at the folk down the hill and had evidently forgotten we were not alone, "is that lady one of your sisters?"

The lady in question was of short and slight build. Her hair was concealed under an elegant veil and she held her head regally high. Her arm was linked with that of a rather grand-looking man in a blue cloak. She was a younger version of my mother. "It must be Deirdre," I said. "I don't think any of the others would be here." And as Doran confirmed that it was indeed Deirdre and that the man beside her was her husband, my father stepped out into the middle of the circle and passed something to Ciarán, perhaps marking the end of the ritual.

Ten years. Deirdre had changed in that time and so had I. I had grown into a woman. I had learned hard lessons about myself and the world I must live in. I had become brave because the alternative was unthinkable. Now, as I gazed on the familiar, well-loved figure of my father, the wounded child within me stirred uneasily. I had been too sick to take in much during the time after the fire, when my eldest sister, Muirrin, was tending to me in the keep, before Aunt Liadan came to fetch me away. Day and night had been a blur of pain and terror: Muirrin's white face and red eyes as she did what had to be done, changing the dressings, making me move my fingers; Mother's voice, murmuring, *It's all right,*

Maeve. You'll be all right, as if by repeating the words she could make them true; my sisters' shocked, disbelieving faces when they were finally allowed in to see me. My cousin Fainne's tight, closed features. And my father, overcome with grief and guilt, for he had rushed to the rescue, had saved my life, but he had come too late to prevent me from being burned. I knew how that felt; I had failed Bounder altogether. I had been too slow, and I had lost my best friend.

The ceremony was over. Now the crowd was coming up the hill, following the path marked out by a double row of flaming torches. Folk carried oil lamps and candles in holders. Druids came quietly in their long robes, one or two in white, most in gray or blue, denoting the lower ranks of the order. With them walked serving men and women, farmers and grooms, richly dressed people who were perhaps visitors from the holdings to north and south of Sevenwaters, though the story I had heard about the Disappearance made me wonder how many friends my father still had among the chieftains of the region. There was a woman druid in a girdled robe. There was a group of children running back up the hill, and a little spotted dog doing its best to keep up. And now, moving at a more stately pace, here was my family.

It was always going to be awkward. The circumstances made it more so: my parents surrounded by their distinguished visitors, the fading light, our arrival a day earlier than expected and at the time of the ritual for Uncle Conor. This must inevitably bring back a host of tangled memories. Best get it over with quickly.

"Father," I said, stepping forward as their party came up onto level ground, my father walking with Deirdre's husband and two druids, my mother and sister in the group just behind them. "You may have seen us ride in. I—"

There was no need for introductions. There was no need for anything. My father turned chalk white; then a blazing smile lit up his face. Tears glittered in his eyes. He took two strides forward and gathered me into an embrace. I had promised myself I would not weep. In the warmth of his arms, it was a hard promise to keep.

"Maeve," Father murmured. "My girl. You've come home."

By the time he released me, holding me at arm's length as if to make sure I was real, others had gathered around us and a babble of excited conversation had broken out. Folk had seen us ride in but had assumed we were guests arrived late for the ritual. Here was my mother, hugging me in her turn; here was Deirdre, every inch a fine lady, kissing me on either cheek and introducing me to her husband, Illann, and her two children, each clutching the hand of an attentive nursemaid. Other folk were introduced, guests, attendants, druids. How would I remember all their names? My head was awash with them. A treacherous memory of my chamber at Harrowfield visited me, a chamber situated on the quietest side of that house, with a glazed window looking out over the garden. There had been children in that household, too, and servants, and visitors. But it had been possible to retreat. Everyone had understood my need to be alone.

"You must be weary, Maeve. Is this your maidservant? Come, we'll get you indoors at once. The house is quite full with our guests here for Conor's farewell, but I've made sure your old chamber is ready for you."

That was my mother, leading me by the arm toward the keep, talking as she went, gesturing to various serving people at the same time. I noted their instant obedience.

"Thank you, Mother. I am quite tired."

Father had been drawn aside by one of the druids, but his eyes were on me. Perhaps he feared I might vanish if he turned away. I managed a smile. Gods, he was exactly the same: his steady gaze, his strong features, his air of quiet control. There were more white threads in his hair now, and he looked tired. That was no surprise, what with the Disappearance and its aftermath. I wondered if he would be prepared to talk to me about such things, as Bran and Liadan had, or whether he might think it inappropriate to discuss matters of blood, death and peril with a daughter.

"Maeve, you look so well!" Deirdre came up on my other side, a big smile on her face under the pristine veil. A curl of red hair had escaped the linen and lay against her pale skin. "It's wonderful to see you! There's so much news—ten years of news—I hardly know where to start. Did you hear Eilis has gone to Galicia? Another of Father's uncles lives there, and his daughter came over to see us, and . . ."

"Deirdre, we must get Maeve indoors," my mother said firmly. "Time enough for talk when she's had a chance to rest. And you'll be hungry, Maeve."

"Mother, I imagine you have a grand supper to preside over, with all these guests. I'd be happier if Rhian could bring me some food on a tray, to eat in my chamber. I am too weary to sit at the family table tonight." After a moment I added, "I mean no disrespect to Uncle Conor; I remember him with affection. But I'm so tired I would probably disgrace you by falling asleep in the middle of the meal."

We were in the courtyard now and heading for the main steps. "Eithne!" Mother rapped out, summoning her own personal serving woman. "This is my daughter Maeve, and this is her maidservant—"

"Rhian, my lady." As she spoke, Rhian bobbed a little curtsy. This brought a smile to Mother's lips.

"Please show Rhian how the house is laid out, then ask Nuala to give her some supper on a tray for herself and my daughter. Maeve will be in her old sleeping quarters. And Rhian—"

"Rhian will share with me," I said. "She helps me with everything—eating, washing, dressing. I need her close by."

"Of course," Mother said, and for a moment her gaze went to my clawed, useless hands. "Oh, Maeve."

I felt my jaw tighten. "We manage well," I said, lifting my chin and looking her straight in the eye.

"After ten years of your Aunt Liadan's example," Mother said quietly, "no doubt you manage very well indeed. Shall we go in?"

Did I detect a coolness in her voice? Disappointment that I had chosen to stay away so long, through all the years of my growing up? Or was she merely tired and disturbed by everything that had happened here lately? I felt a gap between us, a space that had not been there with Father, who had needed no words to convey how much he'd missed me.

Once inside the keep, I was whisked away upstairs before I could think about the last time I had been in this house. It came to me that my weariness and my mother's efficiency might result in one very important thing being forgotten.

"I haven't met Finbar yet," I said, hesitating outside the door to my old chamber, the one I had shared with Sibeal and Eilis.

"I'll send him up with your maid," Mother said. "He's a quiet child. Much like Sibeal was at that age. You look almost asleep, Maeve. I'm sad that you can't join us for supper, but I don't expect that of you. Most of our visitors are leaving in the morning. We'll have a good talk then."

"Mother," I said very quietly.

"What is it, my dear?"

"Never mind," I said, finding the mountain I had to climb too steep for now. Explaining what I could do, what I couldn't do, why I was uncomfortable in company, why I might be an embarrassment to them at a time when things were already difficult, my intention of heading back to Harrowfield as soon as I possibly could . . . "We'll talk tomorrow."

Comforts were provided with remarkable speed: our bags brought in, a tub of warm water for bathing—that was utter bliss after the long ride—and then a very good meal on a tray, fetched by Rhian only after she, too, had made use of the bathwater, at my invitation. The opportunity seemed too good to waste. When we were halfway through eating there was a tentative tap on the door.

Rhian opened it to reveal two figures outside: my brother, all big eyes and dark unruly hair, and the druid who had been at his side during the ritual.

"I hope we're not disturbing you," this man said. He had a voice like honey and shadow, a voice surely made for the telling of stories. "Lady Aisling said you wanted to see Finbar. I am his tutor, Luachan."

There was a brief silence. Rhian appeared dumbstruck, and I understood why. Not only did Luachan have the softest, most melodious voice I'd ever heard, he also strongly resembled the handsome hero from some old wonder tale. His features were harmonious in every particular, his eyes a liquid blue, his hair falling in wavy locks the hue of oak bark, with a narrow plait here and there in the manner of the brotherhood. As Rhian and I stared, his grave demeanor was broken by a decidedly undruidic smile. "We thought we should wait until they took away the bathwater," he said.

An answering smile curved my lips despite my better judgment. If that was not an attempt to flirt, I did not know what it was. I had little experience with druids, but I was quite certain women did not entertain them in their private quarters. Especially this manner of druid. "Thank you," I said. "It must be close to Finbar's bedtime. Perhaps you could come back for him in a little while."

Luachan inclined his head courteously, then retreated. Finbar hesitated in the doorway as if not quite sure whether to come in. He did not look the kind of child one could sweep up into a hug. Besides, he did not know me, and my hands belonged in the kind of story misguided folk sometimes told to warn children of dangers. *Don't go into the woodland after dark, or the girl with claws for hands will get you.*

"Come on in, then," Rhian said, taking the initiative. "Have you had supper? We're still eating ours."

My brother advanced to the middle of the chamber. He stood there watching, his expression thoughtful, as we finished our food. He seemed especially fascinated by the way Rhian passed me the meat and bread piece by piece so I could feed myself, and the way I waited until the soup had cooled, then lifted the bowl between my wrists and drank directly from it. I wondered what question he would ask, but when he finally spoke he surprised me.

"May I look at your hands, Maeve?"

That was a little like a fist in the gut. Still, it was better than the face turned away, the avoidance of what was glaringly obvious. I held out my deformed hands for his inspection. To my surprise he took them in his small ones, turning them over, examining them carefully.

"Father told me what happened to you," he said. His voice was a child's in timbre, but its tone was as solemn as any druid's. "Can't you bend your fingers at all?"

"Muirrin made me do a lot of exercises after it happened," I told him, thinking a serious question deserved a proper answer. "I believe she and Aunt Liadan were hoping I would be able to use my fingers a bit, but they stiffened up. They'll always be like this now. I have my own ways of doing things."

"What sort of ways?"

"Well, if Rhian wasn't here to help me eat, I would use my toes to pick up the pieces of bread. But that is not something I can do in the dining hall." I gave him a smile.

"Can you really eat with your toes? Show me." Now he sounded more like a seven-year-old boy and less like a wise old sage.

I slipped off my shoes, dropped a crust of bread on the floor and demonstrated, hoping very much that nobody came in the door. "It's not very dignified," I said as I brought my foot up to my mouth. "And the food has to be in small pieces. Now you try."

The ensuing lesson had Finbar, Rhian and me in fits of laughter. I liked to hear my brother laugh. Seven seemed rather young to have a tutor.

"How long has Luachan been here, Finbar?" I asked.

"He came when Eilis went away. Eilis used to teach me. Reading and writing, and other things, too." His eyes were bright now. They were of an unusually light blue-gray, like shadows on ice or water under an early-morning sky. "She taught me to go over jumps on my pony. I like riding. Luachan takes me every day."

"Did you see the horse we brought from Britain? He's a beautiful yearling called Swift. We could go and visit him in the stables tomorrow." A pause. "If Luachan approves, of course."

Finbar nodded. He was looking at my face now, where the burn scar marked my temple. "You were trying to save your dog when the flames came. I saw you in the fire."

The hairs on my neck stood up. "It happened long ago, Finbar. Before you were born."

"I saw you reaching out for him. I heard you calling: *Bounder! Bounder, come!* But he didn't come, and you put your hands on something hot, and then you fell down. There was fire all around." He was staring straight at me, but what he was seeing, I thought, was Maeve in the fire, little Maeve facing terror and pain like nothing she could ever have dreamed of. "You nearly died," he said. "Father said you must have had a very strong will to live, or he'd have lost you that night."

I wondered that the story had been shared so openly with him. And I thought about those eyes, which were just like my sister Sibeal's. Seer's eyes. In our family, eyes of that color marked a child out as open to the Sight, both curse and blessing. I found myself wishing that Finbar had gray eyes like Father's, or green ones like mine. "I suppose that must be true," I told him, remembering a tale of a young woman whose features were so warty and deformed she resembled a toad, and her long quest to find one particular herb whose application could render her face beautiful. I could not remember ever believing this was true or in any way possible; not even when I was first injured, and desperately praying that I might some day be restored to what I had been. Neither herbs nor potions nor magic spells would take away the scar on my face or make my fingers bend and move like other people's. I had long ago accepted my situation and moved on. If anyone wanted an example of a strong will to live, mine was a good one.

"Bad things happen sometimes," I went on, thinking that I would make time for my brother, tutor or no tutor, and do with him some of the things my sisters and I had enjoyed doing back in the time before the fire. It sounded as if Eilis had made a start with her ponies and jumps, but Eilis was gone. "They happen even to people who have been good and sensible all their lives. Even to little children sometimes. I don't know if it's the will of the gods, or the mistakes of men and women, or simply fate. If it happens to you, you have to go on as bravely as you can and make the best of what you have." I had not lived in the household of Aunt Liadan and Uncle Bran all those years for nothing. My uncle, in particular, had good cause to embrace that wisdom.

"If there was something bad and you could change it," Finbar ventured, his voice soft in the candlelit chamber, "would you?"

This was not the simple question it seemed; there was a shadow in those big eyes, a darkness that sat ill on a child's face.

"Some things can't be changed," I said, glancing at my hands, "and it's a waste of time to dream of it. But if I knew I could undo something bad that had happened, if I knew I could make a difference, I would try." I hesitated. "But it would depend," I said. "There can be a price, and sometimes the price is too high."

I wondered whether Finbar knew the whole story of his own past, how Mac Dara had stolen him as an infant and spirited him away to the Otherworld, leaving a sticks-and-stones baby in his place; how Clodagh and Cathal had eventually outwitted the prince of the Otherworld and escaped with Finbar safe and well. That had happened only after Cathal had offered himself in Finbar's place; and Cathal had emerged safely only after an act of extreme bravery by Clodagh. As for a price, I thought perhaps the price of Cathal's freedom had not yet been fully paid. If Mac Dara was still making mischief all over the region and setting chieftain against chieftain, as my father's letter had indicated, clearly the account was as yet unsettled.

"If people don't pay the price," Finbar said gravely, "the bad things keep happening." His small features looked weary, the pale skin touched with gray.

The tutor would be back soon. I would not send my brother off to bed on such a grim note. It seemed he knew about the Disappearance and had been listening to the tales of bodies found under gruesome circumstances. A child as sensitive as this would surely have seen the effect of that on our mother and father, and on all the household.

"Our family has survived a long time," I told him. "We've weathered battles and transformations, enchantments and floods and fires." I kept my tone calm. "We've endured being sent away, and we've coped with evildoers in our midst. If I were telling a story of Sevenwaters—and it would be a grand epic told over all the nights of a long winter—I would surely end it with a triumph.

A happy ending, all well, puzzles solved, enemies defeated, the future stretching ahead bright and true. With new challenges and new adventures, certainly, because that's the way thing always are. But overall it would be a very satisfying story, one to give the listener heart." How much of that was he likely to understand? I had been speaking as much to myself as to Finbar. Tomorrow I had my own demons to face.

Rhian had been stacking the supper dishes on the tray, wiping down the small table, getting on with the unpacking. Now she straightened, hands on hips and a smile on her face. "I hope you'll tell that tale sometime, my lady. I'd surely love to hear it."

"We all have our own parts of it, like threads in a tapestry," I said. Finbar was standing close to me; I could have put my arm around his shoulders, and almost did so, since he had shown that my deformity did not disgust him. But I held back. With a wary horse I always took things slowly, one tiny step at a time. This felt very much the same. "When all those threads come together in the hands of a skilled weaver, that's when the fabric gains its true strength."

"And that's when you can see the pattern," said Rhian. A ghost of a smile appeared on Finbar's face.

There was a tap at the door. Luachan had come to collect his charge. As Rhian went to let him in, I said, "Good night, Finbar. I'm very happy that you came to see me. It feels good to have a brother."

"Good night, Maeve. I'm happy you came home."

Someone had taught him good manners. I wondered whether that person had been Eilis, whom I remembered as a small whirlwind, far more interested in riding the tallest and most challenging horse she could find than in conversational niceties.

Luachan stood in the doorway. The light from our candles fell across his chiseled features and illuminated his startling blue eyes. "I hope I am not come too early, my lady," he said, demonstrating his own good manners.

"Not at all. In my turn, I hope Finbar will have time to visit the stables tomorrow and see the horse we brought across from

Britain. If he is not too busy with lessons, that is." The more I thought about it, the more ridiculous it seemed that such a small boy should be subject to a formal education. Finbar should be outside playing. He should be riding his pony over the jumps, if that was what he enjoyed doing. He was far too somber for a child of his age.

"Of course," Luachan said with a devastating smile. "We're at your command, Lady Maeve." And with that the two of them were gone, leaving Rhian and me staring after them.

"I'm completely revising my idea of a druid," my handmaid observed a little later, when the door was shut and she was unfastening the hooks at the back of my gown. "Did you see the way he looked at us?"

I made no reply. What had surprised me most about Luachan had not been his stunning appearance, his mellow voice or his mischievous smile, but the fact that he had met my gaze without a trace of either pity or disgust. He had looked at me as if I were a normal woman.

CHAPTER 3

I rose very early. Rhian was stifling yawns as she helped me dress. I suggested she go back to bed until it was a reasonable hour to fetch our breakfast. Then I made my way downstairs.

I should have undertaken my mission by twilight, perhaps; recaptured more closely the way things were on that long-ago night of Samhain. Doors standing open, for spirits roamed abroad as the year made its turning to the dark. Empty chairs at the table, an invitation for lost loved ones to return and sit awhile amongst the living. A great bonfire blazing in the space between keep and stables. Uncle Conor speaking words of power into the chill air, then lighting a torch and passing it to my cousin Fainne, who walked about the house rekindling each hearth fire in turn. Later that night, with the household abed, I'd woken suddenly to hear screaming. Beyond the little round window of my chamber was a tapestry of flame and shadow. At ten, I was not allowed to have Bounder in my room at night, though I had pleaded his case with all the eloquence a child could summon. That Samhain night I'd known my dog was with our druid guests, who had softer hearts than my mother's.

The druids had not been accommodated in the keep, for to be thus enclosed unsettled them. They were sleeping in the annex across the stable yard. When I'd slipped downstairs and out the kitchen door, quiet as a little ghost, it had been to see the annex all afire . . .

I had been brave then; I had acted without a moment's hesitation. Now I was not so brave. I had waited until it was almost daylight to do what I must do. In the dark, the place would be too much the same. It would be all too easy to remember the smoky air catching in my chest and the hungry roar of the flames.

I must retrace my footsteps as closely as I could. On the night of the fire I had not gone out the front door. Just as well, since there was no way I could open it now, with its big iron bolt. I slipped into the kitchen, which was full of the comforting smell of baking bread. Nuala was taking a batch of loaves out of the oven, her hair tied back in a scarf, her cheeks red. Two young assistants were preparing some kind of mushroom dish, their knives flashing with precision. Both stopped when I came in, staring at me round-eyed. Nuala straightened. I saw the flicker in her expression. Doran would have told her what to expect. They'd both been here a long time; she would remember the child I had been.

"Welcome home, Maeve! I should say, my lady. It is good to see you again."

"And you, Nuala." Perhaps I sounded a little too crisp, but I could not help it.

"Girls, back to work!" Nuala snapped, and they obeyed, not without a few sideways glances in my direction. "You're up early, my lady. Hungry after yesterday's journey?"

"Rhian—my maidservant—will come down later and fetch some food for the two of us," I said. "The bread smells wonderful. I want to go outside. Could you open that door for me, please?" A pox on the kitchen girls; they would simply have to get used to me. I gestured toward the door that led directly out to the stable yard and saw Nuala's eyes widen as I lifted my disfigured hand.

"Oh, let me—" She was quick to help, moving across the kitchen, holding the door open for me. "It's cold out there," she said. "Won't you need a cloak?"

"I won't be long." I turned my back and strode off across the yard. I had come out without cloak or veil, my scars on full display. That had seemed a necessary part of my personal rite.

No bonfire now; only the first hint of dawn, rose-gold on the stone walls of the keep, the wattle-and-thatch outbuildings, the woven fences of sheepfold, byre and chicken coop. Shadows clung to the corners and lay across the ground where the feet of man, woman and child had stepped that long-ago night around the ritual bonfire. And farther out, beyond fence and wall, lay the forest, still sleeping under the violet-gray blanket of between-time. Somewhere in the trees a bird called a greeting to a morning not yet arrived.

If it were Samhain now, the keep would be in darkness still. But I had returned to Sevenwaters in a brighter season, with the oaks in their summer finery and the meadows dotted with wildflowers. That did little to quiet the child within. As I walked across the yard she was whimpering in fear. *Hush,* I willed her. *It is over. It was long ago.* And I thought of Finbar's words from last night: *I saw you. You were trying to save your dog. I saw you in the fire.* A shiver ran through me. Was my brother's every day beset by such cruel visions? Was that what set the shadow in his remarkable eyes?

Nobody seemed to be about, but I could hear horses moving in the stables, restless with the first trace of daylight. I hesitated, part of me wanting to go in and check on Swift, the other part recognizing that I was making excuses. I imagined Uncle Bran standing on one side of me, offering me his strong tattooed arm to lean on; Aunt Liadan was on the other side, telling me to breathe deeply and take one step at a time. Saying he and I were the bravest people she had ever met, and wasn't she lucky to have the two of us right beside her? I kept on walking.

Even in the uncertain light of early morning, it was plain that the annex was gone. In its place was a garden, not a practical herb or vegetable patch but a flower garden with a low wall around it, and in the middle a graceful young tree, perhaps a plum. Beneath were bushes of lavender and rosemary, and at their feet I thought I could discern the heart-shaped leaves of violets. In this spot the fire had raged. In this spot, or very close by, an elderly druid had perished in the flames and a younger one had sustained injuries that could not be healed. In this place my beloved Bounder had been trapped, and had howled for me, and had died waiting for me to come.

I sank down on the wall. I could no more stem my tears than hold back a raging river. "I tried," I whispered through the hot tide of my grief. "Bounder, I tried my best."

I stayed there, remembering, as the day crept closer. The fact that I had failed Bounder hurt far more than what had happened to me that night. I had loved my dog more dearly than anyone in my family could understand. How could I have let him die, alone, frightened and in pain? I bowed my head and closed my eyes. I was not sure I believed in any god, but I sent up a prayer to whatever deity might have a special interest in creatures. I prayed that Bounder's spirit had been set free quickly; that he had not suffered much. I prayed that somehow I could make good my failure to save him.

"Maeve?" The deep voice was my father's; he had come up so quietly I had not realized he was there. Now he sat down beside me and took my misshapen hand in his. Well, he could see the tears on my cheeks; he, of them all, would be the one who understood. He had his two wolfhounds with him, long-legged gray shadows. They gave me a glance, then settled quietly at his feet.

"Whoever planted this garden knew all the plants I loved," I said. "Someone even remembered my fondness for plum preserve."

Father nodded. "The violets were your mother's suggestion; she recalled a favorite gown you wore until it was almost in shreds, dyed in exactly that shade. Muirrin said rosemary denotes a strong woman. Clodagh remembered that you loved the scent of lavender. There's a dog rose in the corner there—it may not surprise you that Eilis wanted those. Deirdre thought of the plum tree, and Sibeal worked out the most favorable alignment and shape for the garden, using an arcane druidic formula. Over the years since you went away all of us have spent time here, thinking about you. I wish more of your sisters were here to welcome you home. Even Deirdre is only with us a few days; she and Illann must head back soon with the children. But she's not far away."

"I like the little garden," I said. A dog rose; dear Eilis. That made me want to laugh and cry at the same time.

"It was something I had to do, or I'd have found it difficult to walk across my own stable yard. I often come here in the early mornings. What happened . . ." Father hesitated, his head bowed. "It's still raw, even after so long. Perhaps, now that you are home again, that pain may start to fade a little. My dear, it's so good to see you. My lovely daughter."

"And you, Father." The tears were abating; I wiped my face awkwardly on my sleeve. "I know I have come at a difficult time. Uncle Bran showed me the letter you sent, and he told me about the terrible things that have been happening here. I suppose it's obvious why we've brought the yearling, Swift. The best horse in all Erin could not make up for the loss of a man's sons, but such a gift may smooth your path with this chieftain a little." How could I tell him I was not home for good? His eyes told me he had spent ten years longing for this moment to come. "I have a certain knack with horses, even nervous or difficult ones," I said. "That's why I've come now, even though it might not seem the best time. Swift needed me on the journey. The grooms, Emrys and Donal, are both very capable. But there are things I can do that they can't."

Father did not answer for a while, and I wondered if he had understood the unspoken part of my explanation. "The yearling is remarkable," he said eventually. "It's a pity Eilis is not here to see him, since she's always had such a passion for horses." His smile was wistful, as if he would like nothing better than to go back to the way things were, his daughters innocent children, his domain peaceful, his neighbors allies. "I did know about your gift with animals. Liadan occasionally gives me news through our special link. Without that, I could not have endured your staying away so long."

I said nothing to this. When pairs of twins were born in the Sevenwaters family, they often had the ability to link their minds and exchange their thoughts, even when they were far apart. My sisters Clodagh and Deirdre could do it, as Father and Aunt Liadan could. It was a gift that could be both useful and inconvenient, and I had never been sure how often they used it or how much they told each other.

"Bran and Liadan believe your ability is quite exceptional," Father went on. "I'm grateful to you for helping bring Swift here safely. I've had a word with your fellow, Emrys, and with my stable master, Duald—you may remember him. The creature is fine looking, but he's highly strung, perhaps a danger to himself. That makes me think twice about his suitability as a stud horse, and I imagine Cruinn of Tirconnell would agree."

"Swift is still young, Father. Bran's decision surprised both me and the stable master at Harrowfield. Had it not been for—" No, I could not say I had come home only because of the risk to Swift of traveling without me. "I've worked with Swift for a long time and I know him well. He needs a quiet period at pasture, followed by a little more work in the yard. Then he'll be ready to go on to Tirconnell." Seeing a certain doubt on my father's face, I added, "Swift's temperament is sound, despite appearances. Otherwise he wouldn't have weathered the sea voyage as well as he did. If there's a safe, quiet field where he can graze and a place where we can do some careful work with him, he should be ready to travel before the weather gets too cold."

Father smiled; the somber look lifted. "You speak like a seasoned stable master, Maeve."

"I can't ride," I said flatly. "I can sit behind someone and hold on, but that's about it. I can't put a bridle or a saddle on a horse. I can't lead a creature around the yard or unfasten a stable door or brush out a mane or perform any of the hundred tasks a groom does every day. But people find me useful, all the same. Animals seem to trust me. Even the most difficult ones. I can help with Swift. I don't need hands to do that." After a moment I added, "I hope Mother won't think that's inappropriate. She must see that I will be no help to her with domestic matters."

Father sighed. "I doubt if your mother has thought beyond her joy at having you back home," he said. "If you have concerns, best be open about them. I'm sure she will understand."

I did not share his confidence. In the time of my childhood, domestic matters had been of utmost importance to Mother. Every serving man and woman at Sevenwaters had known what rigorous standards she set. Every one of them had felt her scrutiny; all had no doubt witnessed her displeasure when someone fell short of those standards. She'd been well liked, for all that; she'd respected and praised good work, and treated people fairly. But she'd never had a tolerance for idleness, and I wondered where a daughter who could not work—at least, not at what Mother would think appropriate tasks—might fit into her ordered world. I found myself dreading our first real meeting.

"I talked to Finbar last night," I said, changing the subject. "His tutor brought him up to visit me."

"Luachan is a good man."

I hesitated, not wanting to sound critical. "None of us had a tutor when we were seven years old," I said. "It's because he is a boy and a future chieftain, I suppose. Luachan seems . . . not very druidic."

"Ciarán recommended him. Luachan is a chieftain's son. He's not only well educated; he's expert in various forms of combat, both armed and unarmed."

I blinked at him, too surprised to comment.

"He found his spiritual calling a number of years ago and set all that behind him. But the skills remain. These days he practices regularly with my men-at-arms. He was the right choice for Finbar."

I took a moment to make sense of this. "So he's a bodyguard as well as a tutor?"

"Regrettably, that is necessary. You'll know the story of Finbar's abduction as a very new baby. After Clodagh and Cathal rescued him, Mac Dara left us alone for a few years. We thought he'd ceased meddling. But now . . ." The smile was gone; I could almost see the weight on his shoulders. "If you know about Cruinn and the need for compensation, you know about the event called the Disappearance, I take it?"

"I do. And I know you believe Mac Dara is behind that. So you think Finbar is at risk again?"

"We can't know what Mac Dara will do. His acts of violence are becoming more savage and more frequent. It's as if he is suddenly in a hurry, desperate to get what he wants. Even Conor did not know why that might be. In any event, I felt Finbar needed protection. I was reluctant to saddle him with a hulking bodyguard; the lad is only young. Luachan's presence gives Finbar more freedom. He can go beyond the walls of the keep. He can ride or walk as far as the nemetons or along the lakeshore and do the things small boys love to do." Another sigh. "Your brother is a solemn child, as you've no doubt noticed. Eilis could draw him out, get him laughing, keep him active and happy. But Eilis had the opportunity for an adventure, and we let her go."

"Galicia. A long way."

"A long story, and perhaps not one for me to tell. She went with a cousin of mine. Aisha and her husband will take excellent care of your sister. It will be good for Eilis; she always wanted to spread her wings and fly."

My throat tightened again; I ordered myself not to shed a single tear. What if my own wings were broken beyond repair? I had long ago banished self-pity, since it did nothing but make folk more miserable.

One of the wolfhounds had her eye on me. "What are the dogs' names?" I asked. They could not be the same pair I remembered, who had already been old when I was a child.

"The dog is Broccan—son of my old Brocc—and the bitch is Teafa. She's from Deirdre and Illann's household."

"Teafa," I said softly. "Come here, girl."

She got up, a leggy, elegant creature, and came over to me. Moving my arm slowly, I stroked her neck with the back of my hand, using my knuckles to rub the sensitive spot behind the ears. After a few moments Teafa sat down and laid her muzzle heavily on my knee.

"There are pups," Father said. "Three of them, weaned now and ready for training. If you'd like one for your own—"

"No." My response was so sharp Teafa lifted her head, startled. "I mean, no thank you, Father. I don't want a dog. Teafa, good girl, rest easy."

"It's been ten years," Father observed after a while.

"A person might think that is enough time for the memories to fade. A person might believe this beautiful garden, planted with such love, might wipe away the guilt of that night. But it doesn't. I'll never want another dog." Teafa was drooling in pleasure as my knuckles worked on her; there was a damp patch on my skirt.

"Guilt," Father echoed. "It clings like a burr, and nothing can dislodge it."

It took me a moment to realize he was not talking about me, but about himself. "Father," I said firmly, "you could not have prevented me from being burned; the fire took hold too quickly. You did save my life. I would never, ever wish I had died that night rather than live with my injuries. There is no reason at all for you to feel guilty."

"Nor you," he said. "You tried your best to save your dog. As you said, the fire took hold too quickly. Nobody could have got him out in time. Nobody could have known beforehand what would happen. But our minds do play it over—what if I had made sure there was a guard on the kitchen door so Maeve could not slip outside, what if I had not let Bounder go to the annex for shelter, what if, what if . . ." He laid a gentle hand on Broccan's head. "Bounder would have died quickly," he said. "He would have been overcome by smoke before the flames reached him. If the dog's spirit lingers to watch over you, Maeve, be certain he forgives any wrong you may believe you did him. That creature was devoted to you."

I got to my feet. It was light now; the sun had risen beyond the cloak of trees, and in stables and outbuildings folk were getting ready for the day's work. Rhian would likely have fetched our breakfast by now, and to my surprise I felt hungry.

"Will you eat with us this morning?" Father asked.

"I'll eat in my chamber. That's easier for everyone. I suppose Mother and Deirdre will be in the sewing room later—please tell

Mother I will come and find them. And I promised Finbar I'd show him Swift."

We walked back together, arm in arm, with the wolfhounds padding on either side. At the foot of the stairs we parted. "Father," I said as he was turning away. "You won't need to protect me. I've learned to fight my own battles."

"You're my daughter," he said with a little smile. "A father protects his daughters."

"Then all I'd ask is that you trust me to make my own decisions," I said. "Some of my choices may seem unconventional. But I know what I can do and what I can't. I want to live the best life I can, Father."

"In that, I will always trust you to make the right choices, Maeve. Now you should go to your breakfast. I have a council later in the morning. The arrival of Swift may now play a part in our plans."

I wished I could be part of his council. The matters he faced were weighty indeed, with Mac Dara's acts of savagery increasing and Father's neighboring chieftains one by one turning against him. At Harrowfield I had learned to contribute to discussion about strategic matters; I was not sure how welcome my contribution would be here.

"I'll keep you informed," Father said. "Go on now. You must eat."

By the time Rhian and I made our way to the sewing room, the morning was well advanced. We walked in to find the place full of women. The shutters were wide-open. Slanting sunlight fell on industrious hands, on heads bent with concentration over spinning or mending or embroidery. My sister Deirdre, straight-backed and immaculately dressed, was working on a tiny, delicately patterned garment. Mother got up from her sewing when she saw me, opening her arms in welcome.

"Maeve! Come in, my dear!"

She embraced me; Deirdre got up to give me a kiss. The others greeted me, then turned their attention back to their work. I guessed Mother had instructed them all on how to behave. There were some familiar faces from childhood: head seamstress Orlagh; Mother's maidservant Eithne; the wives of one or two long-serving men-at-arms. I bestowed nods and smiles.

"Sit down with us, Maeve, and tell us about your journey." In company with so many women, Mother was not going to touch on sensitive matters such as what she thought of my staying away for a whole ten years, or how my crippling injuries might affect my future. "You must be tired."

"I slept well, thank you. I have spoken to Father this morning; I met him in the little garden where . . . where the annex used to be. Perhaps there's some handiwork Rhian can help with. She's an expert seamstress."

"But we don't want to take up too much of Rhian's time. You'll be needing her . . ."

"Not all the time," I said firmly. "And she's a very capable needlewoman. She mends my things, though I am no longer the child who used to come home from adventures in the forest with her gowns ripped and muddy." I caught Rhian's eye and suppressed a smile. My time in the stable yard tended to have something of the same effect; she was kept busy darning my stockings and trying to get the smell of horse out of my gowns.

"Orlagh will find you some mending to do, Rhian," Mother said. "We always welcome an extra pair of hands." A moment later she flushed red, realizing what she had said.

I sat down beside her. "It's all right, Mother," I said quietly, under cover of Orlagh's instructions to Rhian about hemming, which I could have told her were superfluous. "It's the way things are. I'm used to it now."

"Of course. But I wish . . ." She was clearly mortified; lost for words. Had she changed so much since the time of my childhood? We had always viewed her as the strong center of our lives. Perhaps my memory was playing tricks.

"Maeve is a grown woman, Mother." Deirdre kept her voice quiet, so the words would reach only Mother and me. "From the little I've seen so far, she seems to be coping rather well."

I was surprised. I did not remember this particular sister standing up for me very much in those early days. Indeed, I recalled her being somewhat absorbed in her own interests. I gave her a smile of acknowledgment. "I gave up wishing long ago," I said. "There's no point in it. Now tell me, Deirdre, what's that you're making? May I see?"

The conversation turned to family, and I was rapidly brought up-to-date on the progress of my various nieces and nephews and the news of what all my sisters were doing. Sibeal was expecting her first child; the little gown with embroidered owls was for her baby, who would be born far away in Kerry, in the spiritual community where my younger sister now lived and worked. In the north, Muirrin had a little boy and Clodagh twins. Then there were Deirdre's children, this morning out on a walk with their nursemaids. The Sevenwaters family was becoming a far-flung tribe.

In my turn I told them about Aunt Liadan and Uncle Bran and the cousins in Britain. But all the time I was aware of industrious hands around me, plying shuttle or spindle or needle, and beyond the windows the sun moving across the sky. I reminded myself that Mother had waited ten years for this conversation. I sat beside her, calm and still, making sure I gave every appearance of enjoying myself. I would not let her know that I was already restless and longing to be out of doors.

Time passed. Rhian finished her hem and Orlagh offered her a shirt to mend. With the torn garment in her hands, Rhian looked over at me suddenly. "Oh, but perhaps I should do this tomorrow," she said. "Lady Maeve, didn't you promise you'd take your brother to see Swift this morning?"

I suppressed a relieved smile. Later, I would thank her for saving me. "How could I have forgotten? I should go now or he'll be disappointed. Rhian, stay here if you wish—I won't need you for a while." I rose to my feet. "Mother, where will I find Finbar at this time of day?" I hoped she would not say Finbar was closeted with his tutor and unable to do anything so frivolous as visiting the stables.

My mother's look was somewhat quizzical, and I realized I had underestimated her powers of observation. "I can't tell you," she said with a little smile, "but I know Nuala's making honey cakes this morning, and both my son and his tutor are extremely fond of cakes. You may find them in the vicinity of the kitchen. Their lessons are conducted in the little room next to your father's council chamber—you remember, where the scribe used to work."

"Used to? What happened to him?"

"Luachan is very skilled. He took over those duties when he came to teach Finbar. Of course, such a little boy does not need formal lessons all day."

"A man of many parts," I said mildly. "Luachan, I mean."

"All children ask questions," Deirdre put in with a smile. "That's what one expects. But Finbar asks questions all day. Luachan is a good teacher for him. I've noticed druids generally answer questions with more questions."

"Finbar missed Eilis terribly when she first went away," Mother said. "Sibeal, too, though he was younger then. A child does not like to see his world change. Sibeal had a particular understanding of him. Luachan has similar insights. And he keeps Finbar occupied. My son is best not left too much alone."

This intrigued me, but I would not ask her to explain further in this company. "Luachan seems a courteous man," I said. "I'd best go now, Mother. Rhian, you could come and find me at the stables when you're finished here. There's no rush."

"Maeve." Mother spoke as I turned to leave.

"Yes, Mother?"

"I hope that in time you'll sit with us in the dining hall for your meals. Rhian can sit at the family table and help you, if that is required." After a moment she added, more quietly, "But I understand you may feel a little awkward about it, and of course it can wait until you're ready."

A strange anger stirred in me. Never mind that this was exactly what I wanted, time to feel my way in my parents' house, time for their people to get used to me. Mother did not know me. She could not know what I wanted. She had sent me away, and I had come home a different person. It wasn't kindness and understanding that made her say these things, but embarrassment. She didn't want her claw-handed daughter at the family table, making an exhibition of herself before the fine guests who had stayed on after Conor's ritual.

"No need to wait," I heard myself saying in a voice that carried beyond my mother and sister to the circle of women, all of whom were busily pretending not to be listening. "I'll be happy to join you this evening. I will need Rhian. Please ask them to make a place for her beside me. Without her help, I don't eat tidily."

"You sat at the family table in your aunt's house, then?" Mother's voice was full of words unspoken, hurts that had been nurtured over those ten years.

"I was there a long time, Mother. Of course I sat at the family table. It would not have occurred to Aunt Liadan to do things any other way. Now, if you'll excuse me, I must go and find Finbar."

I walked out of the chamber without looking back.

CHAPTER 4

y brother and his tutor were not in their study chamber, or in the kitchens consuming cake, or anywhere to be found, so I went to visit Swift on my own. That was just as well. I was wound tight as a harp string and not fit company for anyone. As I walked over to the stable yard I made myself breathe slowly. I should be able to do this. I should be able to sit in a room with a group of women and have a polite conversation with my own mother and sister. It wasn't as if the place was unfamiliar. My sisters and I had plied our needles there day after day under our mother's eagle eye, learning the skills that would make us fit wives for chieftains or princes. But it was hard, harder than Mother could imagine, to sit idle amid such industry. Rhian had seen it and had presented me with a perfect excuse to leave. Why hadn't Mother left well alone? Maybe she thought she was doing me a favor. Maybe she thought I wanted her to act as if nothing had changed. That was half-true: I hated fuss. Yes, at Harrowfield I had sat at the family table, and nobody had taken a bit of notice when Rhian fed me, because it was simply the way things were. Here, it would be different.

I paused to stroke the forehead of an old mare that was housed at the far end of the stables. She nuzzled close, expecting a treat. "What a disappointment I must be to her," I murmured. "But Deirdre married a chieftain and Clodagh a prince—what mother wouldn't be satisfied with that? Though I imagine a prince of the Otherworld is somewhat less desirable as a son-in-law than the ordinary kind. But then, Muirrin married a healer and Sibeal a scholar. And I won't marry at all. Perhaps Eilis will find a king's son in Galicia, one who likes horses. Maybe she'll never come home again. But it's just as likely she'll fall for a lowly groom or decide she can't be bothered with men at all."

What the mare thought of my ponderings I could not guess, but her quiet presence calmed me. I gave her another caress, using the back of my hand. Sounds of activity from the exercise area, a circular space of packed earth surrounded by a chest-high fence of woven wattles, drew me along the stable building to stand by the barrier. I watched in some surprise as one of the Sevenwaters grooms, a man I did not know, led Swift out into the yard. The yearling's eye was uneasy, his gait nervous. My father's stable master, stocky, gray-haired Duald, was by the doorway. He'd always been a hard-looking man, and time had only rendered his features grimmer. What were they doing, bringing Swift out so soon, when he was not recovered from the journey?

"Go slow, lad!" Duald called out now. "Walk forward steadily. Let the creature know you're in charge."

I held my tongue with some difficulty. Where were Emrys and Donal? Swift did not know either of these men, and he was edgy, sweating, uncomfortable. From where I stood by the barrier, I doubted if the horse could see me well enough to recognize the one familiar face.

"Pick up the pace!" Duald called, louder than was quite appropriate. "Give him a touch!"

Swift ran; the groom ran with him, careless of what damage rope and halter might be doing. If the yearling deviated from what was deemed to be a correct path within the circle, the groom corrected him with a light tap on the flank, using a short leather-bound stick. It was not a cruel blow; indeed, such a practice was common in most training yards. We had never used it on Swift. I felt cold sweat break out on my skin.

A small group of onlookers had gathered on one side of the exercise yard. I craned my neck and spotted Emrys at the back, his features tight with anxiety.

Under Duald's commands, the Sevenwaters groom continued to put Swift through his paces. Perhaps they thought they had his measure, for the horse seemed obedient as he was led at a trot and at a canter, then made to halt while Duald came in close to run expert hands over neck, back, rump, flank. But I could see trouble coming. When Duald took the leading rope in his own hand and moved Swift on again, taking him through a series of sharp turns, warning signs were plain in the horse's movement and in his eye. Surely Duald could read those clues? He'd been in charge here since I was a child. Was he the kind of man who must stamp his authority on a creature rather than train it with love?

Emrys would not speak up. Not only was his Irish limited, but a visiting groom, however expert, did not challenge the chieftain's stable master. But he and I both knew that look in Swift's eye; it was a red flag. In a moment the horse would make a bid for freedom, and he was strong. The small group of grooms and serving people stood to one side of the circle. On the other side there was now an audience of two, for Luachan had come up to lean on the fence, a striking figure in his gray robe, and beside him stood my brother Finbar, who was just tall enough to see over the barrier.

Swift halted suddenly, jerking his head one way, then the other. He shied, hooves flailing, and Duald lost his hold on the leading rope. The grooms gasped in unison. A vision flashed through my head, the horse trying to leap the fence, Finbar standing in the way, those hooves . . .

"Swift," I called, using the special tone of voice he recognized. "Swift, calm. Calm." Using my forearms for balance, I put my foot between the withies of the fence and rolled myself over the top, dropping to stand inside the circle. "Calm, my lovely boy. Green field. Still water. Calm now."

"No!" shouted Duald, gesturing me away and sending Swift into an erratic canter about the circle. "Lady Maeve, move back!"

I took a step forward, praying the horse would not knock me down. "No, you move back," I said, not altering my tone. "Emrys, I need you in here."

Swift wheeled this way, that way, the leading rope swinging as he looked for an escape. This barrier would not hold him; he had jumped far higher obstacles in his time.

"What do you think you—"

"Move back, Duald." I did not take my eyes off Swift to look at him, but Duald must have realized I meant business, for he stood still as Emrys slipped through the gate on the far side and approached step by step, saying not a word. "We don't want him to bolt. Let us do this; Swift knows us."

Then I forgot Duald. "Calm, Swift. Beautiful boy. Calm now," I murmured, keeping my voice steady as the yearling ran, as he kicked out at the barrier, tearing ragged holes in the neatly woven withies, as he tossed his head and breathed in angry snorts. "Easy, boy." Emrys stood quiet, waiting for his opportunity.

The two of us had done this many times before, though not under such conditions. We had worked with Swift as he grew from a leggy foal to a fine young horse. It took patience. He would seem to steady; then at the slightest distraction—a man coughing, a clanking of buckets, other horses stirring behind him in the stables—he'd be off again, dancing out of range before anyone could get a firm hold on the rope.

I tamped down my anger at Duald for bringing the situation about. I set aside my ill will toward my mother and my dread of tonight's public appearance. I kept my breathing slow, my voice even and quiet. I did my best to hold Swift's eye. I kept on talking to him. And eventually, as so often before, a time came when he was no longer frightened, but had begun to play a game with us: *Will I give in yet, or will I test them further? Which way will I jump, left or right? Run a little or stand still?*

"Calm now, lovely boy," I murmured, moving in close as he came to a quivering halt, breathing hard. I laid the soft back of my hand against his sweat-dewed coat. "Kind hands and quiet." I stroked his neck, all the while speaking to him. Swift stood still, though the warning wildness was not quite gone from his eye. I laid my brow against his neck. He shifted his feet but made no attempt to bolt.

Emrys did not take hold of the leading rope right away, but waited for my word, as was our practice. When I judged it was safe, I murmured, "Now." Emrys took the rope as casually as if nothing at all had happened, and Swift allowed himself to be led off to the comforting shadow of the stable building.

"Back to work, then!" Duald snapped at the grooms. They dispersed in a flash. The stable master turned to me, where I stood in the middle of the circle. I felt as if I had run a race. "You took a big risk, Lady Maeve," Duald observed. "In my book, an unacceptable risk."

I hardly had the strength to challenge him, but it was necessary to do so straightaway. "It was too soon to bring him out," I said. "I know you are in charge here, Duald, but this is not just any horse. As you can see, his temperament is volatile. He's always responded better to kindness than to strict discipline."

"What you did was remarkable, no doubt of that." I could see no trace of apology on his face, and I wondered whether I had lost any chance of having him listen. A man does not like to be shown up in front of his underlings. "But the creature's at Sevenwaters now, in my stables, and I'll be handling him my way. If he's going on to Tirconnell, he needs to learn some manners in a hurry. You can't coddle a horse of such wayward temper, Lady Maeve, or he'll always think he's in charge, and such an animal isn't safe to keep in a man's stables. Cruinn of Tirconnell knows his horses. Your father won't be wanting to give Cruinn a flawed gift."

I opened my mouth to deliver a withering retort, then caught the interested eye of the tutor, Luachan, across the barrier and thought better of it. "I'm sure you are entirely expert in these matters, Duald," I said. "I did have a conversation with my father about the yearling earlier this morning. He concurred with my suggestion that it might be best for Swift to be kept quiet for a few days, and then to be pastured awhile on his own, away from the keep. What you say about Cruinn is undoubtedly true. But there's more than one way to win the trust of a difficult horse. With this particular animal, kindness does seem to work best."

Duald looked at me in silence for a few moments. "A few days, maybe. Then we'll see. Hope you didn't tear your gown getting over the fence, my lady. There is a gate on this side, you know."

"There was no time for gates," I said. "I'll remind my father to discuss the matter with you, Duald." I was tempted to add that I would give Father a full report of this morning's happenings, but I needed to win Duald's trust, not annoy him further, so I held my tongue.

"Where did you learn to do that?" the stable master asked as we moved toward the gate. "To calm a creature with just your voice? The only time I've ever seen that done before, it was by one of Dan Walker's traveling folk. And they're a breed apart where horses are concerned."

"I don't know. It's just something I can do."

He moved to open the gate for me, but there was Luachan, smiling all over his handsome face, unlatching it and holding it for me to come through, and there was Finbar, fixing his unnervingly intense eyes on me as I approached.

"Could you do that with a bull? A frog? A wild boar?"

I smiled at my little brother. "I've never tried. I expect a truly wild creature would be much harder to reach. I suppose it might work with a bull, if you started when it was young. But I only use it when I really need to."

"Swift was frightened. He wanted to go home."

I knew better than to ask him how he knew this. "He doesn't like change," I said. "It's hard to leave everything that's familiar." It was all too easy for me to understand Swift's longing for his world to go back to the way it had been. "I hope I will be able to spend a lot of time with him, helping him to settle down."

"We were heading out for a walk in the forest," Luachan said in courteous tones. "Would it please you to walk with us, Lady Maeve?"

I was finding Lady Maeve something of a stranger. "You may call me Maeve. Yes, I'd like a walk." Anything rather than go back and be cooped up indoors. I should let Rhian know where I was going. But the green shade of the forest called me, and I could not face returning to the sewing room to find her. As to whether it was quite proper for me to go off on my own in company with a young man, it could be argued that a druid was a safe companion. And Finbar might be viewed as a chaperone.

"I couldn't help overhearing what you were saying to Duald." Luachan fell into step beside me as we headed down toward the lake. "There are walled grazing fields close to the nemetons, housing cows, goats, a flock of geese. The creatures supply the druid community with milk and eggs. It's very quiet there. An ideal spot, one might think, for an animal needing time to come to terms with its life being turned upside down. Not that I can claim any expertise in the management of horses."

"There needs to be someone to watch over Swift," I said, weighing my words carefully. If Luachan had been employed partly as a bodyguard for Finbar, he must know about the Disappearance. "Father has his guard posts on the borders, of course, and the forest looks after its own. But this horse is particularly valuable, and . . ."

Luachan looked at me sideways. "You fear the creature may spark the interest of a malevolent party already dwelling within this forest? That is possible, of course. But if I were wanting to house a precious item in the place least likely to attract such interference, the place I described is the one I would choose. We are not mages, of course, only druids. But the hand of Danu stretches over us and our modest dwellings. The goddess no doubt extends her protection to every creature within our place of prayer."

Clearly he understood the situation with Mac Dara. I wanted to question him, but I would not venture into such dark matters in Finbar's hearing. "That could be a good arrangement for Swift," I said. "But only if someone can stay nearby and watch over him. And I don't suppose your druid brethren have time for that."

Luachan grinned. "Too busy with meditation and prayer, you

mean? In fact, some must milk the cows and goats, collect the eggs, shut in the chickens at night. And even druids eat, sleep and occasionally wash themselves and their garments. Our lives are not spent entirely in memorizing passages of lore or conducting scholarly argument."

"Really?" I said as we reached the lakeside track and proceeded westward. "From what I remember of my years at Sevenwaters, that was more or less exactly what druids did."

"Ah," said Luachan. "But when you left here you were a child of—what—seven? Your understanding was not what it is now, I imagine, unless you were unusually perceptive for your age." He glanced at Finbar, who was not running ahead or dawdling to poke sticks into interesting holes or skip stones across the water, but walking quietly along beside us.

"I was ten," I said. "And I don't suppose I was any more perceptive than most children are at that age. Whatever is usual for a druid, I suspect you have stepped far outside its borders, Luachan. Do you live in the keep all the time now you are teaching Finbar?"

He smiled again, perhaps realizing I had deliberately turned the conversation away from myself. "I go between your father's house and the nemetons. A few days with Finbar, a day or two of prayer. While at the keep I assist Lord Sean with his letters and documents. I learned to read and write both Latin and Irish as a boy and I am teaching your brother the same skills."

My brother's silence was starting to unnerve me a little. "Perhaps you, too, are headed for the druidic life, Finbar," I said lightly.

He turned his big eyes on me. "I'm the only son," he pointed out. "I can't be a druid."

I had spoken without thinking, and I regretted it. I knew the arrangement. Johnny, eldest son of Bran and Liadan and leader of warriors, was my father's heir. Finbar would be Johnny's heir when the time came. There were several reasons for this line of succession to the chieftaincy, one of which was that Finbar had been born relatively late in my parents' lives. It was possible my father might die before his only son was a grown man. I had not until now considered that being chieftain of Sevenwaters, with the heavy weight of responsibility that role carried, might not suit Finbar at all. He looked such a frail child, shadowy and insubstantial, as if he bore a load too heavy for such small shoulders.

"Do you know how to skip stones across the water, Finbar?" I asked.

He looked at me as if I had said something silly. "That's for little children."

"Oh, big ones, too," I said calmly. "There's no rule that says you have to stop having fun when you turn six or seven, you know. My sisters and I used to compete to see who could get the longest distance or the most skips. Clodagh usually won, but I was second best."

"Show me."

A little pause; Luachan did not step in to help me. "I can't do it anymore, Finbar," I said. "You'll have to skip them for me, and Luachan can be your competition. Let's see if we can find some good stones. Flat ones go best. Not too heavy and not too light. About the weight of a small egg."

"You'll get your shoes wet," observed the druid as I moved off the track onto the pebbly shore and crouched down to hunt for the perfect stone.

"You're afraid of wet feet?" I challenged. "Or concerned that a seven-year-old might beat you?"

In a moment he was hunkered down beside me, finding his own stone. "Best of three," he muttered. "Believe it or not, I used to be good at this."

Finbar took a long time selecting his three perfect stones. It seemed to me he chose as much for color and pattern as for anything. Each of them he brought to me and made me lay it on my palm to feel the weight and to give it my approval. The one I judged too heavy was laid carefully back in the spot where he had found it and replaced by another of the same dove gray.

"Ready?" asked Luachan, who was standing by the water's edge—his sandals were indeed wet, as was the hem of his robe— with his stones in his hand. "Maeve, I rely on you to be an impartial judge."

"Finbar should have a few practice throws before you start."

"That's all right," said my brother, his tone all calm composure.

The druid gazed out over the shining waters of the lake, weighed his first stone in his hand, drew back his arm and flicked the stone expertly across the surface. It was impossible not to see what a fine stance he had, what economy and power of movement. If I had not been told already that he was something of a warrior, I thought I might have guessed in those few moments. The stone skipped across the lake surface, once, twice, five times before it sank.

"My turn now." Finbar did as I would have done, squatting down to throw. In view of the lack of rehearsal, I expected his missile to bounce once if he was lucky. He drew back his hand, and with an economical movement of the wrist released the stone. It hardly seemed like a throw, but the stone danced over the water, bouncing four times, then vanishing like a diving bird.

"Remarkably good for a first attempt," I said. Clearly, no concessions were required. "Luachan wins the first round. Ready for the next? You should go first this time, Finbar; that's fair."

In the second round Finbar's stone bounced six times, Luachan's five again.

"Third and deciding round," I said.

"No more." Finbar's small voice was firm. "It's time to walk on now."

"Are you sure?" He had surprised me again. Was this game too simple for him?

"Yes. Thank you for showing me, Maeve." Solemn as a little owl.

"That's all right. I know a lot of games. But it's a while since I played most of them."

We walked on, my shoes and Luachan's sandals squelching as we went.

"Did you play games with Bounder?" Finbar asked.

A silence drew out, punctuated by our footsteps on the pathway and the gushing of a nearby stream. What to answer? The easy lie: no. The bare truth: yes. Or the difficult answer the question deserved? *Come on, Maeve. I thought you prided yourself on honesty.*

"I remember Doran making me a ball out of hide strips," I made myself say. "Bounder liked chasing it, but he wasn't so keen on bringing it back. And he loved a good tug-of-war." Ten years, and it still hurt to talk about him.

"Teafa had puppies not long ago," Finbar said. "Three of them. You could keep one if you liked."

"Father already offered and I said no." It came out too sharply. This wasn't Finbar's fault. "What about you? Don't you want a dog of your own?"

He shook his head solemnly. "The chieftain of Sevenwaters always has a pair of wolfhounds. Father told me. But that's not for a long time yet. If I got a dog now it might die before I needed it."

He had shocked me again. "But you might want one, just because it's lovely to have a dog for a friend and companion. That's why Father has Broccan and Teafa, I'm sure, not because it's . . . expected."

"If it's lovely," Finbar said, "why don't you want a puppy?"

"Enough, Finbar." Luachan had not contributed to this conversation, but now his tone conveyed an order. "I'm sorry," he murmured, glancing at me.

I felt somewhat annoyed that he thought to protect me from my brother's piercing honesty. "It's all right, Finbar," I said. "It's because I miss Bounder too much. He can't ever be replaced." And since I had gone so far, I might as well give him all of it. "Besides, after what happened that night, the night I lost him, I don't think I can trust myself to look after another dog. I'd always be worried that I might do it again. Or something like it."

The two of them looked at me as if I'd said something ridiculous. "It makes perfect sense," I said, fixing my gaze on the path ahead.

We walked on in silence to a point where the track branched, one path continuing along the lakeshore, the other heading up into the forest.

"We could take you to see the place I mentioned," Luachan

said. "The pasture, the animals and so on. It's a longish walk. You may be tired."

"We have food," Finbar put in, glancing at the bag the druid had slung over his shoulder.

"Honey cakes," said Luachan. "A flask of mead, watered to suit young tastes. Some apples. We're planning to eat when we reach the nemetons."

I wished I had waited for Rhian. Still, when it came to the point I could always say I wasn't hungry. "I'd like to see the place. But I mustn't be away too long or Rhian will worry about me. I told her I'd be at the stables."

"Duald saw us all together," Luachan said easily. "Your maid-servant will doubtless ask him and reach the right conclusion. Shall we move on, then?"

It was a long way, but I was used to walking. The cool damp air of the forest, the crunch of the first fallen leaves underfoot, the high chorus of birdsong calmed and restored me. My companions did not attempt further conversation, either with me or with each other. As we made our way up and down the paths, over gurgling streamlets and under venerable oaks, I thought about Bounder, and why I could not forgive myself for what had happened. Bounder had been first in my prayers every night since he had come into my life as a six-week pup; prayers were not an easy habit to break, even when one hardly believed in any god. He was still first. Father had been right when he said guilt was hard to get rid of. Perhaps I would still be mourning Bounder's loss when I was an old woman. People would think me crazy, with good reason. That vision came to me again, my figure on the stairs of the keep, and visitors muttering my story in voices hushed with pity. I did not much care for the image.

A pox on it, now I had to relieve myself. Why hadn't I waited for Rhian?

"I'm sorry," I murmured. "Could you wait a bit? I need to . . ."

The very poised Luachan surprised me by blushing. Finbar sat down on a fallen tree. He eyed me. I could see him wondering whether to offer help and deciding not to.

"I won't be long."

The business was a little awkward, what with the need to hold my gown out of the way, deal with my stockings, and make sure I returned before anyone came looking. I had ways of performing certain essential tasks, ways I'd had to develop. I was crouched there, clawing up a stocking, when something moved in the undergrowth not far away. I froze. If anything was going to spring out and surprise me, I surely didn't want it to happen when I was at such a disadvantage.

Nothing. Whatever it was, it had become still when I had, for there was not the least movement now amid that profusion of ferns and bushes. The light was dim here; I was well off the track. Luachan and Finbar were out of sight behind the bole of a massive oak. I bent to finish my work with the stocking. There was a furtive rustling, a sound made by something a great deal larger than a bird or squirrel or hedgehog. And now, as I straightened, I saw it for a moment, dark, solid, padding swiftly away under the trees. A dog. A big black dog.

No need to wait until you're old, I told myself, hauling too hard on the second stocking. My fingers tore a hole; Rhian would not be pleased with me. *You're crazy already.* My mind was so much on Bounder that I was seeing him everywhere. If there was a dog running wild in the Sevenwaters forest, it wasn't likely to be a perfect copy of my long-dead friend. It had probably been a pig. Or my mind conjuring up what I wanted to see. I rose to my feet.

Another black form slunk across my vision, a little smaller than the first but shaped much the same. Head down, tail down, shoulders hunched, ribs stark under the pelt . . . It was gone. Two dogs. Two Bounders. This was ridiculous. I would fix my mind on something completely different, such as how to coax a smile out of my little old man of a brother. I checked my gown to make sure it was not caught up anywhere, and walked back to my companions. "I'm ready to go on." I was tempted to tell them what I had seen, but held back. I could just imagine what questions Finbar could get out of that.

At a certain point the forest thinned out, and we walked into a broad clearing ringed by tall trees. In the center stood a great circle of mossy stones. The grass around them had been scythed short; it was clearly a place of ritual. I glimpsed various low buildings set back under the trees, but nobody seemed to be about.

"We'll walk down to the place I mentioned," Luachan said, "and eat our provisions there. The track goes through that way." He pointed ahead toward a stand of birches. "You can take a look, Maeve, and see if you think your charge might be happy in our fields."

"The decision's not up to me," I said, following him along the path he'd indicated. "This is quite a distance from the keep. It's possible Father might think it's too far."

"After what you did at the stables earlier," said the druid, "Lord Sean will at the very least listen to your opinion. It was remarkable. Your audience was deeply impressed."

"It's a useful skill." His praise made me feel awkward. "It counts little against the things I can't do."

Luachan raised his brows at me. "You keep some kind of tally?"

I pressed my lips together so I would not say something discourteous. What could he know, with his fine healthy body and his handsome face, his life as druid and tutor and scribe and guard? A man blessed with natural advantages and opportunities could not possibly understand what it was to be me.

"I don't need to," I said. "I see the tally in people's eyes when they look at me. And don't say you're sorry. That was a simple statement of fact, not a bid for sympathy." I changed the subject before he had a chance to respond. "Luachan, do you know my uncle Ciarán at all well?"

He walked in silence for a little before he answered. "Everyone knows him. A man of hidden depths, I believe. Do you remember him from before?"

"Not clearly. I was young. I suppose we will be reintroduced. Father was saying Ciarán might become chief druid now Conor is gone."

"Perhaps."

"Only perhaps? Are there several eligible people? How is such a choice made?"

"I'm told time is allowed for prayer and reflection, and then there is a discussion. If the brethren are not in agreement, a vote may take place." After a moment he added, "Ciarán is generally thought to be the most likely choice."

I sensed a *but* in this statement; Luachan did not offer more, however, and it did not feel right to ask. Perhaps Ciarán's heritage made some people hesitate. He was the son of a Sevenwaters chieftain, certainly. He was also the son of a dark and twisted woman of the Fair Folk, my great-grandfather's second wife. I did not know a great deal about Ciarán's life before he joined the brotherhood. In my judgment, what lay in his past was less important than what kind of man he was now. But perhaps druids weighed up these things differently.

We made our way through the birch grove, walking beside the stream, and emerged to a broader clearing divided into three walled fields. In one section a few cows grazed, each attended by a trio of geese. In the second, a flock of plump hens was searching busily for insects in the grass, overseen by a watchful cockerel. The third contained a solitary goat. There were water troughs and sturdy-looking shelters. On the other side of the fields a larger hut stood under the oaks, with a walled area for a garden and a lean-to that might provide refuge for creatures in stormy weather. No smoke arose from the hut's chimney, and the shutters were closed. It had a forlorn look, somewhat like that of the goat.

"Who lives there?" I asked.

"Nobody at present," said Luachan. "It's used mainly for visitors, since it's situated somewhat apart from our own dwellings. Most recently it housed that cousin of your father's, the woman from Galicia, and her husband. They stayed here awhile at Ciarán's invitation. He—Conri—was uncomfortable among folk, at least at first. The hut suited them, modest as it is. We might sit on the steps to eat our food."

The awkward moment came, when we were settled there and Luachan had spread out the provisions on their cloth. He offered me the mead flask first. It was somewhat too heavy for me to manage easily, but my arms were strong, and I held it between my wrists, tipped it up and drank without spilling the contents over myself or dropping the flask on the ground. I looked the druid in the eye as I passed it back, and he said nothing at all.

"Did you know Maeve can eat with her toes?" said my brother. "She's good at it; I've seen her."

There was a brief silence. "Impressive," said Luachan.

If he expected a demonstration, he was going to be disappointed. "I'm not very hungry," I said. "Please, go ahead and eat."

Finbar met my eye; his expression told me he saw right through my lie. He busied himself breaking up a honey cake, then taking a knife and slicing off pieces of apple as if he'd fed a crippled sister hundreds of times before. When he reached toward me with a bite-sized piece of cake in his hand, I let him put it between my fingers. Of course, he had watched Rhian doing this very thing for me.

"Thank you, Finbar," I said. "Perhaps I do feel a little hungry."

My brother was meticulous: one mouthful for me, one for himself. Luachan made no comment, but sat quietly eating his own share. Peace settled over me once more. In the fields the animals foraged or grazed in apparent content, and a chorus of birds sang in the trees all around. While the depths of the forest were dark and shadowy even on a bright day, here in this open place the sun cast its light on mossy stones and verdant grass, on the nut-brown pelts of the cows and the bright flowers that grew wild at their feet. There was no sign of any druids, though now I could see the smoke from a hearth fire rising a short distance away.

"It must be good to live here," I said. "Not that I have any sort of spiritual vocation, unlike my sister Sibeal, of whom you've doubtless been told. But I like the quiet of it. I like being close to the forest."

Luachan lifted his well-shaped brows. "The keep is surrounded by forest," he observed.

"A keep is a keep. Ladies are generally expected to spend a good deal of their time indoors, or at least within the protective walls, performing various useful tasks." I had talked myself into another trap. I did not know this young man well at all, and I had no wish to reveal myself further to him. "I prefer the outdoors."

"You like horses, don't you?" Finbar observed. "Are you sad that you can't ride?"

"Not really, Finbar. I was never a keen rider as a child, not like Eilis. At Harrowfield they let me help a lot in the stables. I may not be able to rub a horse down or muck out a stall, but I do seem to be able to talk to animals, even the difficult ones. All the same, I don't think Duald appreciated my help this morning."

Luachan finished eating his apple and threw the core over the wall into the cow enclosure. "A man of Duald's kind doesn't like being shown how to do his job," he said. "Especially not by a young woman, I imagine. He would have felt some shame in front of that particular audience, since every one of those grooms knows horses and their ways."

I was not sure whether he was offering a compliment or criticism. "If I hadn't acted when I did, Swift would have been over the wall and away, possibly kicking a few heads as he went. Quite apart from the likelihood that he would have hurt himself or one of the onlookers, letting things go on the way they were could have undone much of the work we've put into training him. Long months of it."

"Long months of training and the horse is still as flighty as that?"

"Don't judge, Luachan." Perhaps I was not quite as calm as I had thought. "Swift's been taken away from everything he knows. He's had a sea voyage, which is unsettling for any horse. Of course he's upset. He doesn't need to be put through his paces in the ring and prodded by strangers. He needs a rest. Time to himself. Time to recover." I glanced around the clearing. "This place does seem ideal. Whom should I ask about it? Ciarán?"

"I don't suppose you want my advice," Luachan said with more delicacy than I expected after his previous comments. "But I'd suggest you put it to your father first, and let him deal with both Duald and Ciarán. I don't say that because I doubt your judgment in any way. After seeing you quiet the horse, I recognize that you know what you're doing. But there's a way of going about these things that allows men to keep their pride, and I think that's the best way to follow."

I attempted to digest this statement. "You're telling me that women can make decisions, but that they have to let men think they've made them," I said. "Forgive me, but that sounds quite undruidic. It suggests a degree of dishonesty, even deviousness."

"What's deviousness?" asked Finbar, passing me a slice of apple.

"Going about things in an indirect way, in order to keep the truth from someone," said Luachan. "I don't believe I'm being devious, Maeve. Merely thinking that your arrival at Sevenwaters may be a little like a sudden storm in a calm sea—not easy for the inhabitants to accept."

"I didn't want to come," I said without thinking. The expression that appeared on my brother's face made me cringe with shame. "But I'm glad I did now," I added hastily. "It feels good to have a brother."

If Finbar saw through this, he hid it well. "I have lots of sisters," he said, "but they keep going away. Are you staying at Sevenwaters, Maeve?"

I drew a deep breath. "I don't know," I said. "I'll be here until Swift is settled, at least. Then I'll see." In the long term, the truth would be less cruel than a comforting lie. "I know it's hard when people go away." It was just as hard to leave the people you loved behind, I thought. In the ten years I had lived at Harrowfield, Bran and Liadan had been father and mother to me. I missed his quiet strength, her wise and loving advice. No wonder Sevenwaters did not feel like home.

"I went away once," Finbar said. "When I was little. Mac Dara took me to the Otherworld. But I can't really remember. Not clearly." He passed me another piece of apple.

"Not at all, I should think," I said, wondering when I would get used to his odd manner of talk. "Weren't you a newborn babe at the time?"

"There was a fire. Someone screaming. Mac Dara threw the baby in the fire. Not me, or I wouldn't be here. The other baby. It burned all up." His eyes looked into a different world.

Who had told him this? Whether the terrible tale was true or not, it was clear that Finbar believed he had seen it. "Did Clodagh tell you the story?" I asked. I wanted to change the subject completely. I wanted to take that look off his face by whatever means I could, even if it meant making a fool of myself in front of Luachan. But Finbar was too subtle to be taken in by such an obvious ploy.

"I've never met Clodagh," he said. "Not since I was a baby. She stays away, because of Mac Dara. But she told the story before she left, and Eilis told me."

It was hard to believe that Eilis would burden a child, especially this child, with something so disturbing.

"Finbar," said Luachan, "the other baby was not all burned up. Remember? It was not a human baby, and after it was scorched in the fire, your sister mended it and breathed life into it, and then gave it back to its mother. That part of the story had a good ending." His tone was gentle. It sounded as if they had been through this explanation many times before.

"So you know the whole story, too," I said.

Luachan gave me a crooked smile. "It was deemed appropriate, in view of my current duties. Of course, the bare bones of it are common knowledge: the abduction of a chieftain's son does not go unnoticed. The details I had from Ciarán, who heard Clodagh's account after her return from the Otherworld."

"That baby was hurt," Finbar insisted. "He went all black and shriveled, and one of his eyes fell out into the flames. Clodagh burned her hand picking it up. And when Cathal poured wine on him to put out the fire, smoke came out of the baby's mouth."

"Perhaps you did see it, Finbar," I told him, and I put my arm around his shoulders. He did not shrink from my touch, but under it he was strung tight. "But you couldn't remember it. People don't remember what they saw as little babies."

"I see it in the water. I see it in the smoke. I can't help it. It's there waiting for me." He hesitated, clearly wanting to say more but for some reason holding back. He glanced at Luachan.

Suddenly I was angry: angry with my family for burdening this child with the whole dark story, furious with Luachan for allowing his charge to dwell on the hurts and cruelties of the past.

Surely if Finbar were kept busy with riding and running and games, he would not be eaten up thus by worries. At his age, Eilis had been fearless and full of life. Finbar was an anxious little wraith. I had seen snatches of a different boy once or twice, and I made up my mind that I would extricate him from his cloud of trouble whether his tutor approved or not.

"But I'm sure it's true that the other baby was mended and went safely back to his mother," I said briskly. I would seize an opportunity to speak to Luachan alone as soon as I could. He did not seem an unreasonable man. He was kind, clever, able. But not, it seemed, especially sensitive, or he would surely see how unhappy Finbar was. "If there's one thing I remember about Clodagh, it's that she would never tell a lie, not even to make someone feel better. By now that baby will be an Otherworld boy of your own age, Finbar. I wonder if you'll ever meet him?"

A tear rolled down Finbar's cheek. He did not seem to notice it.

"I must head back to the keep," I said, rising to my feet. "Rhian's probably still stuck in the sewing room mending shirts. Finbar, thank you for helping me with my food. You did a good job."

That won me the ghost of a smile. "Rhian's nice," my brother said. "You're lucky to have a friend."

CHAPTER 5

t the supper table I was placed between my sister and Rhian, with a big dish full of fruit in front of us. Someone had judged things finely, since this obstacle was just high enough to screen my platter and my hands from most of my fellow diners, but not so high that it would stop me from meeting someone in the eye while conducting a conversation. In short, it was perfectly placed to assist me without embarrassing me. I glanced at Deirdre and she winked at me. My spirits lifted.

There were still many guests in the house, so the dining hall was almost full. The family table stood on a raised area. The most important guests sat there with us. Tonight they included Ciarán—who was family, of course, though he did not live at the keep—and a pair of local chieftains with their wives.

Everyone else sat at the three longer tables on the lower level. At Sevenwaters the whole household ate together, save for those who cooked and served the meal, and those required to watch over young children. And guards, of course; with the threat of mischief hanging over Sevenwaters, their armed presence around the keep would be maintained constantly. Indeed, I noticed that the women this evening greatly outnumbered the men.

Finbar sat by Luachan. Ciarán was on his other side. If his white robe did not make it obvious, his bearing—almost kingly— and his dark red curls confirmed his identity. It was hard to think of Ciarán as Conor's brother. Conor had been an old man even before I left Sevenwaters. Ciarán looked younger than my father. It was the fey blood, I supposed. Liadan had explained to me that a person born of an alliance between humankind and Fair Folk lived far longer than an ordinary man or woman. I thought what a hard choice it must be to wed such a person, as Clodagh had. When my sister was old and gray, Cathal would probably still look like a man in his prime. I supposed they had thought this through before they decided to marry. There was a world of sorrow in such a choice.

Eating without drawing undue attention was not easy, even with the fruit dish as a screen. As a result, I contributed almost nothing to the conversation. Deirdre talked about her children with love, pride and humor. I saw a warmth and wisdom in this sister that had not been evident when she was younger, and I found myself sad that she was returning home in the morning. Illann asked me some perceptive questions about Swift, which I answered politely; while I was speaking, Rhian avoided passing me anything. I saw Ciarán watching me, but he made no attempt to engage me in talk. Indeed, he was saying even less than I was. Father and the two chieftains were avoiding any topic likely to swing around to the regional conflicts and the shadow of the Disappearance, which no doubt hung heavily over them all. People talked about the meal, the weather, the autumn culling of stock, the need to arrange clearing of undergrowth along a certain path through the forest so laden carts could pass more easily between Sevenwaters and Illann's domain to the south.

Then my father and Ciarán turned the talk to Conor. Ciarán spoke of his half brother's kindness, his wisdom and humor. Father mentioned the many times his uncle had visited Sevenwaters to offer good advice on everything from growing vegetables to tackling a strategic challenge. Illann confessed that he had gone to Conor for advice on how best to approach my father when asking for Deirdre's hand in marriage.

"And what did he say?" Deirdre asked her husband.

"Ah," said Illann. "That's a secret. But it worked, gods be praised."

"He said this: tell Lord Sean that as he has so many daughters, he can easily afford to let one go." My father delivered this outrageous statement with a solemn face.

"Father!" Deirdre protested. "I'm sure he said no such thing!"

"It was a great deal more respectful than that, or your father would have given me short shrift," Illann said, smiling at his wife. "I did approach him with much trepidation. In fact, Conor told me I must appear confident even if I was shaking in my shoes. He was a good man, wise and kind. A wonderful storyteller."

"His tales were full of light and shade," my mother said. "One moment you'd be laughing fit to burst; the next he'd have you on the verge of tears."

"Speaking of tales," said my father, "what better to honor his passing than a fine one tonight? Ciarán, I was hoping you might oblige us, once the meal is finished."

"Of course," Ciarán said. He had eaten very little, I noticed; perhaps that was part of the druidic discipline. Luachan, too, had partaken only sparingly of the meal. As for Finbar, I had not heard a word from him all through supper. I tried to remember at what age we had been expected to sit at the family table rather than take our meals in a corner of the kitchen, overseen by Nuala or a maidservant. I'd liked those kitchen feasts. Bounder used to sit by my feet, where I could slip him tasty morsels. I glanced around the hall, noticing various children seated by their parents. All looked older than my brother. Deirdre's children were already in bed. Emer was five, Oisin only three.

When the meal was finished, tables were moved to make an open space before the hearth. People moved, too, seating themselves around that area ready for the evening's entertainment. Mother was trying to catch my eye. Perhaps she had chosen a spot for me, somewhere I could be unobtrusive. But I had my own plan. I sent Rhian to find space on a bench while I headed straight for Finbar.

"Come and sit with us," I said. "I need you to tell me who everyone is." I shepherded him away from the two druids and into the spot Rhian had chosen, not too close to the hearth with its roaring fire, but near enough so we could hear the story clearly.

When we were settled, Finbar whispered in my ear, "I'm supposed to sit with Luachan. Mother said."

"Tell her I made you do it." He hardly needed a bodyguard right inside my father's hall.

"Shh," hissed Rhian, for Ciarán was beginning his story.

"I offer this tale in Conor's memory," he said, his deep, compelling voice drawing his audience in with the first words. "He was especially fond of it. The story contains a geis, which you will know is a form of curse, though sometimes it can be a blessing in disguise. If a geis is pronounced over a person, sooner or later it will catch up with him, however careful he is to avoid it. Take the case of the famous hero, Cú Chulainn. He had the ill fortune of being subject to two geasa. The first said he must never refuse food offered him by a woman. The second said he must never eat the flesh of a hound. There came a time when a woman offered him a joint of meat, and he ate it. Only afterward did he discover that it had been dog flesh, and that he had complied with the first geis only to violate the second. To do so meant death; the untouchable warrior became vulnerable from that moment on, and soon after was slain.

"A geis does not always set out the terms of a man's death, of course. It can be more along the lines of this: *On the day when you walk under a leafless birch with three crows perched in its branches, you will lose all that is dear to you.* A geis may doom a person to silence or servitude or blindness. It may offer a hope of redemption, provided certain requirements are met. It depends on the will of the person pronouncing the geis. That person is more often than not a woman: a powerful woman, such as a sorceress. Thus it is with tonight's tale."

Ciarán looked around the hall, taking in his whole audience. I had forgotten what unusual eyes he had. The shade was a deep red-purple, like ripe mulberries.

"There were once two chieftains," Ciarán said. "One was named Maelan, the other Torna. Each lived on a wooded hill, and around each hill lay good grazing land. The best grazing of all was to be had in a place right between the two territories, along the banks of a fair stream that passed through the fields. That stream was known as the Silverwash, and it had its source in the Nameless Wood, a place so full of magic that no man or woman had ever dared set foot across its margin. Folk knew *something* lived in the perilous forest, something strange and frightening. Many were the tales of its nature and its deeds, so many that there was no knowing what was truth and what imagining. It was a beast; a ghost; a monster; a dragon. More than one, perhaps. Ten. A hundred. A thousand. Folk told the stories around the fire at night, in whispers, glancing over their shoulders into the shadows behind. Children grew up on the tales, and that was why nobody from either territory ever journeyed up the Silverwash beyond a certain point, and nobody drank the water from the stream, though it sparkled in the sunlight, clear as dewdrops.

"Cattle being cattle, and the boys who tend to them being boys, sometimes a cow or two would stray over Maelan's border, or over Torna's border, and wander down to the Silverwash. And since the beasts of the field know nothing of frightening tales, the cows would drink from the stream while they were there. They seemed to take no harm from it. Indeed, both chieftains bred cattle that were the envy of all Erin—sturdy, glossy-coated, gleaming with good health. Their milk had a sweet, rich taste found nowhere else in the land, and the children of those two territories, growing up on the milk and butter and cheese from those contented cows, were especially bonny and rosy-cheeked, though perhaps they suffered just a little from nightmares. Maybe folk thought about what it all meant. Perhaps they were happier not thinking about it.

"For years the two chieftains had been peaceable neighbors, as their fathers and their fathers' fathers had been before them. But then there came a season of cold and storm in which supplies ran low and tempers grew short. Torna's cattle were housed in his barns for the winter, sheltered and warm, if not as well fed as usual. Maelan's cattle went between barn and fields, for on the rare days when rain and sleet did not fall from the lowering sky, he preferred his stock to roam out of doors, gleaning what nourishment they could from the waterlogged fields.

"Now, it happened one day that the lad who was with Maelan's cows had his mind on something else—his mother was sick with a racking cough, and he was worried about her. So he did not notice his hungry charges crossing the border of Maelan's land, splashing through the Silverwash and heading off into Torna's fields. When he saw them the boy ran after them, wading through the swollen stream, racing onto Torna's land, herding the cattle back home. But the damage was done. While the cows had been trampling all over Torna's fields, they had been seen. Torna's son, a lad of sixteen summers, happened to be passing and caught a clear view of the herd and its frantic attendant. If he'd known what the result might be, he would likely not have mentioned this to his father. The rain would have washed away the evidence, and a great deal of unpleasantness would have been avoided. But this was a responsible lad—Finn was his name—and he went straight to Torna and told him what he had seen.

"It was a small enough incident, and at any other time a simple apology and a promise of increased vigilance in future would have been enough to soothe any ruffled feathers. But this was a hard winter, and tempers were already frayed. Such is often the way of territorial disputes: they start with a rolling pebble and become landslides."

I saw one of Father's visiting chieftains nodding in agreement, while the other wore a smile of appreciation. Both Finbar and Rhian were perched on the very edge of the bench, their attention fixed on Ciarán.

"Torna said this was a deliberate plan to steal the last fodder from his fields, so that when he finally let his herd out, they would grow thin while Maelan's cattle were fat. Maelan accused his neighbor of stirring up trouble for no better reason than jealous spite. The insults and accusations flew one way, then the other. There were covert raids; an outbuilding was set on fire. Then the raids became less covert and more in the nature of outright attacks, and before very long at all, the two chieftains were at war.

"The lovely valley of the Silverwash was gouged and split and ruined as the measured passage of grazing cattle was replaced by the violent activities of conflict. Horses' hooves ripped up the grass. The boots of fighting men did their work. Fire scorched the birch groves and blackened the undergrowth. In place of the gentle chorus of birdsong, the screams of dying men rang out across the fields. The Silverwash ran red.

"By springtime the valley was a wreck, and the losses to each household were immense. Many had fallen, not only men-at-arms, but grooms and kitchen boys and bakers, called to fight when there was nobody else to stand against the enemy. In both households women grieved. Torna's elder son, who had been betrothed to Maelan's elder daughter in the time of peace, was slain, and young Finn became the heir to the chieftaincy.

"Spring hardly dared show its face in such a ruined landscape as this. A cautious bud on the cherry tree; a bluebell hiding beneath an oak still bare-limbed from winter. A blade of grass, standing brave and green in the blood-soaked soil. Torna vowed vengeance for the death of his beloved son. Maelan swore he would stand against the worst his enemy could deliver. Maelan's elder daughter wept.

"Now, there was also a younger daughter. Her job was to tend to her sister in her grief. This meant very little rest, since the bereaved girl woke often in the night needing to be comforted. One morning, just after dawn, the younger sister, Baine, had settled her sister back to sleep and was standing by her tower window, looking out over the wreck of the lovely valley and away up the Silverwash to the Nameless Wood. She gazed and blinked, not believing her eyes. She looked again. A great tide was rushing down the stream from the forest, a monstrous wash of water that spilled over the banks and gushed between the trees and spread out on either side, heedless of margins. Birds screamed; creatures bolted; Baine stood transfixed, her eyes wide, as the wave came down over the land before her, and the water rose, and rose, and rose again. It swallowed the banks where the cattle had stood to drink. It engulfed the little grove where she and Finn had played as children, the place where they had made a treehouse, the dam they had built on a side stream, the big rocks where they had balanced and jumped and challenged each other. It ran over the shallow cave where they had continued to meet in secret, early in the mornings, after their fathers became enemies. The water kept on rising. It ate up Maelan's grazing fields, the fields that had produced the finest cattle in all Erin. It gobbled Torna's fields on the other side. It washed over the places where young men had died in their blood. It laid a silent blanket over the hollows where they had lain screaming for their mothers, or crying for their comrades, or begging the gods to put an end to their pain. The water rose and rose until it came to the very foundations of Maelan's keep. A broad lake filled the valley from side to side. Gazing across its expanse, Baine thought it stretched from her father's front door to Torna's. If she'd had a boat, she might have rowed all the way across to Finn. Not that anyone in that household would receive her now."

Ciarán paused, as if thinking hard about what was to come next. Or perhaps he was waiting for us to absorb the deeper meaning of the story. I was wondering when the geis was going to come in.

"The lake did not drain away over time, as an ordinary flood does. The water stayed just where it was, robbing both chieftains of any useful grazing land, and at the same time cutting off the main road. Nobody could attend the High King's council in Tara. Nobody could go visiting. There was no way to convey stock to the markets. One thing was beyond doubt. The flood had been sent by the malevolent dweller in the Nameless Wood. The creature was bent on mischief and destruction. In Maelan's hall and in Torna's, the talk turned to punishing the evildoer, perhaps with fire, or perhaps by felling trees, or perhaps by hiring a mage or sorcerer powerful enough to drive it out. But when it came to the point, nobody was prepared to act. The folk of that region had been listening to tales of the Nameless Wood for generations, and their fear of it was lodged in the bone, too deep to cast out."

"Master Ciarán?" It was Finbar who spoke, his tone clear and confident.

"You have a question, young Finbar? Ask it."

"Why didn't the two chieftains go over in boats and talk to each other? Didn't they see that the flood was a punishment for what they had done?"

"Ah," said Ciarán with a smile. "One might wish they had been so wise; one might wish each had been prepared to listen to his younger child. Instead, they struggled on awhile as things were, though the fighting was over—the new fight they faced was to live at all, now the lake had robbed them of the grazing land that had sustained them. Torna went into a decline; he had not been the same since the loss of his elder son. More and more, the management of household and land fell to young Finn, and it was not an easy job, for folk were now both fearful and angry, seeing that it was Torna's misjudgment that had turned their lives sour. At Maelan's keep the situation was hardly better, for Maelan had suffered a grievous wound in the fighting, and ill humors seemed likely to kill him before the summer came. In that household there were no sons, only the two girls, and the future looked grim indeed.

"Now, Finn and Baine had not seen each other since the Silverwash flooded, but they had been close friends since they were small children, and they had long-established ways of exchanging messages. So, one morning at around the time when they used to meet in their secret place, Baine hung a blue cloth out of her tower window—*A meeting*—and Finn, on the other side of the strange lake, hung a green cloth out of his—*Tomorrow*—and each knew the time would be just before dawn, so that nobody would see them slip away. The next day, at the spot where the lovely birches had been drowned, there was Finn in a little rowing boat, and there was Baine in another, and—oh, surprise!—one slender branch of the tallest birch stretched up above the lake's gleaming surface, so the childhood friends could moor their craft while they talked. Finn and Baine reached out to clasp hands; the boats rocked gently.

"'I missed you,' Baine said.

"'You are in my heart, every moment,' replied Finn. 'Will we go to make things right?'

"'We must,' said Baine.

"'Now?'

"'Now. Step over into my boat. If we row together, the journey will not seem so long.'

"It was long, nonetheless, and arduous, but not so hard as it would have been for man or woman alone. They rowed and rowed, and the lake stretched on and on, and by the time they reached dry land at the fringes of the Nameless Wood, dusk shrouded the mysterious trees and concealed whatever might lie beneath them. Finn had brought a knife and a flint. Baine had brought a lantern. They tied up their boat at the edge of the lake, lit their lantern, and walked into the dark wood.

"There was a path of sorts, though neither Finn nor Baine knew if it was the right one. Under the circumstances, it seemed best to trust to the natural magic of the place, magic strong enough to turn a peaceful stream into a destructive torrent, and no doubt do far worse things, if the stories were to be believed.

"'Are you afraid?' Finn asked Baine.

"'If I were not afraid,' she said, 'I would be a fool. I am glad you are here with me.'

"'And I that you are beside me,' said Finn. 'You give me courage.'

"'You've always had that,' Baine said, for she knew him better than anyone.

"It was a long, long walk, and the two encountered many strange and frightening creatures on the way, but eventually they reached the heart of the Nameless Wood, and it will be no surprise to you"—Ciarán glanced at Finbar—"to hear that there was a clearing, and an ink-dark pool, and strange, big-eyed creatures watching from the trees all around. And while their passage through the woods had been illuminated only by the glow of their small lantern, here in the clearing they were bathed in the silver light of a full moon. In the middle of the clearing stood a little old woman, leaning on an oak staff.

"'Ah,' the crone said. 'You're here at last.'

"It wasn't much of a welcome, but then, they weren't expecting one, having come more or less as penitents. The two of them introduced themselves—Maelan's daughter, Torna's son—and the old woman dismissed this as if she knew them already and wasn't especially interested in who their parents were. Then Baine surprised Finn by rummaging in the bag she had brought and fishing out something very small, which she offered to the crone on the palms of her two hands.

"'We brought you a gift,' she said. It was a tiny metal cup, with a handle on each side: the kind of vessel a child drinks from when he is first learning to feed himself and not to spill. The cup was old and battered; clearly, it had been well used.

"The crone's eyes narrowed. 'You think you can get around me with gifts, young woman?' she said, and there was a crackling of anger in the air, as if she wore her own storm. 'With the earth torn up and the trees burned? With the river fouled and the valley heavy with the memory of pain and death? No gift can alter what was done. No sacrifice can make it good.' The oaks around the clearing shivered in a sudden breeze; the creatures whispered among themselves.

"Finn did not like the mention of sacrifice, and he moved a little closer to Baine, his hand going to the hilt of his dagger. But he had listened to the tales; indeed, he had done so with more wisdom than most. If he bared cold iron in the presence of a fey woman, likely she and her creatures would vanish forthwith, and he and Baine would be alone in the wood, in the dark, with no answers at all.

"'It is a gift, no more, no less.' Baine held out the cup again, and this time the old woman took it, inspecting it closely, shrewd-eyed. 'I would tell you what this cup means to the two of us, but I will not insult you by offering an explanation that you do not need.'

"The crone nodded. Indeed, she seemed almost to smile. 'Broke the rules, the two of you, more than once,' she observed. Her gaze went from Finn to Baine and back again, and no doubt she noticed that the two of them were especially fine, healthy-looking young folk, Baine with her rippling mane of golden hair and the lovely curves of her body, and Finn with his glossy curls, proud carriage and forthright blue eyes. 'Didn't your mothers tell you never to drink from the Silverwash?'

"Baine smiled. 'They did, and a lot of other things besides, mostly about the terrible monsters that dwell in this forest, with their rending teeth and their little pattering feet and their capacity to swallow men and women whole.' She glanced at Finn. 'We used to talk about it, in our secret place down near the Silverwash. Some of it we believed and some of it we didn't. Drinking from the stream didn't seem to do the cattle any harm.'

"Finn cleared his throat. The old woman was looking almost benign, though he was still deeply afraid of her. But they had come on a mission, and now that Baine had offered the gift, he must ask the question. 'We are deeply ashamed of what was done in the valley,' he said. 'You say no sacrifice can make it good again. But if the waters receded, and if we worked as hard as we could until the land was restored to itself, it could be healed, at least in part. If rituals were performed in the place of death, the valley could be cleansed of sorrow.'

"The old woman simply looked at him, and in his mind he heard her saying, *And?*

"'If new tales were told,' said Baine, 'tales that were true in their heart, and if children were taught that they must remember, then folk could learn from this. They could learn that it must not be allowed to happen again.'

"The crone threw back her head and cackled. Birds flew up in alarm from the dark trees all around. 'Taught that they must remember?' she mocked. 'And who will do that, when you have forgotten the most important thing of all, the wisdom observed by generation after generation until some foolish chieftain neglected to pass it on to his children, and another dismissed is as old wives'

88

rubbish? How can I trust you when you have forgotten the geis?' As she spoke the word, the old woman grew tall, and her shabby clothes became a robe the hue of midnight, and her eyes were so full of power that Baine and Finn wondered if they might be burned to ashes right where they stood.

"Finn found his voice first. 'A geis? I have heard nothing of this.'

" 'Will you tell us what it is, please?' asked Baine. Under the courteous tone, her voice was shaking. A geis could not be good. Not when so much ill had been done.

"'It is simple enough,' the sorceress said, for there was no doubt that was what she was, now that she had revealed herself. 'I would have thought even humankind could remember such a simple thing, but at some point it seems it was forgotten. It is a double geis, like that laid upon the hero Cú Chulainn. *Cross the Silverwash in enmity and death will be quick to find you. Drink of its waters and you will never be the same again.*'

"Finn and Baine looked at each other. There were many questions to ask and neither was confident that the sorceress would answer all of them. Which should they ask first?" Ciarán turned to look at us, his mulberry eyes intense, his face pale in the firelight. I thought he was going to speak to Finbar again—my brother sat so still beside me, he might have been in a trance—but he chose me. "What question would you have asked, Maeve?"

I hesitated, not especially happy to be singled out, since it meant every person in the hall was looking at me, but pleased that he thought my opinion worth having. "It seems to me the most important thing to know was: On whom was the geis laid?" I said. "If only on the chieftains of those two domains, then their children would be able to start setting things right. If on every person who lived in the valley, then all the men who'd been drawn into the fighting would soon die and the community would fall apart. I do not know if Finn took part in the battle, but if he did, he would be cursed along with his father, and I don't suppose Baine could have wrought a miracle on her own, though no doubt she would have tried her best."

I was rewarded by Ciarán's smile, a smile with no trace of condescension in it. He was genuinely pleased by my answer.

"That was the question Baine asked, and the sorceress was happy to provide an answer. The geis had been laid on the chieftains of those two domains and on their descendants. It therefore affected Maelan and Torna, and it also lay over Finn and Baine. How fortunate that despite his father's accusations of cowardice Finn had refused to fight.

"'My father—' Baine said, and at the same time Finn said, 'But—'

"'A geis is a geis,' said the sorceress. The young people heard a terrible sorrow in her voice and knew that it gave her no pleasure to mete out this ancient justice. 'These warring chieftains will fight no more. Guilt and sorrow have claimed Torna; you, Finn, are already chieftain in all but name. Baine, you must be brave. You will not see your father alive again.'

"White as a sheet, with Finn's arm around her, Baine managed to find words. 'My father has no heir,' she said. 'My sister and I are unwed. The law forbids that a woman become chieftain.'

"The sorceress of the Nameless Wood looked from Baine to Finn and back again. 'The future is in your hands,' she said. 'Live your lives wisely. Teach your children the geis. Do not forget. And be glad you disregarded your parents' warning when you were children playing in my clear waters and climbing my trees and singing songs with my birds. Be glad you drank of the Silverwash, for you will need every drop of the strength it gave you. Walk home now, and as you pass through my woods and over my fields, draw courage from them. If you are brave, good and wise you can face any challenge.'

"There was no need for her to spell out the obvious: that the two territories could become one through marriage, and that the geis had delivered both doom and priceless gift. Finn bowed low; Baine dropped a deep curtsy. 'You are a being of great power,' Finn said, 'and rightly feared in these parts. Yet instead of harsh and cruel punishment, you have given us justice and kindness.'

"The sorceress looked him straight in his honest blue eyes, and she said, 'The punishment your fathers have brought down on their land and their people is far crueler than anything I could devise. Besides, you are children of the Silverwash. Off with you now, or you won't be home by morning.'

"Oddly, the path through the Nameless Wood seemed far shorter on the way back, and the moon that had shunned them earlier now lit their path. When Baine and Finn reached the spot where they had left their boat, it was to find the vessel lying aslant on dry ground. The lake was gone; the Silverwash ran as it had in times of old, a lovely, splashing stream, bright under the soft moonlight. Hand in hand, Finn and Baine began the long walk home across the sodden fields. There would be a funeral, perhaps two. There would be explanations to make and alliances to re-build. There would be a wedding. There would be hard work and renewal. And when there were children, they would be taught the geis, and there would be peace."

The story was ended. Ciarán's audience afforded him the re-spect due to a great storyteller, which was a few moments utter silence before they showed their appreciation with the clapping of hands, the drumming of feet and shouts of acclaim. As for Ciarán himself, I could see he was exhausted, though he concealed it well. His eyes held a wish to be somewhere else, somewhere as quiet and peaceful and hopeful as the valley of the Silverwash had been that night when the young couple had walked home by moonlight. I looked at Ciarán as I might look at a troubled crea-ture, and I saw beyond his strength and composure.

"Finbar," I whispered in my brother's ear, "make room for Un-cle Ciarán here. And don't ask him too many questions." As Fin-bar squeezed up toward Rhian, I caught my uncle's eye and signaled that he should come and sit beside us on our bench.

He did so readily. My instincts were likely correct; they had never failed me yet, though they were more commonly applied in the case of horse or dog than man or woman.

"Uncle Ciarán, would you care for some mead?"

Rhian was off to fetch it before he finished nodding his head. I sat beside him quietly until she returned with a full goblet and put it in his hands. "That was a very fine story, Master Ciarán," she said, blushing a little.

"Thank you. As I said, it was one of my brother's favorites."

"A good lesson," I said. "An important tale to keep telling, I think. Uncle, I was asked to pass on a respectful greeting to you from Aunt Liadan. Uncle Bran also sent his regards. He said to tell you he remains forever in your debt." There was a tangled story in their past; the debt went both ways.

"I am happy to meet you again, Maeve. Ten years, is it not? That is a long time to be away from Sevenwaters. Did you feel the pull of the place from over the sea in Britain?"

He had the same approach to questions as Finbar, though he was somewhat subtler in the manner of asking. I spoke quietly, not wanting anyone else to hear. "Perhaps I should have done; I know this place has its own magic. But the honest answer is no. My feelings about Sevenwaters have been colored by what happened to me. I understand the magic, but I do not feel it, Uncle Ciarán." Seeing that Finbar was saying something to Rhian, I added, "Those ten years have made me a stranger here."

Ciarán considered this a moment, looking down at the goblet in his long, graceful fingers. "I should say, you are family, and family are never strangers here. But that is not true for everyone, as you have discovered. We might speak more of this another time." He glanced at Finbar, who had stopped talking and was quite plainly waiting to ask a question. "What is it, Finbar?"

"Uncle Ciarán, what if Finn died before any children were born? What if Baine was too sad to remember about the geis? Or what if another chieftain attacked them and Finn had no choice but to cross the Silverwash in enmity? What if . . ." He glanced at me and fell silent.

"Finbar," said Ciarán calmly, "I am sure Luachan has explained to you the difference between factual truth and symbolic truth. Figurative truth, that is."

If he had explained that, I thought, my brother was getting a remarkable education.

"So it isn't a true story," Finbar said. He spoke flatly, as if unsurprised to find that happy endings exist only in the imagination.

Before I could say anything, Ciarán spoke. "Ah! I did not say that at all. Perhaps the events of the story did once happen just as I told them. And perhaps not. A story may be pure imagining, yet at the same time be truer than fact. A tale exists in as many forms as there are folk to hear it. Finbar, shut your eyes and take two deep breaths with me—slowly, slowly, that's good. Now open your eyes again and tell me, what is the learning in this tale? Give me a short answer, not a long one."

There was a small pool of quiet around us, though in the rest of the hall the crowd enjoyed its mead and exchanged its news with robust good humor. Luachan had detached himself from the main group and had come to stand by us, still and silent.

Finbar opened his mouth and shut it again with not a word spoken. I put my arm around his shoulders, heedless of who might be looking at my hands.

"That we should respect the earth," my brother said.

"And you, young lady?" Ciarán looked at Rhian.

Rhian was no ordinary maid; she flushed a little, surprised that he would include her, but found a ready answer. "Never disregard a geis, Master Ciarán."

"Good, good," he said, smiling again.

"And more," I said, though he had not asked me for a contribution. Looking at Finbar, I went on. "The story teaches us that love can heal the most terrible ills. And that even in times of death, destruction and ignorance, there are still good people who can make a difference. If that answer is too long, I apologize."

"It is not too long, Maeve. Say more if you wish."

"What I liked best were the words the sorceress spoke to Finn and Baine. *If you are brave, good and wise you can meet any challenge.* The story is worth hearing for that alone. I understand why Uncle Conor loved it, and I thank you for telling it in his honor, Uncle Ciarán."

"Thank you, Maeve." He inclined his head gravely. "You speak straight from the heart, with courage. I should not be surprised by that, knowing you were fostered by Liadan and her remarkable husband. She is a brave and forthright woman. He is what he is: one of a kind. You will miss them."

I said nothing. If I chose to stay at Sevenwaters, I would miss them badly. If I made the choice to return to Harrowfield, I would bring down further sorrow on my parents. No easy choice lay before me. As for being brave, good and wise, there were times when I failed on all three.

"Finbar," Luachan was speaking in my brother's ear, "you know the rule: you must sit with me in the dining hall, and when I am not here, you stay close to Doran."

"It was my fault," I said. "I asked Finbar to sit beside me; he did explain the rule. If I've transgressed I apologize."

"The rule is for his safety," Luachan said. "Your father . . ." He did not finish the sentence.

I wanted to argue the point, but this was not the time. Finbar was too good at seeing the shadow at the heart of every story.

"I understand," I said. "I'll have a word with Father on the matter." Let Luachan make what he liked of that. "Uncle Ciarán, will you be staying here at the keep for a few days?" He seemed a wise and interesting man. In many ways he reminded me of Conor, but there was more to him, I thought. Mysteries, secrets; always that inner reserve. I would like to talk to him alone sometime.

"Luachan and I will both be returning to the nemetons in the morning. He'll be back here in a few days, as usual. I have some duties among my brethren that cannot wait. But I hope to speak with you again soon. You are welcome to visit us there, provided someone accompanies you—we have our eyes open to danger these days. Luachan tells me you are a keen walker."

It was on the tip of my tongue to ask him about the grazing fields and Swift, but on that matter, Luachan had been right: it was best that my father do the asking. "Thank you, Uncle. I'd like that."

"Uncle Ciarán?" It seemed Finbar was not finished with his questions yet. "You know what you said at the start, about Cú Chulainn? I know that story. He was a great hero. He knew about the geis on him, but he can't have been frightened by it, or he wouldn't have kept doing brave deeds. Geasa always come true, don't they? Wouldn't he have been thinking about it every day, wondering when it was going to happen, maybe trying to make sure it didn't catch up with him?"

Ciarán took his time in answering this. A little frown had appeared on his brow. "It seems not, in Cú Chulainn's case. But he was somewhat exceptional. As you say, a great hero. Perhaps he *was* afraid, Finbar. Or maybe, being so fond of heroic deeds, he simply made sure he performed as many of them as he could before the terms of the geis came to pass. The tales do not give us the answer."

Later, in our chamber, Rhian brushed out my hair, over which I'd worn a veil at suppertime. Rhian had observed, not for the first time, that it was a shame to cover up such lovely hair—many was the girl, my maid said, who'd kill for a head of red-gold curls like mine. That might be true, I'd told her flatly, but the head of curls needed a pretty face to carry it off, or at least a face not marked by livid scars. I might be prepared to visit the stables with those scars on display, but making my first appearance at my parents' table was a different matter. *Brave, wise and good.* In this decision I had perhaps not been as brave as I could have been, but I had almost certainly made the wise choice. When I had bid Mother good-night, before Rhian and I made our exit from the dining hall, she had put her hands on my shoulders, kissed me on either cheek, and murmured, "Well done, Maeve." So she did understand one thing at least: that even after so long, I must screw up my courage before I stepped out in front of strangers.

"Rhian," I said now, "you have younger brothers. Don't you think Finbar is unusually solemn for a boy of his age?"

The brush continued its steady work. "He is rather quiet," Rhian said. "But he's the son of a chieftain; he's not likely to be ripping his pants on blackberry bushes and having mud fights the way my little brothers used to."

"I don't think my sisters and I ever had mud fights. They sound like fun."

"Washing the clothes afterward is no fun at all, so don't get any ideas."

"I have ideas already, Rhian. Luachan won't be here for the next few days. It's a good opportunity for Finbar to be a little boy for a while. But I'll need your help. It's all right. I'm not planning anything outrageous. They're concerned for his safety, so I imagine he's not allowed to stray far when Luachan's not here to keep an eye on him. We could borrow a guard, I suppose. I must speak to Father about that, and about Swift."

Rhian had finished the brushing and was taming my curls into plaits, ready for the night. She said nothing.

"What?" I knew her; her silence spoke eloquently.

"Nothing. But . . . maybe you should wait a bit before you start trying to change things here. Especially if we won't be staying long." She fastened one plait and started on the other. "There's nothing wrong with spending time with your brother. And of course arrangements have to be made for the horse. But you don't have to do everything yourself, and you don't have to do it right now. There are other things . . ."

"Go on," I said.

"You sound cross. Like a queen daring a kitchen maid to keep on speaking above her station."

"Oh, stop it," I said, swatting her awkwardly. "Just tell me. I see all sorts of things wrong here, things done in a way I don't like, and I don't understand why it's happening. Certainly my mother used to run a tight household, but always with good judgment. My father was widely admired for his wisdom and restraint. People came to him for advice on making peace with their neighbors."

"You believe that has changed?"

"Perhaps not. But something has crept in here, something that shows in small ways, like Duald deciding to bring Swift out into the yard and put him through his paces when I'm certain Emrys must already have advised against it. And Finbar. There's something not right with him, but I'm the only one who seems to see it."

"Not all boys want to spend their time running around and getting into trouble."

"A child can be naturally quiet without being . . . Well, I can't quite say what I think it is. A sadness. As if he's constantly worried."

Rhian sighed.

"What?"

"It's not up to me to tell you what to do," she said.

"You could give me some advice, since it's plain you think I'm wrong."

"My advice is to wait. You want to set everything right, and that's good, but you're forgetting that your mother and father had only short notice that you were coming home. They're still getting used to having you back. And you're planning to tell them they're bringing up their son all wrong. And besides, their stable master isn't doing things the way you want them done."

"Well, he isn't. And that needs attending to right away, Rhian. It can't wait."

She was finished with my hair. Now she began to unfasten the hooks at the back of my gown. "You know," she said, "your uncle's only just been buried. And they have other things on their minds. Terrible things, with that Disappearance, and the search still on for the missing men in the woods."

I glanced at her sharply. "Who's been talking about that?"

"Everyone. Nuala told me they're shorthanded in the kitchen and in the fields because so many of the men are spending all day out on the search. They do it in shifts. This chieftain, Cruinn, the one whose men were lost, they're saying that he threatened to come here with his men-at-arms and mount his own search if your father can't find the last four missing men before winter sets in. And everyone's worried about that. Not only is it more mouths to feed, but they're not going to be friendly ones. Eithne said the fellows who are doing the searching are all having nightmares. The way the dead were found . . . I can hardly bring myself to say it."

"I know how they were found. No wonder Finbar's looking like a ghost, if everyone in the household is talking about this openly. He's probably having his own nightmares. That does it. I'm speaking to Mother in the morning." I stood up and slipped out of the gown. "Don't look like that, Rhian. He's my brother. Someone has to do something."

"Arms up."

I obeyed, bending forward, and she slipped my under-shift over my head.

"You know," she said, holding up my night robe so I could put my arms through the sleeves, "if my daughter had been away for ten years and I had just got her back, I'd like her to come and sit with me awhile, and maybe ask me if I was happy. I'd want her to tell me she missed me, but that she was all right. I'd want the chance to tell her how much I'd missed her, and how my life was a little sadder for her absence. I'd want—"

"Stop it!" I wriggled into the night robe and folded my arms, unable to keep the glare off my face. "You're saying I should tell lies to make my mother feel better?"

"Not at all." Rhian spoke calmly; she was used to me. "I'm saying go slow. Talk to your father about the horse; that's one thing. Ask your mother nicely if we can take Finbar out for a walk, or take him riding, or whatever you'd like to do. And that's all. He's her son. If there's something wrong, do you think she hasn't seen it, too?"

That was exactly what I did think, since nobody seemed to be doing anything about it. But enough was enough. Suddenly I was tired. I sat down on the bed and Rhian knelt to take off my shoes.

"I'm sorry," I said. "I don't deserve you."

"No, you don't," said Rhian, grinning up at me. "But here I am, with my ready advice. Just as well your mother can't hear me, or I'd be dismissed for insubordination."

I could not speak to Father about Swift, because Father rode out straight after breakfast to escort Deirdre and Illann and their attendants to the Sevenwaters border. A considerable number of men-at-arms went with them. I could not take up the question of Finbar's education with Luachan, since he and Ciarán had not even waited for breakfast before slipping away into the forest, back to the nemetons. But I did find Finbar in the kitchen patting the dogs and talking to Nuala, so I took him with me to find Mother. That meant my talk with her was not the one I had planned. She was in the upstairs hallway talking to Orlagh about clean linen, but she paused when we appeared.

"Mother, I have a favor to ask."

"Of course, Maeve."

"Since Finbar's tutor is not here today, I wondered if he could come out with Rhian and me for a while. Rhian suggested we might go riding. Not far; you can tell me what is permissible. Or we might weed the little garden or go looking for nuts. May he spend the morning with us?"

A small frown creased Mother's brows. She was looking pale; her freckles stood out against her skin. "There are some rules you must follow. Finbar knows what they are. When Luachan is away, Finbar doesn't go riding unless he's with his father."

"But didn't Eilis take him when she was here?"

"That was before." She did not need to say *before the Disappearance*. "Besides, if anything should go amiss . . ."

"I won't be able to cope, because of my hands?"

She flushed with embarrassment. Orlagh was suddenly very busy folding a sheet. "Maeve, I didn't mean—"

"Let's both be honest about this, Mother. If you don't think I'm capable of looking after my brother for a morning, just say so."

"Mother, I am a good rider," Finbar pointed out. "Doran said I was unusually capable for my age. And of course Rhian will come with us. Anyway, Maeve has her own ways of doing things. She—"

"I think we can cope," I said, cutting him short. "What if we stay within sight of the keep?"

"Finbar, if you had explained this to Maeve you would have avoided all this trouble. There is no riding without Luachan."

"A walk, then?"

"If you walk out of sight of the keep, you must take a guard with you. And we're short of men."

The search. I could not argue with that.

"Why don't you do something indoors?" asked Mother.

Because this child needs to run and climb and jump and get the roses back in his cheeks and the ghosts out of his eyes.

99

"Finbar could read to you," she added. "Luachan tells me he's remarkably accomplished."

For one fleeting moment I saw on her face a look so full of love and pride and sadness that my heart bled for her. This was her only son, and perhaps she did know how troubled he was, and wished she could make it better. Hadn't she said something once about it being bad for him to be too much alone?

"Maeve? Is something wrong?"

How could I answer that? "No, Mother. For today, we'll walk only as far as the lakeshore. Come on, Finbar. Let's find Rhian. Maybe we'll go and visit Swift first—what do you think?"

It was a good day. I remembered that later, when everything began to turn dark. We obtained provisions from Nuala, including carrots for the horses. While Rhian and Finbar distributed these I spoke to Emrys and discovered to my surprise that the possibility of housing Swift at the nemetons had already been suggested—by whom, Emrys did not know—and that the main concern was a lack of men to maintain the required watch over him. With many of my father's regular stablehands out on the search for Cruinn's lost men, Emrys and Donal were setting their hands to whatever work Duald had for them, and there was plenty of it.

After that we walked down to the lakeshore, and as far along it as we could go while still retaining a view of the keep—in fact, two of Father's men-at-arms seemed to be maintaining a patrol not far from us, and I wondered if Mother had sent them—and Finbar showed Rhian how to skip stones. I did not point out to him that a girl with a clutch of younger brothers was likely to be an expert in this kind of thing. They had a competition, which Finbar won easily. Again his stones seemed to move of themselves, bouncing over the water with an unusual grace. I wondered why he was happy to compete with my handmaid but not with his tutor.

By midday the three of us were grubby, tired and in fine spirits. My plan to get Finbar out of his shell for a while had been a great success, mostly thanks to Rhian, who proved to have talents not only at stone-skipping, but also at balancing along walls, climbing trees and running races, as well as more sedate pursuits such as weaving grass stems into a basket or a little man. Finbar stopped asking questions and applied himself to action for the morning. Sometimes he smiled, as when Rhian made a curious creature from the grasses, with a long neck, a flared snout and a feathery brush of a tail. He might think some pursuits were for little children, but he was not too proud to slip this creation into his pouch before we headed home.

I had done my share of balancing and running, and was feeling comfortably weary. Finbar had some writing to do for Luachan. He headed off to make a start on it—one morning of play had not turned him into a completely different child. I waited in the hallway outside the kitchen while Rhian went in to fetch provisions for the two of us. It had been a satisfying morning. Perhaps the difficulties I saw at Sevenwaters were all in my mind. Maybe I really could fit in here.

Voices drifted to my ears from the little chamber where game was hung—two men talking as they worked. I was about to move away when I caught what they were saying.

"... never find a husband for the girl. Her face is pretty enough. Much like her ladyship. But have you seen those hands?"

"Just think of that against your skin. It'd turn your manhood limp in a moment."

"Makes my flesh crawl to think of it."

The door to the kitchen swung open, and Rhian emerged carrying a laden tray. The men were still talking, but their voices had dropped and I could no longer hear the words.

"Maeve? What's wrong?"

I drew a deep breath.

"Maeve?"

"It's nothing. I'm wearier than I thought, that's all. What kind of soup is that?"

Rhian was not fooled. When we were upstairs and behind the closed door of the bedchamber, she set the tray on the little table, then swung around to face me. "You're upset. What happened?"

"I don't want to talk about it. And I don't want any food."

"You're having some," Rhian said. "Sit down there. You'll feel better with a full belly, trust me."

I ate in silence, with my head full of images of myself on my wedding night, and my husband—his face was not clear—turning away in disgust when I touched him. It didn't matter that I had already accepted I would never marry. It didn't matter that the words had not been intended for my ears, or that the speakers had probably meant no harm by them. I felt dirty, ugly, worthless.

Rhian said nothing at all until our meal was finished and the dishes were tidied back onto their tray. I was sitting on my bed, a pillow held against my chest. My handmaid seated herself on her own pallet, opposite me, and turned her limpid eyes on mine. "If you can't tell me," she said, "who can you tell?"

"I thought I was strong." It was as if something heavy had rolled over me. I had to squeeze the words out. "For ten years I've learned how to be strong. I've practiced and practiced."

"And?"

"I heard something not intended for my ears, and I feel . . . Never mind."

"What did you hear, Maeve? Who has upset you so much?"

I tried to arrange my features in a reassuring smile.

"Maeve, what?"

"It doesn't bear repeating. The fault is mine for letting it disturb me. I should be armed against casual cruelty—I've experienced enough of it." It had been such a good day up till now.

"If you won't tell me, is there anyone else you can talk to? Your mother?"

"No!"

Rhian sat quiet, waiting while I struggled with myself. Try as I might, I could not banish those images from my mind: the marital bed, the tender gesture, the moment of recoil. Who hadn't heard such tales as a child, relishing the shivering chill of terror? The beastly wife. The loathly bride. The monster in the bed.

"Maeve," Rhian said, "you once said to me, look on what scares you as a challenge to be met, a problem to be solved. You just need to work out how. I see you doing that all the time."

I examined my hands, the palms covered with red-purple scarring, the fingers hooked like the talons of a raggedy old bird. Vile.

Hideous. I turned them over. The backs of my hands had escaped the fire; there, the skin was soft and pale.

"You are brave," Rhian said. "You're the bravest person I know. Make a plan. I'll help."

Brave, wise and good. All very well for Finn and Baine in the story. They had not only been healthy and unmarked, they had been of more than usual beauty and grace, thanks to their child-hood draughts from the magical stream. No such handy remedies for me. I had long ago learned to work with what I had and not waste time longing for what I might have had. I had dealt with hundreds of cruel comments. I had stared down discourteous men, thoughtless children and objectionable old ladies. What was wrong with me, that all I wanted to do right now was run away and hide so nobody could look at me and be repelled? I thought I was stronger than that.

"A plan," I echoed, thinking that maybe all I needed was more time: a breathing space, so I could become brave again. Like Swift. A solution came to me. It wouldn't be running away, since I would have a useful job to do, one nobody else had time for. "I do have a plan, Rhian, but I don't think my mother's going to like it."

Not long after that, we were in Mother's private chamber, where— unusually—she was taking a little time for herself. Not that she was ever idle. She had been reading from a small book bound in dark leather, but she set it down when Eithne let us in.

"Mother, may I speak with you in private?" *Back straight; shoulders square; feet planted firm. Look your adversary in the eye.* Uncle Bran's lessons in appearing brave were useful at times like this, when I wanted nothing better than to hide in a corner and will the world away.

"Of course, Maeve. Eithne?"

Mother's personal maid went out quietly.

"Is Rhian to stay?" Mother asked. It was a fair question, since the two maids were of equal status.

"I would like her to be here, Mother, if you don't mind."

"Very well. Sit down, my dear. You look rather serious. Did you enjoy your morning with Finbar?"

Only yesterday, I would have thought this an ideal opportunity to put to her all my concerns about my brother's education, and his sadness, and his lack of opportunity to be a little boy. "Yes, thank you. I think Finbar enjoyed it, too." I cleared my throat. "Mother, I need to speak to you about something else. I have a . . . a suggestion to make. And a favor to ask. You may be upset. If you are, I'm sorry."

She folded her hands on her knees, waiting. She was Lady Aisling of Sevenwaters; it would take a lot to disturb that calm composure.

"Mother, I must be honest with you. Although it's been wonderful to see you and Father and Deirdre again, I'm finding it difficult to be here in the house. There are so many bad memories for me. I thought it might be like this. That is one reason I stayed away so long." I paused to gulp in a breath, rehearsing the next part in my mind. Mother's eyes were fixed on me. I could not tell whether she was upset or not. "I was afraid. Afraid that being here might undo all the work I have put into being brave and learning to cope with the limitations I have. Mother, there are many things I can't do; all the things you would want your daughters to do as well as you do them. No, please don't," I said as she made to say something. "It's true; there's no denying it. But I do have one strength, one thing I can do better than almost anyone, and that's my knack with animals."

Mother gazed at me. The silence went on until it was almost uncomfortable. Then I realized she was courteously hearing me out.

"I don't know if Father told you," I said, "but there's a perfect place for Swift—the yearling—to be put out to pasture until he's recovered from the journey. It's down near the nemetons, a safe place, Luachan says, protected from the reach of Mac Dara. And there's a little house down there, right beside the field. I know the household can't spare a groom to go and stay there. But I could go. Rhian and I. I could watch over Swift, and Rhian could be my hands, and the druids could help with feeding and so on when they tend to their own stock."

Mother's brows had risen rather high. "What an extraordinary idea," she said.

"I feel very uncomfortable in the keep. Not only can I not help with the work, I . . . I would rather be somewhere quiet, without a lot of folk, without the confinement of stone walls. I'm sorry, but it's better to be honest with you now than try to hide this. The place is within walking distance, so Emrys or Donal could come down when Duald can spare them, and we could pick up Swift's training where we left off, once he's ready. He's quite disturbed at present; his whole world changed more or less overnight."

Mother gave me a very direct kind of look. For a moment I felt like a slovenly housemaid or errant workman about to feel the sharp edge of her tongue. I stiffened my spine and met the look with one of my own. Bran had been a renowned and feared leader of fighting men before he found himself master of Harrowfield. He had trained me well.

"You're referring to the cottage where Conri and Aisha stayed for a while?"

"I believe it's the same one. It needs a little tidying up. Rhian has said she will do that, and perhaps find a boy to help with the heavier work."

"It's my turn to be honest, Maeve. You may have a talent with horses, but what about the practicalities? Won't this prize yearling require feeding and watering, brushing down, cleaning up of hooves and so on? You can't expect the druids to do all that, and Rhian will have her own work. Besides, I've been told the animal is particularly difficult." Mother scrutinized me and my maid in turn. "Look at the two of you. You can't do this on your own."

"Could we put this to Uncle Ciarán? I am prepared to abide by whatever he says."

Now I really had surprised her. "Ciarán?" Oddly, I thought I heard a note of disapproval in her voice.

"He must be asked about accommodating Swift anyway."

"Your father wouldn't like this. It's very unconventional." She made to say something more, then checked herself. *It's the sort of thing Liadan would do*, perhaps. Though Liadan had been her friend, back when they were young.

"I was hoping you might help me persuade Father," I said. It was a calculated move, and I felt bad making it.

"Are you really so unhappy, my dear? You've barely arrived here—surely, given more time, you will start to feel at home again. It was too much for you, coming to supper with so many folk—"

"Please, Mother. It's costing me something to ask this of you, knowing it must seem as if I'm trying to run away. But I need the quiet. I need to be away from the keep for a while. Not long. Until Swift is ready to move back to the stables, or to be sent on to Tirconnell. I know I cannot stay in the cottage forever."

"That would most certainly secure our reputation as an eccentric family," Mother said dryly. "A twenty-year-old daughter, living out in the forest like a hermit, with only a horse for companionship."

Rhian cleared her throat quietly.

"Besides," Mother went on, "what about Finbar? Didn't you express an interest in getting to know your brother better? How can you do that if you're not here?"

It was a fair argument. "It's easy enough to walk or ride from here to the nemetons. Luachan can bring Finbar to visit us. That falls within the rules, doesn't it?"

Mother's sigh was inaudible, but I felt it. "Don't mock the rules, Maeve. They exist for a very good reason. You left here before Mac Dara rose to power in the Otherworld, but the things he has done, or has caused to be done, have been . . . They've been truly terrible, bad enough to drive ordinary people mad with grief, bad enough to make grown men weep and tremble. I still cannot talk about the time when Finbar was taken. I try to find the words, and straightaway I am there again, lying on my bed staring at the wall and wondering why I am not dead yet. It was . . . Never mind. I should not burden you with this. You have your own sorrows."

I must have been staring at her, too astonished to say a word, for she added, "You must not make light of the rules. Finbar needs constant protection. I thank the kindness of the druids every day that my son can go safely between here and there; that at the tender age of seven he is not banned from riding his horse or walking in the woods, provided he has the right companion and does not venture into the shadow, beyond the guarding hand of Danu. What I cannot combat is the shadow within. I fear Mac Dara set a curse on my son, during the dark days when my baby was stolen away. I see something in Finbar that is not of this world, and it frightens me."

Stunned surprise turned me mute. It seemed the imperturbable exterior of Lady Aisling concealed a woman with fears and doubts, a loving, troubled mother. She was more like me than I had ever dreamed.

"It was doubly grievous when Finbar was taken," she said quietly, "because we had already lost you."

Oh, gods. What could I say to that? "I'm sorry," I whispered. *Sorry I misjudged you. Sorry I did not miss you more, these last years. Sorry I think of Aunt Liadan and Uncle Bran as my real parents.* That would break her heart. Besides, it was no longer entirely true; had not been since the moment my father walked toward me by torchlight, his arms wide-open. "Some things . . . they stay with us, whether we want them or not."

"Best that this does not fade." My mother's neat features were somber. "It can be hard sometimes to give Finbar the freedom a child must have. I want to keep him close, to wrap him up, never to let him out of my sight. But he must live his life."

I made myself say it. "And so must I, Mother."

There was a tap at the door.

"What is it, Eithne?" asked my mother without getting up.

"Nuala is asking if she can speak to you about the flour, my lady."

"Later."

When Eithne was gone, I said, "He's some kind of seer, isn't he? Finbar, I mean. That isn't something Mac Dara made happen; it's the way he was born. He's like Sibeal."

"Curse and blessing." Mother's lip twisted. "So it seems,

Maeve. It's a heavy burden for one so young. Sibeal managed it far better in those early years. Perhaps it helped her to have the rest of you about, reminding her what it was to be a child."

I remembered Sibeal well. We had been close; she was the next sister down from me, two years my junior. Sibeal's manner had been considered, like that of a much older person. She had possessed an intense stillness. Often she had chosen to sit quietly under a tree, watching, as the rest of us got wet and muddy and tore our clothes on brambles. She would gaze into the water of a pond, or frown over the little wax tablet where she wrote her notes, while I was playing with a ball or running about with Bounder. Sibeal at eight had been very like Finbar was at seven: finely made, dark, with those big, strange eyes that seemed to look right inside you. But, unlike our brother, she had been a creature of poised quiet, serene and confident. There had been no trace of shadow over her.

"Maybe," I said. "I hope we helped her; she surely helped us, with her wise solutions to problems." Another image passed through my mind: my sisters gathered around my bedside, looking down at me. Faces chalk white; eyes wide with horror. Deirdre with tears pouring down her cheeks; Clodagh with her arm around little Eilis. Sibeal as pale as the rest of them, but holding on to her composure. What was it she had said? *The gods honor your courage, Maeve.* She had tried very hard to keep her voice steady. And later my eldest sister, Muirrin, perhaps welcoming a change from the grueling job of keeping me alive, had helped the others make me a doll; they had all worked on it, even Eilis, who hated sewing with a passion. That doll was sitting on my bed back at Harrowfield. She had seen me through some testing times.

"I'm sorry they aren't here," I said. "Sibeal in particular. I would have liked to see them all."

"You will in time. They will come here to visit, or you will go to Inis Eala, or even to Kerry."

"Mm." Or I would go back to Harrowfield and never see any of them. "Mother, about Swift and the cottage—will you think about it, at least? And speak to Father and to Ciarán, if you decide you can allow it?" I hesitated.

"What is it, my dear?"

"I have shadows too; memories that remain with me, no matter how hard I strive to lay them to rest. It has been hard to come back here. Being in the cottage will help keep them at bay. And if I can work with Swift, that will be even better. It is the one gift I can offer; it provides me with a purpose. And a purpose gives a person faith in herself. I'm sure you understand that."

"I understand all too well," my mother said. "Rhian, you've been very patient. Would you go down to the kitchen and ask Nuala for some refreshments for us? And tell Eithne she can come in now."

Rhian bobbed her charming curtsy and went out.

"That young woman is a jewel," Mother said. "As for the other matter, I will speak to your father when he comes home. If he agrees, we'll put it to Ciarán. I'm not sure whether you are just very determined, Maeve, or a little addled in your wits. Time will tell, I suppose."

CHAPTER 6

"ell, then," said Rhian, looking about our new domain with evident satisfaction. Her hair was tied back under a kerchief, her sleeves were rolled to the elbows, and a voluminous apron wrapped her small form. "I think it's nearly done. I'll just wash the floor and then we can light the fire and make a brew. Why don't you go and sit outside until I'm finished?"

It had been hard watching her work. At times like this I had to remind myself of the wisdom of *Do not waste time longing for what cannot be*, and *Do not feel guilt about what you cannot change*. Rhian could manage perfectly well without me; I knew that. She did not expect me to wield a duster with my toes or stack firewood with my forearms, though I was capable of doing both. She welcomed my awkward contributions while seldom asking for them. In my heart I knew the job of transforming the hut into a cozy residence would be done far more efficiently if I got out of her way.

I went out to sit on the front steps. It was late afternoon and shadow lay over the fields, for the autumn sun had sunk below the tree line. Soon, whichever novice druid currently had the job would come to usher the chickens into their coop and tend to the other animals. These now included Swift, who was grazing in what had been the goat's field. Among the domestic stock the yearling stood out like a lily in a bed of cabbages. The displaced goat was currently in our walled garden area, feasting on the weeds that had burgeoned there since the hut's last tenants departed. Rhian planned to plant winter vegetables, provided Swift and Pearl—thus the druids had named their goat—learned to share a field. Having seen the look in Pearl's eye when she was shifted out to make room for the horse, I thought it might be a long time before we dined on our own carrots and turnips.

There was no need to put food out for Pearl; the weeds were a veritable feast, and she would get our kitchen scraps as well. Rhian would cook for the two of us, with my help. I had overruled Mother's suggestion that our meals be sent down from the Seven-waters kitchen. That idea was ridiculous. The point was to put distance between myself and the keep, not create more work for the already busy serving folk.

It did make more work for Rhian. But she seemed happy to meet the challenge, and at least she did not need to dress me up for public appearances anymore, or fetch and carry up and down the stairs. We could walk to the keep for supplies when we needed them, and the druids had offered us fresh vegetables until our own garden was established. I did not tell Mother this last part, since it implied Rhian and I would be at the cottage for some time.

Pearl had paused in her foraging and was gazing at me over the wall, her eyes soulful. I went over to stroke her forehead and rub behind her ears, while speaking to her quietly of such matters as I imagined might interest a goat.

"In the sunniest area, cabbages and kale. Along that side, a strip with juicy carrots and beets . . ."

Pearl leaned in, the better to let me reach an awkward spot between her ears.

"It's a pity men can't be more like creatures," I murmured. "My hands don't seem to bother you at all." The goat's eyes were half-closed in pleasure as I attended to the troublesome spot, using my knuckles. Since Ciarán had given his approval for us to move here, and since my parents had agreed to let me do it, I had worked hard to forget that conversation I had not been meant to hear. I had forbidden myself to see the scene it conjured of a wedding night gone hideously wrong. Now, fleetingly, I imagined myself touching a man with the same tenderness I used for Swift and Pearl. Using the soft backs of my hands, where I could still feel the subtlety of a caress; using my lips, perhaps, or my tongue. Such thoughts were perilous. They brought a lump to my throat and tears to my eyes. They edged me close to self-pity, and that could not be allowed.

"Maybe I'm not as brave as I thought I was, Pearl," I said. "Maybe I have more to learn than I imagined."

Pearl lowered her head and butted me affectionately in the chest. As I stepped back I saw them again, the two dogs, in the shadows beneath the trees about a hundred paces behind the cottage. The leader was uncannily like Bounder, with a big sturdy body and a strong-muzzled compact head. The creature ran with swift purpose, keeping an eye out for danger. The other came behind, an animal with the same night-black coat and solid build, but a little smaller. This one moved awkwardly, as if sick or hurt. They were both thin. They looked as if they had been running wild for some time.

"So I didn't imagine them," I whispered to Pearl, keeping as still as I could. "They're real dogs that have strayed from somewhere. Where, I wonder?"

"All done!"

At Rhian's cheery call both dogs bolted, vanishing swiftly into the darkness of the forest.

They were on my mind as I went indoors, and as Rhian made a brew that we drank in celebration of the move into our new home. A temporary home, of course; I might entertain dreams that my family would allow me to stay on here when I no longer had Swift as an excuse, but I knew I would be battling to persuade them. There were so many arguments against it, arguments that made me long for the spiritual vocation that would allow me to stay at the nemetons without folk thinking Father had lost his good judgment to allow such an eccentric arrangement. Not least of these arguments, I thought, was that people might believe I was here because my parents wanted me out of public view.

"I saw two stray dogs out the back," I said some time later as Rhian chopped vegetables and I made an untidy effort to knead dough.

"Mm-hm."

"I saw them the other day, too, when I was out with Finbar. Big dogs. They look as if they might be someone's hunting animals gone wild."

Rhian gave me a penetrating look. "They'd have had to stray a long way. It took us a long time to ride in here, and I gather the forest stretches out on all sides of the keep." Her knife moved with practiced speed; an onion fell in pale shreds. "They'd be after the chickens, no doubt." She glanced out the window, where the shutters still stood open. "It looks as if that young druid has already put them in the coop. We'd best warn him tomorrow."

I worked the dough, punching with my knuckles, then clawing the mass over with my stiff fingers. A small struggle was going on inside me. *They're hungry. You have food to spare. You don't even need to see them, just put it out before you go to bed.* And on the other side, *Don't even think of it. One step down that road and you're setting yourself up for a broken heart. Besides, you've just moved in here—what are the druids going to think if you encourage chicken thieves?*

We were both tired, Rhian with a great deal more justification than me. After supper, with the meal cleared away and the leftover pie set on a covered platter for tomorrow, we washed in a basin—Rhian had brought water from the well earlier—and put on our nightclothes with hardly a word spoken. Rhian performed the evening ritual of brushing and plaiting my hair. She had already bolted the door, which meant I could not go outside unless she opened it for me.

"Anything you need me to do before we put out the lamp?" she asked.

I wondered if the sound I heard from the forest outside was a creature whimpering in pain, or only the cry of a bird in the dark trees.

"Maeve?"

I wondered if the subtle scratching I heard was made by the claws of an animal on the stone pathway outside our door, or merely branches brushing the wooden shutters.

In her night robe and shawl, Rhian went over to the shelf where she had set the platter of leftover food. "Yes or no?" she queried, brows raised. Sometimes she understood me better than I did myself.

"I'll take it," I said, "if you'll open the door for me. And maybe you could bring the lamp so I don't fall flat on my face."

"What about Pearl?"

She did not mean that Pearl might want this treat for herself—though that was without a doubt true—but that my actions might be putting the goat in danger. "I'll leave it well away from here."

As we walked over to the trees, Rhian lighting the way, I following with the platter balanced on my forearms, the two parts of my mind were still arguing, and I knew quite well which of them I should be heeding. Sensible Maeve said, *It's foolish to encourage wild dogs—those fields will be like a full larder to them. You're asking for trouble, and for what? Because one of those creatures looks like the pet you lost as a child? What if something happens to Swift?* But Wild Maeve whispered, *They're cold, they're hungry, they need you. Would you let them starve because you refuse to let go of the past? What happened to living the life you have instead of regretting the life you lost? Besides, if you give them food they won't need to eat the chickens.*

I set the platter down on a flat stone at the edge of the forest. The pie was already in two pieces.

"Of course," Rhian said as we headed back, "some other creature may eat it. Those dogs may be far away by now. They can't know what a soft heart you have."

"Soft heart?" I glanced across to see a smile on her face. "I don't recall ever doing anything like this before. In fact, I keep thinking that moving out here must have made me slightly mad."

"Mm-hm," said Rhian.

It was good to lie on my pallet in the little cottage, with only the embers of the fire for light, listening to the cries of owls from the forest, mournful and strange in the deep night stillness. I could hear Rhian's soft, steady breathing from where she lay tucked in her own bed. I imagined Swift standing asleep in his field, his lovely coat silver under the moon. I thought of the chickens on their perch, a row of tidy round forms with heads under wings. I pictured Pearl in her makeshift lean-to, dozing peacefully on dry straw and dreaming goat dreams. My mind turned, inevitably, to the black dogs. Were they still padding through the forest, restless, hungry, driven by a fierce will to survive? Were they curled up somewhere in the bracken or in the shelter of a fallen tree, pressing close to each other in the chill autumn night, their bellies aching with hunger? Beyond the security of the nemetons, out in the wild woods where every shadow might conceal an enemy, did they dream of home? *Be safe*, I thought as sleep laid its soft blanket over me. *Wherever you are, be safe.*

In the morning the platter had been licked clean, and there were canine footprints in the soft soil around it. Wolves could not have crept so close without chickens and goat raising an alarm. I was a light sleeper and would have heard that.

We had a rabbit hanging, thanks to the Sevenwaters kitchen. I suggested a stew for supper, since this would stretch the meat further. Rhian obliged without asking questions. During the day I walked back up to the keep and listened to my brother reading. He was remarkably competent for a boy of his age, which no doubt owed something to his tutor. I saw a group of men coming in from the search and another group heading out. From lad to grizzled elder, all of them were well armed and grim of expression. Back at the cottage, Rhian cooked a generous pot of rabbit stew with barley and vegetables, and a little before nightfall we went out to the trees to leave a portion for our nocturnal visitors.

"Sometimes it's better not even to start," Rhian commented, even as she fished a crust of bread out of her pocket, broke it in two and set it beside the bowl. "A creature gets used to being fed, and then when you go away the animal can't look after itself anymore, or it's learned to trust and puts itself in danger."

"This is only for a few days. I expect they'll soon move on."

"Not if they take a fancy to my cooking."

"If you think this is a bad idea, why did you make extra stew?"

"Because I knew that was what you'd want. Maybe we're both fools. If these dogs are as big and strong as you say, why can't they hunt for their own food in the woods?"

There was no good answer to this question, save that perhaps the two of them had been someone's household companions, without any need to hunt. Perhaps they had been as close to someone as Bounder had been to me. That gave me an uneasy feeling, as if an unknown hand was stirring the tide of affairs here, setting me up to make an utter fool of myself. Rhian had not actually seen the dogs yet. Neither Luachan nor Finbar had spotted them the first time. But if they were only a fantasy, what had made those footprints?

"One of them seemed hurt. Perhaps the other is too busy protecting its mate to go off and catch rabbits. As I said, this is only for a short time. To tide them over."

"Until what?"

But I had no good answer. So, night by night we set out provisions for them, and morning by morning we went out to recover the empty platter and to see the marks of their paws printed in the earth. As the days passed, I began to place the offering a little closer to the cottage, and to set it out earlier, wondering if they would dare come out before night could cloak their presence.

Swift grew quieter and fatter in his field, soothed by the deep stillness of the nemetons. Every day I spent time with him, talking to him, bringing him treats, making sure he did not lose the trust that allowed me to approach and touch in perfect safety. Either Emrys or Donal had been coming down every second day to do some work with him—a turn or two around the field, wearing a soft halter, followed by a gentle rub-down. On the seventh day after Swift came to the nemetons, we put Pearl in the field with him. He danced about uneasily; she kicked up her heels and ran to and fro as if to scare him away. Then they both put their heads down and got on with cropping the grass.

There were other visitors. Luachan came often with Finbar, and the two of them generally stayed for a meal and a chat. Sometimes they rode from the keep, sometimes they came on foot. Rhian was good for Finbar. She never gave him a chance to say he was too grown-up to make little figures out of bread dough, paint patterns on the front door with whitewash, or look for frogs in the stream. I guessed she had led her young brothers in and out of trouble for years.

That left me to entertain Luachan. He might have been quite willing to fish and paint and play with the others, as an escape from the rigors of life as a druid, not to speak of his duties as a bodyguard. But I did not want that. Finbar's time with Rhian was a precious return to the childhood he should be having, and it would work far better for him if his tutor was not there.

So, when Luachan asked me if I wanted to walk, I said yes. I made a point of choosing conversational topics likely to engage the attention of a man who had started life as a son of privilege: lore, history, politics, strategy, poetry. This was not so much of a challenge as it might have been for some young women, for the household where I had lived for the last ten years was a place of free and lively debate. On spiritual matters I was perhaps a little shaky, but Luachan was ready enough to provide guidance. He was, after all, both druid and tutor.

Sometimes Luachan annoyed me. He seemed altogether too perfect, with his good manners, his handsome face, his strong shoulders and ready smile. For every dilemma I posed, he had an answer. I found I was longing for him to make an error, to be forced to admit he was wrong, or even to trip up and get his robe muddy. I wondered, once or twice, if I had imagined that game of stone-skipping and his readiness to wade into the shallows to prove himself.

But more often I enjoyed his company. I liked walking; a brisk outing along the forest paths was a pleasure, not a burden. I enjoyed robust conversation, for I was missing Uncle Bran and Aunt

Liadan more than I could have imagined. I began to look forward to his visits.

There was only one topic of conversation Luachen shied away from, and that was his family. It had seemed natural enough to ask him which part of Erin he came from, and whether he had brothers and sisters, and whether he ever saw them now he had joined the brotherhood. After all, he knew a great deal about my family, including some information that was not common knowledge beyond our household. For instance, the fact that my brother-in-law Cathal was the son of Mac Dara. The fact that the well-loved and respected Ciarán was the son of a fey sorceress. I did not imagine Luachan's family housed any secrets of that kind. I learned, because he was too polite to refuse an answer to a direct question, that he had a brother and two sisters, and that his family lived somewhere in the south. Anytime I tried to go deeper, he changed the subject. So I stopped asking. Maybe his father had not wanted Luachan to follow a spiritual path. Maybe his mother would have preferred him to stay at home. Perhaps he was a disappointment to them. I decided it was none of my business anyway.

Rhian and I saw one or other of the druids every day. They greeted us with courtesy and brought us offerings from their gardens. Among them were women, all of them quite old, and I was glad for Sibeal that her life had taken a surprising turn, setting her on a spiritual path that allowed her to wed and become a mother as well as spend her life serving the gods. Deirdre had said everyone in the family had liked Sibeal's husband, a Breton scholar whom she had met on an implausible-sounding adventure in the far north, culminating in an encounter with sea monsters. I had always thought Sibeal would lead a solitary, contemplative life. It made me wonder what lay ahead for Finbar.

And the dogs. Ah, the dogs. They did not show themselves by day; they never appeared when Luachan was at the cottage, or Finbar. But they weren't far away. Rhian stopped talking about chicken-eaters and began regularly cooking more than the two of us could consume. She put bones aside. At the end of the day, there would always be something ready for me to set out for our wary visitors.

I was working on trust: every day the dish closer to the cottage; every day the food out a little earlier. If I had doubted my sanity, if I had thought they might be a strange dream conjured by my own mind or by some malignant power, I ceased to do so on the day the bigger dog ventured beyond the shelter of the woods in daylight. I had been waiting since I took the platter up. I was sitting on the ground with my back against the stone wall that surrounded our garden space. My cloak was the same gray as the stones; I was good at keeping still. So I saw him pad out, cautious and watchful, to snatch one of the two meaty bones, then turn and bolt back under the trees. I stayed where I was, wondering if the smaller dog would follow the other's lead. But no: when a dark form came out from concealment, it was the same dog again, the fitter, bolder one. He took the second bone in his jaws, then lifted his head, suddenly still as he looked down the rise straight at me.

I, too, was still. I made sure I did not meet his eye direct. For the space of three long breaths he examined me; then he fled, carrying the food with him.

Later that evening Rhian remarked on how quiet I was. Inside me the two voices were having a small war again. *Don't name them,* said Sensible Maeve. *They are someone else's animals, and feral. You never intended to stay here. Not at the nemetons, and not at the keep. When Swift is gone, you'll go home to Harrowfield.* But Wild Maeve said: *A name is such a small gift.* And indeed, I knew their names already. The big, strong dog: Bear. The damaged, weaker one: Badger.

The day Ciarán came to visit me, I had been helping Emrys with Swift and was sitting on the back steps of the cottage with my gown tucked up, my hair half-down, my shoes off and a cup of Rhian's herbal tea beside me. Halfway between cottage and wood was Bear, hunkered down in the long grass watching me. Our silent friendship was moving on step by step, but progress was slow, and that troubled me. If Badger was sick or hurt, I needed to have a good look at her as soon as possible. Thus far she had shown herself as no more than a dog-shaped darkness under the oaks, a pair of frightened eyes caught by the candle flame, her loyal guardian's shadow.

And now here was Ciarán, coming to lower his tall form down beside me with no trace of embarrassment at my bare feet and disheveled appearance. Bear was up and gone in a flash.

"What was that?"

"A dog, Uncle. There are two of them; I have been gradually winning their friendship, or trying to. I think one of them is injured."

"You love creatures."

Suddenly I felt like weeping. "They see what a haven this place is, I suppose. I owe you a debt, Uncle, for allowing us to stay here. Without this, I would have . . ." Hard to finish this. I would have coped. I always did. But I would have been unhappy, and I would have made my parents unhappy. "I know we can't stay here forever," I made myself say.

"Stay as long as you need, Maeve." Ciarán looked up toward the forest, to the place where the dog had gone into cover. "Swift seems to be doing well. I spoke to Emrys, and he believes the yearling will be ready to go back to the stables sooner than anyone imagined. Perhaps these dogs are your new challenge."

"I doubt if Mother would think them sufficient reason for me to stay here, especially when the autumn chill starts to bite. I'm content in this place, Uncle Ciarán. But perhaps I am hiding." It did not seem to matter that I had not spoken to him much; that we had not had time to develop the familiarity I'd had with Uncle Conor, back in the early days. Something in Ciarán's presence inspired trust. With him, it felt safe to talk. "I've discovered I'm not as brave as I believed."

He considered this awhile. "You think?" he said eventually. "I would point out that in the past you have shown great courage, a kind of courage most of us are not called upon to display in our whole lives. You might consider yourself something akin to Swift, and the purpose of your stay here similar to his. It is time to rest, time to recover, time to know yourself better. Its true meaning may not become clear to you until long after you have moved on.

This is a place of healing, Maeve. Tend to your dogs, help them, and perhaps you will find healing yourself."

"I'm fine," I said more sharply than I intended. "I'm as well healed as I can be, and I've learned to live with what cannot be mended."

"Ah," said Ciarán, and took my damaged hand in his. "It is not these wounds I speak of, but the ones that cannot be seen. The hurt inside. That, I think, is not truly mended, though you do a fine job of convincing yourself, and the world, that it is."

"You and Finbar," I said, finding a smile from somewhere, "share a particular gift for speaking the most painful truths. I do wonder if there are some things that we can never make our peace with. Wounds we carry for our whole lives." I thought of Mother, and the look in her eyes as she spoke of Finbar's abduction. I thought of the bone-deep weariness that had shadowed Ciarán's face as he finished his story that night in the hall. "Maybe a druid can learn to accept even those," I said.

A slow smile curved his lips. "I suspect it runs in the family."

"What?"

"Speaking painful truths. A druid learns self-control. He learns to open his mind to the wisdom of the gods. Even so . . . even so." The smile had faded. The mulberry eyes gazed into the distance, as bleak as a bare field in winter.

"You do such good," I ventured. "Everyone speaks well of you."

"It is one part of me."

"They are saying you will be the next chief druid."

"It has been suggested, yes." A long pause. "If I am offered that honor, I will decline."

For some reason, I did not feel surprised.

"That's between you and me, Maeve. If no formal request comes, I may not need to take that step."

"Of course." After a moment, I asked, "Will you tell me why?"

Ciarán looked down at his hands, loosely clasped in his lap. "I'm not sure I know the answer. Call it a hunch, a feeling. I believe another path lies before me. What it is, I cannot say. A time of change is coming. Change for all of us. Perhaps your arrival was the key that opened that door. Perhaps not. Only time will tell."

I struggled to understand. "Uncle—are you speaking of Mac Dara? Of the danger that seems to lie over Sevenwaters now?"

"You know, in the ancient tales the Fair Folk appear as noble, wise, almost godlike. Even in the time of your grandmother and her brothers, the time of Conor's youth, those who made their homes within the Sevenwaters forest were of that kind. They were generally well-disposed toward the human folk who dwelled here, perhaps realizing that as the new faith spread fast across Erin and people forgot the wisdom of the old ways, the Sevenwaters family provided one of their last refuges. They expected much from those to whom they chose to reveal themselves, but they also gave good gifts to those who deserved them. Thus it was with your grandmother, who was both challenged and aided by the Lady of the Forest in her time of great need. It was that same Lady, I believe, who visited your sister Sibeal when she was still a child and struggling with her newfound ability as a seer."

"You speak of the Fair Folk as if they are no longer here. But Clodagh saw them when she crossed into the Otherworld to fetch Finbar back. Isn't Mac Dara one of them?"

A bitter smile. "He is of that kind, Maeve, as was my mother, the sorceress. A darker breed, from a flawed line, but nonetheless powerful. And dangerous, since they are completely without scruples. Even the most noble and good of the Fair Folk do not view the world as you might. Their lives are far longer than those of humankind. They find it hard to comprehend that a person might make choices based on love or loyalty or compassion. The Lady of the Forest knew what was best for the future of Sevenwaters. She counseled Sibeal because she saw your sister as a guardian of old truths, wisdom that might be lost if not held in the minds of human scholars. She knew, then, that she would soon sail away from the shores of Erin, and that is what she did, with many others of her kind. Where they are gone, nobody knows. West across the sea, that is as much as I can tell you. Perhaps to Tir Na n'Og. Perhaps still farther, beyond the ninth wave."

"But not all of them went away."

"Indeed no, or the Otherworld part of Sevenwaters would be inhabited solely by smaller folk, clurichauns and tree people and the intriguing race known as the Old Ones, small in stature, great in influence. When the Lady and her companions quit the shore of Erin, they left a gap behind. To Fainne they entrusted a watch over their ancient secrets. Others, such as the druid brethren, hold a part of the wisdom that helps keep Erin safe through troubled times. But in the Otherworld there was no leader, no powerful presence to unite the remnant of the noble folk who had once ruled there and held the inhabitants of that realm in some kind of order. You know, I imagine, what happens when a space is left where, before, there stood a leader, a person of power."

"Someone steps in to fill the space," I said. "If there is no recognized way to appoint a new leader, a person can gain power of his own accord. His reasons for doing so may be flawed, but he rules because there is nobody to oppose him."

"Exactly. That is what happened with Mac Dara. Where he came from, nobody seems quite sure. Whether he was appointed in what you refer to as a recognized way, or whether he simply stepped up and took control, I cannot say, but he assumed power here. Those of the Fair Folk who chose not to go with their old leaders, or who were perhaps not wanted on that last long voyage, became his sycophants, his hangers-on, and in some cases his henchmen. He is clever. He can be charming when he chooses. He had no difficulty in winning them over."

"Uncle Ciarán?"

"You sound hesitant, Maeve. Please ask me whatever you wish. While you consider your question, I will tell you that out of the corner of my eye I see a black dog no more than ten paces away, with his gaze fixed on you as if you were some kind of god whom he both adored and feared. The other is up by the privy, crouched beside the step."

So close. I prayed that Rhian would stay where she was, chatting to Emrys on the other side of the cottage, and not send them fleeing again.

"You were asking about Mac Dara," Ciarán prompted gently. "Or perhaps it was a question about me."

"It was, and please don't answer if you would rather not. I know your parentage is mixed, Uncle Ciarán. Half human and half Fair Folk. And Clodagh's husband, Cathal, is the same—in his case a human mother and Mac Dara himself as a father. I know it means you will live far longer than, say, my father. But . . ." After all, I could not ask it.

"But my fey heritage is of that darker kind, as is Cathal's? What kind of a being does that make me? Is that what you were going to ask?"

He did not sound at all angry or offended, merely a little sad.

"I was, but now it seems impertinent. I apologize."

"Not at all, Maeve. It is rare for me to conduct such a conversation, that is true, but I know you will betray no confidences. Your gift with animals extends, I think, to men and women as well. To troubled small boys. Also to a troubled half man who will never be chief druid. From my father, I inherited the ability to be a leader. Loyalty to Sevenwaters. The capacity to love and to have my heart broken. From my mother I inherited the long life of the Fair Folk, and a certain gift with . . . you might call it magic, or spellcraft, or sorcery. These days I make little use of that craft. I chose to follow the path of light when I returned here some years ago, after the great battle in which both your father and your uncle Bran fought so bravely. Making that choice did not mean I lost my other abilities. They are considerable. They are perilous. Cathal possesses similar gifts, perhaps greater than mine, for his lineage includes a third element, the blood of the Sea People. Between us, we could wield a mighty magic."

My eyes were popping out of my head. I summoned a calm tone. "You mean you could defeat Mac Dara, you and Cathal together? Drive him away from Sevenwaters forever?"

"No war is won without losses," Ciarán said. "Cathal places his wife and children above everything. Clodagh's love transformed his life. I do not think he will take any step that might endanger his dear ones. There is no doubt what Mac Dara wants—if he cannot bring Cathal back by fair means or foul, he will pursue Cathal's son. He has no conscience. He stole Finbar away. He would have discarded the changeling child without a second thought. Those are two drops in a whole well of ill deeds, of which the Disappearance is one of the cruelest and the most public. Could we drive him away? Maybe. Maybe not. A failed attempt could have disastrous consequences. It might leave Sevenwaters, and your father, in far worse strife than would be created by taking no action at all."

This seemed a deeply unsatisfactory answer. "Even the most powerful tyrant must have a weak spot," I mused, putting one hand casually down by my side, where Bear might perhaps creep close enough to sniff it. He was right by the corner of the walled garden, head down, eyes on me, tail tentatively wagging. It was a minor miracle.

"I agree, Maeve. The challenge is finding that weak spot before the damage becomes irreparable."

"Is Mac Dara so very powerful? Cathal and Clodagh managed to save Finbar from his clutches. And when Cathal was trapped in the Otherworld, Clodagh rescued him. I don't remember my sister as being in any way magical, only rather strong-minded."

Ciarán smiled. "Mac Dara underestimated his son's talent, and his patience. He overlooked Cathal's preparedness to harness the goodwill of what Mac Dara would consider lesser races, the Old Ones in particular. He did not understand Clodagh's remarkable inner strength, nor her . . . I am not sure what to call it, but your sister has a power that comes from deep down. She's a remarkable maker and mender. She has a gift that runs very close to natural magic. Her enemy didn't see that. A great error on his part." He hesitated. "Cathal and Clodagh escaped, yes, and Finbar does not seem harmed by his experience. But Mac Dara is not defeated. They won a small battle. The war is yet to come."

A cold nose nudged my hand. "Warm hearth," I murmured, not looking at the dog. "Full belly. Kind hands and quiet." And, when a tongue came out to lick, "Good boy, Bear."

Ciarán smiled. "That name suits the creature." He, too, kept his voice to a murmur. "Did you say you wanted to check the other dog was not injured? If you think he will come close enough, perhaps I could hold him while you look."

"Isn't the other one a female?" As I moved my hand to rub Bear gently behind the ears, I risked a glance toward Badger. She was standing in the open, a few steps out from the tiny hut that housed the privy. She looked a little shaky on her legs, but I could see no obvious wounds. And on second glance . . . "You're right," I said. "Badger's a boy. I won't try to touch him yet; I'll wait until he's prepared to come close to me. Otherwise it's a dive and grab, and that would likely send both of them running straight back into the forest. Whatever has befallen them, it has frightened them half to death. That's it, Bear, good boy."

Ciarán rose to his feet, keeping the movement slow and steady. Bear froze under my hand, a growl rumbling in his throat.

"Ssst!" I made my warning sound, and to my intense surprise, the dog fell immediately silent. Badger stayed where he was, following his companion's lead.

"We'll talk again soon," Ciarán said quietly. "You mentioned Mac Dara's weak spot. I, too, have been considering that, since a remark of Finbar's put the idea into my mind. I have an idea of where to start looking. I should do so sooner rather than later, I believe. At some point your father must have another talk with Cruinn of Tirconnell. He must tell him the most thorough and lengthy search anyone could set in place has failed to find any trace of the four men still missing. I fear even the most splendid horse in all Erin will be insufficient to calm Cruinn's rage. Thank you for talking to me, Maeve."

"And you," I said. "You're a stranger to these dogs, yet they seem to trust you. Perhaps you don't know how remarkable that is."

"There is something remarkable here, yes. But it has nothing to do with me." With that cryptic utterance, my uncle walked around the corner of the cottage and out of sight.

Later, when Emrys had headed off to the keep and Rhian had returned to the house, I got up, told Bear to stay, and went indoors myself. My handmaid was up to the wrists in a sticky mess of boiled barley and shredded chicken, for Emrys had been given a plucked and gutted bird to bring down for us—Mother was not prepared to leave us entirely to our own devices. No doubt Rhian's efforts would result in a tasty meal, however unappetizing the mixture might look at present.

"May I take some of that now?" I asked her, glancing back toward the door, which I had left open.

"Their share's on the shelf." Rhian jerked her head toward a platter of chicken flesh set aside. "I saw they'd come up close; thought I'd better not draw attention to myself. I did set a water bowl out the front."

"Thank you." Her cheeks were looking flushed, and perhaps not only from her labors over the fire. "Emrys stayed a long time today."

"Huh! The man's transparent, the way he tries out his supposed charms on me. It never worked at Harrowfield, so why should it be any different now?"

"Don't ask me," I said, thinking I could see a new brightness in her eyes. "I know nothing about men. Emrys may not be very handsome, with those big ears, but I'd have thought he'd be a reasonable catch for someone. A man who's kind with horses would be kind with women, too. Of course, he's pretty quiet. You'd have to do all the talking. But you're good at that."

"Stop it!" Rhian flicked a cloth in my direction, grinning. "It's a sign of how desperate things are that I bother stopping to chat with the man when I take him his food and drink in the afternoons. A fellow's scarcely at his most appealing when he's all over sweat and stinks of horse. Now off with you and feed your babies out there. I think I see one of them just beyond the door. Next thing the two of them will be sleeping on your bed and you'll be on the floor."

I set the platter down just outside the door, then sat close by it on the step. Tonight's supper could not be seized and carried away, as it was all shreds. If the dogs wanted to eat, they'd need to do it within an arm's length of me.

I had seen Bear close to the doorway earlier, but when I came out he had retreated to the corner of the house. He would not eat before Badger. I sat in silence, making sure I looked away from them, over to the field where Swift was grazing quietly, tired out from his afternoon's work with Emrys. The yearling was making steady progress after the setback of the journey. He walked calmly on the leading rope now, even beyond the familiar field. He was prepared to submit to various indignities such as having his hooves inspected. It might not be long before he could go back to the stables, provided Duald understood he must be trained with kindness. I was going to have to talk to Father.

Bear crept up to the platter, seized a sliver of chicken, padded back to his companion. He dropped the meat at Badger's feet. A snatch, a gulp, and the morsel was gone. Scarcely one mouthful.

"Bear. Come." I pushed the platter a little farther in their direction, not turning.

The silence drew out, punctuated only by the sleepy conversation of hens as they settled for the night, their coop now closed against the fox. It was all a bit upside down, I thought, staring pointedly away from the spot where someone was moving the platter around as if applying an enthusiastic tongue. Lock in the chickens over there and leave the fox hungry; share a chicken with hungry dogs over here. There was no right and wrong about it, only a choice about survival.

"Well, then," I murmured, "the two of you have fallen on your feet at last. You look as if you're overdue for a bit of good luck."

The food was gone, the platter empty. Someone was lapping noisily from the water bowl. Not Bear; he had come to hunker down beside me, as close as he could get without quite touching. Badger lifted his dripping muzzle and lowered himself to sit. He was perhaps six paces away, his eyes always on the other dog. "Good, Bear. Good, Badger. You are safe here. As safe as you can be."

"Safe," echoed Rhian from beyond the open door. As she spoke the dogs raised their heads in unison, but did not move. "Spoiled, she means. Where I grew up, the best the dogs got was a handful of fish guts thrown their way when the boats came in. And they had to fight for that. No lovely ladies coaxing them with tasty morsels of meat and bowls of rabbit stew. All I can say is, the two of you better be on your best manners when she lets you inside. I'm not sleeping with a pack of smelly, flea-ridden good-for-nothings. Catch a rat or two, and I might start to think you're earning your keep."

"They're still right near me," I said. "And Bear's letting me stroke him."

"Don't sound so surprised," said Rhian. "They feel it, the same as Swift does. The touch, or whatever it is you have. They know they can trust you. The question is, can you trust them not to take over the house and have the two of us running around after them?"

"Bear's already responding to my commands. Badger may be more difficult, but all he needs is time. As for flea-ridden, we'll give them a bath before they come inside."

Rhian had come out onto the step, wiping her hands on her apron.

"Easy, Bear," I murmured. Then, "What?" as I realized my handmaid had turned a particular expression on me. Our mutual understanding could occasionally be somewhat awkward.

"You have a new look in your eye," Rhian said, in uncanny echo of what I had felt on seeing her come in from her sojourn with Emrys. "A new brightness in your face. You look . . . happy."

"Is that so amazing?"

"It is, that a little thing like a dog can bring such a change."

"It's not the dog himself, though he is a fine creature. They both are. It's that they are learning so quickly and that I may really be able to help them. Having a purpose makes me content, Rhian. That's all it is." She was right, of course. I had not felt such a surge of well-being since the days back at Harrowfield when Swift was young, and we began to discover what a remarkable creature we had on our hands. "Yes, all right, you're remarkable, too," I muttered in Bear's ear. "And your friend, once he learns to trust me a bit more. Now I'm fetching you a couple of sacks, so you can sleep out here and guard the door. No coming in until you've had that bath."

CHAPTER 7

F allen leaves crunched under my shoes as I walked. Overhead, the green canopy still cast its shade, but that shade was less deep than before, with autumn's touch loosening the summer garments of the oaks and setting shivers through birch and elder. The air was cool and crisp; I had a shawl tied around my shoulders.

I had assured Rhian that I could manage quite well without her on the walk up to the keep, and that if I needed an escort on the way back I would ask for one. She didn't like me to go off into the forest alone in case I should be faced with a challenge that required a functioning pair of hands. She imagined a pack of wolves, maybe, and the need to climb a tree with speed. Or a fall into a hole and a broken leg. Rhian also knew I valued my independence, so when I had said Bear and Badger were more than adequate as a safeguard, and that it was not as if this was an unfamiliar path or a walk by night, she had raised no arguments. Besides, though neither of us had mentioned it, Emrys would be at the nemetons later working with Swift, and he did rather like it when Rhian was there in person to give him his refreshments. If

131

anyone was getting spoiled, maybe it was a certain love-struck groom.

This was the first time I had taken the dogs to the keep with me, but we had been practicing against this possibility. They had walked halfway there and back again with me and Rhian several times now. They had learned to stay quiet and calm while Emrys or Donal worked with Swift in the field or on the tracks around the clearing. They had learned not to bark at the cows or the druids. As for sleeping arrangements, I had not been displaced from my bed as Rhian had anticipated. Bear would have slept inside readily, but Badger did not like to be in the cottage when the door was closed. When night fell and Rhian began to secure our abode with shutters and bolts, he always went out to lie on the old sacks beyond the door. Bear would generally cast a sad-eyed look in my direction as he followed, but he would not leave Badger on his own. I had never before seen a dog with eyes of such a remarkable color as Bear's, a mellow, lustrous gold-brown. Against his black coat, now glossy with good care, they were striking indeed.

There was no doubt in my mind that Bear had once been someone's well-trained house dog, part guard, part companion, for he had swiftly learned the few commands I used: the little hiss that meant *No*, the instructions *Come*, *Sit* and *Stay*. Often he seemed to sense what I wanted from him without my needing to do anything at all. Badger was still wary. With the help of both Rhian and Emrys, and the employment of a tub of warm water and a mutton bone, I had managed to bathe him and check him closely. Quite plainly he'd been half-starved, for his ribs were prominent and his hip bones sharp, but I had found no signs of an injury. Both dogs had been infested with fleas. The application of certain herbs—rosemary, lavender, juniper—helped with that, and good feeding had begun to remedy their general condition, but Badger remained unsettled. Without Bear he could not have survived out in the woods; I was sure of it. Just over halfway to the keep, a narrow plank bridge crossed a fair-sized stream. We had not come so far before, and when they saw the bridge, both dogs hesitated, hanging back. I moved onto the planks, putting my arms out for balance, and walked briskly over. "Bear, come!" I called. "Badger, come!"

Still they held back, and I cursed myself for not testing them with water; it had not occurred to me that a confident dog like Bear might be afraid of such an obstacle. Perhaps it was not the water itself, but a fear of standing on the insubstantial bridge, through whose cracks the swift stream beneath could be glimpsed. I had never used a rope lead with either dog; there would have been no point, since I could not hold on. Any animal I worked with must learn to respond to my voice.

I did need to talk to Father, not only about Swift but about my own future and the tenancy of the cottage. I was also planning to ask him about the dogs—he could make inquiries as to whether anyone had lost such a pair, and we could then arrange to return them. The prospect of that was becoming less pleasing with every passing day. I would not turn back. The dogs must learn to obey even when they were frightened.

"Bear, come!" I used a sterner tone this time. "Badger, come!"

It was quite clear Badger was not going to attempt the bridge; he stood with shoulders hunched and tail down, shivering. Bear solved the problem by splashing into the water, swimming a few strokes and emerging on the bank beside me, where he shook himself energetically. After a moment Badger launched himself after his bolder companion, swimming over to join us on the bank. Immersion in cold water was a lesser evil than being parted from his friend.

"Good boys," I said, breathing a sigh of relief. "Let's run, or you'll both get cold."

We ran awhile, I in the middle, the dogs on either side. I felt my body fill with well-being and my heart with pleasure to be in this lovely place with my two companions, strong and alive. Bear kept looking up at me, tongue out, mouth open in something close to a smile of joy. Badger stayed close to me, which was an achievement in itself. For a while we were in a fine small world of our own.

I do not remember which came first, the sense of wrongness that gripped me or the two dogs halting, frozen on the forest path.

For the space of a breath the three of us stood in silence; then Bear began to growl. Badger edged forward. Both dogs were gazing into the woods with some intensity. Bear's hackles were up; his body was stiff with tension. Badger moved forward again. Unusually, he was ahead of Bear, off the path. I followed their gaze, thinking they might have spotted a boar, a deer, a man wandering where he should not. I could see nothing out of place.

"Stay!" I ordered, for both of them were on the verge of flight. Bear had never disobeyed this command, and what Bear did, Badger copied.

Badger took another step forward; Bear gave a sharp warning bark.

"Bear, Badger, stay!" Curse it, I had thought even Badger obedient enough for this walk. My judgment seldom let me down. "*Stay!*"

A heartbeat, then the two of them erupted in a frenzy of barking, and all chance of control was gone. Badger raced off into the woods with Bear just behind him. Almost before I could draw breath, they were out of sight.

Curse it! This was no simple chase after a rabbit or squirrel, but something far more serious. They'd run at full tilt, heading into an area with no visible tracks. The forest was vast. Could I trust Bear to make his way home to the cottage later, bringing Badger with him? I thought not; the dogs had not been with me long enough. Their time of flight and hardship was too recent. If I took no action, I might never get them back.

There was only one thing to do. Never mind Rhian and her visions of disaster. I was the dogs' friend; they had become my purpose. I might not be able to hold on to a leash, but I could run.

As I raced into the woods I could hear them barking somewhere ahead of me. I followed the sound as best I could. Curse the two of them! They had been doing so well, Bear especially. Why had he suddenly disobeyed? Well, the answer was plain enough, I thought, as a heavy growth of brambles slashed at my skirt. Bear had run because Badger had run: however much Bear might respect my authority, he would always put Badger first. A duty. Unusual, and tricky to work with. But then, Bear was an exceptional dog. I had seen that from the first.

Let me find them, I thought as I ran on, not sure whether I was addressing this to a deity or to fate or simply to myself. *Let them not be lost and hungry and wild again, not after they finally came home.* But that was foolish. The cottage was not home, not for the dogs and not for me. They belonged somewhere else. And I . . . Maybe I didn't belong anywhere anymore.

The thorns were behind me and the ground was becoming more level. Not oaks here but birch and willow. And a path, a narrow way where, oddly, no leaves lay on the earth, nothing at all to conceal the marks of their paws, leading onward. The hairs on my neck prickled. Something odd here. Something not right. The dogs' voices were fading. I gritted my teeth and picked up the pace. I hoped very much that the old theory about family never getting lost in the Sevenwaters forest was actually true. I judged I was going more or less westward, away from both nemetons and keep. Provided I caught up with the dogs, maybe they would lead me home.

It was a long way. I ran until my breath came in painful gasps. I ran until my legs would barely carry me. I ran until my head was reeling and I knew I should sit down before I fell down. Was I imagining things, or was the barking closer now? I reached a little stream and made myself stop to drink. Since I could use neither cupped hands nor vessel, I got right down and put my mouth to the water, somewhat as a dog might. I banished thoughts of being lost. I closed my mind to the things Rhian would say if she could see me. I rose to my feet and ran on. Between the trees, over a heap of mossy stones, nearly losing my footing as I thought I spotted something dark through a gap in the foliage—Bear?

"Bear!" I attempted a shout, but had breath enough only for a squeak. "Badger! Wait!"

They were close. Was that a clearing ahead, a patch of grass in full sunlight? I emerged from the cover of willows and halted at the edge of an open area that was so neatly circular it could hardly be a natural clearing. It was, perhaps, a secondary place of ritual for the druids. A lone tree stood in the perfect center of the circle, an elm whose high crown was studded with the remnants of last season's rook nests. Bear and Badger were running to and fro under the tree as if something there both attracted and terrified them. The frenzied barking went on and on. And now I could see what had drawn their attention. Something was hanging from the elm, dangling just off the ground. A bundle. A large bundle tied with rope, its shape curiously reminiscent of a sleeping human form. Now I was cold all through. In this open, sunny place something was terribly wrong.

"Bear!" I called as I approached, and he came to me. His whole body was trembling; his eyes were wild. "All right, Bear. Good boy." I stroked him briefly with the back of my hand, keeping my tone reassuring, though my belly had clenched tight. That was a man hanging there. Out here in the depths of the forest, far from well-traveled paths, someone had been wrapped up tightly and suspended upside down against the rough bark of the elm. The rope stretched high; the branch over which it had been looped was far above the reach of a tall man. As I walked forward with Bear beside me, I told myself druids sometimes wrapped themselves up in ox hides and suspended themselves in oak trees for whole days and nights, the better to open the eye of the mind to visions. At least, in the old tales that was the kind of thing they did. I willed this to be one such devout servant of the gods, even as I knew it was not. Then we were at the tree, and I paused to stroke the quivering Badger and tell him he, too, had been good. They had known what was here. Even so far away, from the moment they had halted on the track, somehow they had known.

I took a steadying breath, then stepped closer. The bundle moved. My heart turned over; the hairs on my neck prickled. Alive. Against all the odds, still alive. And here was I without useful hands, without a knife, without anyone I could send for help.

I crouched down next to the man. Someone had rolled him in a voluminous blanket and tied him tightly at shoulders, waist, knees and ankles. The ankle rope became the long cord that suspended him. Someone had hauled him up to hang there like a grub in its chrysalis. In just one place the enveloping blankets had an opening, and through that narrow gap I saw his staring eyes, the flesh around them suffused purple-red. His head was an arm's length from the ground; this had been a precisely calculated act of torture. I crouched down beside him, and at that moment the last light left his eyes, slipping away to be replaced by the dull, blank stare of death. Gone. Gone before I could speak a word. Gone before I could cradle his head and tell him he would not die alone. *Oh, gods. Oh, gods, give me today over again so I can make this not happen.*

Bear's cold nose pressed against my hand.

"We have to fetch help," I muttered with tears streaming down my cheeks. "We can't do this on our own." I would have to leave him hanging. I would have to trust I could find him again, for I would not ask the dogs to wait in this place of death. The sun was still quite high; there should be time to get to the keep and back before dusk. "I'm sorry," I murmured, laying the back of my hand against the man's face—still warm, oh gods! His body swung away at the light touch, making me shudder. "I would have spoken words of comfort, at least. I would have asked your name. But there was no time. We'll get word to your loved ones, I promise. We'll lay you to rest with due ritual." I made some promises to myself as well. I would train the dogs to chew through ropes. I would obtain a small, sharp knife and learn to hold it in my teeth and cut cleanly. If something like this happened again I would be better prepared.

No *if* about it; it would happen again. It would happen over and over until Mac Dara was defeated. Each time would be ingenious, cruel, and different from the last. There was, in truth, no way to prepare. The dead man was one of Cruinn's lost riders. My mind might shrink from that fact, but I knew it must be so. Mac Dara had arranged this killing. Mac Dara had been here this very day, in this very spot. Perhaps even now he was watching. And if Mac Dara wanted something, neither well-trained dog nor knife-wielding girl would be able to stop him.

I must go. The sooner I reached the keep, the sooner someone could come and give this man back his dignity. Before I left, I must attempt a prayer. Never mind that I was an unbeliever and not practiced in these things.

I rose to my feet and stretched out my arms as I had seen Ciarán do. I searched for appropriate words. "Danu, lay your hand over this fallen one," I said. "Morrigan, guide him gently through the great gateway. May he find peace. May those dear to him remember his good deeds and not his cruel passing. May they celebrate his life with fine tales around the hearthstone."

I stood there for the space of three long breaths. Then, "Bear, come," I said in a different voice. "Badger, come." We turned our backs on the hanging man and ran for the keep.

Three things to be grateful for. The dogs were obedient to my commands. They found the way for me. And when, after a run I'd thought I might not have the strength to complete, we emerged on the main track, it was to glimpse a familiar figure on a bay mare, riding away from us toward the nemetons.

"Luachan!" I shouted with what little breath I could summon. "Stop!"

What he thought, I could not imagine, seeing me with my clothing all torn from the brambles, my chest heaving and my eyes no doubt red and swollen. My legs felt like jelly; now that I had stopped running, I could barely stand. Luachan swung down from his mount and came striding toward us. In a moment, Bear was in front of me, feet planted square, hurling a fierce challenge. The message was plain: *Lay a hand on her and I'll rip your throat open.*

"Ssst!" I hissed sharply, touching the dog's back. Badger was behind us, growling low. "Bear, sit!"

The barking dropped to a ferocious, subterranean snarl. With visible reluctance, Bear sat.

"What has happened? Are you hurt?" As Luachan reached me, everything began to turn in circles. The druid's arms came out to grasp mine and steady me; but for that I would have fallen. "Breathe slowly, Maeve. You're safe now. Lean on me."

For the space of a few breaths I closed my eyes and let my forehead rest against his chest, feeling a tide of sheer relief run through me that I did not need to do this all by myself. Luachan put his arms around me. It felt remarkably good, better than anything had felt for a long time. Bear was still growling. I made myself stand upright and step back.

"We must fetch help—there's a man out there, dead, killed, and I couldn't get him down—quickly, we must—"

"Maeve. Take a deep breath. Tell me first, are you injured? Has someone hurt you?"

"Someone strung a man up; it's one of Cruinn's lost men—I'm sure of it. We need to get Father—"

"This is something to do with the Disappearance?"

Gods save us, for a druid he was woefully slow to understand.

"Can your horse carry both of us? Come on, Luachan, we must move—"

"Maeve, are you harmed? Tell me. What happened to you?"

"Forget that. I'm fine. We must go. If the horse can't take two, you'll need to ride back for help and leave me to walk. The man is hanging from a tree. He died before my eyes. Luachan, if you stand there staring any longer I'll run to the keep on my own and leave you here with the dogs."

"You can manage on the mare?"

"Would I suggest it if I couldn't?" *Hold on to your temper, Maeve, this is not helping anyone.* "I'll have to ride behind you—that's the only way I can hold on. Apart from that, yes, I can manage provided you help me up. If we don't go now, we may not be able to bring the man's body back before dark."

As we rode to the keep, with the dogs keeping pace on either side, I gave Luachan the story in a more coherent fashion, though it was a wonder I could tell it at all. I knew I was close to collapsing. I did not want to break down and weep in the druid's company, or in front of my parents or the Sevenwaters household. I must hold myself together until I was back at the nemetons and in my own little house with only Rhian and the dogs. My mind kept showing me the moment when I had seen death steal the last light from that man's eyes. That would stay with me forever. Beneath the weariness, beneath the sorrow, deep inside me a flame of anger burned. How dared Mac Dara do this? How dared he pollute our forest, which for generation on generation had been a haven and sanctuary? How dared he indulge in such acts of wanton cruelty right in the heart of my father's domain?

"We have to stop him," I muttered against Luachan's back. "This has to end."

"What was that?"

"Nothing." It came to me then, the realization that perhaps it had all been set up, the dogs somehow alerted and drawn to the place of killing, and I, Lord Sean's daughter, drawn right after them, out of the protection of the nemetons and into the perilous wild places of the forest. Someone had known that if Bear and Badger ran, I would follow. Someone knew me so well he must surely have been watching me since the very first day I came to Sevenwaters. But why would Mac Dara be interested in me? Everyone said he overlooked women, thought them unimportant. It couldn't be me he wanted as a pawn or a hostage; it must be . . . "Finbar," I said suddenly, my heart going cold. "Luachan, where is Finbar?"

"With his mother at the keep." Luachan twisted in the saddle, looking over his shoulder at me. "Maeve, you're as white as a sheet. He's safe, I promise you. I left the two of them, and Eithne, in the stillroom not long ago."

Tears of relief stung my eyes. Safe. My brother was safe, and so was I. But not that man out there, a man who had been someone's brother, someone's son, perhaps a husband and father, too. One of Cruinn's men; perhaps one of his sons. Dead. I had never seen a person die before. I thought I understood those looks now, the looks my sisters had turned on me when I lay burned after the fire, doing my best to bear the pain bravely. They had felt as I had today, when that man had fixed his dying stare on me. Helpless. Utterly helpless.

Luachan may have been slow to understand at first, but when we reached the keep he proved his worth. In the stable yard he dismounted with some grace, tied up his weary horse, then helped me down. Since it was clear my legs would not carry me, he supported me as far as the little garden and settled me on the low wall. The moment he stepped back, Bear and Badger stationed themselves in front of me, their hackles rising as folk came into view between stables and keep. There was a familiar face: Donal, the young groom from Harrowfield, well-known to both the dogs. Luachan called him over.

"Stay with Lady Maeve while I fetch Lord Sean, and don't let anyone bother her." His tone was crisp, and Donal raised his brows.

"Donal doesn't speak much Irish," I said, and translated for him. He gave a nod and took up a position not far from me.

"All right?" Luachan asked me with somewhat more familiarity than was quite appropriate.

"Stop wasting time," I said. "Go."

Very soon my father was striding across the yard toward me, with Luachan behind. The lines around Father's nose and mouth seemed deeper; he looked older. "Maeve, my dear." He spoke with a well-governed calm. "Luachan has explained what has happened. He tells me you are unharmed, but exhausted from your long run to bring us this news."

"I'm fine, Father. I'll need to come with you when you ride out to fetch this man; if he's to be brought home by dusk that must happen straightaway. I can—"

"Maeve. Hush." Father directed a glance of dismissal at Luachan, and the druid went off to tend to his horse, followed by Donal. "You are distressed, and with good cause. But I need you to help me. Not by jumping on a horse and riding off right away, but by giving me the best description you can of the place where you found this man, and the condition of his body."

"But, Father—"

"I know how practical and clearheaded you are. I also know your mother would not forgive me if I expected you to ride out again today, when you're clearly at the last gasp of exhaustion."

"That doesn't matter—"

"Hush, my dear." He might have been speaking to a tiny Maeve, woken in the lonely dark by a sudden nightmare. "Give me your description. I am hoping I may be able to find the place without you. If I cannot, then I will take you with me, I promise. But let's try this first."

I took a deep breath and described the clearing, perfectly circular, and the lone elm. I told him where the dogs had left the main track, not far this side of the plank bridge, and I added as many details as I could recall: the brambles, the variety of trees, the little path that had curiously appeared, without a single fallen leaf on it. I had become almost calm by the time I came to what I had found in the clearing. "He was hanging upside down. It was like a crude imitation of a cocoon. The ropes that tied him—there was no way for me to unfasten them or to cut them. He was so close to the ground, Father—if I'd been there earlier I could perhaps have got something to put under his head and shoulders to take the weight, to keep him alive until I could fetch help . . . He died just after I got there. As if it had been planned that way." After a moment I added, "He is one of Cruinn's lost men. I'm sure of it."

"Dagda preserve us," murmured Father. "So it seems." Then, in a different tone, "I know where that place is. In times past it was used for ritual observance, but it has never been part of the nemetons. There's another way to reach it, an easier way for horses. I am hoping you will trust this mission to me, and go indoors to recover." He glanced around. "I see your mother coming, and I am quite certain she will want to take you under her wing."

Bear growled; he had spotted Mother coming out the kitchen door. I hushed him. "Thank you, Father," I said, rising shakily to my feet. "Of course I trust you to do it. Please be careful."

"I will," Father said. "Not that I believe Mac Dara would attempt a direct attack on me; his strategy seems to be to weaken my authority and turn my allies against me. Luachan!"

Donal had taken the mare, Blaze, off to the stables, and Luachan was waiting at a discreet distance while Father spoke to me. Now he came to stand by us, calmly attentive.

"I want you to ride to the nemetons and tell Ciarán what's happened. Ask if he will come to the keep for supper and stay on for a family council. Perhaps you could escort him back here, if this has not wearied you too much."

"Yes, my lord." A pause. "My lord, Maeve—Lady Maeve—will need an escort home to her cottage. Should I not wait for her?"

A look passed between chieftain and druid. I waited for one of them to drop his gaze, but neither did so until Mother came up and Father turned to speak to her.

"You'll have heard the bare bones of what's happened, my dear. Maeve has run a long way to bring us the news. I must organize a retrieval party." To Luachan, he said, "Lady Aisling will make the arrangements for my daughter. There's no need to concern yourself with that." He strode off across the yard. A moment later the druid, too, was gone.

There was shock in Mother's eyes, but she spoke calmly. "Maeve, you look worn-out. Back to the house with me, then bath, food, rest. No arguments. These dogs must go to the kennels; they can't be left to wander around here."

"No!" I heard the sharp edge in my voice, and felt Bear's body tense against my knee. Badger was behind him now, a silent shadow. I made myself take a deep breath. The man was dead; nothing could change that. Father would bring the body back. He did not need me for that sad duty. I was at the keep and exhausted; I was not going to get back to the nemetons tonight. I would have to manage without Rhian. "Mother," I said, "the dogs must be with me. I don't mind sleeping out in the stables, but I'm not coming into the house and leaving them outside. I need them close by." A rumble of anxiety sounded in Bear's throat. "Hush," I murmured.

"You're a little overwrought, and I understand that." Mother did not like to be challenged in her field of authority. "Once you've had a wash and some food, you'll feel much better. Dogs are dogs, my dear, not men and women. The other hounds do well enough in the kennels at night." There was a note in her voice that made me angry. It said shock and exhaustion had addled my judgment, which was perhaps already askew, thanks to ten years of living with Aunt Liadan and Uncle Bran.

"Mother"—I made my voice level and courteous—"if I can't have Bear and Badger with me, whether it's in my bedchamber or in a corner of the stables, the three of us will walk back to the nemetons. We have plenty of time to get there before dark." Tired as I was, I held my head high and looked her in the eye. "If you don't understand why this is important, think of the night of the fire and why I was burned."

Her fair, freckled skin flushed scarlet. I was sorry I had upset her, but not sorry enough to take back my words.

"After this," she said, and I saw her gathering herself together, the better to sound as the lady of Sevenwaters should, "you surely don't imagine you can go on living out in that cottage, so far away from the keep, with just your maid to watch over you."

My heart shrank. With one hand on Bear's head and the other on Badger's, I said, "I didn't find the man in the nemetons, or on the main track. He was miles out in the forest, away from everywhere."

"Then how was it you found him?"

"Bear and Badger found him. They raced off; I ran after them." It did not sound good and I knew it. "I've worked hard to earn their trust, Mother. I didn't want to lose them. And if I hadn't followed, I wouldn't have found the man."

Mother looked at Bear, as if daring him to utter so much as the smallest growl. Bear gazed back, his amber eyes shining in the afternoon light. He did not make a sound. Behind him, his shadow was hunkered down as if trying to be invisible.

"You know I don't allow dogs in the bedchambers," Mother said. And, as I opened my mouth to respond, "Can they be trusted to behave themselves?"

I could not tell an outright lie. "Badger is uncomfortable behind a closed door. Bear is very protective. They've been hurt and it still shows. If they are with me, I'll make sure they behave."

Mother looked at me quizzically. "You seem to inspire great loyalty, my dear."

"You mean the dogs? I helped them, that was all. I took time for them."

144

"Not only them," Mother said, offering me her arm. "Let's go in, shall we? There's your maid, and those two grooms who won't hear a word spoken against you." She went on quickly, as if realizing this remark implied something she would rather not have passed on. "Ciarán speaks highly of you. Finbar talks about you incessantly. And Luachan, as you just saw, was somewhat put out that he was not to escort you back to your cottage in person."

"That's only because he was the one who brought me here."

"I disagree."

"He's a druid. He's just being polite."

"If you say so, Maeve."

At the kitchen door I halted, and the dogs halted with me. "Mother?"

She answered the uncertainty in my voice without needing to hear the question. "I will help you with your food. Eithne will assist you with the bath and some clean clothing, if that is acceptable. And I've already sent for Rhian."

I nodded, tears pricking my eyes. "Thank you," I said. "I'm sorry if I was discourteous. I do need the dogs . . ." I fell silent, since my voice had begun wobbling perilously.

"Upstairs," Mother said. "As for you"—she glanced at Bear and Badger, and I imagined they quailed at the iron in her voice—"the least misdemeanor and you're off outside. And don't for one moment imagine you'll be sleeping on the bed."

I woke to find Rhian sitting beside me, working on some sewing. No doubt she saw my puffy face and reddened eyes and realized I had cried myself to sleep once Eithne had left the chamber. Bear was on the bed. He had jumped up when I began to weep and arranged himself next to me, so I could lay my arm over his warm body and he could dry my tears with his tongue. I had slept secure in his presence, knowing I was not entirely alone with my dark thoughts.

Beyond the window it was night. "Did they find him?" I croaked, struggling to emerge from my heavy sleep. "The man who died, did they bring him back?"

"They did." Rhian set down her handiwork and passed me a cup of water; I sat on the edge of the bed and drank it thirstily. Badger was on the floor, as close as possible to the bed. I had asked Eithne to leave the door open a crack so I could get out if I needed to, and Rhian had left it that way. Badger's eyes had been turned toward that narrow opening, but now he got up and came to rest his muzzle on my knee.

"Lady Aisling said to tell you that the council tonight will be for family only, apart from Luachan and your father's chief man-at-arms. It's in the small council chamber. Your mother said she expected you'd want to be there even if you were too tired to keep your eyes open."

"I was not very considerate of her feelings earlier. She tried to make me put Bear and Badger in the kennels for the night. You'd better not mention that Bear slept on the bed."

"His lordship will be expecting that every night now, I suppose," Rhian said, eyeing Bear where he still lay comfortably on the blankets. "Here, I have some fresh clothes for you; Eithne said I could take them from your sister Eilis's storage chest."

She helped me dress in a skirt of dark green, a soft shirt, an overtunic embroidered with birds. It felt odd that Eilis's things fitted me. In my mind she was still that white-faced child who had stood by my bedside, her eyes wide with horror. Supper was waiting for me on a tray.

"You know," said Rhian, "for a girl who not long ago was swearing black and blue that she didn't want a dog, you've done a good job of falling in love with this one. Makes me feel almost sorry for the other fellow." She glanced at Badger. "Just as well he doesn't get jealous."

"I think his heart is elsewhere."

"What if you find out that's true and someone comes to claim the pair of them?"

"Then I'll hand them over, I suppose." I could no longer imagine this.

When I moved to the little table to eat my supper, Bear jumped down off the bed and went to wait by the door, as if anticipating that we would be going out.

"Bear seems to think he's going to the council with you."

"We need to take them outside anyway. Will you come downstairs with me?"

Rhian rolled her eyes. "Somehow I don't think this is part of the regular duties of a personal maid. But since I'd rather not have to clean up dog mess indoors, I'll go along with it. Now, eat up that food. I know it's been a bad day, but you won't have the strength to deal with such things if you don't eat. Here, let me help."

"You'll make a fine mother some day, Rhian," I told her as she began passing me morsels of cheese and leek pie. "Kind but firm. I expect your children will all be as capable as you, and as good with animals as their father. And they'll all have big ears."

I wondered whether I had gone too far, since she did not answer for a moment. Then she burst out laughing. "I'm getting quite fond of the ears," she said.

Later, it occurred to me that Rhian in her wisdom had been working hard to keep my mind off the difficult events of the day. I was still tired. There were bruises all over me, bruises I could not remember getting, though doubtless I had bumped into many rocks and branches during my wild flight through the forest. We made our way downstairs and out through the kitchen, where Nuala and her assistants were scouring pots and pans and wiping down tables, setting all in place for tomorrow morning's baking. I complimented Nuala on the pie. She made no comment about dogs in the kitchen. We took Bear and Badger outside and stood in the yard awhile. They wandered about; we gazed up at the moon.

"Swift's on his own," I said.

"No, he's not. Master Ciarán arranged for one of the druids to stay close by and keep an eye on him. He knew you'd be worried. And Donal will go down first thing in the morning. You don't have to arrange everything yourself, you know."

This silenced me.

"I'm sorry," Rhian said after a while. "I didn't mean it to sound that way. But I was worried. We all were. It's all very well to want to do things on your own, but sometimes you . . . Never mind."

She sounded awkward, and I understood that. We were within earshot of the kitchens and of guards stationed outside the keep, and the easy way we talked in private would not be understood by the Sevenwaters servants or, most likely, by my family. I found myself wishing Deirdre had not gone home so promptly.

I walked into my father's council with Bear by my side. Badger stationed himself outside the door, and faithful Rhian settled on a bench beside him.

The council chamber was lit by oil lamps hanging from hooks on the walls. Their light set a warm glow on the faces of those seated around the central table. In this chamber, Father was accustomed to conducting private meetings, studying his maps and charts, writing letters and, I remembered, sometimes sitting quietly by himself, deep in thought. But perhaps that had changed, since the smaller chamber that led off this one was now used by Finbar and Luachan for their daily lessons.

Everyone looked somber. Mother's lips were pressed into a thin line, and Doran, leaning across to pour ale for Father, had the air of a soldier who knows war is looming. Ciarán was calm, as always. So was Luachan, who appeared none the worse for wear after his double journey earlier, though he sprang to his feet when I came in, earning another look from my father. With my arrival it seemed our gathering was complete, and Doran moved to shut the door. I hoped Badger would not explode in a frenzy of barking and try to tear down the barrier. It is not so easy for a dog to learn the command, *Wait*.

"Thank you for being here, Maeve," Father said. "You must still be weary. Doran, come and sit down with us."

Father glanced around the table, meeting the eye of each man and woman there in turn. Broccan and Teafa were not with him tonight. I wondered whether the presence of my dogs had caused his to be sent to the kennels early.

"We are gathered tonight," Father went on, "because I anticipate a response to what has occurred today, and I want to be as well prepared for that response as I can be. Maeve said to me earlier that she was in no doubt the man whose body she found was one of Cruinn's lost warriors. I have to tell you, Maeve, that one of my search parties visited that place only yesterday. They went over the whole area surrounding the clearing and found nothing untoward. Doran was among them. Doran?"

"It's true, Lady Maeve. But that may not be a surprise to you. If the man was alive when you found him, he must have been strung up earlier today—he could not have survived in that position overnight. It's been the same with each of Cruinn's men, though the others were found only after they had died. The bodies were warm in every instance. And in every instance they were found in an area that had recently been searched."

"With each discovery it has been harder to convince Cruinn that we're doing as thorough a job as we can," Father said. "He is perfectly justified in arguing that if a man turns up more or less under the nose of our search parties, recently dead, a little more speed or better judgment could have saved his life. If this man proves to be one of his sons, he will be even more desperate to find the other before he, too, is killed."

"Have you sent a message to Cruinn yet, Father?"

"We have sent word." It was Ciarán who spoke, his voice deep and grave. "It will take time to reach him. But we must allow for all possibilities when he receives this news. There's an even chance the dead man was one of Cruinn's sons."

"I helped lay out the young man's body," Mother said quietly. "While I have never met Cruinn's sons, I can tell you this man bore little resemblance to Cruinn himself. Illann would know one way or the other, since he is distant kin to the family. Perhaps we should ask him and Deirdre to return here. After all, Deirdre . . ." She hesitated.

"Deirdre can talk to Clodagh, and Clodagh to Cathal," said Ciarán, leading us into the territory Mother had hesitated to enter, so delicate were the implications.

Father lifted a hand as if to call a halt: "We have two matters to consider tonight. One is Cruinn's likely response to the bad news, and the need to set in place some strategies to deal with that. The second is far graver—the fact that Mac Dara continues to torment us with these killings carried out under the noses of our searchers. Before we speak of involving Illann and Deirdre further, we must consider the safety of our paths, not only those within the Sevenwaters forest, but also those that link us to family farther afield. We know the nemetons are safe. The strategy our enemy is using, which I believe is intended to force me into ill-considered action, has thus far not touched the keep or our immediate surroundings, though I suppose that could change."

His words made me shiver; I laid the back of my hand on Bear's head and he turned his gold-brown eyes up toward me as if to say, *It's all right. I will keep you safe.*

"Ciarán tells me certain protections have been set in place to ensure the path between nemetons and keep remains secure to travel," Father went on. "I cannot be so sure of the road between Sevenwaters and Illann's territory at Dun na Ri. Nor can I have any confidence that the main track north will not be a target for Mac Dara. After all, the Disappearance itself took place on a well-traveled way linking Sevenwaters to the pass to the north."

"You don't believe it is safe for Deirdre and Illann to travel here," said Mother. Under her practical tone there was something akin to desolation. It must be hard, I thought somewhat grimly, with all her daughters away except for the flawed one, the one she had gotten back and now wasn't sure what to do with. Muirrin and Clodagh lived far to the north, Sibeal far to the south. Each had her own sound reasons for not returning. Eilis was gone across the sea. Deirdre, the sister who had done all the right things, with her strategic marriage and her healthy son and daughter, had been no more than a day's ride away. Until this.

"We must still send word." Father's gaze was on his hands, clasped before him on the table. "Both to Illann's household and to Cathal. I'll need Illann's support in dealing with this. He is close kin to the woman who was to wed Cruinn's elder son. This killing may be the last straw for Cruinn, the outrage that turns this from a grim turn of events we share with him to the cause of a bloody conflict. My own forces and Illann's must be prepared for that development, though I hope Cruinn holds back from it. As for the paths and the uncanny threat, I think it best Deirdre does not leave Dun na Ri, and certainly the children should not do so. Our messengers may be stopped. The content of any messages they bear may become known to our enemy. There is no reason Mac Dara would be aware of the bond between Clodagh and Deirdre, and the fact that it allows us to reach Cathal more or less instantly. Best that our adversary does not learn of it, since that would put Deirdre at risk. If he believes her to be of no great consequence, and if she stays behind her own door, chances are he will not think to involve her in his plotting."

I was feeling unnaturally cold. Today, when I had found the body, it had hardly occurred to me to fear for my own safety. "That might not be what Deirdre would choose," I ventured. "If she can help, I imagine she'd want to."

"Not at the expense of her children's safety," Mother said.

"I will carry word for you." Such was the power of Ciarán's voice that every head turned toward him, although he spoke quietly. "We have ways of traveling that keep us out of folk's eyes and minds, though the creatures of forest and farmland know we are passing."

I wondered whether *we* meant druids, or if he was referring to his fey blood.

"Only one message is required," Ciarán went on, "and it need not be set down with ink and parchment. I would go to Dun na Ri and suggest to Illann that he comes to Sevenwaters covertly. At the same time I would speak to Deirdre, asking her to give her twin a message for Cathal. I would remain in Illann's household until Deirdre had Clodagh's response."

"Father, do you think Cruinn will come here?" I asked, imagining the Sevenwaters keep besieged by warriors from Tirconnell, and all of us trapped inside. The questions I wanted to ask were small and selfish: *What happens to Swift? Do I have to move back to the keep? What about the dogs?*

Father seemed to relax a little as he looked at me. "It's all too easy for me to put myself in Cruinn's shoes," he said. "I imagine my children lost, as his sons are; I think of finding one victim after another, and knowing my own son or daughter could be next. Should Cruinn sweep into Sevenwaters followed by his personal army, demanding justice, I believe I will have some understanding of his fury. You'll be thinking about Swift, of course. Under any other circumstances, the yearling would be a remarkable gift for a chieftain, a true peacemaker. But it's too late for that. The only gift that would have any meaning for Cruinn at this point would be getting his sons back alive and well. I am almost inclined to ship Swift home to Harrowfield, and you with him, since you would undoubtedly be much safer there."

"It's too late in the season." Mother's tone was sharp. "Provided Maeve moves back into the keep, she will be as safe as any of us can be. Unless you are suggesting Finbar, too, should be sent away."

"No, my dear. Nor would I seriously consider despatching the horse on another sea voyage when he has taken so long to recover from the last. But we cannot offer Swift as compensation to Cruinn now. Cruinn would most likely see that as an insult. What he'll want is action."

"We've all the men we can spare out on the search already," said Doran. "We must keep the guard posts fully manned. Should Cruinn gain the support of other Uí Néill chieftains to mount an attack against us, we'll be stretched perilously thin." He thought for a moment, then added, "As for Mac Dara, he's a prince of the Tuatha De Danann. The most formidable human army would be hard-pressed to stand up against his forces, even supposing they could be found. How could ordinary men-at-arms fight against the powers of a sorcerer?"

There followed a weighty silence, in which the memory of the odd conversation I'd had with Ciarán hung heavily over me, filling the air with danger. Then Luachan said carefully, "It seems to me the issue of Cruinn is secondary. The enemy who matters, the enemy who must be destroyed, is Mac Dara."

"That is all very well," Father said, "but as Doran just pointed out, this is no ordinary war. Mac Dara won't be defeated with sword and shield. And without the support of our neighbors, those chieftains like Eoin and Naithi who were once trusted allies and are no longer, we cannot summon the manpower to fight on two fronts, should Cruinn and the northerners decide attacking Sevenwaters is the quickest way to find the last of the missing men."

"You believe he is desperate enough to try that?" Mother asked.

"A man will do much for his children," Father said. "He'll perform reckless acts, deeds of bloody vengeance or insane courage. I hope Cruinn is not yet driven to such an extreme, but we must at least consider the possibility. With Johnny and his forces too far north to call in quickly and the autumn advancing, we would be vulnerable."

I thought of the old times, when Sibeal had been visited by the Lady of the Forest, a figure of benign power and goodness, a lamp in a dark world. Once, the chieftain of Sevenwaters could have relied on that greater power to help in time of need, provided he was prepared to be brave and resourceful himself. It was hard to accept that those times were gone.

Luachan cleared his throat. "If I may suggest . . . We agree, I take it, that Mac Dara is behind not only the Disappearance and its aftermath, but the whole chain of trouble that has dogged Sevenwaters since the time of Finbar's abduction years ago. Since Cathal first came to Sevenwaters and Mac Dara realized his son had grown into a fine man and had wandered back within his reach." He waited for a response.

"That is undoubtedly so," Ciarán said. "The events surrounding Finbar's capture and rescue made it quite plain." He paused. "This is well known to you, Luachan; it is for precisely this reason that you were chosen as Finbar's tutor and protector."

Luachan smiled faintly. "I speak thus for Lady Maeve's benefit, since she is newly arrived here and may not be fully aware of the facts. Also to point out that it makes more sense to uproot the weed than to spend time picking out its thorns. I believe there is no point in continuing the search; no chance at all that the last of these men will be found alive and brought home safely. You should direct your resources not to placating Cruinn but to the destruction of Mac Dara."

"Go on." Father's tone was carefully neutral. Had I been in Luachan's shoes, that tone would have made me think twice about saying another word. "I assume you have a strategy to suggest, one that is not beyond our capabilities?"

"I do. No army. No allies. No war. Offer Mac Dara what he wants. Lure him out. Trick him, then destroy him."

The silence felt dangerous. I admired the young druid's boldness. I was not so sure about his judgment.

"What are you suggesting, Luachan?" Father made no attempt to disguise his shock. "That we should risk Cathal's safety, or that of his infant son, in order to draw Mac Dara to us? Attempt a bluff when we lack the ability to follow through?"

"Luachan," Mother said, "what happened to Finbar marked him. I see the shadow of that experience on him even now; the brightest light in all the world cannot banish it. How can you believe we would use another child as a pawn in Mac Dara's evil game?"

"I do not suggest Cathal's son be involved. The boy is too young to play a part in such a ruse. Cathal himself is a different matter. From what I have heard, Mac Dara's son is a warrior of some note, and adept in the magical arts. To preserve the future of Sevenwaters, would Cathal not come forth from his bolt-hole in the north and challenge the Lord of the Oak? Who better to trick the trickster than his own son?"

Another silence. I wondered if I had misunderstood Luachan's position in the household, or in the nemetons. His youth did not necessarily make him a junior player in the game of strategy. And after all, what he was suggesting was more or less the same thing Ciarán had spoken of that day when he had talked to me at the cottage.

"Cathal would not risk Clodagh or his children by bringing them here," Mother said, as if there were no argument about it. "And he would not come alone, leaving them on Inis Eala, even though that place is considered as safe as our nemetons, perhaps safer. We've heard this from Johnny more than once, and also from Clodagh, through Deirdre."

"May I say something?" I looked around the circle of troubled faces. "You dismissed the idea of involving Deirdre openly; if she helps, it must be secretly, from behind the safe walls of Dun na Ri. Mother is saying Clodagh must stay at Inis Eala with her children. And it sounds as if Cathal isn't prepared to leave her, so that means he can't come, even though that is what Luachan suggests must happen—that the son must be here to battle the father, whether that's a battle with sword and shield or a battle with magic or merely a test of wills. Of course nobody wants to put their loved ones in danger. But I think Luachan may be right. We should deal with the sickness itself, not only the symptoms. And we must be prepared to face risk; there's no escaping it, unless we all hide away and hope Mac Dara will eventually tire of his quest. I don't believe that will happen."

Perhaps seeing that my mother was becoming distressed, Ciarán spoke next. "In one respect, Luachan is absolutely correct. We cannot defeat Mac Dara by force of arms. What we must seek to do is to outwit him. His activities have increased markedly of recent times. He seems to be in a hurry to achieve his goal. I would very much like to know why. Does he fear that the longer Cathal stays away, and the more settled he and his family become on Inis Eala, the harder it will be to lure him out again? Does he suspect his son is spending his time up there perfecting his magical craft, the better to return and defeat his father? Or is this something else entirely?"

"Does Mac Dara need reasons?" put in Luachan. "The Disappearance could be an act of pure mischief. He may simply be entertaining himself. Such a creature does not think as you or I might. With respect," he added somewhat belatedly.

"I wish I knew the answer to your question, Ciarán," Father said with a grim smile. "It might prove part of the key to defeating him."

"Mac Dara is old, isn't he, even by the standards of the Fair Folk?" I said. "Can his kind die, or do they go on forever?" Ciarán had said the Lady of the Forest and her kind had sailed away into the west. A kind of death, perhaps. Or a new adventure. Maybe both. "If he feared his reign was nearing its end, he might be desperate to have his heir ready to assume power. And it seems important to him to see Cathal, or Cathal's son, take his place." The issue was awkward, since Ciarán himself was the offspring of one of the Tuatha De.

"He will not die," Ciarán said, "but he will . . . fade. The Tuatha De do not retain their power and vigor eternally. In time Mac Dara will diminish, and another will take his place." A pause for consideration; he looked unusually somber. "Though I have to say, the clever use of spellcraft can lead to the demise of such a one, especially if that one is caught off guard. I have seen it done."

"Indeed," murmured my father, glancing at him. Neither of them chose to elaborate.

"Even Mac Dara must have a weak spot," I said. "To trick someone as clever and devious as he seems to be, you'd need to know as much as possible about him. Though where you would find out about a prince of the Fair Folk, I'm not sure. You'd have to go back to old tales, I suppose."

Ciarán nodded; everyone seemed to be listening with interest. Encouraged, I went on. "And Cathal must know about his own father, even though he didn't grow up with him—he did spend some time as his captive, in the Otherworld, before Clodagh went to fetch him back. We should ask him." I realized how that sounded. "I mean, you could ask him, Uncle Ciarán, through Deirdre. If you found out what Mac Dara's weak spot is—I'm not speaking of those tales in which a dragon or monster is defeated because it is missing a scale under its chin or between its toes, but about a chink in a different kind of armor—that could give you the means to trap him. You might be able to turn his own cleverness against him."

"You are something of a strategist, Maeve," Ciarán murmured.

I felt my cheeks grow warm. "You can blame Uncle Bran for that. He encouraged my interest in such matters. Fintan did as well. As Aunt Liadan's son, he could hardly fail to learn that women can be as strategic in their thinking as men, even if they may be destined to use those skills to organize a household, not an army." I caught Mother's eyes on me; she was not smiling, but I sensed her approval.

"If you agree, Sean, I will go to Dun na Ri," Ciarán said. "I will ask Deirdre to communicate with Clodagh and, through her, with Cathal." He hesitated. "Illann can bring word of the result to you. I have another journey to make before I return to Sevenwaters. Finbar asked me about geasa and put an idea into my mind. Has it occurred to you that such a curse may lie over Mac Dara himself?"

A geis! That, I had not considered. I saw from the expressions of my companions that the notion was a surprise to everyone, save perhaps Luachan. It wasn't easy to surprise a druid.

"A remote possibility," Ciarán added. "But a possibility nonetheless."

"A geis could explain the increase in Mac Dara's hostilities of recent times," Father mused. "Such a thing must catch up with a person eventually; as the years pass, there must be an increased urgency in the wish to set one's affairs to rights. And that would include having a successor in place before the terms of the geis came to pass."

"How could you find out?" Luachan asked Ciarán. "Who would know such a thing?"

"Ah." Ciarán's expression was grave; I thought he was looking deep into the past. "I cannot be sure of that. But I know where I would begin to seek answers. In his pressing desire for a son and heir, Mac Dara fathered many daughters over the long years of his life, until at last Cathal was born. Very many daughters. Some are ordinary women, some not so ordinary. Some believe themselves to be fully human; some know of their fey parentage and the gifts it brings. If answers are to be had, I will find them among those women." He glanced at my father. "It may take some time."

"We could provide you with a riding horse and an escort," Father said. "But I imagine you will refuse both. You'll wish to travel by your own paths."

"I've just thought of something," I said.

"What is it, Maeve?"

"Father, when Cruinn's men first went missing, they were on horseback, weren't they? What happened to their horses?"

"Most were found unharmed, close to the track from which the riders went missing. Two had wandered back toward Tirconnell and were sheltered by folk along the way—Cruinn instituted a thorough search of his own. Three were found within the next few days by my men, loose in the forest. They had some scratches and were tired and hungry, but all recovered quickly and were returned to Cruinn. The others . . ."

"Two were never found, Lady Maeve," Doran said. "Another we discovered dead, quite some time later and quite some distance away from the area where the others were located. Wolves had attacked it; there wasn't much left."

"Why do you ask?" Ciarán had his eye on Bear, who had risen to his feet as if to suggest it was time for us to leave.

"Bear and Badger had been wandering in the forest for some time before I found them. Their condition made that plain. It's obvious they belonged to someone. They are not wild creatures; Bear obeyed my commands almost from the first. I wondered if . . ." I really did not want to say this, did not want to set in chain a sequence of events that must end with my losing them. "I wondered whether Cruinn's lost men had dogs with them when they rode out. It's common enough for hounds to run alongside such a party. It would mean Bear and Badger had been in the forest for longer than I thought, but it seems possible. And . . . their behavior earlier today was unusual. They were deeply disturbed by the sight of that man hanging from the tree."

"Death is always disturbing," Mother said. "Even for a dog, I imagine. The two of them are closely attuned to you, Maeve. They felt your distress, perhaps."

"It was more than that. They seemed to know where the man was, or to sense it. Otherwise why did they bolt from the path when he was much too far away for them to see or smell? It was almost . . . uncanny."

Silence. Everyone looked at Bear. Bear looked only at me. His eyes were pools of liquid amber in the lamplight.

"There's another possibility." Father spoke with obvious reluctance. "One I have heard suggested in this household. That they are Mac Dara's creatures, sent to lure you off the path and expose you to danger. Spies in our midst; bearers of secret messages. I see your repugnance, Maeve, but the idea must be put in the open. Didn't we just say we must learn as much as we can about our enemy? Imagine how it might be: Mac Dara looking for a weak link among us, observing you, knowing, perhaps, the circumstances under which you left Sevenwaters as a child. He might have noticed how much you love creatures and want to help them. How better to manipulate you than by placing in your path a pair of starving dogs needing food, shelter and love?"

You will not lose your temper, I ordered myself. *You will stay in control.* I rose to my feet. "That isn't so," I said, summoning every technique Uncle Bran had taught me for keeping calm. "I would know."

Luachan, too, had risen. "It cannot be so," he said quietly. "The nemetons are protected against the powers of evil; the hand of the goddess lies over that place and all who dwell there. Maeve first saw the creatures within the borders of our sanctuary. If these are creatures of Mac Dara, they could not have entered there."

I cleared my throat, wishing I did not have to correct him. "In fact, I first saw them as we were walking from the keep to the nemetons, you and Finbar and I. And they were some distance off the path. They only entered the nemetons after I coaxed them closer."

"Don't distress yourself, Maeve," Ciarán said. "Your parents and I have already discussed this theory; indeed, we did so some time ago, when Lady Aisling had cause to reprimand someone for airing it publicly. I said I thought it unlikely, since it depends on Mac Dara having a true understanding of such qualities as compassion, love and loneliness. To conjure in this way, a man must surely know what lies deep in the human heart. While he has a better grasp of such matters than many of his kind, I do not believe him capable of that."

"I see," I said more bluntly than was perhaps polite. "Will you excuse me? I'm tired; it's been a long day. I think it's best if you continue this without me." So they'd been talking this over for some time. Discussing my behavior behind my back, without bothering to speak to me first. I squared my shoulders and lifted my chin. "Bear, come."

It was not possible to sweep out of the room in regal style, since I could not open the door on my own. But Luachan was lightning quick; he reached it before I had to call out to Rhian, and opened it for me to go through. If there was the trace of a smile on his well-shaped lips, I chose to ignore it.

Rhian was still seated on the bench outside the door, and beside her was Finbar. They were making something elaborate with knotted string. Badger sprang up when we came out.

"Finbar," I said, my hurt pride forgotten in my surprise. "Isn't it past your bedtime?"

"Finbar wanted to tell you something, Lady Maeve," Rhian said, trying to convey a message with her eyes as she slipped the string into her pocket. "But not here—my back's sore from sitting on this bench, and I'm thirsty. Why don't you go on up to our chamber, and I'll fetch the three of us a little something from the kitchen?"

So, Finbar had something to say that must be conveyed in private, or at least, not so close to the council. Who was it he did not want listening? Mother? Father? Luachan?

"That's a good idea," I said briskly. "How about warm milk with honey?"

"I'll do my best."

Up in the chamber, my brother seemed more inclined to sit on the floor stroking Bear's belly—Bear was all too ready to roll over and submit to his attentions—than to spill out whatever important news he had to share. I settled cross-legged beside them and told Badger what a good boy he had been, and other things of the same kind, and he allowed me to fondle his ears and rub under his chin, though there was still a tension in him. I wondered whether the dogs really had come from Cruinn's household. Perhaps they had belonged to his sons; maybe they had seen what had happened to them. Had they stood their ground and challenged the attackers? Or had Mac Dara's forces whisked the men away in an instant, using some fell charm, and left Bear and Badger suddenly alone? No smells to guide them; no tracks to follow; no whistle or kind word from a beloved master. Nothing. Nothing but each other.

"Maeve?"

I started at Finbar's voice; I had been far away. "Yes, Finbar?"

"I don't know if I should tell you this."

What was coming? I felt my way cautiously. "If it's someone else's secret, something you've promised not to talk about . . ." No, that wouldn't do. He'd asked to speak to me. "I promise not to pass it on to anyone," I said. "You can trust me, Finbar. I'm your sister."

A grim little smile. It disturbed me to see such a look on his face, but I held my silence.

"Luachan says it's better not to tell. What I see in the water, or in the fire, or in dreams, I mean. Because it might look like one thing but mean a different thing. Telling can upset people. It can make them angry or afraid. Then they might make wrong choices."

"It's safe to tell me, Finbar."

"Luachan says when I'm older I'll learn to put the things I see in a story, so people can understand it better. That's what druids do."

I thought again about the tale Ciarán had told, of the warring families and their destruction of the beautiful valley that provided their livelihood. The brave young lovers; the wise crone in the wood. "That sounds like good advice," I said. "But sometimes you do need to tell someone, especially if what you've seen is . . . worrying, frightening in some way."

"Maeve." My little brother turned his strange eyes on me. His hand stilled against the dog's dark hair. "What are you most afraid of? What scares you more than anything in the world?"

A chill ran down my spine. This required an honest answer; Finbar was not a child one could placate with comforting half-truths. On the other hand, he was only seven. "I can't pick out just one thing," I said, stalling for time.

Finbar waited, pale as a little ghost.

"Being helpless," I said. "I mean, unable to help when someone I care about is in trouble."

"What if you had to choose?" my brother asked, and it seemed to me his words had a prophetic tone to them. "What if Swift and Bear were both in deadly danger, and you knew you could only help one of them?"

Now he was really scaring me. "Is that what you saw?" I demanded. "Tell me! Tell me what was in this vision you had!"

"Luachan wouldn't want me to tell all of it. It would only scare you."

"Believe me, it's far worse to get hints and not the full story," I said grimly.

"I shouldn't have said." His head drooped, showing the white skin at the back of his neck. Now he would not meet my eyes.

I made myself draw a long, calm breath. "It's all right, Finbar," I said. "You must tell as little or as much as you think is right. I'm sorry I snapped at you. I've had a horrible day, and I'm tired and out of sorts. But if you think Swift or the dogs may be in danger, I would like a warning about it so I can do something to protect them."

He looked up then, sad-eyed. "I thought you would say fire," he said. "After what happened to you, aren't you afraid of fire?"

"Very much afraid. I of all people know how destructive and dangerous it can be. But we need fire for light and warmth; without it we would die. Right from the start, Aunt Liadan taught me how to live with my fear and not let it rule me. I've had ten years to practice. Fire is not my first terror anymore, only my second."

The silence drew out. It seemed to me there was something more he had planned to speak of and now held close. I did not want to ask a small boy what he was most afraid of, especially just before bedtime. I sensed, though, that this might be what Finbar expected.

"Luachan's wise," I said quietly. "It's easy to frighten yourself with stories, and I imagine it is the same with visions. I have often woken with my heart hammering after a dream I can't even remember. I should think the hardest thing about learning to be a seer might be keeping track of it all. Working out what is fact and what is . . . ideas, symbols and so on. I'm sure it is very confusing."

That sounded patronizing, which was not my intention. "It's good that you have Luachan to help you understand it."

"Mm." Finbar was closing up on himself again. He had laid his head down, using Bear as a pillow, but there was nothing sleepy about his eyes. "Maeve," he murmured against the comforting warmth of the dog, "what if Mac Dara put a geis on me? He could have done it when I was a baby, too young to know about it. He could have done it easily. What if the geis said I was going to die if I went past a certain place in the forest, or if I stroked a gray cat by moonlight, or if I climbed an oak tree with a knife in my pocket? Or it might be that I had to do those things or something bad would happen to you or Deirdre, or to Mother or Father."

Morrigan save us, the boy had too much imagination by far. Could he have overheard what we were discussing at the council? I must ask Rhian. "That could have happened, I suppose," I said, keeping my voice calm. "If there really is such a thing as a geis. They are mostly in the old stories, and there are other things in those stories—three-headed monsters, talking animals, men with sheepskin growing on their backs—that make me wonder how much is true and how much is just . . . story. That tale Ciarán told, about the flood—perhaps someone invented it to remind us that we should listen carefully to our elders' wisdom and respect the earth with all her bounties. And that we must be brave and resourceful and love one another. A story need not be true to teach us those things. The best tales have a deep kind of truth. It makes no difference whether they actually happened or not."

"You sound like Uncle Ciarán." Finbar's voice was very small.

"Have you spoken to him about this?"

Finbar sat up abruptly. "You said you wouldn't tell." His eyes were on me, clear pools in shadow.

"I won't, Finbar. I keep my promises. But Uncle Ciarán is very wise, and he's kind, too. You seem worried by this and I don't think you need be. He would explain it far better than I ever could. Or you could talk to Mother."

"No." There was an iron strength in the childish tone. "Mother would be frightened. She's already frightened; that's why they got Luachan."

"Finbar," I said as gently as I could, "I understand why you feel afraid. I'm sure there is nothing to worry about. I mean, there's no evidence that Mac Dara pronounced a curse over you, is there?"

He simply looked at me, and my stomach tied itself into a slow knot as I gazed back. He'd been only an infant, no more than a few days old. If he'd seen it happen, he wouldn't have remembered. But we weren't talking about memory. He had said, *in the water, in the fire, or in dreams.* We were talking about a seer's knowledge. I opened my mouth and shut it again. Suddenly, any words at all felt perilous.

"Here we are." Rhian's cheery voice came from the doorway, and the chamber seemed instantly lighter. "Warm milk and oatcakes with soft cheese. Finbar, get up off the floor. Dogs in the bedchamber are one thing; eating supper amongst them is quite another."

I rose to my feet, reminded of how awkward things must be for Rhian sometimes. Finbar was not the kind of child who distinguished between servant and sister. Another chieftain's son might have taken offense if a maidservant gave him orders, however kindly. He might have had her punished for insolence.

"Thank you, Rhian," I said, "for reminding us about our manners, and for bringing us such a sumptuous feast. Finbar, when we've eaten this you'd better get off to bed or Mother will be cross with both of us." I wondered if the council was still meeting behind closed doors. I should not have walked out. If people were starting to say strange things about Bear and Badger, or about me, losing my temper wasn't going to help.

"I'm not hungry," Finbar said, predictably enough.

"No? Look—apart from the milk, this meal can be eaten entirely with the feet. Shall we try?"

He was, after all, a seven-year-old boy. By the time Luachan came to fetch him, the council being over, Finbar had eaten well, if untidily, and was in much better spirits. I bade him good night and hoped his sleep would be visited only by good dreams, dreams of throwing a ball for a dog, for instance, or picking berries, or making boats from leaves and bark and floating them down the stream. When he'd left,

I asked Rhian if our voices had been audible through the door of the council chamber, and she said she hadn't heard a thing.

As she helped me to wash and get into my night robe, as she brushed my hair, as I lay in my bed staring up at the rafters, I conjured images of myself at Finbar's age. Those had been happy, busy times. I saw myself with Clodagh and Deirdre, climbing trees while Bounder explored below. I remembered running along the lakeshore with Sibeal and Eilis, with Bounder racing ahead. And a fine autumn day when all six of us, even Muirrin, who was almost grown-up, had picked apples, and even Eilis had come home with a full basket. That was the day the kittens were born. I remembered crouching quietly beside the stall where the mother cat lay, and watching with breathless delight as the little ones kneaded her belly and snuffled for milk. My sisters had been around me, equally entranced.

"It was a long time ago, Bear," I whispered, not wanting to wake Rhian, who had been tired under her brisk cheeriness. "But I still remember how perfect that day was. It's in me forever, helping keep me strong." I lay awake a long time, staring into the dark. I thought about Finbar. What had he seen in his visions? What had made him believe he was cursed? Weren't the images seers glimpsed in flame or water hard to interpret even for someone like Ciarán, who had had years and years of practice?

All the while, deep inside me where I had hidden it away, I heard him asking, *What if you had to choose?*

"I couldn't choose," I murmured, feeling the warmth of Bear's slumbering form against my back and listening to the sound of Badger's steady breathing from the floor beside the bed. The door was open a crack, and the lamp in the hallway outside sent a narrow shaft of light across Rhian's sleeping form, peaceful under her blankets. "How could anyone choose?"

DRUID'S JOURNEY: NORTH

He comes down the hill between the beeches in afternoon sunlight. The old woman is by her campfire, her mottled hands stretched out toward the flames. A pack lies to one side, a blanket to the other, with a raggedy old cat curled up on it, washing its ears.

"My respects to you, wise woman."

She turns milky eyes on him. "And to you, druid. Will you share the warmth of my fire awhile?"

"I will, for I have come to speak with you." He settles opposite her, opens his bag, takes out the offering. "Will you share some mead and soft cheese?"

"Ah. You come with gifts. You want something."

"The gifts are freely given, wise woman. I come with a question, yes. Perhaps more than one. Answer if it pleases you to do so, or hold your silence. The fire will remain warm, the food and drink tasty."

"We will eat and drink first, then, and enjoy the silence."

Some while later, the modest repast is finished and the cat, sated with cheese, has fallen asleep on the blanket. The druid adds wood to the fire, then takes time to gather more fallen branches and stack them for the old woman. "For tonight," he says.

"Thank you, young man. You've saved my bones some weary work."

"Young?" the druid echoes. "I am hardly that."

"Beside me, you are a green youth," she says, chuckling. "Ask your question."

The druid settles once more, cross-legged, by the fire. "I seek a rhyme," he says. "Or it might be more in the nature of a charm. A potent one. I seek a particular storyteller who may be able to give me this. She would be one of many sisters. The charm or rhyme concerns their father. A long-lived person, with a single son. He, too, appears younger than his true age."

The old woman waits.

"This form of words," the druid says, "may be of particular importance in righting a wrong. In making a change."

"That would be quite a rhyme," observes the crone. "A weighty one. A very weighty one. Too heavy for one old woman to hold."

After a while, the druid speaks again. "It is my observation that brothers share burdens with their brothers, as do sisters with their sisters. The rhyme might perhaps not be too weighty for three old women to support between them. Or four, or five. No more than that, I hope, for time is short."

"In one particular," she says, "you speak with some foreknowledge, I believe."

A shadow passes over the druid's strong features. "Perhaps," he says.

"As to what you seek, I cannot give it to you, not in full. You must go to my sister who lives in the east. You will find her in a cave on a cliff. Look out from that place at dusk and you will see the selkies dancing in the foam. Or so they say."

He is silent a long time.

"Your kin, one or two of them," she murmurs. "If the tale I've heard is true."

"True enough." His voice is full of sadness. "I must move on if I am to find this sister of yours. I thank you for your patience."

"Ah." Her tone arrests his movement. "Not so quickly. You brought gifts here; not only the tasty meal, but your kindness, your courtesy and the strength of your arms. I have something for you in return. It isn't much. Have you a good memory?"

The druid smiles.

"Here it is, then," says the crone. "*Sever now the ties that bind, Brothers in purpose and in kind.* I cannot tell you what it means, nor where it comes in the verse or charm or rhyme. But that is my share."

The druid nods, his lips moving as he repeats the words, the better to remember. This is treasure. It is power. Or will be, when he learns the rest.

"What sparked this journey?" asks the wise woman. "What brought you here?"

"A child's questions. My own observations. So I'm right about this? The verse, in full, might prove a mighty weapon?"

"It might. Best make haste. My sister's cave is far from here, and the dark is coming."

CHAPTER 8

On the tenth day after our council, Cruinn's army arrived at Sevenwaters. My father did not know they were on the way until a man-at-arms rode in on a wild-eyed, sweat-lathered horse to tell him Cruinn's forces had come right past the northern guard post and would by now be halfway to the keep. The men on watch had let them through. A team of six border guards is no match for an angry chieftain backed by fifty well-armed retainers. The guards had explained the rule, the messenger gasped—no passing through the Sevenwaters forest without an escort—but Cruinn had announced that he cared nothing for Lord Sean's rules and restrictions, since all they had achieved was to stop him getting his lost men back alive. There had been no good answer for that.

In the brief time between the messenger's arrival and that of Cruinn, my father called the household together and, with Doran on his left and my mother, white-faced, on his right, gave a set of orders. Everyone was to stay calm. This was not war. Cruinn's men had not attacked the border guards or fired the watchtowers. The gates of the keep would not be closed against the troop, since that would suggest Sevenwaters expected hostility. Cruinn was angry, and with good reason, but most likely he had come only to talk.

Nonetheless, my father continued, and at this point I heard a subtle change in his tone, as a precautionary measure all the women and children were to go immediately to the upper floor of the keep. Doran would direct the men-at-arms to their posts in the courtyard and before the gate. The other men of the household, those not out on the search, would be armed with whatever could be found for them, and would form a second line of defense inside the keep. The women were to follow Lady Aisling's instructions.

Then Mother spoke. Yes, there was a possibility of an attack. Everyone must remain calm and pray that it would not be so. Should that threat not come to pass, the household might well find itself needing to provide food and lodging at short notice for more than fifty men and as many horses. After such a long ride, Cruinn's party was likely to stay at Sevenwaters for a few nights at least.

What she wanted to see from the women of the household, Mother went on, was backbone and commonsense. The situation would be made clear once Cruinn had arrived and spoken with Lord Sean. Nuala and her assistants might soon find themselves very busy indeed. Now we were all to go upstairs and keep quiet until she gave the word.

It was a cleverly considered speech, which almost certainly had the effect of turning most of the women's thoughts from whether they and their children were about to be cut down by armed warriors, to how they might stretch the available foodstuffs to feed twice as many, or whether Cruinn's men might be prepared to sleep under horse blankets. As I retreated obediently inside I felt a quiet pride in both my parents.

Folk set to work with a calm purpose that was almost eerie to see. Reluctant to go upstairs before I must, I lingered in the hall with the two dogs by my side and watched a man-at-arms handing out knives, pitchforks and lengths of wood to an assortment of kitchen boys and grooms. Luachan, assisted by Finbar, was carrying armfuls of scrolls and documents out of the council chamber and into a little room used for the storage of winter vegetables. An ordered pattern of activity in and out of the kitchen suggested fires were being banked, cook pots taken off the heat, baskets of food and waterskins carried upstairs, as if we might be there for quite some time.

The irony of my situation did not escape me, even at such a moment. I had been working hard to persuade my parents that I should return to the cottage, for a host of reasons. I thought Father was inclined to say yes, but thus far Mother had proved adamant. Rhian and I must remain in the safety of the keep. So here we were, and the sudden arrival of Cruinn had made the keep a place of peril. Underlying my father's confident suggestion that the northern chieftain had only come to talk was the real possibility that Cruinn was here to exact retribution for the loss of his men. If we'd been at the cottage, within the protection of the nemetons, we'd undoubtedly have been safer.

Leaving the gates open seemed to me somewhat foolhardy. Wouldn't it be better to wait until Cruinn announced his intentions before letting him in? Perhaps Father thought a battle was preferable to a siege. Or perhaps he knew that with so many men off on the search, he could not possibly mount an adequate defense against Cruinn's forces. Either way, the orderly nature of the preparations taking place all around me was quite remarkable. There were white faces aplenty, but fear did not stop the folk of Sevenwaters from carrying out their duties as my mother had taught them. I'd best follow their example before someone ordered me to move.

"Bear, come. Badger, come."

The chamber farthest from the top of the stairs had been allocated to the children. Rhian was helping watch over them. I went to the sewing room. Since it was the biggest space, most of the women were gathered there. Mother had not yet come up. When she arrived, I thought, she'd probably set everyone to spinning, weaving and embroidery. Even in a siege, she'd be unable to tolerate idleness.

The women of the household stood or sat around the chamber,

exchanging nervous glances and whispered words. We could hear sounds of running footsteps in the yard, heavy items being shifted downstairs, metal scraping and clinking. Closer to hand, I caught Finbar's voice from along the hallway, asking a question, and Luachan's in reply. Of course, Luachan would have to be up here with the women and children. Finbar needed a guard, not only against the dark prince of the Otherworld, but against more ordinary kinds of attack. Cruinn had lost his sons. If this proved to be a war after all, my father's only son would be vulnerable.

"Excuse me," I murmured, and slipped out of the chamber with Bear and Badger close behind me. Finbar and his tutor were in the upper hallway, looking down to the entry below. The only weapon I could see on Luachan was the knife at his belt.

"Finbar could come in with us, Luachan," I said quietly. "You, too, of course. The sewing room door can be bolted from inside and there's a window that overlooks the courtyard."

"Thank you, Maeve." Luachan neither looked nor sounded afraid, and I took heart from that. "I suggest we station ourselves by the tower stairs and look out the narrow window there. It's a more strategic spot than the sewing chamber." He spotted my mother coming up the stairs and, without waiting for me to comment, went over to speak to her. They conducted a brief murmured conversation; then Mother entered the sewing room and closed the door behind her. "Let me show you," Luachan said to me as he strode back over.

"I know where it is. I grew up here."

Bear caught the irritation in my tone and began to growl. Badger bared his teeth.

"I'm sorry," I made myself say. "Yes, we should move now." It was indeed a strategic choice. If the keep came under attack and the men-at-arms downstairs failed to repel Cruinn's forces, Finbar and I could retreat up the little stair that led to the roof, and Luachan could maintain a good defense for as long as his strength lasted, since only one person at a time could mount the stair. The thought of this made my belly churn. Finbar. So little, so vulnerable. Hurt, captured, killed. Bear and Badger, launching themselves against men with spears and swords. Luachan fighting to the point of exhaustion and falling in our defense. It didn't bear thinking about. "Father seemed confident that Cruinn had come only to talk," I said, making sure my voice was as calm as Luachan's. But the druid said nothing.

The window was in a small alcove. It was narrow indeed, since its purpose was to give cover for an archer without exposing him as a target. I let Finbar stand in front of me so he could see out. Luachan stood beside me, his arm brushing mine until Bear thrust his head between us and planted a large paw on my foot. Badger was somewhere behind us.

Then we waited. Below us in the courtyard my father was waiting, too, a cloak over his shoulders and his sword at his belt. I could not see all the men-at-arms from where I stood, but it seemed to me there were not many of them. I thought of various things I wanted to say to Luachan: that I wished Ciarán had returned from his journey, since his wise presence might have made all the difference today. That I hoped the druids would remember to feed Swift and to talk to him if none of us could get back to the nemetons. That what I really wanted was to be in the cottage with Bear and Badger and Rhian, with Swift grazing peacefully in his field, and for this not to have happened at all. I said none of it.

Time stretched out. The silence was full of little sounds, a chink of metal from down below, Badger scuffing at something on the floor behind us, the voice of a child raised momentarily from along the hallway. A horse neighing down in the stables; a dog barking. Bear's hackles rose at that, and I spoke a word of calm, resting my hand on his head. Luachan stood still, eyes fixed on the courtyard below. Finbar matched him. His concentration was as intense as a hunting owl's. I was the one who needed to stretch from time to time, to walk along the hallway and back, to crouch down and give Bear a reassuring hug. Why weren't they here yet? Let them come, and let this be over one way or another.

Just when I thought I could not wait a moment longer, there came a great rumbling sound, as of many hooves on the road. Birds rose up, startled, from the trees all around the keep.

Luachan cleared his throat. Finbar's stillness gained a further intensity, and I was possessed by a mad idea that he was about to launch himself out the narrow window, as if he were a bird or an arrow. For a moment I saw it, the leap, the long descent, the terrible aftermath . . . And suddenly, without a word spoken, Luachan knelt down and put his arm across the window, making a barrier in front of my brother. Out beyond the walls, the thunder of hoofbeats grew louder. My father kept his position on the steps, unmoving. There were guards around him. I did not think they could defend him long if Cruinn rode in with murderous intent.

"All right?" Luachan looked up at me, his eyes warm with concern.

"Mm. How about you, Finbar?"

Finbar did not seem to hear me. He was intent on the scene below, where at last everything had begun to move. Riders poured into the courtyard through the gates Father had ordered to be left wide-open. His men-at-arms stepped forward, spears crossed to protect him from assault. Dust arose under the hooves of many horses; the air was filled with the jingle of harness, the scrape of weapons drawn from scabbard and sheath, someone shouting, "Halt!" In the midst of it all, Father stood quiet.

A lull in the general din. A voice ringing out; a deep, furious voice that must without a doubt be that of Cruinn of Tirconnell.

"Sean of Sevenwaters! You sent me ill tidings indeed. Are your searchers blind, deaf and crippled, that they cannot follow a scent to find a living man within your own borders?"

The dogs, so good up till now, became suddenly agitated. Bear got up on his hind legs and started pawing at the window ledge, shoving Finbar out of the way. Badger began a high, troubled whining. I hissed at him, signaling quiet, but he did not obey.

"Lord Cruinn, welcome to Sevenwaters." Father did not smile or move forward. His tone was perfectly controlled, the effect cool but courteous. "You've come a long way. Doran, please ensure that these men are offered food and drink, and have their horses seen to." Now he moved, taking two steps forward and looking up. "Will you dismount and allow my grooms to tend to your horse? We should discuss this matter privately."

"Pretty manners won't bring my sons back!" Cruinn roared.

Bear barked sharply, scrabbling at the wall as if wanting to leap out. Badger's whining became something akin to a shriek; he was trembling. "*Ssst!*" I paired the command with a stamp of the foot. Luachan put a hand on the frantic Bear's collar as if to pull him down, then muttered an oath as Bear snapped at his fingers.

"It's not good enough, Sevenwaters!" Cruinn was saying. "Your men have demonstrated that they can't search effectively, so I had no choice but to bring mine to do the job for them. If you choose to take exception to our presence on your land, you'll find out what a man's prepared to do when he's robbed of what is most precious to him and left with a bunch of useless folk who don't know a search from a sack of turnips." During this impassioned speech he had moved into view, a big, broad-shouldered man on a tall gray horse. He swung down now to stand with legs apart and hands on hips. "A pox on it, Sevenwaters! You've driven me to this! You must have heard what's being said about uncanny perils and magical beasts in this wretched forest, and all kinds of foolish excuses for a case of simple incompetence! A man can tolerate only so much—"

Bear turned and shoved past me, baying. In a moment he and Badger were off along the upper hallway and down the stairs, making enough noise for a whole army of dogs. Morrigan's curse! They could not have chosen a worse moment.

I sprinted after them. The situation down there was already on a knife-edge. Let it not be my dogs that tipped it over into chaos. I took the stairs two at a time, sweeping past a pair of ashen-faced serving boys—not frightened by me, but by the spectacle of Bear in full flight—and across the lower hallway to the main door. "Bear!" I yelled at the top of my voice. Since the dogs were making enough noise to wake the dead, there was no longer much point in keeping quiet. Perhaps, by some miracle, they would obey this time. "Badger, wait!"

I ran out the door at full tilt, emerging on the steps behind Father, hardly seeing what was around me, for Bear and Badger were heading straight for the imposing, dark-bearded figure of

Cruinn. A man-at-arms with a club stepped forward on the chieftain's right side, a fellow with a spear on his left. Cruinn reached for his dagger.

"Bear! Stop that this instant!" I shouted, hurling myself across the space between Father and Cruinn. *"Bear, stop!"*

An arm's length from Cruinn, Bear halted. He stood quivering in place as if held on an invisible leash, looking at me, looking at Cruinn, looking back at me. Behind him, Badger dropped down onto his belly. Relief flooded through my body. My heart pounding, I moved in beside Bear and laid the back of my hand on his neck. Neither the man with the spear nor the man with the club could strike him without striking me as well.

"Good boys," I gasped, for obedience should always be acknowledged quickly, while a dog understands what he is being praised for. I sucked in a breath. I could not look at Father, so I looked up at Cruinn instead. He appeared . . . bemused. It was not the look of a man who had just gotten his long-lost dogs back. Behind him a wall of warriors on horseback regarded me with a variety of expressions.

"Bear, calm. Badger, calm." First things first. "My lord, I offer a sincere apology." I straightened my back, meeting Cruinn's eye in a way I hoped Uncle Bran would have been proud of. "The dogs mean you no harm." If they were his dogs, he would surely have said something by now. He would not be staring at me as if he could not decide whether to shout with rage, howl with laughter, or pretend I was not there.

"Maeve—" my father began, but Cruinn spoke over him.

"You're his daughter. Sean's daughter, the one who was sent away. Yes?"

"I am Lord Sean's daughter Maeve, my lord. Recently returned here from Britain. I am very sorry about the loss of your men, and your sons especially. I cannot imagine how heavily that must weigh on you." In fact I could imagine it all too well; I saw it in his eyes, dark eyes that had perhaps once been bright and forthright, and now were all grief and fury. "Please accept my father's hospitality, which he offers in good faith. We will do everything we can to help with the search."

Cruinn stared at me for a little longer; I did not drop my gaze. Then, with a quick gesture, he dismissed the two hovering men-at-arms. "They are handsome dogs, Lady Maeve," he observed. "But if you do not train them better they'll get you in trouble one day."

"They are learning quickly, my lord. I have not had them long." *Stop chattering, Maeve, and go back inside where you belong. What is Mother going to think of this?* Oh gods, she was probably watching every moment of it from the sewing room window. I forced myself not to look up there. "I had thought . . . I had thought perhaps they might be yours. That they might have been with your missing men. I found them wandering in the forest." I was right by his horse's head; I stroked the gray's cheek with the back of my hand, and the creature nuzzled at my neck.

Cruinn's features softened. Perhaps, before the terrible sorrow that had befallen him, he had been a kind man, a reasonable man like my father. "These two are not from my household, Lady Maeve," he said. "But I see they have found a kind home with you." He turned toward Father. "Well, Sean. Here we are, and I suppose we must sit down and talk the situation over. I'll bring my councilor indoors with me, and your fellow can make arrangements with my master-at-arms concerning accommodation for the men and horses. It's just as well we left our scent hounds outside your gate; your daughter's creatures would have torn them limb from limb."

He spoke with remarkable good humor, though the jest was not to my taste. "They are not savage, my lord," I felt obliged to say. "But they do not yet fully understand that the dark time is over and that they are safe."

Cruinn gave me a nod of acknowledgment, and then my father was ushering him up the steps and inside, where I hoped the serving boys had set down their weaponry and applied themselves to looking hospitable. As for me, I could feel the scrutiny of too many eyes: the curious eyes of Cruinn's men—*That is Lord Sean's daughter? Did you hear her shrieking like a fishwife? What about those hands?*—and the eyes of my mother from the window up there, no doubt full of shock and disapproval.

"Bear, come. Badger, come." I followed the two chieftains inside, and the dogs came with me, obedient now, though clearly all was not well with them.

"As for you," I muttered, "you have more to learn than I realized. We're going to be practicing obedience until suppertime."

A flood of women was coming back down the stairs, spurred into action now it seemed this was not war, only the sudden arrival of a large number of unexpected guests. Food, drink, bedding, space for men and horses . . . It would all be done, of course, and done well.

Mother stood at the top of the stairs, looking down as folk scurried off to various parts of the keep. I waited until the way was clear, then went up. Rhian was still with the children; I could hear her singing something about ducks and geese, and small hands clapping in time with the refrain. I halted one step below my mother, with Bear and Badger on either side of me.

"I'm sorry, Mother. They bolted for no reason. It seemed better to try to stop them than let them cause a . . . an incident of some kind."

Her brows rose. "You caused quite an incident yourself."

"I made a judgment. There wasn't much time to do so. If I had left the dogs to their own devices something extremely unpleasant might have occurred."

"You will gain a reputation as eccentric. Wild. That is not the kind of young woman a man wants as a wife."

For a moment I was speechless. Then Aunt Liadan's training reasserted itself. I stood up tall. "I don't think we need concern ourselves about that, Mother," I said quietly. "No suitor will ever offer for me. The most ladylike manners in all Erin couldn't render a man blind to my hands and face. I long ago accepted that marriage was out of the question. I'm surprised you consider it a possibility." More words were on my lips, hurtful words: *Or are you just trying to make me feel better?* I managed to hold them back.

She said what I was willing her not to say. "Oh, Maeve."

"I'm not asking for sympathy!" I snapped, my self-control proving more fragile than I had thought. "Only to be accepted as the woman I am and recognized for the things I can do. If it hadn't been for Bear and Badger just now, and my 'wild' behavior, Cruinn might have made a declaration of war. His men might even now be killing ours out there. Instead he's sitting down to talk to Father. But since you're not happy that I stopped my dogs from attacking a visiting chieftain, why don't I go back to the cottage and take them with me? That will get us right out of your way."

Out of the corner of my eye I saw Luachan and Finbar coming along the upper hallway, deep in conversation. Luachan was going to be busy, too, I thought—with so many strangers at Sevenwaters, he'd need to maintain a constant watch over my brother.

"I may give that idea fresh consideration," Mother said, surprising me. "But you won't be going anywhere today. Since Cruinn has met you, if under less than ideal circumstances, it would seem odd if you were not at the family table for supper. I don't want to give him the impression that we were ashamed of your performance just now, or that we want to hide you. It is odd enough that you prefer to be apart from the household. To disappear on the very day an important visitor arrives would appear . . ."

"Eccentric? Wild?" I suggested as Luachan reached us. He stood quietly waiting, while Finbar sat down on the stairs and stroked Bear's ears. "Very well, I will be at table for supper. Mother, I hope you will give some more thought to letting me return to the cottage. I'll only be in the way here. Besides, I can't risk Bear and Badger creating a scene again. Down there, I can work on their training. And Emrys will be busy, so Swift will need me." When she said nothing, I added, "I think Luachan wants to speak to you."

"My lady." Luachan's voice was all honey. "With so many men at the keep, the household will be stretched to its limit. Tempers may be short for a while. I think it appropriate not only that Lady Maeve and Rhian return to the cottage tomorrow, but that Finbar and I move to the nemetons at the same time. We know the hand of Danu stretches over that place, protecting it from both worldly and fey attackers. Cruinn made it clear that his forces have come to take over the search. They'll be everywhere. As Lord Sean's only son, Finbar should be housed among the druids until the truth about the Disappearance is revealed one way or another. Ciarán made it clear to me before he departed that he wanted both Finbar and Maeve to be kept safe. He believed placing the two of them under druidic protection would be desirable."

We were in the way. Serving people threaded an awkward path around us as they ascended and descended the stairs, carrying piles of bedding, laden baskets, buckets and cloths. Every time someone passed, Bear and Badger growled.

"You will stay here tonight," Mother said. "We will discuss this tomorrow. Finbar, you'll have supper with the other children and go to bed straight afterward. Luachan, I want you with him at all times."

"Yes, my lady," Luachan said, and if I saw the glimmer of a smile in his eyes, it was gone in an instant. "Finbar, we'd best retrieve our documents and then get back to our studies." Halfway down the stairs he paused, turning his head to look up at me. "That was entertaining," he remarked, and now the smile was quite clear.

"Believe me," I said, "it was not my intention to make an exhibition of myself. I simply didn't want anyone hurt."

"You achieved both, I think," the druid said. Before I could summon a word, he was down the stairs and off, with Finbar scurrying to keep up.

"We're wasting time." Mother's tone was tight. "I'm needed elsewhere."

"Don't let me stop you," I said, moving to one side to let her pass. "Bear, come. Badger, come."

"You think more of those dogs than of your own kin," Mother said as she went by me.

Not more, I thought. *Just differently. Their love is blessedly uncomplicated. It forgives all. It never falters. For humankind, to love or to receive love is far more difficult. That's why I cannot tell you how much I admire your strength. That's why you don't simply hug and kiss me, and say how sad it was for you when I went away and took ten years to come back. That's why we keep playing these stupid games instead of speaking to each other honestly. You are a good mother. You always were. But right now, you are not the mother I want.*

With Cruinn and his troop in residence, Sevenwaters changed overnight. There was no escaping the presence of the Tirconnell men, whether it was in the dining hall, where they were fed in shifts, or the stable yard, with horses and riders constantly coming and going and my father's grooms working sullenly alongside the fellows Cruinn had brought with him.

When we had come to Sevenwaters, Emrys and Donal had expected to be tending to Swift for a short while and then returning home. Now their stay was beginning to look endless—at least, that was what Rhian told me Donal had said—with all hands required simply to keep up with the routines of feeding, watering and mucking out, and the challenge of accommodating more animals than there was proper room for. Emrys had not complained about the need to stay, and it was clear this had a lot to do with Rhian's presence at Sevenwaters. But he could not visit the nemetons as often as before. That left both Swift and Rhian neglected, and Emrys himself out of sorts. He argued with Duald and with Cruinn's grooms, and when we saw him he had quite lost his cheerful demeanor.

I knew I had been exceptionally lucky in being allowed to return to the cottage, and that my good fortune owed more than a little to Luachan. He had persuaded both my parents that Finbar and I would be best out of the way of Cruinn's activities, and the day after the force from Tirconnell had descended on Sevenwaters, we'd returned to the nemetons. Finbar was housed in the druids' living quarters along with Luachan, but my brother spent a great deal of time with Rhian and me, helping with various household chores and taking some pleasure in feeding Pearl and the chickens and collecting the eggs. Now that he was not under my mother's eye, Luachan seemed to be applying a less rigorous approach to his tutorial duties, and I was glad of it.

Illann had come from Dun na Ri to support my father, bringing his own modest force of mounted men. This added to the overcrowding, though I knew Father would welcome his presence. Illann told us Ciarán had stayed in that household a few days, then moved on, saying he might be gone some time. At Ciarán's request, Deirdre had contacted Clodagh mind to mind. She had passed on Father's message for Cathal: that the situation at Sevenwaters had become sufficiently dire to warrant his return, despite the risk. She'd added that the family thought it best Clodagh and her children stayed where they were. According to Deirdre, Clodagh had become angry and had broken the link, shutting her twin out. It seemed Cathal would not be returning to Sevenwaters anytime soon.

The search went on, grim, relentless. Cruinn's men rode out in all weathers, working in shifts as my father's searchers had, combing the forest from dawn to dusk, sometimes staying out overnight and recommencing at first light. There was a little hill crowned with oaks not far from the clearing where our animals were housed, and from the top of it we could see the lakeshore and the broad tracks that skirted it on either side before branching off into the forest. The view was more open than it had been; autumn was advancing, and the trees were losing their fine cloaks of russet and brown and gold. Drifts of fallen leaves swished around our feet as we walked. They flew beneath the horses' hooves as one or another party of men-at-arms headed out from the keep.

There was a stone seat atop the hill, carved with symbols I could not interpret and half grown over with mosses. The dogs liked it there; the knotted roots of the old trees housed myriad scuttling creatures and the area was full of fascinating smells to be investigated. It was there that I saw Badger wag his tail for the first time. It was there that Bear got a thorn in his paw and rolled over on his back to let me take it out. I was glad Luachan was not present that day, only Finbar, since my method in such emergencies was to find the prickle with my tongue and extract it with my teeth. Finbar, too young to be given the job of taking out the thorn, held Bear's leg still for me while Badger, crouched nearby, whined with anxiety. Afterward, I thought how woefully unrealistic it was for my mother to think I would ever marry. Finbar accepted my ways of doing things because he was a child, and an unusual one at that. Rhian accepted them because she had been with me from the beginning and because she was my sister of the heart. But a man would look at what I had just done and feel only disgust. And whatever Mother might have in mind for me, I would never give up my little freedoms for the sake of respectability.

After a very awkward supper on the night Cruinn arrived at Sevenwaters, I had watched the Tirconnell chieftain as he rode out on the search with his men, head high, shoulders square, and as he came back again at the end of the long day, his sorrow and frustration plain in every corner of his body. Luachan said the search was a waste of time. He was sure the last three men must be dead already, and if not, Mac Dara would eventually do with them what he had done with the others. I hoped he was wrong. Cruinn's sorrow disturbed me. It was like seeing a strong oak gradually destroyed by some canker, or a fine horse going lame day by day. Such was the insidious poison of Mac Dara's touch.

I did not know how much of Mac Dara's story had been revealed to Cruinn, who was a Christian and might find it hard to accept the truth about those who shared our forest with us. Father must have told him some of it. Nobody in his right mind could imagine, now, that the Disappearance had been an abduction or attack carried out by one chieftain's fighting men against another's. Everything about it smelled of fey involvement.

That created a tricky situation. Finbar and I were at the nemetons because it was safer than the keep. It was known that Danu laid her hand over the sacred places of the druids. In addition, Ciarán and his brethren had set protective charms here. Ciarán had hinted at this, and Luachan had confirmed it for me. He believed that the circle of enchantment was strong enough to keep out even Mac Dara.

It was therefore impossible that the three missing men would be found here, unless, of course, they were being hidden by the druids, and there would be no reason for that. But Luachan told me Cruinn was not satisfied by that explanation, nor by Father's refusal to allow his searchers entry to the druid community.

I was not completely surprised, therefore, when on a day when Luachan and Finbar were closeted together studying and Rhian had made a rare trip to the keep for supplies, I heard hoofbeats approaching as I stood in the field with Swift. I looked up to see three men riding along the track toward me: my father, Cruinn and Cruinn's bodyguard, a hard-faced man of about five-and-twenty.

I had Swift circling the field, altering his pace at my spoken instructions. Bear and Badger were hunkered down at the foot of the stone wall, keeping an eye on the proceedings. In a corner, Pearl was making her way through a heap of vegetable scraps. The dogs scrambled up at the sound of the horses approaching, but we had been working hard on obedience, and when I bade them be silent, they both obeyed. Bear stayed on his feet, ready to protect me.

I did not imagine the men had come to the nemetons to visit me, and the exercise Swift and I were engaged in was best not interrupted, so I kept working, bidding the yearling in turn to walk, trot, canter and then to halt and stand. I was aware that the three men had ridden up to the other side of the wall and dismounted from their horses; I saw the unease in Swift's eye, the nervous tremor in his movements, the old urge to sail over the wall and away strong in him. But he held still. I'd worked with him every day since Cruinn's arrival, save for those rare times when Emrys could escape his other duties and come to take him out onto the tracks. The yearling's ability to stand in the presence of strangers and strange horses was pleasing evidence that my work had done some good.

"Easy, Swift." I gave him the soft touch he had earned, stroking his neck, resting my cheek against his, murmuring words of praise. He was tired. He needed a rubdown, but that would have to wait until the young druid came later. "Good boy. All done."

I turned and walked over to the wall. "Father, how good to see you. Welcome to the nemetons, Lord Cruinn." I was dusty and sweaty, the hem of my gown was very much the worse for wear, and my hair was pulled back into a single plait. I wore no kerchief;

it was easier to dispense with it when Rhian was not there to tie and untie it for me. That meant my facial scarring was on full display.

The bodyguard avoided looking at me. Father greeted me, then opened the gate so I need not leave the field the way I had entered it, by setting a foot between the stones and rolling up over the wall on my stomach. Badger followed me through. Bear took the wall in an enthusiastic leap and ran a few circles around the three men and their horses before coming to sit beside me in a manner that pleased me greatly. I had not forgotten Cruinn's remark about ill-trained dogs.

I glanced at the Tirconnell chieftain now, wondering if he'd come here to perform a search. He looked five years older than he had the day he rode into our courtyard and was greeted by my baying duo. His loss weighed him down. Yet at this moment there was a brightness in his eye. This had nothing to do with me. His attention was all on Swift.

"That is a very, very fine young animal, Lady Maeve," he observed after a while.

"He is, yes." Had Father told him why Swift had been brought to Sevenwaters? I'd best not speak of that until I knew one way or the other. "Bred in my uncle's stables at Harrowfield, in Britain. Swift is very like his dam, who has the same silvery color, the same conformation and the same rather difficult temperament." That was perhaps a little too honest. "His sire was a fine riding horse, also a gray, belonging to the chieftain of Northwoods, my uncle's neighbor. Father will have told you, I expect, that we have Swift here in the nemetons so he can recover fully from the sea voyage, and to allow more training before—before he moves on. I regret that I was too involved in that training to offer a greeting when you arrived, my lord."

"Not at all," said Cruinn absently, his eyes still on the yearling. "I saw that you were working. You have a remarkable gift, Lady Maeve. Difficult temperament? There was no sign of it just now. Where did you learn to train a horse that way, using only your voice?"

"I have no other way to do it. I taught myself, I suppose." I laid my hand on Bear's head. "I can't take all the credit for Swift's training. The two grooms who came over with us from Harrowfield have done a great deal of the work. Emrys, in particular, has an excellent touch with the horse."

"I see you have taken my advice to heart," Cruinn said, tearing his gaze away from Swift to look directly at me for the first time. "Your dogs did not try to kill me today."

"No, my lord." He was smiling. That seemed a minor miracle. "They are good dogs. They needed time and love, that was all."

"I see your Swift is somewhat weary and could do with a rubdown, which I imagine would be difficult for you to manage without some help. I'd be happy to perform the task, since I'd like to inspect the animal at closer quarters, but only if that is acceptable to you, of course."

With an effort, I managed not to gape at him. "Of course. Thank you. But I'll need to be in the field with you. Swift is unpredictable with folk he doesn't know." I glanced at Father, who was looking as surprised as I felt. The bodyguard was staring off into the distance, disapproval written all over his face. "There are some cloths up there by the door of my cottage," I added. "Perhaps your man would fetch them for us."

Father cleared his throat. "I want to visit my son," he said. "I might walk over to the druids' quarters now and come back after I've spoken to Finbar, if that suits you, Cruinn."

"Take your time," Cruinn said.

The bodyguard brought the cloths. Clearly, he was staying in case I attempted some act of violence against his employer. I had wondered if his instructions were to shadow Cruinn closely at all times, but when the chieftain and I went back into the field, the guard stayed outside the gate. The three horses had dropped their heads and were cropping the grass by the track. Badger stayed by them, as watchful as the man. Bear came with me.

When Cruinn had first appeared at Sevenwaters, I had thought him formidable. He had seemed a figure of power, the kind of man who would not bend. Now I was obliged to reassess my judgment. Perhaps it was that he knew and loved horses. Perhaps it was that, for some odd reason, he had decided he liked talking to me. Perhaps it was being away from other folk, doing a simple job with his hands, surrounded by the green quiet of the nemetons. He went about the rubdown with the strong, gentle touch of the most expert horseman. He listened to all my warnings about Swift and heeded them. I stood at the yearling's head and murmured to him, and Cruinn worked on until Swift's coat was dry and glossy and his eyes were dreamily quiet.

"We haven't found a trace of them." Cruinn spoke into a long silence, making my skin prickle.

"Your sons?" I asked quietly.

"I've only the two boys, Lady Maeve. We've had our disputes and disagreements over the years. Those petty squabbles, a fight over the use of a piece of land, a falling-out over an unsuitable friendship—they faded to nothing when I lost them. I would give my life to get them back."

"What are their names, my lord?"

"My heir, Tiernan. My younger son, Artagan." His voice cracked. "There," he murmured, laying his hand against Swift's back and turning his head away from me. "I'm an old fool. I can hardly bear to speak their names."

I gave him some time to compose himself. Then I said, "Nobody would think less of you for that, Lord Cruinn."

"There's a third lad still missing. I remind myself that he, too, has grieving parents. Tiernan's friend Daigh, the son of my chief councilor. I refused to bring his father with me on this journey. That man has a wife, and she needs him by her side. My wife died before this sorrow overtook us. I never thought I would see that as a good thing, Maeve, but this would have been too heavy a burden for her. She was a woman like a meadow flower; she was never strong." He straightened his shoulders, stiffened his spine, lifted his head. "There, my lovely boy," he said, addressing Swift. "All done."

"Your sons are strong and resourceful, I'm sure." I searched for words that might comfort him. "You must hold on to hope, Lord

Cruinn. That you have not yet found them may not mean the worst. It may be that they are . . . on a journey. They may be in a place where ordinary searchers cannot find them." I hesitated, not sure how much it was safe to say. "In time, perhaps they will make their own way home."

"Hope, hope," muttered Cruinn. "Sometimes it's hard to believe in. I think it's anger that keeps me going. Your father says his woods are full of uncanny beings, portals to the Otherworld, traps and tricks that make the very paths turn and twist, forming a new pattern each day. My searchers have found neither fey creatures nor eldritch doorways, but they tell me the story about the paths is true, so I suppose I must give some credence to what Sean says . . . If my boys have been abducted, if they have been taken into a realm beyond the human, how can I cling to hope? If I do not find them alive, I have failed my boys, and I have failed their mother." He drew a ragged breath. "What is this adversary your father alludes to, Mac Dara? A prince, Sean said. What manner of prince steals fine young men from their fathers for no good reason? What manner of man kills them as a kind of joke? One seemed to think he could fly; one tried to commune with bees; one was imitating a fish or frog when he drowned. Young Niall, the man you were unfortunate enough to find, was strung up like a grub in a cocoon. Why? What fiendish imagination devises such hideous games?"

From across the field, the bodyguard had his gaze fixed on us. Pearl had approached him and stretched out her neck across the wall. Any fool could have seen she wanted him to scratch between her ears, but the man did not seem to understand.

"I know less about Mac Dara than my parents do, Lord Cruinn, since I have been away from Sevenwaters ten years. I don't think he has acted out of any particular malice toward you or your men. His intention is to force my father into action." I hesitated. It was not for me to tell Cruinn about Cathal, or mention Ciarán's hope that Mac Dara's son would return to Sevenwaters and challenge his father. "He abducted my little brother when he was a baby," I said. "My sister and her husband went to the Otherworld to get

Finbar back. It's not talked about much; people find such stories hard to believe. But it proves that people do sometimes come home safely from that other place. Finbar was only an infant. And he is fine now." Fine outwardly, at least.

"If I knew," Cruinn murmured, "if I knew where they were and how to find them, I would go to the ends of the earth to bring them back. The others were all killed. I'm forced to ask myself why these last three would be any different."

Since I had no good answer to that, I held my tongue.

"You said, *force your father into action*. What action?"

"My lord, you should speak to him about that. I don't believe Father would want me to be the one to explain it to you. Though I am a daughter of the household, I am new here. In many ways I am more stranger than family."

Instead of replying, Cruinn offered me his arm, something men seldom did.

"Thank you," I said. "You love horses; I can see that."

"My wife used to say I should have been a groom, not a chieftain," Cruinn said as we went out the gate. "I believe she was joking, but there was truth in the jest. My boys are fine riders. Our stables are something of a passion. Not that it means much now. Nothing seems important anymore. Only them. Only finding them." He looked back at Swift. "Thank you for allowing me to do that," he said very quietly, and if I had not known he was an Uí Néill chieftain, which meant he was second only to the High King in power, I would have thought him overtaken by a bout of shyness. "And for listening to me. You're a kind girl." Still awkward, he bent to stroke Bear rather than look me in the eye. "Who's a fine boy?" he murmured. "Who's a good boy, then?" Badger crowded in, uncharacteristically, making sure he got his share of attention. The two of them had been quick enough to recognize Cruinn's affinity with animals, even if their initial greeting to him had looked more like an attack.

"Lord Sean's on his way back, my lord." The bodyguard had spotted my father walking down from the druids' dwelling house, with Luachan on one side and Finbar on the other. Luachan was holding forth, gesturing as he illustrated some point; Finbar and Father were both smiling.

"A lucky man," Cruinn said, straightening. "A man with a son who walks by his side, safe and well. I did not understand the worth of that when my boys were children."

"I often tell myself, there is no point in wishing certain things had not happened. We can't change what has been, only do our best with what is to come." After a moment I added, "I don't mean any discourtesy, my lord. It is simply something I have often found helpful, since I have had some cause to feel sorry for myself over the years."

"Thank you, Maeve. I understand the wisdom in that, but find myself unable to be philosophical. Instead I am angry and bitter. Above all, I am overshadowed by the fear that I will find them as you found poor Niall: a moment too late."

"I wish I could have saved him." I would never forget watching the light go out in his eyes. I would always remember that I had not managed to speak to him before he died.

"You were there," was all Cruinn said. "You witnessed his last breath. In death, he was not alone."

Scant comfort, I thought, if the dying man did not know I was by his side. But perhaps he had sensed it in the moment before his last breath left him. I hoped very much that this was so. I found myself possessed by a powerful, and entirely inappropriate, urge to rush off and find Tiernan, Artagan and Daigh all by myself, and ordered myself to stop being a complete fool. I was behaving as Bear or Badger might once have done, racing off the track at the first sniff of a scent. The conclusion to the sorry tale of the Disappearance must come through Mac Dara, Cathal, the Otherworld. It involved a sorcerous prince, a senior druid and a pair of chieftains. An impulsive girl with useless hands was not likely to make much of a difference.

Some days had passed since Cruinn's visit to the nemetons, when the chieftain of Tirconnell had surprised me with his openness. I was at the back of the cottage, watching as Bear and Badger chewed through a strip of linen Finbar had tied between two benches at my request.

"They're getting much better at it," my brother commented.

He was right; with rigorous training and daily practice, both Bear and Badger had learned to chew through bonds of linen, leather and woven straw in turn. It had been hard work, but necessary, since I'd never be able to untie knots on my own. With my mind on that man Niall and his hideous, suspended death, I'd resolved that since I could not rescue someone who was tied up, I'd make sure Bear and Badger could do it for me.

"Maeve."

"Mm?"

"If someone really was tied up, it would be much harder. How could Bear and Badger bite through the rope without biting the person?"

"I'm not sure how we could teach them that," I admitted. "Perhaps you can work out a way."

"I could tie you up," Finbar suggested.

"It might be better if you tied the rope around something else. Shall we try it now?"

We did so. Bear and Badger obediently freed two turnips, a stool and a bag of flour from their bonds. I knew in my heart that it was most unlikely I would ever have to put their new skill to real use. There might be three men still missing, but the odds of my being the one to find them were slim indeed, and Mac Dara's method of dealing with the lost men had been different in each case. Why had he devised such bizarre endings for them? Simply to entertain himself? I shuddered to imagine what the fey prince might try next.

Later, we took the turnips over to Pearl, since they were no longer at their best. While the goat picked at them, we leaned on the wall watching Swift frisk around the field, as graceful as a swallow and perfectly at ease. He seemed a different creature from the nervous, fearful horse we had brought to Sevenwaters. I found myself hoping Father would give him to Cruinn after all. The journey might be hard for him, but I knew Swift would be well loved in that stable.

193

"Maeve," said Finbar in a tone I knew well. A difficult question was coming.

"Mm?"

"Have you ever seen . . . When you go walking in the forest, do you ever . . . No, it doesn't matter."

"Have I ever seen what?" I wasn't going to let this go. His hesitancy troubled me. This was not the first time I had wondered if he was afraid. "Are you thinking of Mac Dara and his kind? You do know you're safe here in the nemetons, don't you? Luachan must have explained that."

"Not Mac Dara. The other ones, the good ones."

"Do you mean the Lady of the Forest? The Fair Folk? Aren't they all gone now, Finbar? That's what Uncle Ciarán told me, and it's what most people believe. The way he said it, they sailed into the west, never to return."

"They might not be gone. Not all of them." Finbar's little face was fierce with the will to make it true. To banish the bad things and restore the good.

I could not bring myself to explain that Ciarán had made it clear the good ones were all departed, and that if anyone knew about such things, it would be him. "I can't say, Finbar. I suppose there are still all manner of folk living in the Sevenwaters forest, even though people don't see them as often as they once did." I was sure I could remember strange beings floating in sunbeams or dancing among cobwebs; I thought I recalled distant winged presences that were neither birds nor insects. But perhaps that had only been a child's imagination.

"You might meet one of them one day." Finbar's tone was grave as an old sage's. "You might be walking down the path and there she would be, just like the old days. What would you do?"

"Probably turn and run," I said with a grimace. "What about you?"

"Why would you run?"

"I was joking," I said. "I simply meant that with the search taking place all over the forest, I might not be inclined to trust anyone straightaway, even if that person appeared to be . . . a beautiful goddess. Or one of the Tuatha De, the good ones." This was an odd conversation.

"Of course, being beautiful does not make a person good." Finbar had evidently thought about this, or had been taught it.

"And being ugly does not make a person bad," I said, feeling my mouth twist. "I know that lesson very well, Finbar."

He turned his gaze on me, and in his clear eyes I saw myself as he saw me, a beloved sister, perfect in every way. I saw that he had no idea what I meant.

"You're the best brother in all Erin, Finbar," I said.

"How do you know that? You only have one brother."

"I know it the way dogs know things. Inside. In my heart."

"That's good," Finbar said. "I can't say you're the best sister, even if it is true, because I have lots of sisters and it would not be right to say any of them was the best."

"Very tactful of you," I commented. "I think Rhian may have that nut cake ready by now. I can smell it from here. Shall we go and see?"

Luachan was busy with his fellow druids—he had not explained what he was doing, but I imagined he needed time for prayer and study—so Finbar was with Rhian and me for the whole afternoon. We sat in the cottage awhile enjoying Rhian's baking. Bear and Badger got a generous share, since their cooperation in the biting experiment had earned them a treat. When we were finished, I gave Rhian leave to walk up to the keep with some cake for Emrys and Donal, bidding her be sure to get home before dark. I'd have been happier if she had not been alone, but I knew she wanted to see Emrys, and the path was considered safe. Rhian, in her turn, was more willing to leave me if I had Finbar to act as my hands.

We lingered awhile before the fire, my brother and I, on the floor with the dogs. I sat with my back against the bench; Bear was asleep, his big head resting on my knee. Finbar sat cross-legged, staring into the flames. Badger stretched out on the mat with one eye half-open.

"Can I tell you a story?" Finbar asked.

"I'd like that."

"Are you sure? It has a fire in it."

After a moment I said, "All right."

"Once there was a great forest, and in the heart of the forest there lived a white dragon. You know how dragons live in caves and breathe flame? This dragon could breathe fire all right, but she didn't like dark caves, so she lived on a high hill in a grove of oak trees. This was a dragon who loved the light."

My brother paused as if thinking out the next part of his saga. I could hear that he already had a druid's gift for storytelling, and I sat quiet, waiting for him to go on. Bear's head was heavy on my knees; he was sunk deep in his dreams.

"The white dragon watched over all the smaller creatures of the forest and kept them from harm. So it went for a hundred years, two hundred years and more. Then the dragon grew old and tired. One day when the birds and mice and squirrels went up the hill at daybreak, they found that she had flown away. All that was left was the warm hollow under the oaks that had been her resting place.

"That made the animals sad. Now there was nobody to protect them from hunters, or keep them warm in winter, or listen when they squeaked and chirped out their little tales. But life went on. They learned to manage without their white dragon. Until one day, when the small creatures came out from their roosts and their burrows and their hollows, they found that a new dragon had come to watch over the forest: a dragon black as night."

Finbar paused for dramatic effect.

"What happened next?" I asked.

"The black dragon didn't make his home on the hill, but down in the shadowy depths of the forest, out of reach of both sunlight and moonlight. He hunted by night and slept by day, curled around the roots of a great oak. All the other creatures were afraid of him. He didn't look after them the way the white dragon had. When they dared to come close, he burned them with his fiery breath or crushed them to splinters.

"The black dragon ate up all the larger creatures of the forest:

badger, wolf, wildcat. Hunters didn't come there anymore, because there was nothing left to hunt."

Morrigan's curse! My brother had a dark imagination.

"Under the black dragon's rule, the peaceful forest became a place of fear and flight. Nobody came in; nobody went out. The little creatures lived in terror for their lives. They were too scared to look for food; too scared to leave their young ones in the nest. Surely they would all die. The age of the black dragon was dark indeed."

Finbar looked at me as if concerned that his story might be upsetting me. "Shall I go on?" he asked.

I nodded, wondering if this was indeed a story of his own invention, or something he had discovered during his studies with Luachan. Part of becoming a druid, I seemed to remember, was memorizing a vast body of lore, including ancient tales. This might be one of those, retold in Finbar's own words. I suspected it was not.

"You might think, Maeve, that the story ends with all the creatures dying and only the black dragon left. But that wasn't what happened. One night the black dragon thought, *I am master of this whole forest and all that lives in it, except for that one hill where the white dragon used to hold court. That hill should be mine. I will go there and claim it.*

"Of course, there was nothing much on the hill. Only a few oak trees. But the white dragon had left something behind: her spies, a flock of doves that nested in the shelter of the trees."

"Wouldn't they have died long ago?" I asked. "The white dragon had been gone years and years, hadn't she?"

"They were the great-grandchildren of the first doves," Finbar said gravely. "You must know about wisdom being passed down from father to son and from mother to daughter, Maeve."

"Oh," I said. "Yes, of course." I wondered what my mother had passed down to me. As I would never have children, it probably didn't matter if I remained as ignorant as my little brother clearly thought me. "What did the spies do?"

"The bravest dove flew all the way to the island where the

white dragon had gone to rest, and told her what had happened. That island was far, far away, beyond the setting sun."

Lulled by Bear's warm presence against me, I had been enjoying the tale for what it was, a good story told well. Now a curious feeling was creeping over me, a sense that the tale my brother was telling had nothing much to do with dragons.

"The dove begged the white dragon to return to the forest and challenge the black dragon. Only she, the dove said, could drive him out and bring back peace. But the white dragon did not want to do it. She was old and tired, and all she wanted was to rest. Besides, she told the dove, it wasn't easy for one dragon to defeat another. If it came to a straight-out fight they'd probably burn each other up. When the dove heard this, she said, 'I have flown to the end of my strength to bring you this message. I have given my last breath to find you. Please help us.' Then she fell to the ground, stone dead."

Was this in fact a tale about Sevenwaters and Mac Dara? A grand, symbolic version of the way Finbar wished our story might unfold? He had fallen silent now, his gaze on the flames. While he was telling a story, I forgot that he was a child of seven, for he spoke with an assurance beyond his years. But he *was* a child. He had a child's frailty and a child's limits to understanding.

"Did the white dragon come back then?" I asked, no longer confident this tale would have a happy ending.

"She did," Finbar said, "and it made the black dragon so angry he set many trees alight with his fiery breath. Then he realized that would only make it easier for the white dragon to find his lair. So, for a while, he did nothing at all, and the white dragon settled into her hollow atop the hill as if she had never been away. She slept by night; he slept by day. Dragons sleep deeply. In their sleep they get their strength back, so they can fly and hunt and feed when they wake up.

"Because of the black dragon's greed there wasn't much left to eat in the forest, and he was not prepared to share even a vole or marten with his rival. He plotted and planned how best to be rid of her, and decided he would make a fire by night, all around the white dragon's hill. It would be so bright she would wake up, thinking it was day, and take wing immediately. But she would be weak after so short a sleep. Then he would attack her and tear her to pieces.

"So, by night, he felled many of the great trees within his forest. He carried the massive logs in his talons to a place close to the hill but hidden from his rival. This would be a fire of fires, a great con—" He struggled for the word.

"A great conflagration," I suggested quietly.

Finbar's eyes were distant; he was caught up in the story. Watching him, I was reminded strongly of Ciarán, and I was convinced this tale had some meaning that went far beyond the rival dragons. The black dragon was surely Mac Dara. But who was the white dragon? My brother couldn't really believe the Lady of the Forest would come back to help the human folk of Sevenwaters, could he? In the old tales, when the Fair Folk sailed into the west, it meant they were gone forever.

"Now, though the brave dove had given her life to bring her message to the white dragon, her flock still lived in the oaks on the hill. The morning after the black dragon had knocked down the trees, one of these birds was wandering across the white dragon's back, pecking out the troublesome insects from between the creature's scales, and as it did its work, it told the dragon how her rival had spent his night. *Logs, logs, a hundred logs, two hundred he piled up, and a thousand birds lost their homes. All night he worked. These forest giants lie waiting not far from your hill. But for what, I cannot say.* When the white dragon heard the dove say this, she knew what the black dragon was planning.

"The white dragon was furious. How dare the black dragon ruin the beautiful forest and harm the creatures she had protected? How dare he try to trick her? She wanted to spread her great wings and fly over the forest so she could blast the black dragon with her fiery breath as he slept. But she did not, for that would make her no better than he was. And a battle might end with both of them dead. Who would protect the other creatures then? The white dragon needed some advice.

"Not far from her hill there lived a wise woman, old as the oldest oak, her face all wrinkled, her hair long as a horse's tail and white as moonbeams. She was a friend of the white dragon from long ago and knew the answers to many questions."

I looked at Finbar, and he looked at me. "But—" I began.

"The crone had fey blood," my brother said. "Such people live far longer than you or me, Maeve."

"Quite right," I said. "Go on. I want to know what happened."

"The white dragon told her friend the evil things the black dragon had done and asked what was the best way to be rid of him, and the wise woman said, 'Aha! So you don't know?'

"'Know what?' asked the dragon.

"'About the geis,' said the wise woman. 'The geis is the key to everything.' It turned out someone had spoken a curse over the black dragon when it was just out of the egg, though not many folk knew about it. That kind of thing is too complicated for mice and hedgehogs and birds to remember. The crone knew, just as her great-grandmother had known, but nobody had thought to ask her because, after all, she was only an old woman." My brother fell abruptly silent. He did not look at me, but stared off into a corner of the cottage as if he hardly knew where he was.

It seemed to me Finbar had reached some kind of sticking point, and although I was keen to hear the rest of the tale, I could read on his face that going on would be difficult. "What was the old woman's name?" I asked.

My brother mumbled something I could not quite catch. Willow?

"It's all right, Finbar," I said. "It is a long story, and you tell it very, very well. If you want to save the rest for another day I can wait, though I do want to know what happens."

"I'm not sure what happens," my brother said. His voice was no longer that of the seasoned storyteller, but had become that of the little boy, and an uncertain little boy at that.

But he had told it with such confidence. I remembered what he'd said that other time—that Luachan had told him he should not share his visions, but that when he was older he might learn how to retell them in the form of stories. "Did you dream of those two dragons, Finbar? Did you see them in the water or the fire?" He had said it would be a story of fire, but there had been only the threat of fire in it. What had he left out?

Finbar seemed to shrink into himself, making me regret that I had spoken. "I'm not supposed to tell," he said. The house seemed momentarily darker, as if a shadow had passed over us. Bear raised his head, then with a sigh laid it back on my knee.

"Then I won't ask any more questions," I said briskly, "though I will think about the story, and when I've worked out how I believe it should end, I'll tell you. I always prefer happy endings to sad ones, and I like stories where people show courage and think out clever answers to their problems. Finbar, I need to go out to the privy. You could feed Pearl if you like. Rhian's left a bowl of scraps on the table there. I won't be long." Pearl would do him good; goats were uncomplicated creatures, pleased by simple things, and she was a particularly kindly sort of goat.

"All right." My brother took the bowl and went out, leaving the door ajar for me.

Bear came with me; Badger went with Finbar, which pleased me. My shy second dog was starting to emerge from his shell. Sitting on the wooden privy seat, with Bear waiting beyond the door, I pondered the story Finbar had told. The most troubling thing about it had been the sudden ending before the tale was done. *I'm not supposed to tell.* What did that mean? Was it only that Luachan and Ciarán had warned him visions were perilous to share because they could be so misleading? Or was it something more sinister? Was my brother keeping a secret, and if so, whose?

I was midway through the laborious task of tidying my clothing when Bear started barking. The warning note in it made me thrust open the privy door and stumble down the step with my stockings halfway up and my skirt awry, expecting to find Cruinn's searchers streaming along the track or some wild creature attempting a raid on the chicken coop. Bear was agitated, hurling his challenge with hackles up, and now I could hear Badger barking, too, farther away. Much farther away. Cold sweat broke out on my skin.

From here, the cottage blocked my view of the field where Swift and Pearl were housed. It blocked the spot where Finbar would be standing to feed the goat. I could hear Pearl now, bleating loudly. I ran, and Bear ran with me, soon outpacing me in a headlong hurtle down to the fields.

No sign of Finbar, but he might be back in the house already. No sign of Badger, though his voice, fading fast, could still be heard somewhere in the forest beyond the fields. Pearl was running to and fro in her enclosure, uttering cries of distress. And Swift was gone.

"Finbar!" I shouted. "Finbar, where are you?" I leaped up the step, shoved open the door, saw immediately that he was not in the cottage. As I turned to go out, wondering how fast I could run to the druids' quarters for help, I saw a flash of white under the trees across the clearing, and over the sound of Badger's barking I thought I heard my brother calling.

"Here! Maeve, here!"

Oh gods. By the time I ran to the druids to raise the alarm, and someone went up to the keep to fetch people with horses and bring them back here to start a search, Finbar might have gone far into the forest and become completely lost. What if Mac Dara was out there waiting for him? But if Bear and I ran after him now, he'd still be within shouting distance and we could quickly bring him back. No time to waste. *Didn't you promise not to go off into the forest?* asked Sensible Maeve. But Wild Maeve said, *I like stories where people show courage.*

"Bear, come!" I said. We ran.

CHAPTER 9

I collapsed between the roots of a great oak, my breath coming hard.

"Wait . . ." I gasped. "Bear . . . wait . . ."

Badger's voice had long since died away, and it was some time since we'd spotted the glimmer of white that was Swift. Perhaps I'd imagined Finbar's call. Maybe he'd run up to the druids or been collected by Luachan in that short time when he was out of my sight. He couldn't have come so far so fast, surely. I prayed that I'd been mistaken and that he was still home and safe.

Bear had stopped running now and was pawing at something on the ground. He made a little sound, a courteous reminder that we were in a hurry and that I was wasting time. I dragged myself to my feet and went over to him.

And there they were: my brother's footprints in the soft earth, deep enough to tell us Finbar had been running at full tilt. I blinked back sudden tears. This was no time for weakness.

"Well done, Bear," I said. "On we go."

We followed Finbar's tracks for some time, until we came to an area where deep leaf litter blanketed the way and there was no longer any visible sign of his passing, or indeed of Swift's or Badger's. But Bear had the scent, and he led me onward. Uphill, downhill, through thickets swarming with little biting insects, across muddy streambeds inhabited by strange-voiced frogs, under prickle bushes, over the great dark forms of fallen trees, their crevices inhabited by night-pale fungi and scuttling, many-legged creatures. Bear found the way; I followed him. Where I needed help, he was there. He pushed aside hanging foliage to let me through. When we had to wade across a stream on slippery stones, he stayed close so I could steady myself with one hand on his neck. When we had no choice but to scramble up a steep bank, he provided his back as a support for my foot. Without him I could not have made the journey. It no longer seemed adequate to say *Good boy*. He was so much more than that.

There came a point where Bear knew I must rest or be unable to go on. He paused beneath an oak, eyeing me, then flopped down, tongue lolling. I lowered myself to a sitting position. Stopping was perhaps not such a good idea. Every part of me was hurting. Worse, the moment I ceased the effort of walking, my mind was full of voices. Sensible Maeve said, *It's late in the day. You have no water, you have no food, you told nobody where you were going, and Finbar is out there on his own. How are you going to look after yourself, or him, if one of you gets hurt? What if you're stuck out here overnight?* But Wild Maeve said, *Finbar. Badger. Swift. Run.*

Even when a person feels so exhausted she can hardly set one foot before the other, she can always find more strength somewhere. *Set aside everything that's in your way*, Bran had said. *Anger, guilt, grief; the pain in your body, the doubt in your mind. Keep going. Find the flame inside yourself.*

"Time to go, Bear," I said, rising awkwardly to my feet. "I'll try to keep up."

But I could no longer go so fast, and Bear slowed his pace to accommodate me. At the next stream we stopped to drink, the two of us lapping side by side, Bear much more capably than I. We paused on a rise to look across the terrain ahead, mostly oak forest, the limbs half-clothed in their autumn raiment, and here and there a thicket of elders or birches whose leaves had already fallen, allowing light to penetrate to the forest floor beneath. I saw no clearings, no tracks, no stone walls, no evidence of human presence at all. Up another rise, where an oddly shaped rock formation stood gray against the fiery hues of the foliage, the low sun caught something white, moving fast. Almost as soon as I had seen it, it was gone.

"Swift," I muttered. "It's Swift. We can reach him, Bear." *Finbar.* My heart was tight as a clenched fist. Even as I spoke, I knew my brother could not have come so far on his own. The first part, maybe, if he was trying his very hardest. But this distance, a distance greater than I had covered the day Bear and Badger led me to the dying man? Impossible. He could not be riding Swift; Swift had never been trained to the saddle. Either Finbar had already come to grief, or someone had taken him.

We ran on, down the hill, across a little valley all springy, thorn-armed branches, up the other side toward the rocks. The sun had sunk almost below the treetops now, and it would soon be dusk. What was I to do if I could not find my brother before dark? "Be there, be there," I muttered, as Sensible Maeve said, *Turn for home right now, or you'll be stuck out here all night with no warm clothing, no food and no means to make fire. Not that you could do that even if you'd thought to bring flint, knife and tinder. Run back and fetch men, horses, lanterns. If Finbar dies of cold, it will be your fault for rushing off and trying to do everything yourself.*

Finbar was not by the rock formation or hiding in the shallow caves beneath it. He was not at the top of the hill or anywhere to be seen in the place that lay beyond it, a little valley of tall stones, their shadows lying long and eerie across the ground. There were no trees here, only squat, misshapen bushes growing at random. After the leafy depths of the forest this was another world, a place of sharp corners and treacherous, pebbly slopes. A chill wind whistled up the valley toward us, like the breath of a great cold giant.

"He's not here." But I had seen Swift. I was sure I had.

Bear was sniffing the ground, seeking the trail. He went one way, then the other way, then came to stand beside me, head down.

"Finbar!" I told him. How could I make him understand? With darkness almost upon us, we must concentrate on my brother's scent and set Swift and Badger aside. They, at least, were not likely to perish from cold in a single night. No, I would not even think of that. "Find Finbar. Go, Bear!"

But Bear would not go on. He padded a few steps forward, then halted, looking at me over his shoulder.

"Go! If he went that way, we must follow!" *You probably lost his trail long ago*, said Sensible Maeve. *Turn around. Go home.*

Bear did not understand. He was a dog; how could he? I had thought he was following Finbar's scent, but it had just as likely been Badger's. And Badger might have been on his own all along. Never mind that. *Hold on, little brother*, I thought. *I'm coming to find you.*

"All right, Bear," I said. "If you can't find the trail, we'll have to take the likeliest path, and that leads right down this valley. If it gets dark we'll go back and shelter in those caves for the night." Without food, water or blankets. I hoped very much that Badger was still with Finbar. I hoped . . . No, I would not think of Mac Dara. *The age of the black dragon was dark indeed.*

The valley was narrow and steep. To either side stood the tall stones like ancient sages, moss-cloaked. Some of them bore grooves across their corners, patterns of threes and fives and sevens, or characters that resembled forked twigs or combs or little men. Were they the Ogham signs used by druids, or an older, stranger language? Sibeal would have known. Perhaps the signs were warnings: *Step no farther. This way lies death.*

About halfway down the valley, Bear left the path and began scuffling beside one of the stones. He ran back to me with something in his mouth.

"What is it, Bear? Show me, good boy."

He dropped his find at my feet. The light was already fading, and at first I thought he had picked up no more than a few wisps of dried-out foliage. Then I looked again, and saw that it was a little animal fashioned of grasses, a familiar creature with a long snout and a fronded tail. Although somewhat the worse for wear, it was unmistakably the one Rhian had made for Finbar that day at the cottage. He must have kept it in his pouch all this time. He had passed this way.

"Well done, Bear. Good boy." I stroked his head; he leaned against my leg for a moment. "Down to the bottom there. We just have time. You try to pick up the scent, and I'll look for footprints."

For a little while it seemed we had found what we were seeking, for Bear moved forward with confidence, nose to the ground, and I thought I could see the marks of small feet here and there among the great stones, as if my brother had taken time to stand by each and read the signs carved there. But when I came to the third stone and looked more closely at the prints, I saw that they were much too small to be Finbar's, and that in addition, the foot that had stood here had been unshod, and its owner had only had three toes. *You're imagining things*, said Sensible Maeve. *You're conjuring monsters out of dusk and guilt and fear.*

"Bear," I said, coming to a halt. My heart was cold. "We're not going to find him before dark and it's too late to go home. We must walk back to those caves and get through the night as best we can."

We turned and went back up the valley. As we did so it came to me how quiet this place was. Uncannily quiet. At this hour, back in the nemetons, all manner of birds would be winging to their roosts and the forest would be alive with their cries. Here not a single bird called. The place seemed empty of life, save for my dog and me. *Logs, logs, a hundred logs, two hundred he piled up, and a thousand birds lost their homes.* "A pox on it, Finbar," I muttered. "I'm never letting you tell me a story again."

Before it grew quite dark we reached the shallow caves at the foot of the rock formation. Rain had formed a pool in the hollow of a stone that might almost have been set there for the purpose. I crouched down to drink; Bear lapped with unusual restraint. He could have gone off to hunt for supper—I had no doubt he had provided for himself and Badger as well as he could during their time running wild—but he would not leave me. We wriggled into a little cavern, Bear on his belly, I on knees and elbows. When we were as far in as we could go, we curled up together on the earthen floor. Beyond the opening the sky grew dark. I tried and failed to curb my imagination. Finbar, crouched in the forest somewhere, shivering, white-faced, staring out into the night. Or worse: Finbar in the clutches of whoever had taken him. Finbar perhaps already dead, treated with the same arbitrary cruelty as Cruinn's lost men.

"He can't be dead, Bear," I murmured against my dog's warm back. "I told him the story would have a happy ending. I'm not letting Mac Dara make a liar of me."

Swift out in the forest, running, running, eyes wild, racing forward in sheer mindless panic. Swift crashing over a bank, misjudging a fence, smashing into a tree. Swift with his leg broken, writhing on the ground. *You will not think it*, I ordered myself. *You will not see it*.

Badger all alone. Badger lost again, this time without Bear to provide for him, to be his strength, his companion, his guardian. Badger, who had come so far and done so well, suddenly back in his old nightmare, and all because he had done the right thing. I was sure he had gone after Finbar, sensing there was no time to run and fetch us. "Good boy, Badger," I whispered. "Be strong. If you are with him, keep him warm tonight. We'll find you, I promise."

The moon rose. The night grew bitterly cold. Here, away from the valley of the standing stones, there was at least the reassurance that we were not the only living beings in the forest, for I heard an owl, and later another creature, not a bird but something that shrieked high in pain. Bear lifted his head.

"Calm, Bear. Safe haven. Kind hands and brave hearts." I spoke as much to myself as to him. I could not stop the bouts of trembling that shook my body; I could not banish the nightmare thoughts, try as I might. I should have fetched help. I had been utterly foolish. This was all my fault.

Bear did his best to help, but he was cold, too. We pressed close together, Bear's nose against my neck, my arms around his body. Oh, for a blanket, a cloak, a shawl, an old sack, anything at all to cover us! The night air was like winter's sharp teeth on the skin; it turned the blood to ice. Bear shuddered against me; even he could not fight the chill. It came to me that the two of us might die tonight, and that nobody would ever know what had befallen us. We might lie in this little cavern until we were no more than bones and teeth and hair.

"Bear," I whispered, "you're the best dog in the world." I realized something had been changing within me, almost without my knowing it. When I thought of Bounder, it was as the dear friend of long ago, the companion of my childhood. Though he would never lose his place in my heart, he was gone. This dog who lent me his ebbing warmth, this creature who shared with me each shuddering breath, was the loyal, courageous friend of today and tomorrow. "We're not going to die," I told him. "We're going to live until morning, and then we'll go out there and find Finbar and Badger and Swift. It's not going to end like this, in a miserable, pathetic death caused by my own stupidity. I won't let it happen."

Bear licked my cheek. His tongue felt cold. I nestled closer, hoping I was not making a liar of myself.

The night wore on. Worse than the biting cold was the fear that filled my mind with dark visions, stretching my courage thin. I did not sleep and nor did Bear. I told him stories through chattering teeth. My family's history was full of acts of bravery, and I faltered my way through every one I could think of, from the tale of my grandmother, who had undone a sorceress's curse over her brothers, to Uncle Bran's imprisonment and torture and Aunt Liadan's amazing mission to save him. I told him about Clodagh and Cathal and the changeling baby Mac Dara had left in Finbar's place. "You know, Bear," I muttered, "I'm sure you and Badger have a story that's just as remarkable as these, if only you could tell me what it is. What sent you running out into the forest on your own? What made you wild, when it's plain you are a house-and-hearth kind of dog? I suppose I'll never find out."

Stories, I could just manage. Making a sensible plan was beyond me. There was no thinking beyond the rising of the sun and the time when we could creep out of our bolt-hole and go. Staying alive until the morning seemed a high enough mountain to climb.

It was the longest night of my life. Time passed in a sequence of slow, shivering moments, punctuated by the cries of birds and the occasional passing of something on furtive, padding feet. It was dark; out there the moon must be veiled by clouds. I ran out of stories, but it felt important to go on talking, for to fall silent seemed to be taking one step closer to death. I chanted their names like a prayer: "Finbar, Badger, Swift. Finbar, Badger, Swift." After a while, remembering Cruinn's sad, strong features and his kindness, I added some other names. "Tiernan, Artagan, Daigh." Still alive? Was it possible? If the small magic of naming could win them one day longer, one hour, one moment more of life, I would do it. If remembering them helped keep them strong, I would remember. "Finbar, Badger, Swift. Tiernan, Artagan, Daigh." It came to me how puny I was beside the might of Mac Dara, and how foolish my small effort was against his malevolent power. "All the same, Bear," I whispered, "a name is strength. A name is something to hold on to. A name is something to fight for."

Bear sighed and pressed his muzzle against my neck. He was close to slumber. I did not want him to fall asleep. My mind had already shown me an image of myself at dawn, waking to find him lying stone cold beside me, never to rise again.

"Stay awake, Bear," I said, prodding him. "I need you—"

The words dried up in my mouth. Out beyond the cave entrance a light had appeared, not cool moonlight, but the warm gold light of a lantern. Someone had found us.

Bear struggled to rise in the cramped space, a growl sounding in his throat. I hissed softly in his ear, a warning to be still. If it was a search party, my father, Luachan, Doran, why hadn't they called out to us? Whoever it was had approached in complete silence. I had heard no footsteps on the rocks beyond our refuge. My heart pounded.

"Maeve!" The voice was a woman's, clear as a church bell and sweet as nectar. "Maeve, come out! I have a warm cloak, a blanket, food and drink. Come out, my dear."

I neither moved nor spoke, but Bear, disturbed, let out one warning bark before I hushed him.

"Maeve," the woman said, "I am a friend. It is safe to leave your hiding place."

I sucked in an uneven breath. How I longed for that warm cloak. Almost enough to risk everything. The speaker was close to the mouth of our shallow cave, perhaps bending to peer inside, for the glow from her lantern set twin golden points alight in Bear's wary eyes.

"I can help you find your brother," she said.

We came out. There was no dignity in it, what with the need to wriggle on elbows and knees with my skirt caught up in awkward folds and the dust of the cavern floor everywhere. Bear emerged ahead of me and a fanfare of barking broke out. I came out into the night and rose shakily to my feet. "Ssst!" I hissed as my eyes struggled to accustom themselves to the lantern light. The barks subsided to growls and then to an obedient silence as Bear came to stand beside me, his flank pressed against my thigh.

The woman was tall, taller than most men. A hooded cloak of deep blue concealed much of her form, but her face was illuminated by the warm light of the lantern, which she had set down on a stone. It was a lovely face, perfectly oval, the eyes large and lustrous under fine arching brows, the mouth sweet as a rosebud. The woman's skin was remarkable, for it seemed to hold a light within it, as if she herself were a lamp. It was not possible to look on such a person and believe her anything but good. And yet . . .

"My lady," I managed, feeling the hard thumping of my heart and willing myself to stay calm, to listen carefully, to think clearly. "My brother—Finbar—you know where he is?"

The woman smiled. "Half-frozen, covered with cuts and bruises, all alone in the dark, and the first question you ask me is this? Come, child, wrap this cloak around you and take some refreshment. The night is cold and you are far from home." Somehow there was now a dark woollen cloak over her arm where before she had held nothing at all. In her other hand was a little basket, cunningly woven, from which the most delicious smell arose, like fresh-baked bread hot from the oven. Bear made a tiny sound.

"My brother," I said, not moving an inch, though every part of me longed for the cloak's warmth around my shoulders. "Finbar. Please tell me where he is. He's only seven, and it's cold—I need to find him quickly."

"Is my kind so soon forgotten," she said, "that a daughter of Sevenwaters does not know me? Can it be that Lord Sean's daughter is too proud or too foolish to accept help in times of peril?"

Every instinct told me to apologize, to take the cloak, to accept food for Bear and myself, and only then to seek answers. It was Uncle Bran's training, perhaps, that held me back even now. "Forgive me," I said, wrapping my arms across my chest in a vain attempt to stop shivering. "I mean no discourtesy. But I don't know you. I have never met you. And I have no cause to trust strangers right now, even when, as you point out, I could do with some help. What I need is to find my brother and take him safely home. If you can assist me with that, I would welcome it."

She smiled. "You will not be strong enough to find him if you refuse to accept warm clothing, food and drink, Maeve. Here."

Somehow the cloak dropped itself around my shoulders. I was suddenly warm, oh, blissfully warm, the feeling spreading from the roots of my hair to the tips of my toes. It felt so good that for a few moments I was speechless. I lifted the side of the garment to accommodate Bear.

"Thank you," I said when I could speak again. "Will you tell me your name?" She was fey, no doubt of it. This was my first encounter with the Tuatha De, and it seemed as though she expected me to know who she was. The only names I knew were the Lady of the Forest and Mac Dara. White Dragon and Black Dragon. But the Lady had gone away years ago, and despite Finbar's story, I did not imagine this was she.

"Eat first, Maeve," she said, placing the little basket beside the lantern and unfolding a delicate cloth all embroidered with tiny images of forest creatures. "And drink." There was a flask there, too, though I had not seen it a moment ago. The stopper was off, as if she had anticipated what my difficulties might be with using such a vessel. Oh, that smell of new bread!

"No, Bear," I warned as he edged forward. "My lady, I cannot eat or drink these offerings."

"No? This flask would be easy for you, Maeve. As for the food, I can help you if that is needed, but it is all in small pieces."

I found myself somewhat disturbed by this. She had not simply stumbled on me, but had prepared carefully for our meeting.

"That isn't what I mean," I said. "It seems to me that this may not be food and drink from the human world. And although I have been long absent from Sevenwaters, I did live here as a child, and I have heard stories about what it means to eat such food. I would rather stay hungry than touch a mouthful of it."

"Ah," the woman said lightly. "You are proud, then. And wary. What of this hound? His eyes are hungry. You may choose to go without, but surely you will not deny your faithful friend his supper?"

"And see him trapped in the Otherworld forever? I love him too much for that. He will not die of hunger in a single night, my lady, and nor will I. We are made of sterner stuff."

Her brows rose. "I see," she said, and her tone suggested she was genuinely surprised. "Then it may help if I tell you we are not in the Otherworld—not yet—but still within your father's forest. When dawn breaks you can walk home, if you choose, without crossing any margins save those of humankind. As for these provisions, they are of your own world, obtained with the assistance of a local cottager. You and your friend can eat and drink without fear of falling under a spell. I speak only the truth, Maeve. There is no need to be afraid of me."

I bit back my first response, which was to tell her I was not in the least frightened. That might be a display of courage, but it would also be a lie. "Please tell me who you are," I said, "and how to find Finbar. He'll be lonely and scared. He's the one who needs a warm cloak."

"Take this blanket," the woman said. I did not see her lift anything, but now there was a folded blanket across her outstretched hands. It looked as soft as swansdown, and in the lantern light its color was dove gray. I took it from her awkwardly; it weighed almost nothing. "Carry the basket over your arm. I see you will not eat in my presence, and that I understand. You have your reasons to want privacy. But maybe you will quench your thirst and satisfy your hunger when you are alone with your staunch companion there." She glanced at Bear, who stood half-shrouded by the cloak, his hair on end as he stared back at her. The forest was full of shifting shadows; beyond the circle of light cast by the lantern, the darkness seemed alive with presences unseen. Birds. Bats. Insects. Stranger things. When I did not move, she said, "You are indeed slow to trust. Is it the hurt that was done you in childhood that makes you like a hedgehog before hunting dogs, a creature all prickles?"

"Tell me your name," I said, squaring my shoulders under the cloak. I would have liked to shrug it off, but my shivering body would not allow me that gesture of defiance. There is not much point in pride when you are freezing to death. "And tell me how to find Finbar. Then I might consider trusting you."

"They call me Caisin Silverhair," the woman said, slipping back her hood. A waterfall of long tresses flowed down her back, gleaming moon-pale in the lantern light. "I am a friend, Maeve. I am kin to those who showed your little sister the ways of the seer; I am kin to those who guided your grandmother through the long, cruel task the sorceress's curse laid on her. I will help you find what you have lost. For you seek not only your brother, I think, but two others that are precious to you."

Badger. Swift. "Where are they?" My voice shook.

"Find the child and he will lead you to the others. When dawn comes, go down the valley of the stones and over the bridge of withies. Your brother sleeps as the squirrel sleeps; if you follow the signs, you will find him safe and well. Ask him what he dreamed of, slumbering in the heart of the oak." She stood quiet a moment, watching me. I said nothing, for I had heard enough old stories to know that every detail must be remembered, every instruction acted upon. I did not like the sound of *sleeps as the squirrel sleeps*; it put me uncomfortably in mind of Cruinn's lost men.

"You're sure Finbar is safe?"

"For now."

Oh gods, what did that mean—that I should rush off in the dark lest he perish before I find this bridge and this oak? But then, if I'd been told to go at dawn, then leaving too early might mean I walked on and on all day, with never a bridge or an oak to be seen. My head spun. Within the folds of the warm cloak, my heart was cold.

"Put down the blanket, Maeve," the woman said, and her tone was all compassion. "Eat and drink from the basket. Lie down and sleep until the sunrise. All will be well." The air stirred, a shadow passed, and she was gone. On the stone, the lantern burned on.

I put down the blanket, and Bear lowered himself onto it with a sigh, as if he had only been waiting for me to show some common sense. Then, feeling like a traitor, I lifted down the basket and settled beside him. I took a mouthful from the flask, and then another. It was some kind of cordial, its flavor that of every berry of the forest mixed together. Its effect was immediate and startling, for those two sips were enough to put new heart in me. I shared the food with Bear. When we were finished he licked my fingers clean. Then we lay down, the two of us, and I drew the cloak awkwardly over us, and we slept until morning.

I never considered running back to the keep. Caisin Silverhair had given the kind of instructions people get in stories, and I knew well enough what happened in the old tales when folk disobeyed. It seemed to me that when dealing with the Fair Folk, stories might be a more reliable guide than plain common sense, though I hoped to apply the latter as well.

"Down the valley of the stones," I muttered as Bear and I moved on. I had the blanket under my arm and the flask in the pouch at my belt; I'd managed to get the stopper back in with my teeth. Caisin Silverhair had left us sufficient food for that one meal only, which meant the cordial was all I had for Finbar. I hoped he would find the strength to walk home today. "Over the bridge of withies." I would not think of the time when Bear and Badger had refused to cross another bridge. Would it break Caisin's rules if Bear decided to wade or swim instead? Might so small a departure from the instructions spell my brother's doom? "And look for a big oak tree." Let this not be one of Mac Dara's tricks. Let me not find Finbar curled up like a squirrel, cold and dead.

"That's an odd name," I murmured, putting out my free hand to stop myself from slipping over on the uneven, pebbly ground. "Caisin Silverhair. Maybe I should call myself Maeve Dog-Friend. Or Maeve Claw-Hands. Not an everyday name, a story name." Gods, let this not be a terrible mistake, and the two of us heading straight into a trap set by Mac Dara. Let us not be walking boldly forward into one of those tales where human folk get trapped in the Otherworld for a hundred years and come home to find their families long dead and buried.

"Bear the Brave," I said as he headed downhill, leading the way. "Bear the Beautiful. Faithful Bear." And although I liked the last one best, it troubled me. It was all too easy to imagine a tale in which those to whom Bear was so loyal came to grief, and he sat vigil beside their bodies, fading day by day from a fine healthy dog to a bony, sad wraith. "We're going to find them," I said, squaring my shoulders and lifting my chin. "Today we'll find them all and bring them home."

At the foot of the little valley we found a path. It snaked forward into a dense, dark area of forest where the low sunlight barely penetrated. Pale nets of spiderweb festooned every tree. These were not oaks, but gray, spiky things of no kind I recognized, their branches thrusting out like hostile arms to block our way. If we kept to the very center of the narrow path we could avoid being scratched. When I forgot to duck I got cobwebs in my hair. There was a faint rustling all around us, as of countless small creatures busy with mysterious work. Above us, from time to time, I caught a snatch of words spoken in a whisper, though the language was unknown to me. Bear padded on bravely; I followed in his footsteps, trying not to think about situations from which I would have trouble extricating myself. I had only to trip and sprain an ankle or get my gown irretrievably snarled on one of those thorny branches and I would be in real difficulty. I must stay alert. I must not stumble. I must make no errors of judgment.

Before we found the bridge, we heard the river. I did not remember a river from the Sevenwaters of my childhood, but the rushing sound told me a sizeable one lay not far ahead. We came up over a rise and there it was. I drew in a shocked breath. The river was broad, perhaps fifty paces across, and it looked deep. Shreds of mist drifted above the water. On the other side stretched a great tract of oak forest: strong dark limbs, tattered remnants of autumn robes, sun gold, blood red, butter yellow. Hundreds and hundreds of oaks.

And there, not far along the riverbank, was the bridge: a fragile structure of woven withies, broad enough to walk upon, but without rope, chain or rail to keep a person from falling. It sagged in the center, dipping perilously close to the swirling water. The basket-weave surfaces looked sodden, slippery and uneven. For me, it would be an exercise in courage and balance. For Bear it would be impossible.

My gut twisted. "Bear," I said, "I'll have to go on without you. She said oaks, and the oaks are over there." As I spoke I made my way to the spot where the flimsy bridge met the bank. It seemed to be only resting there, without any anchors. A gust of wind might snatch the entire structure up and rip it into fragments. If I didn't do this quickly, I would be too scared to do it at all. Caisin Silverhair had made it clear: cross the bridge, find the oak, save Finbar. There was no choice about it.

I would have taken off my shoes if I'd been confident I could get them back on again. Bare feet would give me a firmer purchase on the treacherous woven surface. Never mind that. I managed to sling the blanket over my shoulder so I'd have both arms free for balancing. I stepped onto the bridge.

"Bear," I said, turning my head to look back at him. "Stay."

He gazed at me with his heart in his eyes.

"*Stay*," I repeated, making it a command. I stretched out my arms and took a step along the bridge, away from him. Bear could not swim this river; if he tried it he would be swept downstream in a moment and drowned. Best that he wait for me where it was safe, and when I brought Finbar back, Bear could find the way home for us.

I fixed my gaze on the far bank. I would be brave. I would ignore the rushing water, the chill spray, the slippery surface underfoot. I would set aside the strangeness of this place and the fact that I had told nobody where I was going. I would forget it all . . . But I could not shut my ears to Bear's voice. His anguished howl rang out behind me, tightening my throat and filling my eyes with tears. I did not look back.

The withies were uneven and slick with moisture, and even with arms outstretched I teetered and wobbled as I moved gradually forward. I made myself breathe slowly. When the bridge seemed to bounce and shake beneath me, as if in protest at my crossing, I told myself sharply to stop being silly. I set one foot in front of the other. Now I was in the middle. Now I was more than halfway over. Now I was nearly there . . . I reached the far side and stepped off the bridge to collapse in a trembling heap on a shore carpeted with perfectly round white pebbles. Gods! Let me not have to do such a thing again, at least until I was heading home with Finbar. Bear's howling had ceased. Had he settled to wait for me or decided to run for home? I looked back across the river.

Bear was halfway across the bridge. He stood frozen, staring down between the loosely woven withies at the raging water below. Faithful Bear.

I was up again before I had time to think, walking out onto the bridge, standing to face him. "Bear, come!" I called, stretching out my arms in the sign he knew and making my tone calm and confident.

Bear looked up. His amber eyes were full of trust, though he was shivering so violently I feared he might fall.

"Good boy, come on!"

Step by slow step I talked him across. I held his gaze; I pushed down my fear and filled my voice with warmth and welcome. "My best boy. Come on, now. Good Bear. Brave boy." As he advanced toward me I backed slowly to the end of the bridge.

He ran the last few paces, sending my heart into my throat, but he reached me safely and almost knocked me over with his exuberant greeting. For a few moments, as I threw my arms around him and felt the rough caress of his tongue on my face, I was filled with sheer delight. Then I stepped off the bridge, and Bear came down beside me, and we faced the oaks. I was reminded of the moment when I had looked up from dealing with my disobedient hounds to see Cruinn's mounted warriors staring back at me, a hostile wall of men.

There were so many trees: a great army of oaks. A person might wander here all season long, checking one trunk after another and finding nothing but last season's nests and the leavings of mice or beetles. I took a deep breath and made myself let it out slowly, counting up to five.

"Very well, Bear," I said. "We're here, and we're going on. Let's not think about what we can't do, but what we can do." The chance that Finbar had been brought over this very same bridge seemed most unlikely, but Caisin Silverhair had said I would find him among these oaks, so that was where I must look. The task was daunting. But I did have Bear, and Bear had found a trail before.

I hitched up my skirt, then crouched to feel inside the pouch with my mouth. I lifted my head, the little straw creature held in my teeth.

"Find Finbar," I said, kneeling to drop the thing on the ground in front of Bear. "Find him."

It seemed he understood, for he sniffed at the little creature and pawed it, then took a few steps toward the trees before looking back over his shoulder at me, as if to say, *Are you coming?*

I got the straw animal back up and into the pouch. I would not leave this token of my brother behind. I rose to my feet. As I did so, the sun edged over the treetops, turning the river to a stream of silver and the oaks to a dazzling curtain of red-gold. To a person who believed in omens, this would have been a good one. "All right, Bear," I said. "Let's go."

We walked for a long time. Once, I stopped to take a drink from Caisin's flask, which by daylight showed itself to be of a metal I did not recognize, bright as moonlight and chased with strange figures that were neither men nor creatures, but something between. The vessel was of an ideal size and shape for me to manage between my wrists, and the stopper could be put in and out with my teeth. Luck or good preparation? The fey woman's knowledge of me had been unsettling. Could the Fair Folk read our minds? Were they privy to our most secret thoughts? I did not like that idea at all. Indeed, the more I thought about our encounter, the more it troubled me.

"Why wouldn't she bring Finbar to us, if she knew where he was?" I addressed this question to Bear, who took no notice but continued moving on. "Why did she wait until we were half-frozen to come and rescue us, since it seems she knew exactly what was going on? And if she is kin to the Lady of the Forest and her kind, the benign type of Fair Folk, where was she when Mac Dara was establishing his hold in these parts?"

Bear had nothing to say. We were deep in the oak forest now; the rushing sound of the river had long since died away. Fallen leaves lay ankle-deep on the path, slowing our progress. If anyone was about, they would hear us approaching by the crunch of our footsteps. Should I be calling Finbar's name as I walked? The forest was vast; he might be anywhere.

No sign of Swift today. No evidence that a horse had passed this way, or a dog for that matter. More likely they had been separated soon after they left the nemetons, for unless Swift had been led away from his field—unlikely given how soon he had vanished—he would have quickly outpaced both boy and dog.

We came to a rise, and Bear helped me climb up. The moment we reached the top he ran on.

"Bear, wait!" I bent over, my sides aching. I felt sick. "Bear!" A pox on it, I would have to sit down and catch my breath before I could go any farther. "Come back!"

He obeyed, padding back to lie down beside me. He was panting; even he could not go on forever. I would not give him the cordial, for despite the fey woman's assurances that it was quite safe for us, I had some misgivings about it. I could not think of any drink available to humankind that produced such an immediate sense of well-being, and it seemed to me that so powerful a gift would not come without a cost. I would take that risk for myself, if it meant getting Finbar back safely. I would take it for my brother if it was the only way he'd have the strength for the walk home. There was no need to subject Bear to the same peril.

"I think I must be hungry," I muttered, stroking his back. "It feels like a long time since breakfast, if that was what it was." I had abandoned Caisin's little basket on the far side of the withy bridge. If there was a special reason why she had bid me carry it over my arm, that was too bad. Getting across the bridge without falling into the river had seemed more important. "We must find him soon, Bear," I whispered. "The sun's quite high already. I wonder if folk are out looking for us."

They would be, of course. I pictured Father, silent and grim-faced; Luachan, horrified that his charge had gone missing, even if it was not on his watch. Folk from the keep, diverted from the search for Cruinn's lost men. Perhaps even Cruinn himself, for he would understand Father's anguish all too well. I imagined how my family would feel if Finbar never came back, or if he was discovered dead as Cruinn's men had been. "Tiernan, Artagan and Daigh," I murmured. "I hope they survive where the others could not." Bear licked my face. "They have the strength of grown men, at least. But Finbar isn't very strong, Bear, and we must find him quickly."

Bear got to his feet, understanding the meaning if not the words. I rose more slowly. I prayed that we would find Finbar soon. And I prayed that when we found him we would find Badger and Swift as well. Because if we did not, I would have to take Finbar home and leave them behind.

"Bear, come." It no longer felt right to command him thus; in this hunt, he was the leader and I the follower. "Show me the way, good friend."

We walked on. The sun reached its peak and began to sink again; the sky clouded over and rain began to fall. The half-clad trees provided some shelter, but soon enough both Bear and I were damp and cold. He still seemed to be following a trail, and it seemed more and more likely it was not Finbar's scent but Badger's. My brother could not possibly have come so far. Not on his own. Yet Caisin's words had not suggested Finbar was a captive. *He sleeps as the squirrel sleeps.*

"Kidnapped by squirrels," I murmured, trying to keep up my spirits. "If I get him safely home again, I'll make up a song about that. Rhian would probably enjoy it, even if nobody else did. Only I imagine she'd prefer clurichauns."

The light began to fade. The clouds thickened, threatening heavier rain. Even if we found him right now, we could not reach home before dark. It would be another night in the open, without food or fire. I had carried Caisin's blanket over my shoulder all the way from the bridge. Once or twice I'd been tempted to abandon it, for even a small burden grows heavy when a person is weary to the bone. Now I was glad I'd kept it. Its warmth might be the difference between life and death for a little boy on a cold night.

Bear's eager gait had become more of a resigned plod. I was full of a longing to be back home and by the fireside, warm and dry, with a full belly, and I despised myself for it. Such thoughts were not only selfish, they were weak. Bear had not given up. I would match him. But as the rain increased, persistent enough to soak us even through the protection of the trees, and as the sky turned to a bleak stone gray, it was harder and harder to stay strong. *Believe in yourself,* I muttered, digging deep for some of Uncle Bran's wisdom. *Trust yourself, and know you are never quite alone.*

True enough; I did have Bear. And now my companion had halted in front of me, his head up, his body tense with anticipation. What had he seen?

Around us, the curtains of rain hid everything. Water poured off the thinning foliage of the oaks and pooled around the drifts of fallen gold beneath. The air was filled with a wet, earthy smell. The birds were quiet.

"What is it, Bear?" He had not moved. He stood intent, staring ahead into the obscurity.

Then I heard it. Barking; barking getting rapidly closer.

"Badger?" I whispered, unable to believe that at last we had found one of our own.

Bear barked a joyous greeting, running forward until the rain concealed him from me. A few moments later, the two of them came rushing out of the veil, chasing and jumping and playing together like young pups, until Badger ran up to me, planted his muddy forepaws on my chest and licked my face. It was a first.

"Badger, my lovely boy! Where have you been?" I blinked back tears, hugging him and at the same time doing my best to check whether he was hurt. "Good boy, Badger, fine brave boy. You, too, Bear." Oh, how I longed to turn around and head for home with the two of them, to get my boys to safe shelter and let someone else continue the quest. I suppressed the feeling quickly; it shamed me.

My elation at Badger's arrival soon drained away. Surely all this rain would erase any trace of Finbar's trail. Here we were, miles and miles into an immense tract of forest—I could not remember it being part of Sevenwaters at all—and perhaps there was now no way to find either Finbar or the path home. Rhian's voice sounded in my mind: *You don't have to do everything yourself.* But that was exactly what I had chosen to do, and now here I was, with only the dogs, and I must keep on looking for my brother until . . . I would not think of that.

"Bear, come. Badger, come."

We walked on until it was almost dark. My legs were shaking; they could barely carry my body forward. The rain eased, then stopped, and a chill wind came up in its place, sending probing fingers under my wet clothing. Beneath the oaks, vapors rose and twisted, clothing the knotty roots in shrouds of white. Here and there misshapen fungi sprouted alone or in clumps, like tiny wizened men in fantastic hats. Once or twice I thought I saw a taller figure, a person clad in gray or green or brown, but when I peered closer there was nothing but the oak trunks and the gathering dusk.

"A fire would be good," I muttered. "But even if I could kindle one, where would I get dry wood?" We would have to stop and find a place to shelter before it grew too dark. The oaks stretched off into the distance. Each way I turned, the vista was the same. "A tumbledown cottage," I murmured. "A fallen tree. Some rocks. A hollow. Anything that might keep out this wind." I wondered if Finbar had been out in the rain like me, and whether he, too, was cold to the marrow. "Where is he, Badger? Where is Finbar?"

The two dogs looked at me as if I was a little touched in the head.

"All right," I said. "We're not walking any farther. Let's find somewhere to sleep." Oh gods, Finbar out for another night, all by himself, without even Badger to keep him warm. How could he survive this? *I'm sorry, Mother. Oh, Father, I'm so sorry.*

Just when it seemed we would walk on forever, there was a fallen tree, and a hollow within it large enough to accommodate the three of us. Water was no longer hard to find. Bear and Badger lapped from puddles on the ground; with a certain difficulty, I did the same. A little later, as I was squatting to relieve myself, Bear hurtled off into the darkening woods with Badger close behind. *Finbar*, I thought, knowing in my heart how unlikely it was. I tried not to think of the possibility that the dogs would not come back.

It was a lonely wait. I laid the blanket in the hollow, ready for the three of us to lie on. Oddly, it was not sodden like my clothing, but felt dry and warm. The cloak Caisin had given me was drying, too, though everything I wore underneath it was wet. Magic. I would not think too hard about that. It seemed to me that if the fey woman were to appear now and offer me Otherworld food, I would devour it with scarcely a second thought. My belly felt hollow, my head dizzy. Given the choice between being condemned to live in the Otherworld or dying of cold and hunger, I was fairly sure I would choose the former. Besides, those old tales might be wrong. They might be inventions designed solely to stop children from sampling every berry they came across.

I wondered if any of those fungi we had seen earlier were edible. They were not like the ones that grew near Harrowfield. Those, Aunt Liadan had taught me to recognize. *This is beneficial for the shaking sickness, and this for irritations of the skin. This one can be eaten in a stew with no harmful effects, but raw, it will give you a powerful bellyache. A bite of this red spotted one will kill you.* If I found the right plants, I could probably pick a few, using my feet. Or I might crouch down to graze like a sheep. Finbar would find that amusing. "Where are you, little brother?" I whispered. "Be safe. Be warm. We're getting closer." I prayed that this was true.

A rustling in the leaves beyond the fallen tree and here were the dogs, tails wagging, eyes bright. Bear was in the lead. He came up with something in his mouth and dropped it at my feet. A rabbit. It was limp, bloody and not long dead. Though the light was almost gone, I could see that Bear was immensely proud of himself. Badger danced about behind him, celebrating the catch.

"Good boy, Bear." I stroked him behind the ears, in the way he loved. "Well done. Eat now."

He stood waiting. Looked down at the little corpse. Looked up at me.

I shook my head. "I can't," I said, thinking that by tomorrow I might not be so fussy. "Bear, eat. Badger, eat." I edged farther into the hollow and turned my face away from them. I listened as they devoured the meat.

When they were done, the two of them squeezed in with me. It was only when they were settled, one on either side, that I realized Bear had brought a bone. It was one of the larger ones, a haunch, with a good amount of flesh still clinging to it. He did not gnaw it, but placed it on my chest with some care. The golden eyes gazed into mine. I saw his thoughts as clear as day. *Eat. You must eat, dear one.*

I had done my best not to weep. I had tried not to feel sorry for myself. It came to me that it is not trials and travails that bring us down, but unexpected moments of kindness.

"I can't," I whispered.

But I could; Bear helped me. He was insistent, holding one end of the bone in his teeth while I gnawed the other, then, when I realized I was indeed hungry enough to eat raw meat, watching me intently as I held his offering between my wrists and stripped it of flesh. I was beyond caring about blood on my clothing, or about what anyone might think of me. If I were to have the strength to go on in the morning, I needed food in my belly. Bear was my provider. Not to accept his gift was to throw his love back in his face. So I ate, every scrap of meat, and then I chewed on the bone until my companion, with a sigh, put his head down on his paws as if satisfied. On my other side, Badger was already asleep. Beyond our little shelter the rain had stopped, the breeze had died down, and the moon was peering between clouds. Its light transformed the wet forest into a fey realm of glittering light and deepest shadow.

"Good night, little brother," I murmured. "Be warm. Be safe." I pulled the cloak across the three of us as best I could, then lay down with my face against Bear's shoulder and my back warmed by Badger's sleeping form. And despite everything, very soon I, too, was asleep.

DRUID'S JOURNEY: EAST

He reaches the coast at dawn. The air is cold as a knife, slicing to the bone. He descends by a cliff path; finds the woman on a ledge outside her cave, swathed in a blanket, warming water over a little fire. Huddled though she is, she looks tall, straight, young enough to be the other's daughter. Down on the pebbly shore below a lean gray dog runs to and fro, playing at chase; the gulls tease him, hovering just within snapping range, then rising at the last moment. By the time the druid reaches the ledge, the dog has sprinted up the path to give him close inspection.

"Get in, Slip," the woman says, and the creature settles by her, its bright eyes never leaving the visitor.

"My respects to you, wise woman."

"And to you, druid." She speaks without glancing up; her gaze is on the curling flames, the wisps of bark she is feeding into the fire's heart. "You are just in time for breakfast. We can offer you a share of a fish."

"Thank you. I have bread enough for all." He settles cross-legged, getting out the loaf, a small knife, his flask of mead.

No more talk, then, until the fish is sizzling over the fire, the bread lies ready on the platters and the two of them have a cup of mead apiece in their hands.

"My sister sent you," she says.

If he is surprised that this woman of middle years is sister to the crone of the north, he shows no sign of it. "She suggested the wisdom I seek might be found with you, yes."

The woman reaches to turn the fish, using a pair of sharpened sticks. Her cooking pan is black with use, her platters chipped and cracked. The dog makes an anticipatory sound.

"Some of that wisdom. Not all. You have a long journey ahead of you, druid, and time runs short."

He waits, holding his silence. The sun creeps up, turning the expanse of water before them into a glittering carpet of light. He gazes out over the sea toward an island veiled from the eyes of humankind. The old woman had spoken of selkies.

"Your kin," says the woman, as if she knew his thoughts. She passes him a platter of fish and bread. "They come in here from time to time."

He nods, not finding any words.

The three of them eat their meal, the dog quickly, the others more slowly as the sun moves higher. It is still very early in the morning. The shore is empty of seals.

"You'll be wanting this," the woman says, indicating the remains of the loaf.

"Keep it for supper. The mead, too."

"If you say so." She packs the things away in the cave, tidily. "Let us go down."

They walk on the shore awhile. The woman throws sticks for the dog to chase; the creature is in bliss. Gulls swoop and dive, fishing offshore.

"If you'd come at dusk, you might have seen them," she says.

The dog runs up, panting, its tail scything to and fro. The woman throws the stick again.

"I might," says the druid. Beneath the simple words, a well of sorrow. "But time grows short."

"Then I will give you my share of the rhyme, and let you move on," says the woman. "It is this: *Overcome the fear of flame, Bid the wildest beast be tame.* What it means, I cannot tell you. Within the whole, it lies just before the part my sister gave you."

"Danu preserve us," murmurs the druid. "Can this not be achieved without endangering the innocent?"

"When the stakes are high," says the wise woman, "the risks are also high. For you, I think, especially so."

"My own risk is of my choosing."

"Others, too, make their own choices. Even the innocent."

"You think?"

"I know, druid." She pats the dog, praising its return of the stick, then turns her steps back toward the cave. "Best be on your way, then, and seek out my sister in the south. It is a long, weary way, but for your kind, perhaps not so far. You will find her in a cottage by a deep well. Elms grow all around."

"I thank you. For the words, and for your wisdom."

"It was little enough. I was beginning to wonder if it would simply be forgotten, for in all this time nobody has asked me for it. I wish you well. This has been a dark season; keep your light shining, druid."

"I will. Farewell."

CHAPTER 10

I woke late. Beyond the fallen tree in whose hollow I had slept, it was full day. A watery sunlight touched the forest but failed to warm it. The blanket on which I had lain was dry, and so was the cloak that covered me, but all my clothing was heavy with damp and the garments chafed against my skin. I smelled as a person smells who has been living wild for two days and nights and has not had the opportunity to wash or change her clothing, not to speak of lying on her belly to drink and eating raw meat. If this went on much longer I would become a crazy wild woman, the sort of figure who'd more likely have stones hurled at her than be offered food, shelter and clean garments. Maeve Claw-Hands indeed.

The dogs were out in the open, eating what could only be a fresh kill. The flesh steamed in the morning chill; the sound of crunching bone was loud in the silent woodland. The smell made me queasy.

It was hard to move. My joints were stiff; my back ached; I was desperate for warm water and Rhian's capable hands. I struggled out of the hollow log and made myself bend and stretch, willing strength into my reluctant body. I went into the bushes to relieve myself. When I returned, Bear was ready with my breakfast. He held it in his jaws, an unidentifiable joint of raw meat with fur attached. I wished I'd trained him to gather nuts and crack them open with his teeth, or dig up edible roots.

The look in his eyes made it impossible to refuse his offering. I forced down a few mouthfuls, then passed the bone back to him.

"Enough, Bear. Thank you." My belly was protesting; it was a struggle to hold the food down. I went off in search of water and found a pool that was not quite so muddy as the others. I drank deeply. I vowed to myself that once I got safely home, I would eat every meal offered me with appreciation. "Not that there's anything wrong with the food you provide, Bear," I told him. "It's just that I'm not a dog. If I were, this might all be easier."

He lay down, head on paws, almost as if I had rebuked him. Badger was munching busily, impervious.

"Right, boys," I said with a brightness that was entirely artificial. "Today we find this oak, and we find Finbar, and we go home. The sooner we move on, the better."

My feet hurt. I had not dared take off my shoes for fear I would not be able to get them on again by myself. The leather was sodden, and I could feel a fine crop of blisters developing. *Let today be the day we get safely home. Oh, please,* said a voice in my mind, a weak, self-pitying voice. A stronger voice silenced it quickly. *Why waste your strength in pleas and prayers? Out here, nobody's listening. If you want to get home, make it happen.*

So, put on the cloak. The hardest part was getting it around my shoulders; that took time. Once there, the garment revealed its fey qualities, for the clasp fastened without the need for fiddly finger work, joining together and hooking up with startling ease. I had wondered about it last night, when I removed the cloak, but had been too weary and despondent to think clearly. Now I realized that even in this, Caisin Silverhair had prepared very specifically for a meeting with me. "What was she playing at, boys?" I asked. "What did she want from me? She can't have meant us to be out here for so long. If she knew where Finbar was, why didn't she see him safely home?"

Next, fold the blanket. I could not use my feet without removing my shoes, so I did the job with teeth and forearms, untidily. Before taking the bundle under my arm, I had a drink from Caisin's flask; just one sip. The cordial ran through my veins like fire, rendering me suddenly, startlingly awake. "If she lied about it," I muttered, "I'll . . ." What would I do, set the dogs on her? Tell my father? Put her under a geis? She was of the Tuatha De; I was an ordinary woman with not a streak of magic in me. Besides, if she had lied and the potion was of Otherworld origin, I was already doomed. Or would be, if I had stepped over the border of that uncanny realm. But that could not be; I had not yet found Finbar, and this was not like last time, when Clodagh had followed our brother all the way to the heart of Mac Dara's world to bring him safely home. Hadn't Caisin said I could do it without crossing the borders of Father's land? *Stop it, Maeve, you're thinking too much. The sooner you get moving, the sooner you find him. The sooner you find him, the sooner everyone goes home again.* And the other voice said, *A happy ending, hmm? It's not quite so simple, is it?*

Cloak on, blanket over arm, flask in pouch. I offered the little straw manikin for Bear and Badger to smell. "Finbar, boys. Find Finbar." It was hard work to keep the note of hope in my voice.

Dusk was falling on that third day when we came to a clearing in the forest. Since morning the dogs had followed a scent. How could Finbar have traveled so far? My whole body ached with weariness. Doubt had been rising in me for some time. By now we must surely be beyond the borders of Sevenwaters land. My father's holdings were wide, but not so wide as this. In the south was Illann's territory of Dun na Ri. Somewhere close to Illann's borders was a place that had belonged to my mother's family, but the house had burned down and nobody lived there now. The sun told me we had been traveling roughly westward, and I knew nothing of whose land lay in that direction. Shouldn't we have reached the margin of the Sevenwaters forest and a guard post? Shouldn't we have come upon the road down which Cruinn's men had been traveling when Mac Dara took them? Perhaps my sense of direction was less accurate than I thought. Today's long walk had given me no landmarks, no hills or valleys, no watercourses beyond a small stream or two, no signs of human habitation. Only the oaks, hundreds and hundreds of oaks, stretching out as far as the eye could see. Stretching out forever.

I had eaten wild onions, a meager but welcome feast. I had eaten mushrooms—at least I hoped they were mushrooms—and thus far I had suffered no ill effects. Bear and Badger had found the corpse of something in the long grass under a tree. With a certain difficulty, I had convinced Bear I wasn't hungry.

And now, so late in the day, here was this clearing. A shudder went through me, for it reminded me sharply of the open area where I had found Niall hanging from the elm. This place, too, had its lone tree—not a lofty elm this time, but an oak, a formidable old giant all heavy dark limbs and swathes of autumn foliage. Drifts of fallen leaves blanketed its knotty roots. Birds exchanged plaintive cries in its branches: *The darkness comes, fly in, fly in!* I welcomed their voices, remembering the eldritch quiet of another dusk.

Bear halted in his tracks. Badger halted behind him. Now I heard what they heard: behind the birdcalls, another voice, a human voice, young and urgent.

"Maeve! Maeve, here! I'm in here!"

My heart turned over. He was alive. We had found him. "Finbar!" I called, blinking back tears. "I'm coming!"

The tree. *He sleeps as the squirrel sleeps.* I should have known the moment I clapped eyes on this most formidable of oaks that it was the one we were looking for.

We ran, the three of us, arriving at the foot of the oak breathless and excited. The tree's bole was huge; it dwarfed those of the other old oaks nearby. I craned my neck, gazing upward, but there was no sign of him.

"Where are you, Finbar?" I called. "How do we reach you?"

"Up here!"

I took a few paces back and looked up again. High above my head there was a patch on the trunk that looked curiously like a glazed window, and through it I could see movement—yes, there he was, his pale face, his hand waving. There must be a hollow up there, the kind of place in which a creature might make its winter home. Quite a big creature, if a seven-year-old boy could fit inside the cavity. But what was it that veiled Finbar, rendering his features blurred and indistinct? His voice was reaching me clearly enough. Gods, the place was high: nearly three times the height of a tall man.

"Can you climb down?" I shouted.

"I can't. You have to come and get me."

What did he think this was, a game? Had he forgotten about my hands? I drew a deep, calming breath and hissed the dogs to silence, for the two of them were barking so loudly I could hardly think straight.

"I can't, Finbar," I called. "I can't hold on." Even for a fit person it would be hard; on this side of the tree the lowest branch was well above my head, and the next was high above it. "How did you get up there?"

There was a lengthy pause. Finbar had retreated within the tree; I could see him moving about, doing something.

"Finbar, how did you get up there?"

He was back at the opening, if it could be called that. Was that filmy barrier a spiderweb? A net of some kind?

"You have to go around the other side," Finbar called. "That's where you get up."

Bear and Badger had flopped down in the long grass, obeying my order to be quiet. I made my way around the giant tree, taking care as I stepped over the tangle of roots. Now it seemed we might get safely home after all, the last thing I needed was a wrenched ankle.

There was something odd about this place. Here on the western side of the tree the light was quite different, almost as if it were another time of day. There was a shadowy tinge to grass and rocks and roots, a new chill in the air. Even my skin looked odd, pallid to the point of grayness. Was I so filthy after my days living wild? Had my mushroom meal sickened me without my knowing it?

From this side of the tree I could not see the dogs. I could not see my brother, either, for there was no visible entrance to his bolt-hole, but his voice carried clearly from up above me.

"See on the bark there, someone's carved footholds. And the trunk leans, so it's easier to balance."

"I can't see where you are, Finbar."

"Just climb straight up."

"I can't!" I failed to keep the frustration from my voice. "You come down. I'll stand here and if you lose your grip I'll try to catch you." I could at least cushion his fall. If he had climbed up, he could surely get safely back down. "Come on, Finbar!" Belatedly, I realized there might be another reason for his hesitation. "Are you hurt? Sick?"

"You have to climb up." The little voice was dogged, unshakable. It was the same tone he'd used, once or twice, to say, *I'm not supposed to tell*. My brother might be only seven, but I wasn't going to move him on this.

"If I break my leg," I said, gritting my teeth and looking for a possible way I could do this, "how are you going to get me back home?"

"You have to climb up, Maeve. If you don't, I can't get out."

My skin prickled. Magic. An enchanted oak. What else could this be? I had a hundred questions, but the time to ask them was when I had my brother safely on the ground. And if there was a spell or charm in place that said he could not leave his bolt-hole unless I went up there and fetched him out, that was what I'd have to do.

I tried to recall whether Uncle Bran had any advice on attempting the impossible. Being brave was all very well, but no amount of courage could make my fingers grip. "Believe in yourself," I muttered, looking at the shallow depressions that had been roughly carved into the tree trunk, each two or three handspans above the last. In the curious light on this side of the oak, it was hard to make them out clearly. I must hope I could get up and down before it was too dark to see at all.

I set down my bag and the blanket. I took time to get the flask out of my pouch, remove the stopper, drink a mouthful, put it safely back. With the fire of that draft warming my body, I looked up again.

Finbar was right. On this side the trunk sloped away from me as it rose. If I leaned in as I climbed, perhaps my upper body and outstretched arms might help stop me from falling. I could not use my arms to pull myself up; my legs must do that job on their own. It was a ridiculous thing to attempt; something I would never have dreamed of suggesting to anyone else.

"Finbar, are you quite sure this is the only way?" I shouted.

"I can't get out on my own." His voice was like an old person's, weary, resigned. Perhaps he believed I would not try this, that I would leave him in the tree and walk away.

"All right, I'm coming up," I called. "I might be a bit slow."

It was a scrabbling, painful, gut-churning climb. Each step was a risky heave, my weight all on my legs, my arms hugging the bole as I pushed myself higher. Each step sent cramping pain through my stomach and thighs. The bark grazed my face and tore my shirt. My wet shoes kept slipping. *Concentrate, Maeve. You can do this. You must do it.*

My feet caught in the hem of my skirt, sending my heart into my throat. I teetered, then steadied, using all my strength to lean forward against the trunk. For a moment I let myself rest, drawing a few deep breaths, thinking perhaps I was halfway up, reminding myself that coming down had to be easier. At least the dogs were keeping quiet now. I did not look down.

"Good climbing, Maeve!" Finbar's voice came from above me. "You're nearly there!"

That gave me new resolve, and I pushed myself upward again, body pressed against the bark, arms as far around the bole as I could stretch, legs doing the hard work. I would have a few bruises in the morning. *Let me not fall,* I prayed to whoever might be listening. *Let me get him out safely.* From up here, a fall would do a lot of damage. My thoughts ran to what would happen if I were knocked unconscious, or broke a limb, or worse. Unthinkable. *Keep going, Maeve. Hold on.*

Three labored steps, four . . . Something stabbed into my right arm. I let out a gasp of pain; my eyes filled with tears.

"Maeve! What's wrong?"

"I'm fine, Finbar." A jagged splinter, lodged deep in the flesh. The pain was severe; it made me feel sick. "Just a splinter; nothing to worry about. I'm coming on up now."

In truth, I had not thought I could do it, but eventually I teetered on the highest foothold and got my elbows onto the rim of the hollow. Finbar, crouched on the edge like a little tree creature, held on to my upper arms and hauled, and I managed to wriggle up. I collapsed on the floor of his refuge, breathing hard. Asking even one question felt beyond me.

"I thought you weren't coming." I lifted my head to look at my brother. He was snow-pale, his eyes as solemn as if he were at a graveside.

"You look . . ." He hesitated, eyeing me with a certain wariness. "You look different. There's blood on your face."

"I'm not hurt. A few scrapes and bruises, that's all." I did not mention the raw meat supper, or the throbbing pain in my arm. The splinter could wait until we were somewhere safe, with clean water and good light. "Finbar, we must climb straight back down and head for home."

"It's nearly nighttime." He spoke with perfect calm. "Where will we sleep?"

"We'll find somewhere. I've been sleeping wherever I could. The dogs are down there; you must have seen them. Bear kept me warm, and then we found Badger. You can tell me what happened to you later. Let's get out of here now, before it's too dark to climb down safely." The hollow was big; it could have housed an army of squirrels. There were odd carvings on the wood, almost like the ones I had seen in the valley of the stones, only curlier, more elaborate, halfway between letters and drawings. A man with wings; a frog with a human face; a thing like a cocoon . . . Oh, no, I would not look. It would make good sense to stay up here for the night, since the place was sheltered and dry, but there was a strangeness about it that filled me with unease. I could not wait to get out.

"We should take some of the nuts," Finbar said, and I saw that to one side of the hollow there was a store of them, not only acorns but also hazelnuts, glossy chestnuts, though it was early in the season for those, and walnuts in their wrinkled cases. A fair few empty shells, too; Finbar had perhaps been using the heel of his shoe to crack them. In a corner was a little waterskin. I was sure my brother had not had this with him when he went out to talk to Pearl. Odd, how long ago that seemed now.

"That's a good idea," I said. My belly had ceased churning in terror and was telling me how fine a meal of nuts would be, especially once I got out of this place and could hunker down somewhere with my brother and the dogs. "This looks like a squirrel's hoard; I suppose they're safe to eat. Put some in my pouch and I'll try not to drop them on the way down. Be quick."

As he scooped up the nuts, I asked the one question that needed to be spoken now. "Finbar, did someone bring you here? Is there someone else about?"

He hesitated just long enough to set dread in my heart. Then he said, "I don't think so."

"You don't think so? How could you not know such a thing?" It came out shrill and edgy; I tried for a calmer tone. "I mean, that seems rather odd. Did you really walk all this way by yourself? Did you follow Swift?" Oh, Swift.

"Swift jumped over the wall and ran. I ran after him. Badger came with me."

"Why didn't you fetch me? You should have waited for me."

"I called out. But I couldn't wait. Swift would have been gone."

A weighty silence then. I held back the obvious response.

"He was following something. Swift, I mean. He wasn't scared, more . . . excited. After a while I lost him, and then I lost Badger. I couldn't find the way home. But I found this waterskin and I found the tree. When I first got here I saw a light; that's how I knew there was a shelter. Maeve . . . I don't want to stay here. There are . . . things."

"Things?" I looked more closely at the delicate film that covered that other opening; I followed my brother's gaze upward to see that the roof of the hollow was festooned with gossamer curtains, looped and swagged in an elaborate pattern. Here and there they dipped down to a point, and at each of those points a small, dark object hung, swathed in silver-gray filaments. Not so small as bees or flies or moths. More the size of birds or bats or squirrels.

"Don't look up there," Finbar whispered. "She doesn't like it. Can we go home now, Maeve?"

But I had looked, and I had seen the patch of darkness crouched high in a corner, and the glitter of many little eyes. A presence. A scuttling, dangerous presence. Big. Very big.

"Let's get down now." Finbar's voice was firm, precise. His words sounded almost like a command.

"All right." I attempted breezy confidence, though my heart was thumping. I had never been especially fond of spiders, even little ones. "Bear and Badger will be wondering where I've got to." They were remarkably quiet, considering their earlier excitement. What were they doing? "I'll go first. I wouldn't want to slip and land on you. I may be quite slow."

"That's all right, Maeve."

It was then that the barking erupted below, both Bear's and Badger's voices suddenly at full pitch, warning of calamity. My heart jolted. I looked down through the web-covered opening, but I could see nothing of them. "Bear!" I shouted. "Badger! What's wrong?"

Barking, snarling, scuffling; the sound of a fight. Wolves?

"There's someone there." Finbar was beside me, looking down through the filmy curtain. "The gray-cloak people. They're trying to put ropes around the dogs' necks. I think Bear bit someone."

I was already sliding out the opening on the other side, on my belly, searching for the footholds. There was no time to be scared of falling. I slipped and slithered down the tree, hardly stopping to see if Finbar was coming after me. I heard a thud, a yelp, a high-pitched sound of pain and fear. A snarl, a snap, an oath.

"Leave my dogs alone!" I screamed. "Bear! Badger!"

My feet touched the ground. Finbar scrambled down beside me. We raced around to the other side of the tree.

Nothing. All was silence. Nobody was there.

"*Bear!*" I shrieked.

Finbar touched my arm, speaking quietly. "They're over there, moving away under the trees. See where I'm pointing?"

I couldn't see a thing. The forest around us was all gray shadows. "Where?"

"One man's carrying something," Finbar said. "A bundle maybe. It could be a dog. And two of the others have something between them in a cloak or blanket."

"Bring them back!" I shouted into the deepening darkness. "Bring my dogs back here! How dare you take them!"

"I can't see them anymore," Finbar said.

A sound of rage and frustration burst from me, a wild, guttural growl such as I had not believed I was capable of making. I sank down to a crouch, crossing my arms over my face. There was no way we could follow them with night falling. We would quickly lose them, and likely lose ourselves.

"Maeve." The little voice was calm as before; my brother put his hand on my bowed shoulders. "It's nearly dark. We should look for a place to sleep."

I couldn't find any words. I couldn't make myself straighten up, take decisions, be grown-up and capable. *Bear. Oh, Bear.*

"If we shelter near the tree," Finbar said, "we can go after them first thing in the morning. I can remember which way they went."

As a plan it had many flaws, but through my distress I recognized that a plan was hope, and that hope was something we could not do without. I made myself get to my feet. I scooped up Caisin's blanket, which still lay on the ground beneath the oak. Although the light was almost gone, I could see the earth was disturbed all around us, a sign of the heroic fight my boys had put up before they were taken. Oh, let them not be hurt. Let them be still alive.

Be strong, I willed them. And I wanted to say, *We'll find you,* but that would be a lie. Whatever Finbar might think, I knew that my first task in the morning must be to get him home. If that broke my heart, the more fool me for letting Bear and Badger inside a door that had been so long locked against love.

One thing my brother could always do and that was surprise me. He was the one who found a place for us, under a network of prickly, half-dead bushes. It was hardly comfortable, but it was dryish, well protected from the wind, and big enough for the two of us to squeeze into. Finbar spread out Caisin's blanket, we sat down on it, and my brother draped my cloak around our shoulders. He passed me his waterskin; I took a mouthful and realized to my surprise that it was almost full. After a while I tipped out the store of nuts we had brought, and Finbar cracked some open between two stones.

It was a long while since I'd had a good meal, but I felt so sick and sad that I was hard put to take a single bite. I made myself chew and swallow my share, knowing I needed the strength to go on. When the meal was finished, all I wanted to do was curl up in a ball and cry myself to sleep. But there were questions that must be asked. Where best to start? I did not want him to close off from me, as he had done before when it did not suit him to answer.

"Finbar?"

"Mm?"

"Who are the gray-cloak people? You spoke as if you've seen them before."

"I see them sometimes. They live in the forest. I don't know who they are."

"Are they—" I stopped myself from asking straight out whether he thought they were fey or human. If they were Mac Dara's people we were in deep trouble. "Finbar, why would they take Bear and Badger? What possible reason would anyone have to hurt them?" I must remember that he was only seven; his manner made it easy to lose sight of that. He was neither sage nor hero, but a little boy, and he must be tired, hungry and scared, for all his preternatural calm. "Never mind that," I said. "Finbar, did you cross a bridge to get here?" Something about all this did not add up. He couldn't have walked so far, or found the spider tree on his own. And what was that about there being a light to show him the way up?

"What kind of bridge?" Finbar asked. It was too dark now for me to see his expression, but his voice sounded cautious, as if he were judging how much was safe to tell me.

"A long one made of withies, with nothing to hold on to," I said. "Bear and I crossed it. We hadn't seen Badger since he left the nemetons with you, but much later, after Bear and I had traveled a long way on foot, we found him again. He couldn't have swum over the river; it was broad and swift flowing. But he wouldn't have used the bridge. He's terrified of bridges."

After a brief silence, Finbar's voice came to me in the darkness, solemn, weighty for all its childish note. "There's more than one bridge, Maeve. There's more than one way in and out."

Those words were the small, cold claws of something deeply unwelcome, something perilous. I shrank from them even as I made myself ask, "In and out of where?"

"Here," said Finbar. "The Otherworld."

My jaw dropped. *"What?"*

"The Otherworld. Didn't you know that was where we were?"

"What are you saying? That we are already over that margin, that we left our own world when we crossed that river? Why didn't you tell me before? We've been eating these nuts and drinking the water! I ate mushrooms. I ate—"

"It's all right, Maeve." Finbar's hand came out to rest against my sleeve. "I've eaten things here before and it didn't do me any harm."

"You what?" Horror upon horror. Unless he meant when he was a tiny baby. But I thought the story was that Mac Dara had found him a human wet nurse.

Finbar did not reply. He realized, perhaps, that this was one of the things he was not supposed to say.

"Finbar, look at me."

Perhaps he turned his head; it was too dark to be sure.

"I know you wouldn't lie to me. If you say we're in the Otherworld, I have to believe it. We've lost Bear and Badger, and Swift, too, and we need to get home safely. You must answer my questions. Never mind if someone said you shouldn't talk about this, or about your visions, or about anything at all. Whoever that someone was, he probably didn't foresee that we'd get into this sort of situation. Have you really been here before? I mean, apart from that time when you were a baby?"

"I'm not supposed to tell." It was scarcely more than a whisper. "It's dangerous. You don't understand."

I drew a slow breath. I would be calm. "Dangerous for whom? Or can't you tell me that, either?"

"Everyone," he said simply. "You shouldn't ask me."

"All right, I'll ask a different question. You said a light guided you, showed you the oak tree with the hollow. And you slept there last night. What about the night before? Where were you? Was Badger still with you then?"

"That's three questions."

"I'm hoping you'll answer all of them. Finbar, someone's playing games with us. Someone lured us here. If you know who it was, or if your story can give us any clues, that could be very, very helpful." After a moment's silence, I added, "I have something to tell you, too. I met a woman of the Fair Folk, the first night I spent out here. She gave me this cloak and this blanket, as well as some food and drink. She said it was safe to eat; that I wasn't over the border. And maybe that was true, because Bear and I didn't cross the bridge until the second day."

"Oh." My brother spoke in a tone of complete surprise. "But—"

"But what?"

"But I've only been here one day and one night. I ran after Swift, and Badger came with me. We ran and ran, but Swift was too fast and he went out of sight. We got to the place where I—we came to a little wooden bridge over a stream, and I went over it but Badger splashed across in the water. We walked through the oak forest. Later on, we heard barking—I thought it was Bear—and Badger ran off and didn't come back. I kept walking, and I saw a light in the distance, and when I reached it there was the big tree. I climbed up and found the nuts and the waterskin. I ate and drank and then I went to sleep. I woke up when I heard Bear and Badger barking, and then I saw you."

It was a curiously simple account. "But, Finbar," I protested,

"I've spent two nights sleeping rough; this is the third. I've walked for two days, not counting that first day when Swift ran away. It doesn't add up." *He sleeps as the squirrel sleeps.* "Maybe you were asleep for longer than you thought. Two nights and the whole day in between. And most of today as well." The thought made my skin prickle. On the other hand, sleeping in the tree, he'd been safe from the unwelcome attentions of the gray-cloak people, whoever they were, not to speak of predators such as wolves. Perhaps whoever had put him there was a friend. I thought of Caisin Silverhair's face, uncannily perfect, and those limpid eyes that seemed incapable of guile.

"Finbar."

Silence.

"Why did you say you couldn't get down from the oak tree by yourself? Why did you make me climb up to get you?"

"I'm not supposed to—"

"Finbar, *tell me*." I struggled to hold on to my temper.

A silence. Then he said, "Luachan says I shouldn't talk about what I see in the water or in the fire. He says I get mixed up. I might tell you something was going to happen, and you'd be scared, and it would only be a story." Another silence. "But sometimes it isn't a story, it's true. It was like that with the tree. In the water, I saw myself sleeping up there. I knew I had to stay until you came and got me down, because that's the way it was in the vision. The way things were meant to happen."

He still wasn't telling me the full truth; I was sure of it. "I don't understand," I said. "You say this is how things are meant to happen. But if I hadn't been up in the tree, Bear and Badger wouldn't have been taken, and . . ." I made myself stop, just a little too late.

"I'm sorry." Finbar's voice was small and shaky.

"It wasn't your fault," I said. "If Bear and Badger couldn't fight them off, I don't suppose I could have. Finbar, what Luachan says about visions—that's reasonable, I suppose, since you're still young. But if you see something that frightens you, something that makes you worried about the future, you shouldn't keep it to yourself. Staying silent isn't always the right thing to do." It could be perilous, with Mac Dara playing his evil games. But I did not say that aloud. "Luachan is your tutor, so I suppose you must follow his rules. But sometimes it seems as if you have another set of rules to follow, rules that nobody else knows about. If you would tell me about those, it might help us get safely home."

"It's all rules, Maeve." Finbar edged out from under my cloak and lay down on the blanket as if ready for sleep. "Don't go beyond the nemetons; always sit beside Luachan at supper. Don't go out riding without Father. Stay in sight of the keep." He waited a little, then added, "That's one of the things I like about you. You don't care about rules."

"And look where it's got me." He still hadn't provided an explanation. But I thought that if I pushed any further I would make him cry. And most likely he still wouldn't tell me what I needed to know. "I think I'm a bad example," I said, lying down next to him and doing my best to pull the cloak over the two of us. "I'm sure you never broke rules before you met me. But when Swift ran off, you did exactly what I would have done."

"No, Maeve." In the darkness, Finbar's voice was a forlorn thread of sound. "If you'd done it, you would have caught Swift by now, and you'd be safely home with him, and Bear and Badger, too. You're brave enough to stand up to anyone."

I turned on my side and put my arm over him. "I've been well taught," I said. "But you're brave, too, Finbar. Only a very brave boy would have done what you did. And tomorrow we're going to be brave together."

I waited until he was asleep before I let myself cry again. I wept bitter tears for Bear and Badger, and for the errors I had made, and for the sorrows Mac Dara had laid on my family and Cruinn's. But especially I wept for Bear: for the warm body that should have lain beside mine; for his shining, hopeful eyes; for the love and friendship he had shown me every step of the way. What human comrade could ever be so loyal? What man could ever love me the way Bear did? It did not matter to Bear if I was ugly or beautiful, scarred or perfect, uncouth or demure. He loved me exactly as I was. He loved as only a dog can love, with heart and soul, without reservations. As Bounder had loved me. But this felt different, because I was not a child anymore, and I understood how rare it was and how precious. I knew the value of what I had lost and I mourned for it.

The cold and my sorrow kept me awake, though I snuggled close to Finbar, hoping that between the blanket, the cloak and me, he would be warm enough. My mind went around in circles, trying to make sense of what little he had told me, trying to work out why Mac Dara might want the two of us in the Otherworld and why Caisin Silverhair had given me the instructions that led me to Finbar, without warning me that those same instructions would carry me over the border into Mac Dara's realm. I could not get past the fact that she'd known where he was but had not taken the simple—for her, surely it was simple—step of bringing him home.

In the middle of the night, when I was drifting uneasily between sleep and restless half-slumber, I looked up through the network of thorny branches that sheltered us and saw lights in the sky. An eerie music sounded, like hundreds of tiny bells. I was gripped by an uncomfortable sensation, as if the points of many needles were gently brushing my skin. The lights brightened, their hue now the green of the deepest forest, now the blue of the broadest lake, now the red of a sunrise yet to come. I edged toward the opening of our makeshift shelter, gazing up into a dark, soft sky in which, here and there, a star peeped down between the clouds. The moon was a dim glow behind the veil. The forest lay still around me.

The music grew louder. I could hear a harp and a flute over the tinkling bells, and strange, high singing. The lights drew closer, coming from somewhere under the oaks, perhaps the direction in which the dogs had been taken, but perhaps not. I crouched there frozen, torn between curiosity and caution. Were these the gray-cloak people Finbar had spoken of? Might they be bringing Bear and Badger back? Or had they returned for me and my brother? It was hard to stay under cover and see out at the same time. Should I wake Finbar? Maybe we should run before they came close enough to spot us.

I was not quite sure what I expected to see, but I had heard many old tales in which the Fair Folk moved in formal cavalcade across the land or through the sky by night. Sometimes they had human captives riding along with them . . . There was a tale of a girl who had run out and seized her beloved, and held on as he changed from man to bear to snake to fire-breathing dragon, until at last the fey queen released him from her service. But didn't those rides always happen at full moon? Tonight, clouds veiled a moon that was still waxing.

I listened for hoofbeats, wondering whether the gray-cloak people were behind Swift's disappearance. An uncanny woman like Caisin Silverhair would look very fine riding such a horse—he would match her long locks perfectly. She'd have a hard job training him to the saddle. I prayed that they were treating him kindly. Perhaps the Fair Folk used magic to discipline their creatures. *Bear. Badger. My brave boys.*

Perhaps I really should wake Finbar. It did seem he knew more about this place and its rules than I did, perhaps because he'd had a druid as a tutor. Or maybe something had rubbed off on him during that time as an infant in Mac Dara's hall. But he was sound asleep, peaceful under the cloak. I would wait.

The riders emerged from beneath the trees, a long double line of them, not in gray cloaks, but in glittering, shimmering raiment of gold and silver, in deepest purple and sky blue and emerald, in rose red and oak brown and sunny buttercup yellow. Some bore lanterns; it was the light from these I had seen earlier. It was curiously changeable in color, as if responding to the mood of the party, or perhaps to the music, in which harp, flute and bells had now been joined by the compelling beat of a drum. Filthy, unkempt and heartsick as I was, I felt a tingling in my body, an itching in my feet, and with them a ridiculous urge to run out into the open and dance. The music was a drug; it was as dangerous as those fungi Aunt Liadan had warned me about. I must stay where

I was, in the protection of the thornbushes with my brother sleeping by my side. But despite my better judgment, I edged forward.

The riders were so close now that I could see the silver clasps and ornaments on their horses' harness; I could see the jewels in the ladies hair, formed into the shapes of glinting beetles, iridescent butterflies, brilliant bees. The men were equally dazzling, adorned with golden armlets, glittering bracelets, finger rings studded with gems as big as pigeons' eggs. The folk themselves were uniformly tall. All were beautiful, their faces perfectly proportioned, their skin translucent and without blemish, their eyes lustrous and their hair falling in glossy waves or piled high in elaborate confections of ribbons and gauze and feathers. One lady had a bird nestled in her auburn tresses, as if in a nest; I thought it a toy until it opened its beak and let out an elaborate cascade of song.

I saw a woman who might be Caisin, but she was wearing a hood, and without that waterfall of silver hair I could not be sure of her identity. The women's faces were as alike as those of sisters. Shivering, I tried to pick out Mac Dara; but with no real idea of him, I could not. Was he a man whose features showed instantly the evil at his heart? Or could he put on the semblance of goodness as easily as he might don a hat or a pair of shoes?

A sleek-haired woman had a dog before her on the saddle, a slender white hound in a jeweled harness. Its eyes were bright, but there was something in its demeanor that troubled me. It was not natural, surely, for a creature to stare fixedly ahead like that, as if it hardly saw the whirl of activity around it. Was it deaf to the music and the voices? It perched there perfectly still. Not once did it turn its head, look up at its mistress, shift its pose. But, like the bird, this was no toy; I saw it blinking, breathing. I felt a sudden urge to gather the little dog to me, to pet and soothe it, to gentle it back to itself. Foolish. I knew nothing of these folk or of their creatures.

They would soon ride by and be gone; I might never again see such a sight. I might never again hear the music that tugged me forward, filling my body with the crazy desire to dance. Me.

Maeve Claw-Hands. Out there among those perfect people, making a complete fool of myself.

The riders did not pass me by, but halted not far from my bolt-hole, their mounts drawn into a circle. Or almost a circle, for on the side nearest to me there was a gap that seemed perfectly arranged to give me a clear view to the open ground in the middle of their group. The music grew louder, the drumbeat more insistent. If the instruments could have spoken, they would have been calling, *Come out, Maeve! Come out and join us! Forget your sadness and dance!*

I did not move. Someone had stolen my horse and my dogs. Someone had led my brother astray. Someone had tricked me into stepping over the border into the Otherworld and eating what grew here. Someone had made my brother sleep for longer than any human child should sleep at a stretch. In this situation, I had no doubt Uncle Bran would advise caution. *Stay under cover. Observe. Hold your silence.*

And yet . . . and yet . . . Oh, gods, what was this? I was as still as stone, as quiet as a mouse; I could feel the sleeping form of Finbar right beside me. But at the same time, I saw myself out there, in the middle of that circle of magnificent folk on their stately horses, the object of all eyes as I danced. One foot forward, the other foot forward, turning, prancing, arms up over my head, hands moving with fluid grace . . . A perfect Maeve. No claw fingers there, no disfigured face, for the dancing Maeve was lovely as a wildflower, her pale skin lightly freckled, her fiery curls rippling down over her shoulders, her green eyes bright with pleasure as she followed the heart-quickening beat of the drum. In my hiding place, I wrapped my arms across my chest, clenching my jaw tight to keep myself quiet. I watched her. I watched the lovely vision of myself. She was not clad in the filthy, tattered remnant of a gown that I had worn for the last three days and nights, nor the evil-smelling, damp shoes I had not dared remove. Dancing Maeve was in a gown the color of moonlight, of lilies, of snowdrops. She wore a simple ornament on a chain around her neck; I could not see it clearly, only the sparkle of it as she turned in the light of the fey lanterns.

Now there was a man dancing with her. With me. His hand in mine; his every movement a complement to mine, so that we seemed like two parts of the same being. He was a big man, well built, broad shouldered and tall. Dark haired. Somehow, whichever way he turned, I could never quite see his face. And yet he looked familiar. He looked like someone I should know. The flute soared like a lark; the shimmer of the bells was a waterfall in springtime. The drum beat heart-deep. The singing was over; around the circle, the watchers were silent now, their lovely countenances grave as they observed the dancers. Why couldn't I see the man's face? Who was he? And who was that other Maeve, the one who looked as I might have done if the past had been different? Why would I be shown this?

The music reached a peak and fell to a quiet ending. Flute, bells and drum whispered into silence. Graceful Maeve rose on tiptoes to give her partner a little kiss on the cheek, and I saw the sweet tenderness on her face as she looked at him. *You will not cry*, I told myself. *This is false. It's fey magic. You've known since you were a chid that you couldn't have this. Shut your eyes. Don't look at these lies.*

But I did look. I kept on looking as the horses moved again, and as the uncanny procession re-formed, and as the Fair Folk lifted their lanterns high and rode off under the trees. I kept on looking, hoping I might glimpse the face of that man at whom Graceful Maeve had looked with her eyes soft with love. But both he and she were lost in the group, and if they mounted horses and rode off with the others, I did not see them.

After that I did not sleep, but lay awake staring up at the sky, where stars winked in and out of view between the shifting clouds. I did not weep; I had shed my tears earlier, for the loss of Bear and Badger and for the errors I had made, and now what I felt was a slow-burning anger. Why show me that? Why torment me? I had done nothing to harm these folk, nothing at all beyond stepping over their border uninvited, and I'd had good reason for that. Besides, Caisin herself had bid me do just that when she sent me after Finbar. None of it made sense. I watched the sky gradually lighten, and worked on various theories, including the notion that

Caisin had not been among the folk I had seen tonight, but that perhaps Mac Dara had sent them. Caisin had not seemed inimical; indeed she had been both courteous and helpful, if more detached than a human woman might have been in the circumstances. And if the old tales taught us anything, it was that the Tuatha De did not think or act like humankind. Might Mac Dara find it amusing to tease me with visions of a perfect self?

As the dawn edged closer and the first birds began their tentative chirping out in the oak forest, I fought through the numbing grief of losing the dogs and made myself plan the day as Bran would. The goal. Get over that wretched bridge and back onto Sevenwaters land before nightfall. Reaching home would be a two-day journey. The equipment. What we had was limited, but useful: the waterskin, the remains of Caisin's cordial, some nuts, the cloak, the blanket, which Finbar could carry. The nuts would be adequate to get us through one day, and as we'd already eaten some, it would make no difference if we consumed the rest. I would not touch any other food we found and I'd make sure Finbar didn't, either. Once over the bridge, we could forage safely. At least we were unhurt, though I was tired and sore, and there was a wrenching feeling in my stomach, as if leaving Bear and Badger behind might cut me in two. But I had to get Finbar home. I had to put that first. *They're only dogs*, a little voice whispered in my mind, and sudden, furious tears came to my eyes, but I did not let them fall.

There was one thing I had not allowed for in my planning: that Finbar might have other ideas.

"We can't go home," he said as we ate our breakfast of a few nuts washed down with a mouthful of water. "You wouldn't go away and leave Bear and Badger here, Maeve. And what about Swift?"

"Mother and Father would expect me to take you straight home. That is the right thing to do." It was painful to get the words out.

"Right for them, maybe. But not right for you. You can't leave Bear behind." He spoke simply, knowing exactly what this meant to me. When I was ten I had risked death trying to save Bounder from the fire. I had done so without a second thought. Had ten more years of growing up turned me into a coward?

"I don't want to talk about it," I said. "My plan is that we head straight for home. It's the only sensible choice."

After a moment, Finbar said, "Can I tell you my plan?"

"You can tell me while we walk. I want you over that bridge to-day." I rose to my feet. Beyond our shelter the day was brightening and the solitary chirps and cheeps had become a chorus to the sun.

"Which bridge?"

"Any bridge that leads home. The withy bridge I came over, or the one you used, if you can find it. Yours does sound much easier."

"Maeve."

I sighed and sat down again. "All right, tell me."

"We need to follow Bear and Badger. I saw them go; I can find the way. It's still early. We can rescue them and get to the bridge before dark."

Oh, yes, yes! cried Wild Maeve. I closed my ears to her. "That's not a very good plan, Finbar," I said. "For all sorts of reasons." Reasons I had no intention of discussing with him, lest I frighten him out of his wits.

"But it's the right plan. We came here to find Swift. And now Bear and Badger have been taken, we need to find them, too. Going home now is giving up the mission. You're brave. You'd never give up a mission." There was something in his young face that terrified me: a naked longing to be proven right, and not to have me turn out to be less than he'd believed.

I cleared my throat, searching for good words and finding none. "The mission has changed. My first job must be to make sure you get home safely. You're my brother; you're our parents' only son. And you're a boy. Bear and Badger are dogs." I could not bring myself to say *only dogs*. "They will look after themselves."

"They didn't last time. When you found them they were half-starved and scared to death."

"They are strong now." Stronger, yes. But how easily they might be tipped back into that nightmare. "Finbar, if I'd come down to the field and found Swift gone and you still there, I wouldn't have run after him. I would have gone for help. Fetched Father, or Emrys, or Luachan. I only came here because of you. Because I needed to make sure you were safe."

Finbar sat silent, hunched over, staring at his hands.

"That is the truth. It's the way things are. I'm not giving up on my mission. Of course I want to go after Bear and Badger. I want to so much it hurts. But I can't. I'm not being weak. I'm trying to be strong."

"That means it's my fault." His voice had lost all its assurance; it was small and forlorn. "My fault you're here; my fault you can't rescue the dogs. My fault Swift is lost."

"Hardly." I put my arm around him. "Swift chose to bolt. That's nobody's fault, unless you want to blame Emrys or me for not training him better. As for Bear and Badger, they made their own choices. Come on, we need to move."

"I think we're meant to follow them."

I felt the hairs on my neck stand up. "What was that?"

"I think, if we don't follow them, everything will come out wrong."

Now he was really worrying me. "What do you mean?"

"It's like that story, the one about the valley being flooded because everyone forgot a geis. They did the wrong thing, and it all went bad until Finn and Baine were brave enough to break the rules and put it right."

"This isn't the wrong thing. It makes perfect sense for us to go home. If we follow the dogs we could both get hurt and we still might not find them. And there's something else, something you might not have thought of."

Finbar turned his big eyes on me.

"I'm not especially good at looking after myself out here. I can't even put my shoes on without help. I'm certainly not the best person to look after you or execute a rescue mission."

"You said you came to find me. So it *is* a rescue mission."

Against the odds, I felt a smile creep onto my lips. "Then help me finish it well, Finbar. We must go home. There is no geis on you, or on me, or on Bear or Badger or Swift, unless it exists completely unknown to any of us, and if that's the case, I don't see how it makes any difference to our decisions. Mother will be distraught with worry. Father has Cruinn and his war band rampaging all over the forest hunting for the missing men. You and I are faced with a very simple choice and, because I'm older, I'm making it for us. We're going home, and you're not going to spend the whole day telling me I'm wrong."

My brother got up, and when I, too, had risen, he folded the blanket precisely and put it under his arm, while I struggled into the cloak. I put Caisin's flask in my pouch; Finbar picked up the waterskin. He said not a word, but his mouth was set tight and his eyes were full of trouble. We crept out of our hiding place and set our steps toward home.

DRUID'S JOURNEY: SOUTH

He follows a winding pathway through birch woods, his sandaled feet soft on the damp earth. Fox and badger watch him pass. His progress is the subject of ravens' gossip; larks sing his journey into the morning sky. As the wintry sun reaches its peak the druid sees the elms ahead, and the cottage tucked against a little rise, with a neat garden of winter vegetables to one side. There is the well, as he expected, and there is a young woman drawing up water. A creature is crouched in the long grass by her feet. A big cat or a terrier, he thinks as he approaches, and then, no: a hare. It lifts its long ears, examines the visitor with mild eyes. The woman hefts the bucket to her shoulder and turns to face him.

"My respects to you, wise woman."

She gives him a thorough look up and down. Her features are handsome, her body strong; her clothing is that of a hardworking country wife. Her eyes are a curious shade, neither quite green nor gold nor brown, and their gaze goes deep. "And to you, druid. I'm about to make a brew; I have good herbs for weary travelers. Will you come in awhile?"

"Thank you. I have some honey cakes to share. And I would speak with you."

Inside, she busies herself with the brew while he brings out his supplies and sets them on the table. The hare retreats to a basket, from which it watches him unblinking.

"I'd be surprised by any visitor who did not want to speak," the woman observes after a long silence. "Mostly, it's talk they want, with the brew coming second."

"I'll take what you have to give. I'm come from your sisters in the north and the east, and I seek your share of a rhyme. I expect you know which one it is."

"Ah," is all she says.

While she is chopping her herbs, watching the pot, fetching the cups, the druid takes the bucket and goes back out to the well, drawing more water to save her the trouble later. Under a gnarled apple tree he spots some windfalls and collects the least damaged. Back indoors, he cuts an apple into neat slices and offers it to the hare, piece by piece. The creature eats with some delicacy, as if doing the giver a favor with its acceptance.

"Well, then," the wise woman says when they are seated at the table enjoying their meal, and the hare has settled to rest in its basket—its eyes are still open to slits; it will not relax until the stranger is gone. "This rhyme. A geis, yes? And not pronounced over you, but another. That was many, many years ago. What makes you believe this is the time for it?"

The druid wraps his fingers around his cup as if to warm them. "A change in the manner of things. An urgency about his deeds, as if he sensed time running out. It seemed to me . . ." He hesitates. "It seemed he might have seen something, heard something to suggest the conditions of a geis would soon be met. Perhaps he saw his own death coming."

"What would he do then? Try to prevent those conditions from coming about? A geis is a geis. Sooner or later, it will be fulfilled. He is a prince of the Otherworld. He knows this."

The druid frowns. "He might strive to ensure his chosen successor was ready to take his place."

She ponders this awhile. "That much I understand, for he has long desired to entice this precious son of his back to his side for just that purpose. What I do not understand is how your knowledge of this rhyme can make a jot of difference. That which the geis has set down will in its own time come to pass. You cannot halt it. You cannot change it. You might perhaps delay it, as he no doubt has attempted to do, but what would be the purpose in that?"

There is a darkness in the druid's face, a shadow in his eyes. "Change is coming," he says. "Great change. You are right. I have no power to prevent it. But with the right knowledge, I can alter the manner of that change. My blood demands it of me. My training sets the tools in my hands. I am the son of a fey mother. And I am a son of Sevenwaters, with a bone-deep loyalty to clan, kin and hearthstone. How can I not act?"

She looks at him long. "There's a heavy price to be paid," she says.

"I have paid heavier and lived with the burden."

A silence then. After a while she says, "My share of the knowledge you seek is this: *Evil's defeat demands the price of a brother's sacrifice. As the age begins to turn, that is when the oak will burn.* This would come at the end of the rhyme, I believe, since it deals with the demise of a certain person. As for brothers, I cannot imagine what brothers they mean. Lord Sean has only one son. And you walk alone. I see you no longer have that raven who used to shadow your every move."

The druid gives her one of his rare smiles. "He moved on to warmer climes." His meal finished, he rises to his feet. "I thank you for your hospitality and for your wisdom."

"And you know, I imagine, that the rhyme is yet incomplete. If you would have the last piece in your puzzle you must seek out my sister the storyteller, who lives in the west. You must come full circle. Make haste, for a long journey still lies before you."

"I will." He bows his head to her, then turns and makes the same courtesy to the hare. It observes him through its slitted eyes.

The wise woman walks to the door with her visitor. She stands watching as he slings his bag over his shoulder and heads off up the path.

"A long journey," she says again.

He turns; waits.

"But not such a lonely one, I think," she adds, and her tone holds affection and sorrow and a farewell that stretches long into the future. "Our brother is close by and looking for you."

The druid becomes very still. This, he has not expected. This is both gift and peril, the key to the mission and its possible undoing.

"You will find him five miles to the northwest, close to a circle of stones," says the woman. "By dusk today you should be close to that place. He will be ready to meet you." A long pause. "I wish you well, druid. You have great courage."

"You think?" He smiles again, turns away, is gone.

"Make haste," she whispers to the empty space. "Make haste, brave soul, for the dark is coming."

CHAPTER 11

Finbar, keep up!"

We'd been walking a long time. We were both tired, and our pace had slowed as the morning passed. But Finbar was dawdling. He kept stopping to gaze along the pathways between the oaks, or to look up at a sky now filled with heavy gray clouds, their bellies swelling toward a thunderstorm. Spots of rain were starting to fall. I judged it was around midday, and we were less than halfway back to the bridge.

"Finbar!"

He'd stopped again and was staring off into the distance, perhaps watching something in the trees, perhaps lost in a daydream or vision. I regretted ordering him not to complain on the way home. This snail-slow progress was my punishment.

"Come on! Can't you see it's about to pour with rain?" I failed to keep the frustration from my voice. It didn't help that my arm was throbbing; the splinter I'd picked up while climbing the spider tree had gone deep and the flesh around it had turned an angry red. I should have asked Finbar to dig it out with his little knife before it got so bad. The job would be beyond his skills now.

Besides, there was no time. "Come on! What are you looking at anyway?"

"I keep seeing them. Up in the trees. Those people, the ones all made of twigs and leaves."

Despite myself, I halted and stared into the thinning canopy of the nearest oak. The wind was moving the branches and shivering through the last clinging leaves, but I did not see anything else up there.

"I saw him," Finbar said. "That boy. The one Mac Dara left when he stole me. I'm sure it was him; he's the same size as me. He was waving to me, giving me a signal. I think he wants to tell me something."

I looked again. Dark branches clothed in tattered leaves, blood red, ochre yellow, sunset gold, all withering now, ready to admit defeat the moment the storm came. By tomorrow's dawn these forest giants would be stripped bare. "I don't see him," I said.

"He was there a moment ago. Over there, where that path goes off under the trees—there! He's coming out on that big branch, look—"

For a moment I saw the creature—a spindly, awkward being all fashioned of forest matter, a leaf here, a spray of autumn flowers there, a handful of grass, a cobweb . . . His eyes were unmatched pebbles in a face that had the general semblance of a human boy's, with the correct complement of nose, mouth, ears, in the usual arrangement. Yet he was profoundly uncanny. He waved a long, twiggy arm and Finbar waved back.

"See?" my brother said, striding with confidence toward the tree where the being was perched on a perilously high limb. "He wants to tell me something."

"Finbar, no—"

My words dried up on my lips. Over the rising wind came the sound of hoofbeats approaching, the jingle of harness, and—oh, blessed relief!—a voice that was unmistakably human calling, "Maeve! Finbar!" Luachan. Help had come at last.

In the moment before I turned I saw the twiggy boy go still, then dart back along his branch to vanish into the forest. Whether he'd had something to say to Finbar we would never know; the opportunity was lost. Then Luachan rode up on his bay mare, Blaze, swung himself gracefully down next to me and opened his arms, a look of utter relief on his face.

"Maeve! Thank all the gods! Are you all right?"

I was tempted to throw myself into his embrace; that would have felt good. I held back, though his words warmed me. "I'm fine. Tired and dirty, but otherwise unharmed. Finbar, too. But Bear and Badger are gone, and we never found Swift." I drew in an unsteady breath, telling myself I was not about to break all my own rules and collapse into tears of relief and exhaustion. "It's so good to see you, Luachan," I said shakily. "I don't know how you found us. I was told—someone said that on this side of the bridge, we're in the Otherworld."

Luachan's brows went up. "Then it's just as well I have supplies," he said with perfect calm, unfastening his saddlebag. "I imagine you're hungry. Finbar, come over here—let me look at you."

Finbar was still under the oak where the twiggy boy had perched, craning his neck in vain hope of catching another glimpse. He did not seem especially surprised by Luachan's arrival.

"He's not happy with me," I murmured. "The dogs are lost. Someone took them. He wants to find them before we go home. I told him we must head straight back to our own side of the bridge." My stomach was growling with hunger; my mouth was watering. "Who else is with you?" I asked. No other riders had come into sight. "My father? He must be desperately worried about Finbar."

"And about you," Luachan said quietly, giving me a sideways glance as he brought a cloth-wrapped package and a waterskin out of the saddlebag. "We were all worried. You can imagine what we thought. Lord Sean's out searching for you along with men from his household. And Cruinn's out, of course, with his armed band. But there'll be time enough to discuss all this when you've eaten. You, too, Finbar. You both look exhausted. Sit down awhile; rest your legs and have some of this."

Finbar must have been as hungry as I was, but that did not stop him from taking time to break up my share of the food and pass it to me piece by piece. I was relieved that Luachan did not offer to perform this task. He busied himself getting out a small bag of oats and feeding Blaze, then settled beside us.

"Why are you out here on your own?" I asked when I had taken the edge off my hunger.

Luachan cleared his throat. It was the first time I had seen him look uncomfortable. "When I raised the alarm, I expected to head out straightaway searching for you. Your father made it quite clear that my assistance was not required. His anger was not unreasonable. I had argued for the two of you to be housed at the nemetons. I had failed in my duty of protecting Finbar. So, armed riders set out, and I was not among them. I was . . . somewhat frustrated. Early on the second day I heard that the wolfhounds had lost your trail quite quickly, and that this was looking like the Disappearance all over again. So I headed out without asking for permission. It seemed to me there might be places I could search where others might not venture."

"If you had an idea of where we might be, then it's taken you a while to get here," I said. Luachan was a fit, able man, and he was on horseback. Finbar and I had our reasons to be slow. What did he mean about places where other people might not venture? Did druids make a habit of traveling to the Otherworld?

"I lost the trail." Luachan spread his hands in a gesture of helplessness. His tone was apologetic. "I didn't expect that."

"There's an oddity about the place. A changeable quality. Similar to what happens in the human part of the forest, where strangers often lose their way. It's as if the land itself doesn't want to let intruders go by." I thought of the spider tree, where each side was like a different world. "But I'd have thought that even in the Otherworld part of Sevenwaters Finbar and I would not be considered outsiders."

"It's different now Mac Dara is here," observed Finbar gravely.

I had no answer for that. "Luachan," I said, "we've had some encounters with . . . folk from here. A woman helped me, gave me food and drink and this cloak, and cryptic instructions that allowed me to find Finbar, though it took me a while. I . . . saw some folk by night, riding past. And Bear and Badger were stolen, taken by force while Finbar and I were in a tree and couldn't reach them. Finbar said it was the gray-cloak people, but he hasn't explained to me who they are." On the brink of telling him that my brother thought he had been here before, I held back the words. That confidence was Finbar's to tell, not mine.

Luachan was staring down at his linked hands. Something in his demeanor reminded me of Ciarán, a man who always seemed to have secrets, and most of them unhappy ones.

"Many folk must dwell in these parts, of course," Luachan said. "All kinds, I imagine. Some benign; some less so. The sooner we head for home, the better. Blaze can carry the two of you. I will walk alongside."

"I'll walk," I said a little too quickly. Perhaps that was stupid; I was weary to the bone. But I did not care for the prospect of sitting on a horse, holding on to my young brother for support, and being led home like an erring child. It was no way to complete a quest. "Finbar, you should ride."

I could see Finbar was about to say he, too, would walk, but he seemed to think better of it. Instead he folded up the cloth that had held the food, put the stopper back in the waterskin, then rose to his feet. "All right," he said. He'd stopped glancing toward the trees in hope of seeing the leaf and twig boy again. His manner, his tone, his posture all spoke of defeat.

"Finbar," I said, "you've done a great job this morning, walking all this way and not complaining at all. Don't think I haven't noticed. You know it hurts me to leave Bear and Badger behind. I can't put into words for you how hard it is. But there's no choice. We have to go home."

He turned his big eyes on me. They were full of sadness—not reproach, only sorrow that he had not been able to make me understand. Then Luachan boosted him into the saddle, and we moved off in a direction I judged to be roughly eastward. There were questions I might have asked, such as, *Whose trail was it you lost? Mine? Swift's? Finbar's? And if you lost it, how was it that you found us?* But now was not the time for that. We had a friend and protector and he knew the way home. I didn't have to do this on my own anymore. That made more difference than I would have believed possible. Never mind the cold and wet; never mind the paths that had a curious tendency to change their direction each time a person looked at them. If Luachan led us back the way he had come, soon enough we would be at the Sevenwaters keep. And though it was breaking my heart to leave the dogs behind, I took comfort from the thought of bringing Finbar safely home. So we walked on. Blaze went beside me, with Finbar in the saddle, and on the other side of the horse walked the tall young druid, saying little.

Time passed. Perhaps more time than I realized. Even allowing for the rain, it began to seem oddly dark for afternoon. We had been walking for a few hours, certainly, but it was too soon for the light to be fading. There should have been sufficient hours of day left for us to reach the bridge. I made no comment on the oddities of the light and nor did Luachan, but when I glanced across I saw that his mouth had a grim set to it.

The rain began to fall in relentless sheets, as if seeking to drown every wretched creature that dared move in this forest. There was a bite in the air. The sky darkened still further, as though dusk were already falling. Birds cried out all around us, a song of distress; what was this strange night that swept over the afternoon forest like a dark cloak over a gown of autumn gold?

"We'll have to camp tonight, of course," Luachan said. "Once we're over the bridge we can find a place and I'll make a fire. We won't be able to get all the way back before dark."

I had known this. All the same, I had kept myself moving by imagining my family's hearth fires, Rhian's welcoming smile, the tub of hot water awaiting my weary body; hearing the uncomfortable truth spoken aloud did not improve my mood. At the rate things were going, we might not even reach the bridge before it was too dark to find a way.

"A fire will be good," I said, glancing up at Finbar, who sat hunched on the mare. He had Luachan's cloak draped around his shoulders, the hood concealing his face. The garment was running with water. Blaze walked with her head lowered, no doubt thinking of a dry stable and a manger of food.

The chill wind rose, driving the rain into us like a scourge. Even with Caisin's cloak to shield me, I was cold. My feet were numb; I stumbled over tree roots, stones, unexpected clumps of drenched foliage. I could barely see an arm's length in front of me. My skirt was sodden. It was becoming hard to breathe.

"We'd best stop and find shelter now." Luachan was looking around into the gathering gloom.

"It's like nightfall," I said, shivering. "But it can't be night yet. Maybe when the rain stops . . ." My voice faltered and died as the last light leached abruptly away, leaving us in total darkness.

"Finbar," I said, putting out a hand to reassure myself that Blaze was still there. "Reach your hand down so I can touch you. That's it." What this was, I did not know, only that it frightened me beyond words. "Luachan, there'll be no finding shelter in this."

Finbar's hand was winter-cold against my arm.

"Put your hand on Blaze's back." Luachan spoke with commendable steadiness. "Don't let go."

The best we could do in the complete dark was to get Blaze lying down, then huddle up with our backs against her body and Caisin's blanket draped over all of us. The blanket undoubtedly possessed fey qualities, for like my borrowed cloak it imparted some warmth and kept the worst of the rain out, even in a storm like this. But it was not big enough to shelter a man, a woman, a child and a horse. Water seeped in. The wind lifted the corners, whistling in around us. Briefly, I allowed myself to remember falling asleep with my head pillowed on Bear's warm body, with his heart beating steady and sure against me.

"This storm can't last forever," Luachan said. "We must simply wait it out and then head for home."

Perhaps he thought to reassure Finbar with this statement. The storm was all very well. I had most certainly had enough of being wet and cold, but I could endure a little more of it provided I knew the next thing would be going home. But this darkness, this sudden night at a time when the sun should still be high—what could it be but a fell charm, a thing of Mac Dara's doing? He did not want us to go home. He wanted to trap us here in the Otherworld; I was becoming sure of it. I would not say so in Finbar's hearing. Tucked in between me and Luachan, with the druid's cloak wrapped around him, he was still shivering.

"I think—" I began, hardly knowing what I would say, only that Finbar could not be lied to.

"We're supposed to go back." My brother's voice, shaking with cold, was nonetheless full of certainty. "We're supposed to find the dogs. That's why it's dark and wet. It's to stop us from going home. I told you, Maeve."

A silence. "Supposed to?" asked Luachan over the roar of the downpour. I could feel water pooling underneath me. Blaze shifted against my back. "What do you mean, Finbar?"

Finbar did not reply.

"Finbar said earlier that if we went straight home this would work out badly. I insisted that we go. Finbar, you know that's what Mother and Father would expect us to do." After another silence, I said, "Finbar?"

"Did you see something in a vision, Finbar?" asked Luachan. "I've told you how easy it is to get things wrong, to misinterpret the signs."

"We have to go back." The little voice remained firm. "In the stories, if there's a chance to make things good, that's what you have to do. Father wouldn't mind. Not if he understood how important it was."

I knew nothing in the world would persuade our father that Finbar should be taken deeper into the Otherworld rather than being brought safely home.

"Well," said Luachan, "we can't go anywhere right now, since there's no seeing the way. The best we can do is try to keep warm and wait until it's light again."

If it's ever light again. I felt my spirits plummet. Endless darkness. Had Mac Dara the power to impose that on his realm? The black dragon of Finbar's story had cared nothing for the destruction he wrought in his own forest, nor for the folk he drove out or consumed in his mindless hunger. Would a creature like that be bothered with such small beings as a horse or a pair of dogs or a human brother and sister? If he'd wanted to abduct Finbar and use him as a bargaining piece, as he had long ago, he could have done it far more simply than this. I couldn't think of any reason why he would want me.

"Some mead would be good," Luachan mused. "Alas, I brought only water."

"Oh. I do have a drink—a kind of cordial—that I was given by the fey woman I mentioned. And since I've already drunk from the flask several times, I don't suppose doing so again will make any difference. She said it was safe for us. And she seemed to be a friend. If you want to risk it . . ." I maneuvered the flask from my pouch and held it out to him between my wrists. "Now seems the right time for it. It gave me heart earlier."

We all had a drink, even Finbar.

"You could call her," my brother said.

"What?"

"The fey woman. You could call her, and she might come to help us."

Dear gods, it was the white dragon again; he believed Caisin was the Lady of the Forest come back to save her people from Mac Dara.

"I'm not sure that's a good idea. We should do as Luachan says and simply wait for morning and for the storm to be over."

"I think you should call her. We might be here until we drown in rain. And Blaze is cold. Can't you feel her shivering?"

I could, and I didn't like it at all. It made me think of Swift, out in the forest somewhere running wild. It made me ache for Bear and Badger, captive among cruel strangers or worse.

"Why would Caisin Silverhair come to me if I called her? She's one of the Fair Folk. I'm nobody."

"She helped you before, didn't she?" Luachan said. "I think, on this occasion, that Finbar may be right. It is indeed cold and wet, and night has come some hours early. I don't believe it would do any harm to try."

I was not at all sure I wanted the Fair Folk to help us. Calling Caisin Silverhair felt arrogant. It felt wrong. It felt as if I were starting something that could turn dangerous. "You surprise me," I said. "Isn't it perilous to seek help from the Tuatha De? I mean, Mac Dara is one of them. We might walk right into some kind of trap."

"I weighed this up carefully before I spoke, as we are trained to do." Luachan was still calm. "In my judgment, our situation is sufficiently severe to make a call for help appropriate. This woman helped you before. Perhaps she will do so again. It would seem she has your best interests at heart."

"Calling her is what you're supposed to do," Finbar said. "Please, Maeve. You could save Bear and Badger."

"That's not fair!" I snapped, losing my precarious control. Gods, it was cold and miserable. How could I be expected to make a balanced decision with the rain trickling down my neck and filling my shoes and drenching my gown under me? Despite that mouthful of Caisin's cordial, I felt weak and hopeless. And if I felt that way even with Luachan here to help us, how must poor Bear and Badger be feeling, out there in the storm? If they still lived. "I'm sorry, Finbar." I moderated my tone. "You say, *supposed to*. How do you know? What have you seen? Isn't Luachan right to say visions can be misleading?"

After a moment, Finbar said, "Yes. And no. Please call her, Maeve. I'm cold."

That, and the shivering of Blaze at my back, decided me. "This is ridiculous," I said. "How could she possibly hear me over all this?" The rain thundered down; the oaks creaked and groaned in the whistling wind. "And what do I do—just shout *help*?"

"Of course not," said Finbar. "Call out her name. Be respectful. Like saying a prayer."

"Quite right," put in Luachan.

I slipped out from the blanket's meager protection and stood in the downpour, feeling more than a little foolish.

"Caisin Silverhair!" I yelled. "We need your help! In the name of Sevenwaters and of all that is good, please come to our aid now!" A puny voice, soon lost in the darkness. I would not call again. I crouched down and crept back in with the others.

"You're all wet," observed Finbar, edging away from me.

"Come on this side, Maeve." Luachan reached out a hand and guided me over. Now he was in the middle, with me on his right and Finbar on his left. He put his arm around my shoulders. It was not quite appropriate, but it felt remarkably good. The warmth of his body soaked into mine. Such a simple thing could not dispel the endless dark, but it gave me new courage. We waited.

It was a long time. It was so long that I became quite sure Caisin Silverhair had not heard my summons. Or if she had, she had chosen to disregard it. I could not think of a single time, in the old tales, when the Tuatha De had done the bidding of humankind.

"She'll come," Finbar murmured, as if saying it might make it happen.

"I don't mind if she doesn't," I said, "as long as we get home one way or another."

"One way or another," said Luachan, "I'm sure we will. If not by fey assistance, then by our own efforts. It must be day sometime. Once it's light, we can go on even in this rain." A shudder ran through him as if, in keeping us warm, he had grown colder.

"Are you all right?" I asked him.

"I'm fine, Maeve." There was a note in his reply that forbade further inquiries; perhaps he did not like to seem weak. "I've been out here a far shorter time than you or Finbar."

I thought of him riding in search of us. I remembered the river that must be crossed and the precarious bridge over which Bear had followed me, forcing back his terror to be with the one he loved. The river would be swollen with rain now, coursing wildly, breaking its banks. "What bridge did you use, Luachan? How did you get Blaze across?"

"I only know of one bridge." He sounded surprised. "It's—"

And then he was silent, for the rain was abating, and the darkness was relieved, at last, by a faint light. Luachan lifted up the blanket and I saw what looked like a row of small lanterns, approaching us from deep in the forest. As they drew closer, and as the rain eased from a steady fall to a pattering shower, the lights were revealed to be suspended on poles, each held by a cloaked figure. *The gray-cloak people*, I thought, my stomach churning with unease.

"I told you she would come." Finbar spoke with utter conviction.

"But what if—"

"Maeve of Sevenwaters!"

There was no doubting it now, for the melodious voice that rang out was that of Caisin Silverhair herself. Her greeting was alarmingly formal this time. I reminded myself that I was a chieftain's daughter and must respond in an appropriate manner. I struggled out of the shelter, rose to my feet and straightened my shoulders. I tried to forget that I was soaked to the skin, filthy and unkempt. She stood perhaps six paces from me. On each side of her was a woman bearing a little round lantern hanging from a kind of crook. The glow from these lights gave Caisin's perfect features a rosy tint. Her companions wore their hoods up; what I could see of their faces told me they were like the Fair Folk who had ridden past my refuge by night. Each was as lovely as a wildflower. Behind them stood others of their kind. Their cloaks were not gray but green, brown, deepest blue.

Should I wait for Caisin to speak, since she was my senior, and this was her world? No. I did not want to hear *poor child*, or *oh dear*, or any of those remarks folk tended to toss my way without thinking.

"I regret that I needed to call for your help, my lady," I said. "I would not have done so had our circumstances been less difficult. I found my brother, and I was on my way home with him and . . . a friend. We were caught by the storm and a sudden darkness came down. If you are able to shelter us until it grows light again, we will be most grateful." I hoped the tone of my speech was appropriate: neither too obsequious nor too confident. "And shelter for the horse, if that's possible," I added.

"Let me see your brother and this friend you speak of."

They were already emerging. Finbar paused to fold up the blanket before he turned to look at her. Luachan gave her a graceful bow.

"My lady."

"Ah." Caisin's brows rose. "A druid. A young, comely, well-mannered druid, right here on my doorstep. Now, that is unusual."

"Luachan is Finbar's tutor. He was searching for us. As are many others. I need to get my brother safely home. But we can't go by night."

"You must come home with me, of course, daughter of Sevenwaters. It is not far. We will guide you. Food, drink, warm water for bathing, a soft bed, a hearth fire—these things can be provided for you. And in the morning we will talk."

Warm water. Every inch of my wretched, grubby, itching body yearned for it. But there were some things I needed made clear first. "In the morning, we will go home," I said firmly. "And if any kind of payment is required for your help, I'd like to know now what it is. I'm sorry if that seems discourteous—I am most thankful to you, especially for your help in finding my brother. But I will not enter into any bargains I cannot keep."

Caisin's laughter was a peal of silver bells. I noticed that her cloak was quite dry, though she must have walked here in the rain. "No bargain, Maeve," she said. "It would be churlish indeed if I expected anything of you in return for a single night's shelter. Your company, perhaps, and that of your druidic friend here. No more than that."

Even that, I thought, could mean more than it seemed to. And I wanted to ask, *My company for how long? Tonight? A hundred years? Forever?* But I did not say it, for Finbar was looking like a pinch-faced ghost and Luachan was visibly shivering as he coaxed the cramped Blaze up onto her feet. I must make the choice to trust Caisin. Thus far she had been a friend.

"Thank you," I said. "We accept with gratitude."

"Just one thing."

I might have known it. "And what is that?" I asked, working on calm.

"Your companion must put down his weapons. A druid should know better than to carry iron across the bridge. The child, too, must give up his knife."

Before I could say a word, Finbar had slipped his little knife out of its sheath and laid it on the ground. "I am very sorry, my lady," he said, in a manner that would have given our mother great pride. "There was nobody else to protect my sister."

Caisin smiled. "You are possessed of a courage that well out-weighs your size, Finbar," she said. "Your weapon will be kept safe for you, and returned to you when you need it." The smile faded. "And you, druid."

Luachan looked displeased, as well he might; he had already failed once, as my father had seen it, in his role as Finbar's body-guard.

"You'd better do it, Luachan," I murmured.

He set down his short sword, a dagger, a little knife that had been hidden in his boot.

Caisin lifted her brows. "There is more," she said evenly. Her lovely eyes were fixed on him; she might have been admiring his chiseled features and well-made body or judging him as an en-emy to be watched. I could not read her expression.

Luachan reached into the folds of his druidic robe and brought out a small spiky object that glinted in the lantern light. He threw it down. I could not see exactly what it was. He straightened, look-ing Caisin in the eye. "You require me to remove my horse's har-ness as well, my lady?" His tone was not a druid's, measured and calm , but the assured, challenging voice of the nobly born warrior he had been. "Had I known we would be needing to rely on your hospitality, I would have ridden out on my rescue mission with only a rope bridle."

Caisin regarded him, unsmiling. "Leave the harness; my grooms will deal with it." And, as he made to interrupt, perhaps with a query about tomorrow: "All your belongings will be re-turned when you require them. Now let us walk. You are wet and cold, and the forest is in darkness."

Not, *and it's nighttime*, I thought. Because she knew, as I did, that this sudden night was an uncanny thing. Once we reached shelter, once I was clean and warm again, I would ask her outright if she believed Mac Dara had done it. I would ask whether she thought Swift had been led or coaxed into the Otherworld with the express purpose of drawing Finbar and me in after him. And I would ask if she knew why.

I was curious to know what sort of house a fey noblewoman might inhabit. In the old tales, they dwelled in hollow hills, in caverns rich with glowing insects and floored with animal skins, or in airy dwellings under the trees. In that realm there was an endless summer. Yet here we were, in company with Caisin and her attendants, making our way along a pathway strewn with the debris of today's storm: piles of sodden leaves; scatterings of stones; the sad, small corpse of something that had been dislodged from a nest far above or washed from a snug burrow by the driving rain. Perhaps the endless summer was an invention, along with many other wondrous details of the fey realm. Perhaps Caisin Silverhair and her kind lived in quite modest dwellings. Or maybe they floated around with no need of food, drink or shelter for themselves, their needs constantly met by means of enchantments.

Two of Caisin's attendants led the way, holding their lanterns high. Next, at her invitation, went our little party, first Finbar and me with Caisin herself walking beside us, then Luachan leading a nervous Blaze. At the rear came the remainder of Caisin's companions.

Her house or hall, when we reached it, seemed woven of trees. One of the attendant women gave a high, melodious call, and our procession came to a halt. Around us, in the circle illuminated by the lanterns, I saw only foliage glinting with damp, and dark saturated trunks stretching skyward. Then a voice called back, a man's this time, in words I did not understand, though I guessed they might have meant, *Come forward!* We moved on, and the forest seemed to open and lighten, and we were in a grand chamber roofed with living green, walled with what might have been the silvery trunks of willows and floored in perfect summer grass. The air was warm; it was like the best of sunny days. A shuddering sigh went through me, part relief, part exhaustion, part shock at the utter strangeness of it.

I felt Luachan's hand at the small of my back, just for a moment. "Are you all right, Maeve?" he murmured.

Only a touch, yet it filled me with warmth. I nodded, astonished.

Caisin gave a little wave of her hand, and a young man—human, I guessed from his appearance—came forward. "As you see, we have visitors," she said. "This horse needs food and shelter; see she is well tended to."

Luachan seemed about to protest, but checked himself and passed the reins over without argument. Blaze was led away. I wondered what might bring one of our own kind into this place to work as a groom; had he strayed here by accident or come by choice?

"Follow me," said Caisin, leading us across the enclosed space quite in the manner my mother might do with newly arrived guests.

We followed. The brightness hurt my eyes; I struggled to take in the details. Lamps hung above us, as though floating in the air. Folk stood about in elegant groups or sat on chairs and benches made, not of hewn branches but of living wood, for all sprouted leaves or flowers or berries, and some were cushioned with soft mosses. The people were dressed as those folk had been last night, richly, as if they were at a celebration. Their hair was dressed in elaborate confections, and the women wore slippers that resembled flowers or fruit or, in one case, a pair of hedgehogs whose bright eyes seemed to follow my progress across the floor. Finbar tugged at my arm; I had fallen behind the others, staring.

Caisin led us out of the hall, down a leafy passageway and into a smaller chamber. "I have summoned a woman to help you bathe and dress, Maeve," she said, giving me a thorough look up and down. "After that, I hope you will join me for some refreshment before you sleep. Young man, take Finbar that way"—she pointed through an arched doorway—"and you will find bathing quarters for men. An attendant will bring you back to us when you are ready. We will, of course, provide all of you with clean clothing."

"I don't know—" I began, finding myself reluctant to let Finbar out of my sight even for a moment.

"I will keep him safe." Luachan gave me a reassuring smile.

"Very well." I could hardly insist my brother bathe with me.

The two of them went off, and a girl came. Not one of Caisin's kind, but human like the groom, or almost human. She was young, rosy-cheeked, smiling. I thought of Rhian, and I felt a pang of guilt that my handmaid and friend was back at Sevenwaters not knowing what had befallen me, while I was here warm and safe. But this girl had none of Rhian's vivid, bright-eyed energy. Indeed, although her features were pleasing and her eyes lovely, she seemed somehow . . . distant. As if she were in a waking dream.

"You will help Lady Maeve bathe and dress," Caisin told her. Then, to me, "Enjoy your bath, my dear. Take your time."

The girl beckoned; I followed. Down another hallway was a chamber with a wooden bathtub. Folded cloths, brushes, jars and bottles stood on a long, narrow table. I could not escape the impression that the knots in its wood were eyes, gazing at me as, with the girl's help, I took off my borrowed cloak and then my sodden garments, right down to the filthy, waterlogged shoes. My hair was a hideous greasy tangle. I felt ashamed in front of my companion, though she seemed quite unperturbed.

"Thank you," I said as she helped me into the bath. The sides were high; it was the sort of everyday task that was especially awkward for me, since I could not hold on. I sat down with care. The water was warm and the bath was deep. Gods, it felt good!

The girl let me soak undisturbed awhile, then, when perhaps she saw that I was in danger of falling asleep, came over to help me wash myself. She was not quite as adept as Rhian, or as gentle, but she did a good job with my hair, though she could not comb the tangles out without bringing tears to my eyes. When I was out of the bath and dry, she sat me down on a strange stool resembling a mushroom, then got the splinter out of my arm, probing with a bone needle and using her fingernails to extract the jagged piece of bark. She dabbed the broken skin with a green salve; immediately the pain began to fade.

I had wondered what manner of clothing the Fair Folk might provide for me. They were all so much taller and grander, and their raiment was heavy with decoration—feathers, leaves, jewels, oddities. But the garments the girl helped me into were similar to her own: plain and warm. A shift, good stockings, a gown of very fine wool, a shawl for over the top, with a silver clasp in the shape of a little dog— had Caisin chosen that especially for me, or was it mere coincidence? The slippers were the only item that seemed fey, for although they felt both soft and strong, they had the sheen and hue of butterfly wings.

Perhaps the young attendant was mute. I had said very little beyond thanking her for her help, but she had spoken not a word. She had used gestures to show me what I should do or what came next. Now she motioned me to the stool again, then began to plait my hair.

"May I ask you a question?"

She said nothing.

"Have you lived here all your life? In Caisin Silverhair's hall?"

No reply. Her hands worked quickly, drawing the damp strands of hair into place. I could not see her face.

"I'm sorry," I said. "Perhaps you cannot speak, or are forbidden to speak. I have never been here before—in the Otherworld, I mean. And it seems to me you might be the same kind I am. I wonder . . ." No, best not ask how she came to be here, and the hundred other questions about the place I wanted answers to. "Never mind." Her silence disturbed me. Perhaps I had heard too many old tales. Perhaps she was indeed deaf and mute, and Caisin had provided her with a safe haven and work for her hands. Maybe her own kind had not wanted her. There could be a hundred explanations for her unusual demeanor. I must not treat her the way others had so often treated me, as an oddity to be stared at and whispered about. "Thank you for your kindness," I said.

My hair was neatly braided down my back. I rose to my feet. The girl set down the comb and pointed to the doorway. A moment later, a woman of the Fair Folk appeared there. She towered over me. Her hair was a river of fire, her eyes gems of piercing blue. She wore a trailing gown of gossamer-fine fabric, dotted with tiny glowing stars.

"I am Fiamain Flamehair. You are ready?" she asked, reaching out a long-fingered hand as if to draw me along with her. "You enjoyed the bath?"

"Thank you, yes." I found myself thinking Maeve Claw-Hands would be quite apt if all the folk here had such names.

"Come, then. A small feast has been prepared."

I made no comment. I would deal with the question of food when Caisin was present. Neither Finbar nor I was going to touch a morsel of anything these people offered us, and nor would Luachan if he had any sense.

Fiamain led me to yet another chamber, in size somewhere between the grand hall and the room with the bath. The bathing assistant was left behind us, her presence not acknowledged by the lady with the least word or gesture. I murmured another thank-you over my shoulder as we left. The girl would have to deal with my discarded garments. I wondered if I would get them back, clean, dirty or otherwise. Maybe they would burn them. That was what my mother would have done, without a doubt.

In this new chamber there was a table with benches set on either side. A hearth held a small, smokeless fire, and like the rest of Caisin Silverhair's dwelling, the place was warm. In my fresh clean clothes, with my body scrubbed and my hair smelling of the sweet herbs the girl had used for washing it, I was precariously close to forgetting that we were still not safely home, and that Mac Dara was out there somewhere plotting mischief. I thought I could recall Uncle Bran telling me that when one reaches a certain point of cold and exhaustion, one's judgment tends to go awry. *Keep your mind sharp,* he'd said. *Think twice before accepting the first offer of warmth and shelter.* And he'd explained why, but it was hard to remember. I was almost asleep on my feet.

"Sit here, Maeve," Fiamain said. "Your companions will be with us soon. Eat, drink, make yourself at home. You have come a long way."

On the table there was a flask of fine ruby-red glass and a set of little goblets to go with it. There was a large platter containing, not the intricate fey sweetmeats I had imagined they might offer, but a loaf of crusty bread, a round of cheese and a heap of dried plums. My mouth watered.

"Thank you. I'll wait for the others."

She went out; I saw the little smile on her face. She knew exactly what was on my mind. Alone in the chamber, I resisted the urge to put my head down on my arms and sleep. I must stay alert. I must keep my wits about me. What should I ask Caisin when she came? What knowledge might she have that would be useful? I thought of Father out searching for us. I thought of Cruinn and his lost sons. I thought of Swift, all alone in the forest, perhaps already come to grief. I tried not to think of Bear and Badger.

I was falling asleep by the time Luachan and Finbar came in, the two of them pink-cheeked from the bath and dressed in clean, plain clothing. Finbar's hair was the tidiest I'd ever seen it, his dark curls tamed into a ribbon at the back. Luachan looked different without his druidic robe. The blue tunic they'd given him set off his eyes. The lamplight played on his strong features, and it seemed to me that he was every bit as handsome as those men of the fey with their high-boned faces and glossy locks. I smiled; Luachan smiled in return, ushering Finbar to sit beside me at the table.

"Scrubbed, soaped, rinsed and brushed to within an inch of our lives," Luachan commented, taking the seat on my other side.

"You look lovely, Maeve," said Finbar, and yawned widely.

"Clean, at least," I said, realizing I had not given any thought to the scar on my temple for some time. I had run from Sevenwaters without veil or scarf and had not considered that, with my hair plaited down my back, the livid mark of my burn was on full display.

"You are not accustomed to receiving compliments," murmured Luachan. "Your brother speaks only the truth."

I would have done much to prevent the blush from rising to my cheeks. "I can't fault the two of you on your manners," I said, hoping my tone warned them both that I wanted no more discussion of my appearance. In this household of uncannily beautiful folk, I was a warty toad among sleek silvery fish. Or a cockroach surrounded by gauzy butterflies. Gods, that bread smelled good. "Luachan," I said, "we mustn't eat any of this food. Do you still have your supplies?"

"Fortunately, yes. My weapons were taken from me, as you saw. My meager and somewhat damp supply of foodstuffs appeared to cause no alarm. I have to say that food on the table is a great deal more appetizing than what lies in my traveling bags. This supper appears quite ordinary in every way. One might expect enchanted viands to be somewhat unusual in appearance."

"We're not eating a single crumb. Do you understand, Finbar? These folk have been kind to us. But they are what they are. The important thing is getting home safely. I don't want any of us risking that simply because we're hungry."

Luachan turned his blue gaze on me, somewhat bemused. I wondered if he thought it not quite appropriate for me to make a decision for the three of us. Yet he'd seemed quite content for me to be the one who spoke to Caisin when she first came.

"This might be the only chance we get to speak alone," I said. "This is important. Maybe you don't care if you're stuck in the Otherworld for a hundred years, but it's not going to happen to me and Finbar. And yes, I did already eat some things that were growing in the forest, but that's no reason to start accepting every bit of fey food that's offered me."

"Quite right," said Luachan after a moment, and I heard in his voice that he was struggling not to laugh.

"Don't worry, Maeve," said Finbar. "We weren't going to eat it anyway. We talked about it while we were bathing."

"Oh."

"Maeve," said Luachan.

I looked at him.

"It's going to be all right. You'll be safe, both of you. I promise."

He believed his own words, no doubt. On the other hand, he'd given up his weapons, we were surrounded by magical folk, and outside this haven the uncanny darkness lay over the forest. "It's not Caisin's people I'm worried about," I said. "It's Mac Dara."

DRUID'S JOURNEY: WEST

When the druid comes to the old woman's hut, he is no longer alone. A warrior walks by his side, tall and somber. Keeping pace along the forest track, they might almost be brothers, for each carries something in his bearing of the unknowable Other, a subtle difference that marks him out as not fully of humankind.

His journey has brought the druid back toward Sevenwaters. Forest, keep and family are three days' walk from here, perhaps two for a fit man. The hut lies in a hollow of the woods, circled by leafless willows. No garden here; the place is low to the ground, its stones moss-coated, its timbers erratically patched and its roof thatch dark with the wet. Bushes and briars wrap it close. There's no thread of smoke from the chimney. Nothing stirs but the wind in the trees.

"She's not here." The warrior's tone is flat with weariness.

"So," says the druid, "we rest, and we wait. You've come a long way. Some time for reflection can only benefit the two of us."

They make a fire between stones, prepare food, sit awhile in a silence that is not quite companionable, for each has too much on his mind for that. Eventually the druid says, "You brought them with you, then."

"*Brought.* That is not quite the word. I knew I must come. Clodagh was adamant that if I did so, she must travel with me, and the little ones as well. Believe me, I weighed that risk over and over. They are protected by ancient magic. We must hope it holds." After a moment, the warrior adds, "My wife believes the time for standing back and staying safe is past. We must step forward boldly and confront our enemies, or our lives—long as they may be—will not be worth living."

The druid nods. There's a little smile on his lips. "That does not surprise me. Her sister Maeve put forward a very similar theory not so long ago. And if Sibeal were here—I thank the gods that she is not—no doubt she would tell us just the same." Suddenly he is as somber as his companion. "I admire their attitude, though it is based on an incomplete understanding of the situation before us."

The warrior glances up, his eyes full of shadows. "Oh, Clodagh understands perfectly well. We keep no secrets from each other. She is afraid for me and for our future. But that fear has not made her any less resolute."

They wait some time longer. Nobody comes. The grove grows a little darker. Birds begin to wing their way in, alighting on the roof of the hut and in the bare branches all around. Thrush, robin and swallow. Dove and raven. Even a small owl, though it is not yet dark.

"My bones tell me time is running out," the warrior says, getting up to pace. "What if the wise woman is gone? Her way of life was to wander from one household to another with her stories. If this was her home, perhaps she was seldom here. And she was old. What if—"

"We need the last lines of the geis." The druid speaks in a murmur, as if that telltale word might in itself be dangerous. "Incomplete, it cannot help us. And only she knows them. Exercise patience. Her sister said she would be here. Or implied it, at least."

"What of your own visions? Have you sought wisdom on this matter?"

The druid looks into the flames of their little campfire. "What I saw troubled me. Like you, I feel the sand running swiftly through the glass. Still, we will wait. I am not ready to give up hope."

When the old woman comes, she, too, is not alone. She leans on a girl of perhaps ten years old, a mouse-haired waif in a gown too big for her skinny frame. The child looks too frail to provide the crone with much support, but perhaps she is stronger than she seems.

"Ah, visitors," says the woman. "Greetings. I believe I know the two of you and I believe I know what you're after. A story, hmm? Or a verse?"

"Our greetings to you, wise woman," says the druid with a little bow. "And to your young companion. We do indeed seek a verse, or rather the missing part of one."

The woman ignores him. She's scrutinizing the warrior through narrowed eyes. "How's that wife of yours?" she asks. "I liked her. Got a brood of little ones by now, I expect. She was cut out to be a mother if anyone was."

"Two," says the warrior. "A son and a daughter, lovely as stars. Precious to us."

"Mm." Her look has softened somewhat. "And now you're in a rush to set the world to rights for them, yes?"

A silence unfolds.

"I wish it were as simple as that," the warrior says eventually. "I would that courage alone were enough to make this good. I know that for every victory, a man may expect a corresponding loss. There's a balance about these things, and it cannot give every man what he wishes for. Of course I want them to grow up in a world of justice and courage and mercy. I want them to know that their father was a good man, a man who fought for what matters."

After a while, the druid echoes quietly, "Was?"

But the warrior says nothing at all.

The wise woman does not invite them into the hut, but seats herself beside them on a tree stump, wrapping her cloak more closely around her against the evening chill. The girl goes inside.

A lamp is lit, and sounds of clanking dishes suggest she is preparing a meal.

"My student and helper," the wise woman says. "I'm not getting any younger."

"If there's anything we can do for you . . ."

She smiles, awakening a map of lines on her weathered skin. "Me, ask such as you to fetch wood and water, or mend my roof, or feed my feathered friends? Holly will attend to that, and what she can't manage I'll do for myself. There's only one thing I want from the two of you."

"Tell us what it is, then." The warrior's tone has an edge now; the need to be gone pulls at him.

"Not so fast, young brother. Everything in its own time."

With a visible effort he remains silent.

"I will not invite you to supper. I will not offer you the shelter of my roof. What I want from you is the answer to one question. My gift to you is powerful. Tell me how you will use it."

The men exchange a glance; mulberry eyes and black.

"For change," says the druid. "For good."

"For the future," the warrior says.

"There will be pain in this," says the wise woman. "A measure of sorrow, a measure of loss. There will be sacrifice and a long farewell."

They sit in silence awhile, as the light fades and the air grows chill. The warm glow of the lamp beckons from within the hut; it is too cold out here for an old woman.

"Very well, then," the crone says. "The words you want are these: *Held by hands that cannot hold stands the steed so proud and bold.* A season ago, it would not have been clear to anyone how these conditions might come to pass or, indeed, what they might mean. And now, I hear, Sevenwaters has both an exceptional horse and a young woman with disfigured hands."

"Maeve," the druid breathes. "I was right, then: this does require her presence."

"There's more."

"Out with it," the warrior snaps, then adds, "I'm sorry. Please tell us, and let us move on with haste."

"If you didn't care for the first part, you'll like the second still less. *Chieftain's son with seer's eyes observes the Lord of Oak's demise.* That's all I know, and now you have the whole, if you've seen three of my sisters in turn. I believe my lines come first."

"Finbar," whispers the druid. The blood has drained from his face. "I thought his part in this was done. The risk is high indeed."

"*Observes*," says the warrior. "To observe is not in itself perilous."

"It means, at the very least, that he must be there at the end. That, I like little. I like even less a reference to Maeve and to fire in the same verse. There is a cost in this beyond that which we already know and accept."

"You would not act on it then?"

"If you do not act, and act soon," says the old woman, "another will. And you will like that even less."

The two men become a pair of statues, gazes fixed on her.

"You thought this would be easy? You thought that once you had learned the terms of the geis, you might set them in place and watch your enemy fall victim to the ending this verse laid out for him? These things are never so simple. What man would put a child at risk of his life, or a crippled kinswoman, even with so much at stake? For you, the gain must always be balanced against the risk. Another, without your scruples, might think differently. A human life or two might weigh little in that person's balance."

"Another," echoes the warrior. "What other?"

"A rival," says the druid, comprehension coming fast now. "He has a rival for his place as ruler. Hence the urgency, hence the spate of attacks, the increase in activity. He's panicking, desperate to get what he wants before this person mounts a challenge."

"And it is possible," says the old woman, "that with all his attention on that challenge, he has failed to notice the return of a woman with crippled hands to Sevenwaters."

"How can there be a rival?" the warrior asks. "There's nobody there with the authority, the wits, the power to challenge him. I'm quite certain of it."

"Ah," says the old woman, "but it is some years since you walked among them, and time passes differently in that realm. I should not have to tell you that, young man. I have heard that one is come who will indeed challenge him, and soon. If you would avert this, you must go quickly; the dark is at the doorstep."

"Who?" demands the warrior. "Who is it?"

"My informants told me only that there is a rival, and that this rival is devious, clever and without any sense of right and wrong."

"I thought only you and your sisters knew the geis," says the druid.

"By means of torture," she says, "it seems another party has obtained the verse. Not from one of my sisters, but from a smaller being who had the misfortune to be present when the geis was first spoken. The small one paid a heavy price before she gave up her knowledge."

"So we may already be too late," the druid says.

"Too late? No. But you must act swiftly. My spies believe all will soon be in place."

A silence, then the two men speak as one. "How soon?"

A beam of warm light comes from the door of the hut, where the girl has appeared, wanting to call her teacher in to supper, but reluctant to interrupt.

"All right, Holly, I'm coming. It's too cold for my old bones out here." The wise woman rises slowly to her feet. "Tomorrow," she says. "Walk as a man walks and you will come too late. Run as a deer runs and you will come too late. Fly as a bird flies and perhaps you will be in time. Farewell, and may the breath of Danu lift your wings."

CHAPTER 12

e had not been waiting long when Caisin Silverhair entered the chamber, accompanied by Fiamain and two men of the fey, one young and well made, with russet curls and a merry face, the other much older in appearance and wearing the dark robe of a councilor or sage. That struck me as odd; I had thought the Fair Folk might possess the secret of eternal youth, or at least the magical arts to make folk *seem* young. I'd heard something of that kind about Mac Dara— that it was difficult for folk to tell him and his son, Cathal, apart, so alike they were in looks. Yet Cathal was only part fey. Although Mac Dara was his father, Cathal's mother carried a blend of human blood and that of the Sea People. And Mac Dara was years and years Cathal's senior. He had fathered scores of daughters over the years, but only the one son. The tale was one thread in the complicated family tapestry of Sevenwaters. Mac Dara's quest to retrieve his son, or his grandson, to rule his Otherworld princedom after him, was the stuff of legend.

"My sister, Fiamain Flamehair," said Caisin, seating herself at the head of the table. "My brother, Dioman Owlfriend. My councilor, Breasal Wiseheart. We welcome you. It is late and you are weary. Please, partake of these humble provisions; all are safe for you to eat."

Owlfriend. I liked that name. Stealing another look at the young fey man with his cheery smile and bright eyes, I saw that on his shoulder, half-hidden in his exuberant hair, a small owl was perched, its gaze fixed unnervingly on me. It was so still it might have been a thing created cleverly from feathers and linen and wadding, but I knew it was alive. It put me in mind of the little dog I had seen among those nighttime riders, seated on its mistress's knee and scarcely aware of the world around it. It reminded me of the girl who had helped me bathe. I could not repress a shiver.

"Thank you, my lady." Luachan stepped in when I failed to respond. "We acknowledge your generosity. But we will eat from our own provisions." He had his bag with him, and now he took out the cloth-wrapped bundle that held his store of food.

"So careful." Caisin's eyes were not on Luachan. She was studying me with altogether too much perception. "You still don't trust me, Maeve? Twice now I have given you my aid and asked for nothing in return."

In my mind I heard the voice of Uncle Bran, a man who had gotten himself out of more tight corners than most folk see in a lifetime. *Don't let small things—a flicker of the eyes, a movement of the hand—reveal what's in your mind.* "It is not you, my lady," I said. "In all the old tales I have heard, human folk cannot partake of Otherworld food or drink without some ill effect." I realized as I said this that Ciarán's story of Finn and Baine was an exception, for they had drunk from the forbidden stream, and all that had resulted was exceptional physical beauty. There was a joke in that somewhere, a joke I might make at my own expense. "Since Luachan has brought food from home, it makes sense to exercise caution and to eat that." When she simply regarded me, brows up, I added, "In fact, the first time you offered me food I accepted. My dog and I both ate what you provided and it was welcome."

"This food, too, is from your world," put in Fiamain. "My sister anticipated your caution. You may eat it safely."

"For the love of Danu, leave the girl be," said the young man, Dioman. "If she prefers sodden bread and moldy cheese, let her have it. Or are we to be all night debating the niceties of supper? I'll eat this if nobody else will. What's in the flask, mead?"

He sounded so ordinary, so down to earth, that I was almost convinced the food was safe. But Luachan was passing me a share of his own supply and providing Finbar with the same, and although the bread had indeed suffered a little from rain seeping into its package, it would suffice for now. It was a big step up from raw bones.

The Fair Folk ate what was on the table with apparent enjoyment. Finbar helped me with my food; my hunger was stronger than my need for privacy. Nobody said much until the meal was almost finished. Finbar was struggling to stay awake. His eyes were shadowed in a face wan with weariness. I was about to ask if he could go to bed when Caisin spoke.

"We must speak privately, Maeve. But first, I have something to show you."

"Of course," I said. "But Finbar should go to bed; he's worn-out."

"Oh, I think Finbar will want to see this," Caisin said. "The young man may come, too, if you wish."

She led us through such a maze of passageways that I no longer knew in which direction we were headed. Everywhere those lanterns floated above us, setting a warm light on the birch trunk walls and the leafy roof, above which no sign of the sky was visible. Were we outside? Inside? Somewhere between? This grove, if grove it was, seemed untouched by Mac Dara's eldritch darkness and quite sealed off from the wintry weather that had attended our journey. It was a dream world, the kind of place one might invent for a tale of magic and wonders; a realm to which a lonely, unhappy child might long to escape for a while. All was warmth, light, peace, beauty. There was nothing like the bustle of orderly activity I was accustomed to see in the Sevenwaters keep or in Aunt Liadan's house at Harrowfield, only people strolling in little groups, or drifting along by themselves as if their thoughts were elsewhere.

Caisin's high status in the household was obvious. Folk greeted her with reverence and she was gracious in her responses. Our supper companions had all come with us. I could not imagine what she wanted us to see. The opportunity to talk with her alone might be useful. Perhaps I could summon the courage to ask her about Mac Dara and the Disappearance. At Father's council, everyone had seemed to agree that information was what we needed to defeat him, and where better to get information than in the Otherworld itself? Whether she would tell me was another matter, of course. But I should try.

"This way," Caisin said, and led us through another doorway. I smelled horses before I saw what was before us.

"Come up beside me, Maeve," Caisin said. "There. Now you can see."

There was a barrier of woven withies very much like the one around the training yard at Sevenwaters, and within it an open, grassed area. Even here I could not tell if we were indoors or out of doors; it was noticeably cooler, but there was no wind, no rain, and the place was lit by more glowing lanterns hanging overhead. At one side was an open shelter with a feeding trough and a water barrel. And there, at the far side of the area, stood a magnificent silver-gray yearling. He was somewhat the worse for wear. Patches of blood stained the lovely pelt; his long journey had marked him.

"You found him," I breathed. "Swift is safe." Remarkably, our lovely horse, apple of so many eyes, had survived his wild run through the forest. I must get in there and find out if he had any major injuries. I took a step toward the barrier and halted, seeing the look in his eyes. There was no trace of recognition there. His stance said clearly that the first sudden movement or unexpected sound would send him over the fence to wreak a trail of destruction through Caisin's peaceful hall.

"Our people brought him in earlier today," said Dioman. "Not without some difficulty, I may say. The creature seems more than half wild. He won't eat. He won't stand still long enough to have those cuts tended to. And he's kicked one or two of our folk, done some damage." He glanced at Caisin.

"Charms could have been employed to hold him," she said. "I ordered that they not be used for now. I thought it possible you would pass this way with your brother, going home, and I know this horse belongs at your father's hall."

Swift was sidling across the far end of the enclosure and back again, as creatures do when they feel trapped. He swished his tail and tossed his head.

"He's disturbed by what has happened. This is no ordinary horse; he's highly strung at the best of times. My lady, he needs attention, and quickly. If I can hold him still, perhaps with Luachan's help, can your people provide warm water to wash those wounds, and a healing salve?" I was by no means confident I could get Swift to stay still, let alone hold him in place long enough for Luachan to do what was required. But I must try, at least.

"I can help," said Finbar. "He knows me."

It was true, though at present Swift was refusing to recognize any of us. Still, we must try something.

"We can provide all you need," said Dioman. "But none of us can get near the creature; we stopped trying when it seemed he would injure not only us, but himself."

There was an obvious question: how, then, had Caisin's folk managed to catch Swift in the first place? But with Finbar weary and Swift starting to pace, I did not ask it.

"Very well," I said, assuming control. "Please bring the water, the salve, and a couple of clean cloths. And a halter, the softest you have. Luachan, Finbar, I'll try to talk Swift into calm, the way I usually do when he's upset. The two of you need to do Emrys's job between you. Luachan to get the halter on and then hold Swift. Finbar to tend to the cuts and bruises. When we've got him standing still, I'll try to assess whether there are any deeper injuries. If I need the two of you to help with that, I'll ask you. Once we're in there, speak softly. I'll tell you when to move." When Caisin went to open the gate to the enclosure, I said, "Not yet, my lady. Not until he's calmer."

She stepped back without a word.

"Swift, lovely boy," I murmured, using the special voice he was used to. "Green field. Sweet water. Kind hands and quiet . . ."

I suppose the whole process took quite some time; while I was working I did not think of such things, but judged when to move forward by the animal's demeanor, his stance, the look in his eye. There were steps in it, all of which happened after I had been soothing Swift for some time with my voice, and the others had stood silent to let me work. Open the gate, go through, stand by the wall. Move forward three paces. Finbar and Luachan coming in behind me and going to either side, taking each step with slow care. Move forward another three paces. A halt while a bird flew across above us, making a high trilling sound that sent Swift plunging forward. Our audience of Fair Folk gasped; Finbar and Luachan retreated to the withy wall; I stood exactly where I was, my steady tone never changing. It was something I had taught myself to do. I was not sure if Swift would ever intentionally harm me—I thought not—but he might hurt me by accident. Another fright a little later, when a burst of strange laughter came from somewhere in the house, and Swift tossed his head and whinnied in response. "Steady, my boy. Quiet now. All's well." Were my lips telling him reassuring lies, with Mac Dara's eldritch darkness lying over the forest and keeping us from home? With Bear and Badger still out there somewhere, captive, perhaps hurt? "Soft grass. Blessed sunlight. Smiles and sweet touches."

When Swift was calm again and had halted somewhat closer to me, I took three more steps forward, and I was near enough to touch him. I raised my hand slowly to his neck; laid the back of it to his damp skin; stroked gently. "My fine boy, Swift. My dear good horse." Now there were tears running down my cheeks. Not part of the plan. I was not even weeping for Swift himself. But touching him undid me. For a moment I was back in the nemetons, working in the field with him, and by the wall lay my boys, so quiet and good, waiting for me to be finished so I would come and scratch their bellies and praise them. "Calm boy, Swift. Kind hands and quiet."

Swift started when Luachan slipped on the halter, but I kept touching him gently and humming under my breath, and he quieted.

"I have him secure, Maeve." Luachan kept his voice to a murmur.

"Good. Finbar, you can start washing those scratches. You need to be firm but gentle. And careful. I can't be certain he won't try to kick you." Without looking, I sensed my brother's presence on my right, stepping quietly close, setting his pail of water down, readying his cloth. "If you see any bigger injuries, dark patches, cuts that look too open to be left, tell me." I prayed there would be nothing needing a poultice or a stitch; back at the stables, with Emrys at hand, that might be achievable, but I did not think we could manage it here.

"Good boy, Swift," Finbar said in a creditable imitation of my tone. "Calm boy."

There wasn't a sound from back at the barrier; indeed, I wondered if Caisin and her companions had tired of the lengthy process and left. With all my concentration on keeping Swift calm, I did not look over to see if they were still watching us. The yearling twitched and pulled against the rope when Finbar dabbed at the deepest cuts, but between Luachan's steady hand on the halter and my presence by Swift's head, eventually the job was done.

"I can't see any bad cuts or big bruises, Maeve." My brother's voice was remarkably steady. He must be exhausted. "And he has his weight on all four legs."

"Thank you, Finbar." I gestured to Luachan to hold Swift steady while I performed a quick examination of flanks, quarters, legs and hooves. "You're right; he seems sound. But he's tired and confused. A pity there's no enclosed stall where we can shut him in for the night. Never mind; perhaps now that we've tended to him, he'll eat and rest here, even though it's unfamiliar." I considered offering to sleep in the straw-floored shelter, but I could not do that; I must be close to my brother.

"Finbar, you go out now," I said quietly, "and close the gate behind you."

He obliged without question, tidily taking his bucket and cloth with him. Not only were Caisin's group still watching, but several other fey folk had joined them. What did they think this was, an entertainment put on for their amusement?

"What now, Maeve?" Luachan still held Swift's halter; the leading rope was in his other hand.

"Lead him over to the gate, take off the halter and go out."

"But—" Luachan met my eye and fell silent. "Very well. I accept that in matters equine, you are my superior."

"It's nothing to do with being superior. I know what to do, that's all."

"As you say." He had found a smile somewhere; I heard it in his voice.

Often enough in the past, I had trusted that Swift would not hurt me, and my trust had been justified. So it was again now. When Luachan took the halter off him, Swift stood calm by my side, obedient to the touch of my hand and the soft soothing of my voice as I kept up my litany of all things good and quiet. Luachan went out the gate and closed it behind him. Under the gaze of the small crowd of Fair Folk, I turned and walked the yearling back over to his food and water, keeping the back of my left hand against his neck, talking him gently across the open space. I halted by the water barrel.

"Drink, sweet boy. Eat. You're hungry and tired. Sleep awhile. Tomorrow we're going home."

I stood there a little, until he dropped his head to drink. Then I took my hand away and walked slowly back to the gate. Dioman opened it for me and I stepped through.

The expressions on their faces—Dioman's, Caisin's, those of all their kind—told me that they still did not realize how important it was to be quiet, even now I was beyond reach of Swift's hooves and teeth. Quite plainly they were about to burst into a chorus of amazed congratulation. I opened my mouth to warn them, but Finbar forestalled me.

"Don't speak," he said, his voice clear enough to reach all ears, yet soft enough not to trouble Swift, who was still thirstily drinking. "You have to be quiet until we're well away from here or Swift will be upset and Maeve will have to do it all again." After a moment he added, "My lords. My ladies."

Caisin Silverhair made a gesture and the fey folk who had gathered to watch dispersed in an instant, leaving only her inner circle. Then Caisin put her arm around my shoulders, and Luachan took Finbar's hand, and we made our way back through the leafy passageways. I heard no sound from Swift as we left him, which was a good sign. When we had rounded a corner and were out of the horse's sight, Luachan said quietly, "He'll be fine until daylight, Maeve."

I nodded, but found myself incapable of speech. I was so tired. I wished I had decided to sleep in the straw with Swift, as Emrys might have done. But the day was not yet over. Caisin wanted to speak with me; I must seize the opportunity to get some answers from her. Did *privately* mean without Luachan? Glancing across at him, remembering how reassuring his presence had been earlier, I was not sure I wanted that.

"My lady," I said as we entered the chamber where we'd eaten earlier, "you mentioned that you wanted to talk to me. But Finbar's badly in need of sleep, and . . ." It was too awkward to say aloud. *And I must be sure he'll be safe.*

"And your druidic protector cannot be in two places at once?" Caisin was several steps ahead of me. "A dilemma, certainly, but easily solved. Sleeping quarters are close at hand for all of you. The druid with your brother; yourself in the next chamber. Take time now to settle Finbar, and when you are ready to talk, return here. You may bring the druid; my brother will watch over the child." She glanced at Dioman, who nodded assent.

I found myself unable to summon any argument against such a reasonable arrangement. Indeed, I wondered that I still harbored any doubts about these folk, who had gone out of their way to help us. "Thank you," I said. "I won't be long."

Dioman was already moving to a doorway, indicating that we should follow. The owl on his shoulder lifted a wing and moved its feet as if to mimic his gesture. Dioman led us to a chamber furnished with a pair of leafy hammocks on which soft blankets waited, an invitation to rest.

"Good night, Maeve," my brother murmured. Early as it must still be, he looked exhausted. He climbed into one of the hammocks and snuggled down. "Good night, Luachan. Good night, my lord." This last was addressed to Dioman, who appeared mildly amused.

"Your quarters are there." The fey man pointed to a low archway through which I could see another cozy sleeping place. "You'll be close to your brother. I will watch over him until you are finished your business with Caisin."

Business: that sounded serious. I hoped I was sufficiently awake to ask the right questions and give the best answers. "Thank you," I said. "Please do stay here; I don't want Finbar left alone." There was no need for songs or stories. My brother was already fast asleep, heavy lids closed over weary eyes, blanket up to his chin.

"He needed rest," I murmured to Luachan as we made our way back. "Some very odd things happened to him when he was on his own. But he's always reluctant to explain. Always ready to cut discussion off with *I'm not supposed to tell*, as if there is a restriction over him that I can't possibly understand."

"His gift makes things difficult. It has developed early, and it's strong."

"You think he still has trouble distinguishing between vision and reality? Future and possible future?"

"That is common in young seers learning their craft." He hesitated. "I have on some occasions suggested he keep what he sees to himself. Speaking out when he does not fully understand the nature of his visions could do untold harm."

"Does he talk of these things to you?"

"That is different. I am his teacher."

Luachan folded his arms; he was not meeting my eye. He seemed to have lost his usual composure, though I did not think my questioning had been unduly blunt.

"I believe he's scared," I said. "Scared and unhappy. Something is troubling him badly, and he feels bound not to talk about it. I don't like that, Luachan. He is too young to have to hold such secrets."

"He's exhausted. He's walked a long way, much of it alone. And here in the Otherworld everything is new and strange to him. No wonder he is out of sorts. But children recover quickly. Once we reach home all will be well."

He must have seen on my face how inadequate I thought this was, for he added, "You are tired, too. In the morning this will seem less troubling."

"Don't patronize me, Luachan. I'm not so tired that I can't recognize a real threat where it exists. It's not just the mention of a geis. Finbar seems to know more about the Otherworld than he should. Almost as if he's been here before."

"He has, of course."

"As a newborn baby." I hesitated. "He has a very strong idea about what we should be doing here, and when. As if this has all been . . . foretold. He was certain I should find the dogs before we went home. When I refused he was quite distressed. I know he believes that if we don't go about things the right way some kind of disaster will ensue. But how can I do anything but take him straight back—"

"Maeve?" Caisin Silverhair had appeared at the entry to the chamber ahead. Warm light spilled out around her graceful form, setting a glow on the soft fabric of her gown and turning her hair to a shimmering cloak. "Are you ready?"

No sign of her sister or the councilor this time. We followed her in and seated ourselves at the table.

"The child is safely asleep?"

"Yes, my lady. He's had a long journey and is weary."

"As you must be." Caisin's gaze was fixed on me, as if weighing me up. "But you'll have questions, I imagine. I have heard you are not shy of asking them."

She had? From whom? "How is it you know so much about me?" Too late, I wished I had watched my words, for this was quite the wrong note on which to start.

"You think we who share your forest have no interest in the human folk of Sevenwaters? Wrong. We owe you a debt; all of us know that, save perhaps for one. That one is powerful, and those who follow him adopt his ways for their own protection. We are not all made in his mold. If that were so, you would indeed have cause to despair of the future."

"It's not in my nature to despair," I said. "I've always thought it more sensible to attempt to put things to rights. But we human folk do work at a certain disadvantage, being short-lived and without any magical powers. Will you answer further questions for me?"

"I have said that I expect to do so."

In fact, all she'd said was that she expected me to ask them, but never mind that. Luachan was sitting quietly, chin on hands, as if he assumed that I would be doing all the talking. I would not waste time quizzing Caisin over what had happened to Finbar or why she had not given me straightforward directions to find him. That hardly mattered now he was safe. I must ask about Mac Dara, about how much she knew. I must seek out any information that might help my father. But there was something that must come first.

"My dogs," I said, a lump forming in my throat. "While I was getting Finbar down from the oak tree they were stolen. Taken by force, with a fight. Finbar said he saw people in gray cloaks carrying them away into the forest. Do you know who those people might have been and why they would do such a thing? Is there a way I can get Bear and Badger back?"

Caisin lifted her brows. I had tried to speak calmly, as if this were an ordinary matter, but it had not been possible to keep my voice steady.

"Two dogs?" she queried. "When I first encountered you there was only one."

"It's a long story, but yes, there are two. They were running wild in the woods, scared and hungry, before I took them in, and now . . . Because I must take Finbar home as soon as possible, I had thought I must leave them behind. But since events have brought us to you, I wondered perhaps . . ."

"I have no knowledge of this matter. But I can inquire for you, and perhaps find out what has happened." A delicate frown creased her brow. "What I am about to tell you will not be welcome news,

Maeve. Among our people, each clan has its own colors. The folk in gray cloaks belong to the household of that powerful personage of whom I spoke earlier. He calls himself the Lord of the Oak. They carry out certain tasks for him. They are his minions."

"I see." My heart was like a cold stone. "Then it is not likely I can fetch my dogs back. Not without those magical powers I do not have." Why would Mac Dara take my boys? What possible use could he have for them?

Caisin smiled and reached out to pat my hand. "Magical powers, perhaps not. But you have another gift that is rare, Maeve. The skill you demonstrated with the horse was truly astonishing. I have never seen anything like that. None of my folk were able to get anywhere near the creature."

She was being kind, of course; she could see how upset I was and thought to make me feel better. I asked the question I had held back earlier. "If your folk could not approach Swift, how was it he ended up in your enclosure?"

"You'd need to speak to Dioman. I gather the horse was found grazing with some of our own animals and came in with the others. As I told you, we avoided the use of spellcraft, seeing the creature was already exhausted and hurt."

That was a curiously incomplete explanation, but perhaps Dioman could fill in the gaps. "My lady, is it permitted to mention the true name of that other person, the one whose folk you believe may have taken my dogs?"

"It is not forbidden, Maeve, though the name sits ill on my tongue; it tastes of wrongdoing. Did you wish to ask about him?"

"You have heard of an event my people refer to as the Disappearance, I imagine." She'd said her kind were interested in the human folk of Sevenwaters, after all. "That is, the disappearance of sixteen men from Tirconnell, including a chieftain's sons, on the border of our forest, and the later reappearance of all but three of them within this same forest, each done to death in cruel and unusual fashion. My father believes it was Mac Dara's doing, an act designed to set Father at enmity with his neighboring chieftains, to isolate him, to apply pressure."

"I know of it," Caisin said gravely. "Pressure to do what?"

I looked at Luachan, suddenly wary of saying too much. I was quite sure I did not want to mention the unlikely possibility of Cathal coming back to confront his father, though it did seem that might be central to the whole matter.

"It seems Mac Dara wants something from Lord Sean," Luachan said smoothly. "Something Lord Sean is not prepared to give. And it does appear this Lord of the Oak is in a hurry, or he would not have increased his activities so dramatically of recent times. I believe Lady Maeve was hoping you might know something about his reasons."

"I don't want to see any more lives lost," I said. "Nor does my father. We did wonder if Mac Dara perceived some particular threat to his authority, something that might make him a little . . . desperate."

Caisin threw back her head and laughed; the sound was an unsettling reminder that she was not a human woman. "Desperate? That is not a term I would ever use for that person. He so loves to be in control." Abruptly, the amusement left her face. "Maeve, we touch on matters strange and perilous. Tell me, is your purpose here solely to fetch your young brother back home, out of harm's way? Or do you seek to aid your father and to secure the future of Sevenwaters?"

She sounded deeply solemn, and for a few moments I could not think how to reply. "Both, I hope," I said with some hesitation. I had been fixed on the need to return Finbar safely to our parents. I still was. But what Caisin had just hinted at turned things on their heads. Of course I wanted to secure the future of Sevenwaters. There was no argument about that. She could not mean I might actually play a part in doing so, surely. Me against Mac Dara? Maeve Claw-Hands standing up against the Lord of the Oak? It was laughable.

"Please make yourself clear." The look in Luachan's eye was, if not hostile, then definitely cool. "Lady Maeve is tired, she has come a long way and she's lost her beloved companions. If you have something particular to say to her, I believe she would prefer you to do so plainly and without delay."

Under other circumstances this speech would have annoyed me; I preferred to fight my own battles. It was a measure of how weary and dispirited I was that Luachan's words set a warm glow inside me, reminding me that I still had friends to rely on. "I am indeed tired," I said. "But, my lady, if there really is some way I can help in the struggle against Mac Dara, I would be very glad to hear it explained."

Caisin clasped her long-fingered hands together on the table and sighed. "There is so little time," she said. "So very little. Maeve, I would not tax you with this now, when you are weary and far from home, and have lost the dogs to which you are plainly so devoted. But since I saw you with the horse and realized what you can do, I have no choice but to put it to you. I believe you may hold the key to defeating our mutual enemy. You and Swift between you."

Luachan and I stared at her. I was too astonished to find words.

"Let me explain. For some years Mac Dara has held sway here; many of my folk follow his lead and dance to his tune."

"Almost all, surely. When my sister came to the Otherworld, none of your kind opposed him. Only smaller folk."

"Perhaps your sister saw only those who chose to show themselves: Mac Dara's sycophants and lackeys, dazzled or cowed into obedience. Believe me, there are plenty who wish him gone. More than that: there are those who plan to remove him." For a moment I saw something different in her lovely face, as if there were a fire within, a power seldom revealed. As quickly it was gone, and she was as before, a flawlessly beautiful woman with kind, troubled eyes. "But he is skilled in magic, more skilled than any of us. A challenge of the time-honored kind would almost certainly result in his retaining his authority here. And, of course, that is what he intends to do until he can secure the successor of his choice."

"His son." I realized she had known all along about Cathal. She must understand exactly why Mac Dara was tormenting my father.

"Or another of his own blood. But I understand the grandchild is still a babe."

"You mentioned a challenge," said Luachan. "So there is an accepted way for the leadership to be decided? What is that way?"

"A contest of magical skills. It would be held at the Grand Conclave, following lesser encounters of the same kind. Mac Dara has not been challenged before. It is a single combat, you understand, one mage against another. None of those who oppose him has sufficient power to stand against a practitioner of such singular subtlety and power. If the rules were broken—if, for instance, two of us stood up against him together—that would render the contest invalid, and he would retain his authority regardless of the result. There is a way these things must be done. That is set down in ancient lore."

There was a brief silence while we digested this.

"Explain to me how it is that a girl with crippled hands and a skittish horse can achieve what a group of fey nobles with magical powers cannot," I said. "I'm sorry to be so blunt, but your idea is starting to sound a little implausible."

Caisin smiled. "This time it is different," she said softly. "We have worked for some time to discover a weak spot in Mac Dara's apparently impregnable defenses. It seemed there was no such weakness; that there was no way to bring him down. Until now. By means of spellcraft, we have uncovered a remarkable secret."

The silence had acquired a different quality. The pleasant chamber where we sat was suddenly full of shadows; there was danger in the air. We waited.

"There is a geis," Caisin said. "It was spoken over Mac Dara long years ago, when he was only a child. It set out certain conditions under which he would lose his power. The words were not entrusted to a single individual to remember, but divided among several. On their own, the pieces of this verse mean little. Put together, they are the weapon I have long been seeking: the means to rid this realm of its cruel prince forever."

"A geis," I whispered. Ciarán had been right. So, in his way, had Finbar, though he had thought Mac Dara might have laid a geis over *him*. He'd seen something in his visions and gotten it confused. The curse was not on my brother, but on the Lord of the Oak himself. If Mac Dara had perhaps not known about it earlier, he surely did now. What better explanation for the way his attacks on my father had increased so markedly of recent times? If Mac

Dara sensed the terms of the geis might soon be met, and if he knew he had potential rivals for the leadership, he would indeed be desperate to fetch his son back home. "He thinks he's about to be deposed," I said. "Or that he's about to die." But wait. How could Swift and I possibly be part of a curse that had been pronounced years before either of us was born? "How did you discover this?" Had she sent someone on the same path Ciarán was following, asking the same questions? Might she even know about his journey to find the daughters of Mac Dara? She'd said *by spellcraft*. That might mean almost anything.

Caisin seemed to hesitate, as if choosing her words with care. "We discovered a source of information; one few folk knew about." I heard in her tone that this was all the answer I would get.

"What are the words of this geis, my lady?" Luachan asked.

"As I said, it is somewhat cryptic. But less so now that Maeve and her horse have made their way to Sevenwaters. It runs thus:

Held by hands that cannot hold
Stands the steed so proud and bold.
Chieftain's son with seer's eyes
Observes the Lord of Oak's demise.
As the age begins to turn
That is when the oak will burn."

Luachan looked at me. I looked at him, then down at my hooked fingers, stiff as twigs on my lap.

"*Hands that cannot hold,*" I said flatly. "Based solely on that, you believe I can somehow make this geis come to pass?"

"Not only do I believe it, Maeve, I am certain of it. Into our midst comes a remarkably fine but highly strung horse, and a young woman of Sevenwaters with a certain disability, who happens to be able to control this wayward animal using only her voice . . . It must surely mean the fulfillment of the terms. I believe all that is required is that you demonstrate again the skill you showed us earlier. I am asking you to do so, before my people, in Mac Dara's sight, at the Grand Conclave. Maeve, you can be the key to his downfall. You can win peace and security for your family and your community. Will you do this?"

Morrigan save us. Her eyes were shining with hope; her voice trembled. But . . . me, save Sevenwaters? Bring down an enemy so dark and powerful that his own people shrank before him?

"Wait a moment," I said. *"Chieftain's son with seer's eyes*—that must be Finbar. My brother is only a child. Mac Dara stole him away as a baby; he cared nothing for his welfare. But the words of this verse suggest Finbar must be present when this conclave happens, present for the challenge."

"So it would seem. He is the third part of this, setting it beyond doubt that now is the time for this geis to be fulfilled."

Dear gods. It was almost as if Finbar had known what we were walking into, with his insistence that we must do things in very particular ways. He had been so certain we should not go straight home. He had been so sure . . .

"I don't like this," I said. "I don't want Finbar involved. He's only little. What is that reference to burning?"

"Maeve," put in Luachan quickly, "don't distress yourself. I'm sure there will be time to discuss this, to make sense of it—"

"What does it mean, *the oak will burn*?" My voice was shaking despite my best efforts. "Are you sure that's the whole geis? It doesn't make sense."

"Yes, that is all of it. Such verses are often somewhat obscure. I do not believe your brother will come to any harm. The rhyme says only that he must be present to observe."

"It's not— I don't think—" My mind was awhirl; I hardly knew what to say to her. "My lady, calming Swift with my voice is not as straightforward as it may look. If there was a crowd of folk around, and noise, and bright lights, I might well have no control at all over him. He would be very disturbed. And Finbar . . . It is hard to believe this rhyme requires only that he stand and watch. Simply being in the Otherworld is a risk for him, and going to this conclave, where Mac Dara could see him openly, it's . . ." *It's something my parents would not want to happen, even if it meant defeating their worst enemy.* "My lady, I believe their son's safety would weigh more to my parents than almost anything."

"Maeve—"

"You need time, of course," Caisin said quietly, cutting off whatever Luachan had been going to say. "This is a hard choice for you. You and your sisters have been trained to family loyalty, and of course that loyalty might call you to protect this young brother above all other things. I ask you to consider a wider view. This could save your father's land and his position. It could bring about a time of great change. A new age."

When the age begins to turn . . . "You didn't answer my question about fire," I managed. It felt equally impossible to accept and refuse. How could I risk Finbar? But how could I turn down a chance to end Mac Dara's reign? "The geis mentions burning. In your plans, where does that part come in? You know, I suppose, how much fire disturbs even a placid horse." I found I was shivering, and wrapped my arms around myself. Finbar had spoken of fire when he told the story of the two dragons. But that story had ended halfway through, before we got to the burning.

"I do not believe it means, literally, that our adversary would burn. There is always a fire at the Grand Conclave; that meeting is our most significant gathering. You must be accustomed to ritual fire, since your family is scrupulous in its observance of the old ways."

"I have not lived at Sevenwaters for ten years. But I do have cause to remember the use of fire for ceremonies, yes."

"Of course," she said calmly. "You look cold, Maeve. Will you drink a little of my cordial to restore your spirits and help you with this decision? I promise the draught will not harm you. Besides, you have already sampled it, out in the forest."

The shivering was getting worse; I felt as if I were on a steep slope, sliding downward with no way back. "Very well," I said. "A sip or two." She was right—I had already tasted the potion and it had helped me considerably. I needed a clear head for this.

I had thought Caisin would snap her fingers to summon a lackey of some kind, but she got up and went out, surprising me.

And Luachan surprised me even more, removing the outer tunic he was wearing and coming to wrap it around my shoulders.

"You're shaking," he said. "This is too much to ask of you."

"How can I make such a choice? I can't risk Finbar; it's wrong. I feel it in my bones. But if this really is the only chance to defeat Mac Dara . . . It can't be. It can't be all down to me; that's simply ridiculous."

"The terms of a geis can often seem somewhat ridiculous," Luachan said. "Look at the tale of Cú Chulainn. But, odd as the details may be, the intention is entirely serious. If the verse is accurate, it seems this may spell out the end of an age, no less." His voice was not quite steady. It seemed he, too, was overwhelmed at the immensity of this.

"If Caisin is wrong, I could die," I said. "Finbar could die. And Mac Dara could stay right where he is, wielding power over the fey folk of Sevenwaters and tormenting the human folk until my father's authority is quite gone."

"That is the worst that could happen."

"It's too risky. At the very least, I'd want to consult Father and Ciarán before saying yes to it. We should go home, tell them about this, and if they decide we should go ahead, then we could come back in time for this Grand Conclave. Though I really doubt that my parents would let Finbar do that, no matter what depended on it." *I want to keep him close,* Mother had said of Finbar. *To wrap him up, never to let him out of my sight.*

"Would you go ahead with it if your brother were not required to be present for the fulfilment of the geis?" Luachan laid his hand over mine on the table. "Gods, you're ice-cold! You should go off to bed and forget this until morning."

"In the unlikely chance that I can sleep after this, my dreams will doubtless be full of Mac Dara. Luachan, what do you think we should do? Tell me honestly. Tell me what you would do if you were me."

After a moment he said, "I can't. I can't put myself in your shoes. I know that you are brave and forthright, and that you don't like other folk to make your choices for you. All I can say is that in any decision you must weigh the danger against the prize."

"I don't seem to be able to do that this time. Both seem monstrous, too big to contemplate." I wondered that he had not suggested I seek the wisdom of the gods. As a druid, surely that must come first for him. Perhaps he knew how little faith I had in any deity.

"You don't need me to remind you," Luachan said, "that you've faced a monstrous challenge once before and come through it with admirable courage. Not unscathed, of course, but still fighting bravely on."

This remark confused me. I was not sure whether I cared for it or not. The silence was just becoming awkward when Caisin returned, bearing a plain earthenware jug and three cups on a tray. The style of these, I thought, was calculated to make her potion look as innocuous as possible, like mead or ale brewed by a country wife.

She poured it and passed the cups. We sipped in silence, then she said, "I am sure you have more questions for me, Maeve."

"Only one right now." The cordial had set some fire in my veins. "You spoke before about there not being much time to make the decision. How much time exactly? When is the Grand Conclave?"

Caisin turned her lambent eyes on me. "It is tomorrow."

"*Tomorrow?*" Luachan and I spoke as one.

"You understand, I am sure, why I must see your arrival in our midst at this particular time, with your horse and your brother, as no less than an act of the gods. This is meant to be."

Struggling with the enormity of it, I said, "Or someone might have made it happen this way. Swift would not have jumped the wall and fled from his field without reason. Someone might have manipulated all of us—set it up so Finbar ran after the horse and the dogs and I followed, since there was no time to fetch help. Brought us all into the Otherworld. Lured my brother to the oak tree and put him in an enchanted sleep until I got there. Left Swift wandering where you would find him. Stolen the dogs . . ." Something in the quality of the silence made me falter to a stop.

"I hope you are not suggesting *I* would have done such a thing," Caisin said, folding her hands before her on the table. "And I can assure you that none of those who are of like mind with me would have acted thus, if only because it placed both you and your brother at risk of capture by our mutual adversary."

"I did wonder why, when you found me and Bear out in the woods, you did not lead us straight to Finbar. If you believed Mac Dara might take us . . ."

"At that time I did not know about the horse or about your unusual gift. Believe me, I have come to regret my decision deeply. But you must remember that this world is not like yours. Our ways will never be fully comprehensible to you."

Nor ours to you, I thought. As an explanation, it had been more than a little lacking. "What if Mac Dara did it?" I asked. "He may be several steps ahead of you and determined to destroy us before the geis can be fulfilled. Perhaps he knew Finbar would go after the horse and I would follow him."

"If this were his doing," Caisin said, "you would already be in his grip, Maeve, and your brother with you. He would not have left you wandering where I could come to your rescue. He would have ensured your brother's sleep was eternal."

Somewhere inside me, a little girl was whimpering, *I want to go home*. I knew that child from long ago, and I ordered her to hold her tongue.

"I'm not doing this," I said, trying for the kind of tone Aunt Liadan might use. "Not tomorrow. It's too soon for me to weigh up the rights and wrongs of it. Why can't it wait until the next Grand Conclave, whenever that is?" And when nobody offered a response, I added, "I can't make a decision like this on my own. I need to talk to my parents and Uncle Ciarán. I need to take Finbar home."

Still Caisin said nothing. I wondered if she thought I was not in earnest.

"I'm sorry," I said. "I mean it. I won't do it."

"Young man," Caisin said quietly, "will you leave us for a little? Perhaps you could see if Finbar is sleeping soundly."

What was this? If she thought she was going to persuade me more easily if I didn't have Luachan for support, she thought wrong.

"Maeve?" Luachan had risen, but seemed reluctant to leave me.

"All right, go," I said somewhat ungraciously. I did think he could have spoken up, supporting my decision. Surely he didn't believe I should go through with this?

When he was gone, Caisin leaned forward and took my hands in hers. She fixed her eyes on mine. "I wonder if it has occurred to you, my dear," she said, "that I might have something to offer you? Something that could make an immense difference in your life?"

I sat mute, unable to guess what she was going to say, but fairly sure I would not like it.

"Of course, your . . . difficulty"—a subtle glance down at my hands here, and I wondered if she'd been going to say *deformity*— "is part of the reason why you are so valuable to us all, since the nature of it is woven into the geis. I could see you thought that strange, since this is a verse from long ago, before the time of your father's father. But ours is a different world, Maeve, although it exists alongside your own. Such curses have their own ways of working out, long and intricate ways, and so it has been with this one. To bring about Mac Dara's downfall, we do indeed require a young woman with hands that cannot hold." She moved her fingers gently over the scarred flesh of my palm, making me flinch. People generally did not touch me there unless they had to, and the curious intimacy of the gesture unnerved me.

"It was a sad thing to happen," Caisin murmured. "And you only a child, not much older than your brother is now. A cruel thing. Your pretty face, your lovely hair. And these hands."

"It was a long time ago. I cope well enough. My lady, whatever it is you're trying to tell me, it won't change my mind. I'm taking Finbar home in the morning."

"Oh, Maeve. Has it not occurred to you, as it would to any other human girl in your circumstances, that you might make a bargain with me?"

I felt a sensation like a trickle of ice water down my spine. "My decision is made," I said, withdrawing my hands.

"Perhaps you do not understand just how much I can offer you. If you assist us with this, I can restore your face to beauty. I can render your hands not only unblemished, but as useful as if they had never been burned. Ah"—as I opened my mouth to deliver an outraged refusal—"do not be so quick to throw this back in my face. Think what it would mean. A fine marriage and children of your own. I see how much you love your young brother, and I think you would not be averse to motherhood. Undamaged, you might well wed a nobleman or prince and hold a position of considerable influence. Best of all, this would give you the ability to do what your . . . misfortune . . . has denied you: riding, dancing, playing music, everything from picking flowers to ordering the work of a great household as your mother does. Cannot you imagine stroking your baby's soft skin? Embracing your lover?"

"Stop it!" I snarled, putting my maimed hands over my ears. "I won't listen! Do you imagine I would place Finbar at such risk, and Swift, too, on the strength of a promise to make me beautiful? That's simply wrong! If I were to agree to this, it would be for one reason only: to restore Sevenwaters to the peaceful, well-governed place it was before Mac Dara came here. To make it safe for my family. To make it safe for everyone, your kind included. Your so-called bargain is an insult!"

Gods, this hurt. It was bad enough that Caisin believed I could be so easily corrupted, that she thought me so shallow. Still worse was the longing inside me to say yes, for I did want this. I wanted it so badly it felt as if my heart was being ripped in two. In my mind was that strange night when the Fair Folk had ridden by as my brother and I hid in the forest. I had watched as a perfect version of myself danced with a man, their steps graceful and fine, their eyes only for each other. I had yearned to be that woman. Deep inside, I still did.

"My answer remains the same," I said. There was a little image of Aunt Liadan in my mind now, telling me to be true to myself. I rose to my feet. "I'm sorry to disappoint you, my lady. Now I must go to bed. We'll be leaving first thing in the morning."

"Perhaps," said Caisin, "you should ask your brother what he thinks."

CHAPTER 13

Sleep proved impossible. My belly was a churning mass of anxiety. My body was filled with the urge for action. But there was nothing I could do, not now. The household went quiet. Lights were dimmed. The sounds of voices and music faded as, I assumed, folk went off to bed. Did the Fair Folk sleep as humankind did? I supposed the answer must be yes, or they would not have been able to offer us these comfortably furnished quarters.

Within my chamber I paced, torn by indecision, furious with myself for considering, even for an instant, how wonderful it would be to become magically whole and perfect. To have the use of my hands. How could I not long for that? To ride. To throw a ball for a dog. To hold a baby. I had thought myself beyond wishing the past could be changed, but it seemed that was not so. Silently, so as not to disturb Luachan and Finbar, whose doorway was covered only by a light hanging, I walked to and fro, fighting my own weakness. *In the morning we'll fetch Blaze and Swift, and we'll go straight home*, I told myself. *Finbar can ride Blaze. Luachan can lead Swift. And I'll walk, since there's nothing wrong with my legs.*

I prayed that Ciarán would be back at the nemetons when we got there, for it seemed to me he might be the only one wise enough to offer sound guidance.

"Maeve?" Luachan's voice was just above a whisper. He stood at the curtain; it was drawn slightly aside, and through the narrow gap I caught his eye. "You seem upset. What did Caisin say to you?"

It stretched the bounds of propriety for us to be housed so close. Talking to a young man while the household slept around us was quite beyond anything my mother would have sanctioned. But the circumstances were extreme. I moved to seat myself on the floor beside the curtain, and after a moment Luachan sat down on the other side.

"She made me an offer," I whispered. "Tried to bribe me into doing what she wants at this Grand Conclave. I said no."

"What offer?"

A flush of humiliation warmed my face. I did not want to talk about this. But refusing to tell would be cowardly. "She said she could take away my scars. Make me beautiful. Give me back the use of my hands."

After that, Luachan was silent for quite some time, long enough for me to assume the conversation was over. Then he said, "She offered that and you refused?" His tone was one of complete incredulity.

"Can't you see how wrong that would be? What if I agreed and then something happened to Finbar? She should have known I didn't need bribing."

"How could she know that? You had refused to help her."

I wanted to snap at him for being so calm and sensible, but I restrained myself. "Luachan?"

"Yes?"

"You think I should have agreed to go, don't you? You think Finbar and I should appear at the Grand Conclave."

A pause. "As I said, I would not tell you what to do," Luachan murmured. "You are your own woman; that's plain to me. But . . . You suggested this could wait until the next Grand Conclave. I don't believe it can. I was told by Dioman, when we were bathing, that the conclave is held every third year. How likely is it that in exactly three years from tomorrow, all the components of this rather odd verse will again be assembled here, ready to be brought into play at the right time? How likely is it that three years can pass without Mac Dara learning that his opponents are preparing this trap? Someone will see something. Someone will say something. How much more mischief can the Lord of the Oak work in that time? All the pieces are at hand. This may be the only chance to put them together."

He had shocked me. "But you were hired to keep Finbar safe. That's why you're here. He's only seven years old. This can't be a simple matter of his watching whatever it is that has to happen. It can't be as straightforward as my calming Swift the way I did earlier, even allowing for a crowd and a fire and a lot of noise. Mac Dara's hardly going to stand there and let us do it."

After a silence, Luachan spoke again. "So you still intend to take Finbar home in the morning?"

"Of course that's what I intend! And I'm expecting you to come with us, since otherwise Finbar would have to lead Swift, including getting him across the bridge." I forced myself to be honest. "We can't do it without you."

"Will you tell Finbar about the geis?"

"No! And you shouldn't tell him, either."

"Is that quite fair?"

I had thought I was already cold, but this conversation was setting a new chill in my bones. Could Luachan be right? Surely I must put Finbar's safety ahead of everything else. But perhaps I was making the biggest mistake of my life, an error that would haunt me into my old age. I longed for Bear and Badger. Not that they would provide ready answers, but their warm, strong presence would give me the heart I so badly needed. "I know as well as you do what Finbar would say: that we have to go through with this, that it's the way things must be done. He's been telling me that all along. He said we should take time to find the dogs today before we went home. But the dogs are still lost."

"Finbar is a seer. Sometimes he gets things wrong, yes, because of his age and inexperience. But perhaps in this instance he is right; perhaps he has seen that we must all be present tomorrow or your father's enemy cannot be defeated."

"I won't talk about this anymore," I said, rising to my feet. It was uncomfortable to be reminded of Father's council, where I had supported Luachan's argument that the family must stand up to Mac Dara. Easy enough to do in the warmth and safety of home, with armed guards all around. "I don't want Finbar told about the geis; he can't understand the peril he'd be in if Mac Dara saw him. When he wakes up he's to have something to eat—that's if you have any supplies left—and then we're fetching Blaze and Swift and leaving. If this darkness lingers, if there is no morning, we'll borrow a lantern and leave anyway. And now I'm going to bed."

I turned my back and walked over to my sleeping hammock. His voice came as the merest breath in the darkness.

"Maeve."

"Enough," I said.

"I failed you. I should have brought you home safely, you and Finbar. Instead, here we are. As a protector I have proven myself of very little worth."

"My father would probably agree," I said without turning. "But I don't think you've been fully tested yet. Get us safely home tomorrow and nobody can complain that you've failed in your duties. Push me into facing Mac Dara and all three of us might perish. That really would be a failure."

"Push you?" he echoed. "I don't believe anyone could do that. Once your mind is made up, nothing can change it."

I almost relented then, hearing the defeat in his voice. I wanted to go back to the curtain, sit down again, and offer words of comfort that might ease both Luachan's mind and mine. Then Finbar made a little sound in his sleep, and the moment was over.

"When I said I wouldn't talk about this anymore, I meant it," I said. "We both need rest. By morning you'll be seeing it the way I do. The only wise choice is to go home."

*   *   *

The night passed slowly. There was no more sound from next door. I lay on my hammock, soft bedding cushioning me. Within that comfort my body was a jangle of tight parts and my mind was awash with unwelcome thoughts. I longed for Bear. Images of what might have befallen the dogs beset me, refusing to be banished, along with conflicting visions of a possible tomorrow. I could not escape the feeling that whatever happened in the morning, it would not be a simple ride home followed by a measured council in which Father or Ciarán thanked us for making the right decisions, then came up with a solution that would suit everyone. Perhaps the strange darkness would not lift. Perhaps, outside this lantern-lit place of peace, it would be night forever. Perhaps . . . perhaps . . .

At some point I must have drifted off into a light slumber, for I was jolted awake by a sound like a faint bell. I thought perhaps there had been soft voices speaking nearby not long ago, but now all was silent. After some time the bell-like sound came again: a bird was calling somewhere up in the trees that formed walls and roof to Caisin's hall. Maybe dawn was coming. My head hurt. My limbs ached. And I needed to use the privy. I rose and went to the curtain, drawing it aside to peer into the next chamber. Luachan and Finbar were both fast asleep.

I had slept in the clothes provided for me. Though the lanterns were dimmed, there was sufficient light to find my way, so I headed out to the bathing chamber and the privy that was close by. When I was done, I found myself reluctant to return to the bedchamber and wait, alone with my thoughts, until the others woke. I would go and check on Swift.

A sound of voices drifted to me from somewhere within the house now, but there was nobody in sight. I took the path I thought we had taken to reach Swift's enclosure, but it seemed I chose wrong, for the way wound in a circle, bringing me back to my starting point. I tried again, peering into a series of leaf-canopied spaces, all of them empty, until at last I found the area where Swift was housed. He was standing quiet, a white shadow at the far end of the enclosure. I stood awhile by the barrier, watching him and thinking I was not ready to face a new day. Indeed, I felt ill equipped to make a decision of any kind at all. I found myself wishing I had never left Harrowfield. And yet, the voices of Uncle Bran and Aunt Liadan whispered in my ears, saying that was wrong; telling me I had work to do here, and that if I was not brave enough to do it, then nobody was. *Be true to yourself, Maeve*, Aunt Liadan said. *Confront your fears head-on*, said Uncle Bran. *What frightens you won't go away, but you'll learn the trick of standing up to it.*

After a while Swift noticed I was there. I rolled myself over the barrier and went across to talk to him. He seemed more interested in the feed someone had left for him, and that was a good thing; if he was calm he'd be better able to make the walk back to Seven-waters this morning. I found a place to sit and tried to achieve my own state of calm, while above the leafy canopy the sky began to brighten at last, spelling an end to the preternatural darkness. It seemed the storm that had near drowned us was past and a sunny day was dawning. I was glad of that, for another weary walk through the sodden forest did not bear thinking of. It would be hard enough getting two horses over that bridge without the complication of rain.

Now, that was odd. Where was Blaze? Where were the horses of the Fair Folk, those I had seen passing by at night? This little yard was bordered on three sides by the trunks of tall, slender trees, and on the other side was the pathway back into Caisin's dwelling. I had been so weary and confused last night I had not thought of it, but there was no sign of any other enclosures for livestock. I could see no stables or any obvious provision for the upkeep of the many animals a household such as this must require. Fey horses might have different needs, of course. Dioman might have decided, wisely, to keep nervous Swift away from their other livestock. But I would have thought Blaze, at least, would be somewhere close by. When I saw Caisin I must ask her.

I sat there a long while, watching Swift eat, telling him some of my thoughts, not all, for I did not want him to pick up my anxiety. Eventually I fell silent, listening to the swell of birdsong from above and thinking I must move soon, so I could be sure Finbar had breakfast before we left. Soon. But not quite yet.

"Maeve?"

Caisin's voice startled me. I turned my head to see her standing by the barrier, a blue cloak thrown over her gown, her abundant hair confined in a jeweled net at the nape of her neck. The look on her face brought me to my feet, my heart thumping. "What is it?"

"I need to speak to you. Come closer, my dear."

By the time I had crossed the enclosure and come out to stand beside her, I was shaking. Something had happened, something terrible. "Tell me," I said. "What is it? Finbar—is he safe?"

"Your brother is well and eating his breakfast as we speak. Maeve, you'd best sit down." Caisin gestured toward a bench with her long, ring-decked fingers. I sank down onto it, my stomach in knots. "I'm afraid I have ill tidings for you."

"What tidings?" My mind filled with one unspeakable possibility after another. Mother. Father. Rhian. Deirdre or her children.

"You asked if I could find out about your dogs," she said, and the compassion in her lovely eyes froze my heart. "I know you were very attached to them."

Were. "What? What's happened to them?"

She hesitated. "It is . . . it is distressing news, Maeve. I hardly know how to tell you."

"Just say it!"

"A messenger came early this morning. The folk Finbar saw were indeed Mac Dara's henchmen. The Lord of the Oak is fond of games, and he plays them with cruel inventiveness. I do not understand his motive in this, but he has put both your friends to death."

That wasn't true. It couldn't be. They were lost, perhaps hurt. Locked up. Prisoners. But not this. Bear couldn't be dead; he couldn't be. "No," I heard myself say, and it felt as if I were miles away, looking down on a scene that was not real. "No, it's not true. I don't believe you."

"I'm afraid there is no doubt about it, Maeve. My messenger saw what happened with his own eyes."

"He saw it? Then why didn't he try to stop them? Why didn't he—" I put my head in my hands. Caisin's arm came around me, but it provided no comfort at all. Bear. Badger. Gone. Gone forever. My fault. My doing. I had let them be taken. They had been alone and frightened, and I had not come. It was Bounder all over again.

"Weep all you want," Caisin said. "You loved them. Beyond the usual affection between a woman and her pet, I can see."

I let her hold me. I sobbed like a child; there was no stopping the tears. After a while I made myself draw a long breath and straighten, extracting myself from Caisin's embrace. I wiped my eyes on my sleeve. Enough of weakness. I must ask the question. "You say your messenger was there when it happened. Tell me how it was done. How did Bear and Badger die?"

"It is best if I do not tell you that," Caisin said. "Believe me, you would wish I had not."

"How did they die?" I had not thought I could speak in such a voice: cold, level, dangerous. An iron-strong darkness was filling me up, leaving no space for soft thoughts.

"By fire. Afterward, Mac Dara cut out their hearts and ate them for supper."

In that moment, I knew what it was to want to kill. I sat staring ahead of me, seeing only the vile image in my mind.

"Maeve—"

"Go away. Leave me alone."

Caisin retreated, her skirts whispering around her. Time passed. Swift moved across his enclosure one way, the other way. The birds sang; a breeze stirred the leafy branches high above me. In my mind, over and over, a tall man dressed in black raised a dripping knife to his lips, smiling. In my ears, over and over, sounded the dying screams of my boys. In my heart, a dark desire for vengeance took root.

"Maeve."

I started like a hare as the little voice behind me broke my trance. My back ached. My neck hurt. My head throbbed. I had sat unmoving since Caisin left me. And now here was Finbar, his eyes reddened and swollen, his manner courteous as always. As I turned to face him, he put his arms around me.

He knew, then. They had told him. I hoped they had spared him the details. Somewhere inside me there were good memories: Bear's rough tongue licking my cheek. His bright eyes, his alert pose, his sweetness and loyalty. His courage. His strength. The warmth of him against me at night. But those fine things were beyond my reach. All I could see was that man smiling, smiling as he lifted the gobbet of flesh to his lips.

"Finbar," I said, "I have something to ask you."

The Grand Conclave was, it seemed, sufficiently grand to require a change of clothing for everyone, human folk included. I had been unable to eat, which was perhaps just as well since what remained of Luachan's supplies was barely sufficient to feed him and Finbar. I allowed myself to be escorted back to the bathing chamber, where the silent maidservant washed and dried me, then dressed me in clothing of a kind I had never worn in my life before: a gown of clinging, silvery cloth, and over it a tunic of midnight blue, its edges trimmed with what looked like swansdown. She braided my hair and pinned it up, adding a short, gauzy veil that did nothing at all to conceal my facial scars. The whole thing was ridiculous. I told Caisin so when she came in to admire me.

"The moment I step out in this, I'll draw attention," I said. "How could Mac Dara not realize who I am? And if Finbar is with me, he'll recognize both of us. Doesn't setting up the terms of the geis require an element of surprise?"

Caisin looked, if anything, amused. She, too, had changed her clothes. She was clad in a gown of sky blue, its skirt decorated with silvery streamers that were perhaps intended to give the effect of clouds. Whatever it was made of, it was no ordinary fabric, for the garment had a life of its own, shifting and changing even when the wearer did not move. Looking at it, I found it hard to keep track of my thoughts, and I wondered if there was magic woven into the cloth.

"You seem remarkably calm, Maeve," Caisin observed.

Calm. Yes, I was calm on the surface. Once she had told me about Bear and Badger, once she had broken the hideous news, something odd had come over me. It had changed me into a new person, cold and intent. My fury was no less strong for being well controlled. I still feared for Finbar; that had not altered. But he had chosen this, as I had known he would. *We have to do it, Maeve,* he had said. *This is the way it's meant to be.* And this time I had believed him.

"I need your assurance that my brother will be safe," I said now. "You made Luachan give up his weapons. How can he guard Finbar without them?"

"A man does not enter the Grand Conclave bearing cold iron," Caisin said. "But the druid will be armed. Your brother will be well protected. I give you my solemn word. As for appearances, your small party of three will remain concealed until it is time. You will be able to watch the challenges, but you must keep quiet. When I give the sign you will come forward and the geis will be fulfilled."

"Swift must be with us. I'm the only one who can keep him calm until it's time."

"Maeve, I am a person of considerable power and influence, with many folk at my disposal. I possess some abilities that would astonish you, should I choose to demonstrate them. Believe me, there is no need for you to be concerned. All will be well."

"I agreed to this with some reluctance, my lady. In view of the risk, it is not unreasonable that I seek some assurances."

"Of course not, my dear. Now come, let us find that brother of yours and the companion who guards him so faithfully. We must be on our way."

"My lady?"

She had been heading out the door but turned back at this, arching her brows in question.

"When you spoke of the conclave last night you mentioned a series of challenges. Who will stand up against Mac Dara? If the challenge succeeds, who will take his place?"

Caisin smiled. "There are many who would like that privilege, but only one, I think, with the necessary qualities. Come, Maeve, we should proceed if we are not to draw attention to ourselves by arriving late."

I had myriad questions, but clearly they were not going to be answered. And perhaps that did not matter now, since I was committed to doing this anyway. Whoever the challenger was, if he had the support of Caisin and her friends he must at least be a better prospect than Mac Dara.

I could hardly believe it. Before dusk we might be home again, bearing the news that Mac Dara no longer ruled in the Otherworld. Never mind that the moment we were safely out of this place, the grief I had locked away inside me would emerge and undo me completely. At this moment I was a warrior. If I harnessed my anger, it could carry me all the way to victory.

There were more of Caisin's folk than I had thought: too many to count. In their finery of blue and silver—clan colors, I assumed— they resembled a flock of exotic birds. There was a suppressed excitement in their manner this morning. They murmured and whispered together, gesturing with pale hands. Dioman was there, though today he did not have his owl. I saw the councilor, Breasal, somber in his dark robe. He was the only person not dressed for a celebration.

And now, coming into the central hall where we had gathered, here were Luachan and Finbar, clad in garments to match mine, all silver and blue and feathers. Luachan carried it off remarkably well and I was reminded that he was a chieftain's son. Finbar was pale, his face all eyes, but he held his head high. Gods, I hoped his instincts were right about this.

"You'll be wanting to fetch the horse yourself," Dioman said, coming over. "I'll take you there."

This simple act of courtesy softened my mood. I thanked him, and the three of us followed him through the winding ways to the horse enclosure, where Swift, blissfully ignorant of the trial await-

ing him, was grazing. As we approached the barrier a young man
of the fey came up, holding a soft halter and leading rope. I could
hardly have organized things better myself.

"He'll be best not walking with a large group," I said to Dioman as Luachan opened the gate for me. "I don't think he'll let
anyone but Luachan lead him. And I'll need to go alongside to
help keep him calm. I want Finbar in sight all the time."

"Of course." Dioman did not attempt to join us in the enclosure, but waited by the gate. "You will be concealed on the way, so
Mac Dara's spies cannot see you."

"Concealed?" asked Luachan. "What do you mean by that?"

Dioman spread his hands in a gesture of apology. "A charm.
Think of it as a veil cast over you. You will see and feel nothing out
of the ordinary, and nor will the horse, but you will be hidden
from curious eyes. We can maintain that shield over you until it is
time to reveal our hand. My sister will give a sign, we will lift the
charm, and you will step forward."

"What is to stop Mac Dara from blasting us with some kind of
spell the moment he sees us?"

Dioman favored me with a charming smile. "The Great Conclave is governed by strict rules, Lady Maeve, old and respected
rules. Once a challenge is accepted, both parties must abide by
those rules for the duration of their encounter. You will be safe. If
it were otherwise, believe me, my sister would not have asked you
to help us today."

"What are the rules?"

"They are many and complex. You need know only that they
are intended to keep the challenges both fair and safe."

"You used the word encounter," I said. "And earlier, I remember Caisin speaking of combat. Are these challenges in the nature
of . . . fights? Or are they displays of magic, one participant trying
to outdo the other?"

"Either is possible," Dioman said lightly, as if it hardly mattered one way or the other.

There was no time to quiz him: Caisin had bid us hurry. In the
back of my mind was the knowledge that Mac Dara had never

before been challenged at the conclave. How, then, could anyone be sure he would obey the rules, whatever they were? If he saw the conditions of the geis occurring before his eyes, would any rules stop him from attacking me or Finbar or Swift in order to stop the curse from coming to fulfillment?

"This is the way it's meant to be, Maeve," said Finbar, his voice grave as a druid's. "Do you want me to help with Swift?"

We were lucky. A night in the quiet of Caisin's hall and a good breakfast had done wonders for Swift's state of mind, though the scratches and bruises of his flight through the forest were still apparent. I spoke to him and stroked him while Luachan put on the halter, and we led him out without any difficulty. Despite that, Luachan was even whiter than Finbar, and there was a grim set to his jaw. I saw, now, that he had indeed been given weapons. He carried a knife and a sword, both sheathed.

"Fashioned from bone, or something very like it," he said, observing my interest. "With an exceedingly sharp edge. I won't hesitate to use them. But I hope it won't come to that."

We led Swift to the area where Caisin's people were gathering, and I saw that many of these splendidly clad folk were armed. Indeed, they appeared equipped to deal with a veritable army of assailants. There were willow bows and bright-feathered arrows, sheathed swords and knives, pale spears that might have been of wood or bone. This was both reassuring—we would be well protected—and troubling. Why would they come thus prepared unless they were expecting to fight?

Headed by Caisin, the party moved out into the open forest, though it was hard to tell where her hall ended and the forest began. Remembering that strange procession I had seen by night, I had thought the Fair Folk might ride, but all went on foot. Swift's coat gleamed against the many blues of gown and cloak and headdress. Luachan and I walked one on either side of him, with Finbar next to me. Luachan held the leading rope; I put my hand up to touch Swift's neck from time to time and reassure him that all was well. If he could have known how my heart was drumming he might have walked less easily.

We wound our way between the oaks as the sun rose higher and the birds carolled a greeting to a fairer day. The leaf litter underfoot was saturated, clinging in dark clumps to the pretty shoes I had been given, but the rain was quite gone and the air was still. Provided one walked briskly, the day felt almost warm. *Tonight*, I told myself. *Just get through this, and tonight you will be safely back home, and the job will be done, and you can weep and scream and rage all you want. Be brave. Be as brave as Aunt Liadan would be.* I tucked thoughts of Bear and Badger away in a hidden corner, deep inside me. I must be iron strong. Nothing must get in the way of this mission.

"All right, Finbar?"

"Mm."

"I don't think it's far."

"Don't worry, Maeve," my little brother said. "I'll look after you."

I would have said the same to him, but this was the statement of a man, even if that man was only seven, and I must accept it as such or insult the brave soul he was. "Thank you," I said.

The path began to ascend, heading up a thickly wooded hillside broken by stony outcrops down which streamlets tumbled to lose themselves in the boggy ground below. We climbed for some time. The pitch was becoming almost too steep for Swift when we rounded a corner and the ground leveled. The path broadened. Caisin's folk came in all around us, blocking my view ahead. Dioman and several other tall people had moved to form a kind of guard around Swift. The horse turned his head from side to side and whisked his tail.

"Ask them to stay farther back, my lord," I said to Dioman. "Swift isn't used to so many people; he may bolt again. Luachan, keep a firm hold."

"I have him safe," Luachan said.

All at once everyone stopped walking. I stood there, stroking Swift's face with my knuckles, and after a while Fiamain Flame-hair threaded her way back to us. "Maeve, Finbar, you will wait on the rise up there, by those rocks," she said. "Druid, guard them well. My brother will stay beside you. The veil of concealment lies over you still and will remain until Caisin gives the word." She stood before me, a vision in rich dark blue, her bright hair caught up in a net that seemed decorated with real fireflies, for they danced around her head in a sparkling halo. "You must not call out, or run forward, or do anything that might break the charm. Do you understand? Much rides on this."

I understood all too well. Get this wrong in any particular, and not only might I never reach home again, but Finbar too would be condemned, not to speak of Luachan, who was only doing his job, and poor innocent Swift. "Yes," I said at the same time as Finbar chimed in with, "Of course we understand."

"Very well," said Fiamain, and I thought her voice held a tinge of regret. "You know what you must do when the time comes?"

"Calm Swift with my voice," I said. "That is all I have been told."

"It will suffice. Make sure, when it is time, that you do not lose sight of that simple instruction."

A young man of the fey stepped forward, reaching to take Swift's leading rein.

"No!" I protested.

"The horse can go no farther with you," Dioman said. "He must wait elsewhere; there is no room for him up there and, as you yourself said, he will be disturbed by the crowd. Let Glas take him, Lady Maeve."

"You don't understand. He's not used to strangers; he'll be upset. If I'm supposed to calm him later, this is not—" I stopped myself. The last thing Swift needed to hear right now was my voice raised in anxious protest.

"Glas will take him to a place with food and water, out of sight of the crowd," said Fiamain. "He can wait there until it's time."

"Why can't we wait there with him?"

"No, Maeve." Finbar surprised me. "We need to be here, where we can see."

I hesitated. He was right, of course; if we did not watch the conclave proceed, we might not be adequately prepared for what lay before us. Meeting the challenge was vital. And I could not send Luachan with Swift. He must stay close to Finbar.

"I think we have no choice," said Luachan quietly. Without waiting for me to say anything, he passed the rein to Glas, who led Swift away.

"Come," said Dioman. "I will take you to your position."

The Grand Conclave took place around the rim of a rock basin. The hollow was both broad and deep. After the heavy rains of the last few days it should surely have been full of water, a whole lake of it, but there must have been a drainage point somewhere, for the basin was dry. The bottom was filled with a jumble of round stones each the size of a man's head, atop which was a sizeable mound of sticks and branches. It was almost like a fire laid on a hearth; but this would be a giant's hearth, the flames from which would roar high, hot as a dragon's breath. Oh gods. I looked at Finbar, and he looked back at me. *Logs, logs, a hundred logs, two hundred he piled up . . .*

"Finbar," I whispered, my flesh crawling, but before I could say a word more, Dioman silenced me with a finger to his lips.

We watched in silence as Caisin and her retinue moved out around the rim of the great basin, where many people were already gathered. There was a group in green and another in autumn tones of russet and yellow. At one point stood a somber collection of folk clad all in black. The crowd numbered perhaps a hundred, maybe more. All of them I judged to be Fair Folk, tall, elegant in appearance and somewhat detached in expression. That seemed to me strange. If the Grand Conclave was a gathering at which a ruler of this realm might be deposed and replaced, shouldn't every race that lived here be represented? It was my understanding that Mac Dara ruled not only his own people, but all those who dwelled in the Otherworld part of Sevenwaters. The other races were surely not so insignificant that they would be left out of the conclave. What about the mysterious Old Ones, who had helped Clodagh and Cathal escape from the Otherworld?

What about those tree people, like the boy Finbar had spotted earlier? A circle of old oaks stood guard around this rocky, open place, but if there were folk up in their branches they were hidden from sight.

Our vantage point was a natural shelf on the rising ground leading from the basin to the surrounding trees. We were about six strides from the level area bordering the basin and high enough to see over the crowd. It felt odd to be here in full view, yet clearly invisible to the folk down there, for nobody gave us so much as a glance. We waited. Caisin and her party greeted various people. It seemed to me she must be a person of some status, for as she progressed around the circle, bestowing a word here, a smile there, folk bowed low to her. A large group of people in red and gold drifted in from the forest, swelling the crowd. At a certain point a broad tongue of stone jutted out over the basin. If there had been water below, it would have been a good place from which to launch oneself in a spectacular dive. Nobody stood on the projection, despite the lack of room. Caisin and Fiamain took up places not far from that point with their blue and silver entourage behind them. Several of the tallest men of their clan stood close to the sisters, their stance alert and watchful.

I wished we did not have to wait. Waiting provided too much thinking time. What happened at a conclave, anyway? I had envisaged it as part council, part tournament, though it was hard to imagine either being conducted in a place like this. I glanced at Finbar. He was composed, though still rather pale. Let this be over soon.

I met Luachan's eye and he attempted a reassuring smile. His tense features undermined the intention. I managed a smile of my own, though I was wound tight as a bowstring. Finbar had his gaze fixed on the tongue of stone. I wondered if he had seen this place in one of his visions.

A horn sounded a piercing, eldritch note and from the black-clad group stepped forward a tall man, his garments simple but impeccably cut, his face long and pale, his hair flowing midnight black across his shoulders. His eyes were deep-set, and although I could not see their color, I imagined they were of the same dark hue. The assembled folk fell silent as one.

The man walked out onto the tongue of stone. Behind him came a pair of fey guards, brawny as fighting bulls. Their segmented armor reminded me of a beetle's carapace. The two crossed their pale spears to block anyone from following. Who could this be but the Lord of the Oak? When I looked at him the memory of my boys stirred inside me, in the secret place close to my heart. His foul act shrieked for vengeance; it was a bloody wound. Yet I was not blind to the sorrow on Mac Dara's face, and the weariness. I saw also that his features might be pleasing to some women's tastes. If the tales were to be believed, he was old beyond count of years, but in appearance he was a man in his prime, thirty at most. Some women might favor that lean, dangerous look.

He stood there a few moments before speaking, waiting until every eye in the crowd was on him and every tongue still.

"Welcome one and all!" Mac Dara spread his arms wide. "It is time once again to celebrate the season with song and dance; to test the mettle of our finest combatants; to hear the report of deeds done, for good and for ill, since last we gathered here at the Stone Cauldron." His gaze went around them all, and there was something in it that made me shiver. "This is our day of reckoning; it is our day of accounting; it is our day of challenge. Let the Grand Conclave commence!"

The horn sounded again from somewhere behind the crowd. Mac Dara's guards lifted their spears and the prince moved to seat himself on a throne-like rock over which a venerable oak spread a canopy against both sun and rain. The graceful folk of the Tuatha De shrank away as he passed, leaving an empty space between their prince and the stone basin. Whatever was to unfold there, he would have an unimpeded view. The bodyguards stationed themselves on either side of his seat; other armed men stood close by.

Music played. I heard flutes, a harp, drums pounding a rhythm with beats grouped in threes and fours: headlong, uneven, dangerous. Onto the tongue of stone came a pair of statuesque women, each holding a staff. They wore long gowns—one green, one yellow—over which were leather breastpieces. They faced off and began a leaping, turning, ducking dance in which staves swung and parried, feet kicked and pranced, and the combatants' long hair flew out behind them—gold, russet—like banners of war. I wondered that they could move so fast and stay so graceful. No human woman could have executed such intricate moves at such speed. Each blow seemed certain to strike; each blow was evaded by the merest whisker, as if the women had some means of knowing just where it would fall. Perhaps they did; fey folk would not fight as humankind did. This fleetness of foot, this remarkable ability to make things look so easy, was perhaps not surprising at all.

An odd shadow passed over the tongue of stone, causing one combatant to hesitate. It took only an instant, but the other was lightning swift, seizing the moment, striking low with the staff to catch her opponent across the knees and send her sprawling to the stones.

The crowd roared approval. Finbar jumped, startled by the noise, and I bent to whisper reassurance. By the time I looked back across the basin the tongue of stone was empty. I spotted the winner of the fight among the crowd, pushing her hair back from her face, receiving congratulations. The other woman, I could not see.

Two men came forward next, one dark, one fair. They were well matched in height and build, and each was possessed of the physical beauty shared by all the Fair Folk. I expected weapons, perhaps swords or knives this time, but these fighters had other tools at their disposal. On the stone tongue they faced each other at a distance of six strides, their pose as casual as if they were merely exchanging the time of day. The fair man had a ball in one hand; he was toying with it as he stared at his opponent. The dark man's hands were empty. He gazed back. A hush came over the crowd.

The combatants held their pose, eyes locked, to the count of perhaps twenty. Then, without warning, the fair man hurled his ball, fast, toward his opponent. Before it could reach its target, the dark man's hands moved before him, and instead of a ball, there was a little red bird that spread its wings and flew up and away into the trees. The crowd applauded.

How far away had they taken Swift? Not too far, surely—he must be ready to return here as soon as it was time for us to play our part. He must surely be able to hear all this noise, to sense the crackle of magic in the air. He must be wondering where he was and why we were not there to reassure him. *Calm, Swift,* I thought. *Green fields. Sweet water.* How could any creature be calm in such a place? My belly was tight with unease. If anything went wrong, if we could not put every single element of the geis in place, we would end up in Mac Dara's clutches. My future and Finbar's would be unthinkable. Mac Dara would use us to force our father's obedience. *Don't think of what might go wrong,* I ordered myself. *Don't dwell on the possibility that in your grief and anger you've agreed to something unutterably foolish.*

Now the dark-haired man had a ball. It was fashioned of bright metal. He did not wait as the other had but released his missile immediately, so his opponent was caught off guard. Almost. At the last moment, with the ball speeding straight for his face, the fair-haired man ducked. The projectile hurtled straight toward Mac Dara, who did not so much as lift an eyebrow. The fair man spun around, pointing, and with a popping sound the ball exploded in a small burst of blue and green flames, three strides from the fey prince. Shards of metal fell to the ground; it had been real enough.

Mac Dara's slow applause was as much derision as admiration. The look on his face said, *You call that magic? Wait until you see my magic.* The two combatants bowed politely and moved back into the crowd; it seemed this contest was a draw.

"Cheap tricks," murmured Dioman in my ear, making me start. "They are just for show, to set the crowd at ease. The real displays will be later. There are various positions of authority to be filled; it is customary for folk to challenge for them."

Later. How much later? This could take all day. "Swift won't be able to wait very long," I whispered, "even if he has food and water. He'll become restless. If he bolts, this is over before it's begun."

"No need to concern yourself."

"But there is," I insisted, troubled that he did not seem to understand. "You don't know Swift; I do. If—"

"Truly," Dioman said. "Simply wait; do not distress yourself. And stay quiet; it is possible some of those below may hear our voices."

That surprised me. If he could cast a spell that would render us invisible to those folk down there, he could surely cast one that would stop them from hearing us.

"We should take no risks," he murmured, as if reading my thoughts. "The stakes are high."

The displays of prowess had ceased. The conclave had moved on to a hearing of grievances and delivery of judgments, quite similar to those held by leaders such as my father to settle disputes. There were councilors present from all the clans, and each in turn stepped up to read out a list of complaints. The folk concerned were given the chance to make a case, and then Mac Dara passed judgment. My attention wandered despite my best efforts. I kept imagining a fire in that stone basin, a great fire such as the one in Finbar's story, the flames licking at my face and hands, the smoke filling my mouth and my chest and sending me into a witless stupor . . . I kept thinking of my family, of the terrible blow I would deliver them today if this crazy mission failed . . . They would wish, quite rightly, that I had never come home . . .

Down there they were talking about the duty or right of one man to exact vengeance for the humiliation of his brother. The two parties put forward their arguments, the interchange becoming more and more heated, until, as at a certain point in the preceding cases, a bell sounded a single pure note, signaling the end of the discussion. The voices fell silent, and into that silence came the judgment of Mac Dara.

"Labhraidh, you are the offended party in this quarrel. But you were not without fault; if you had acted swiftly, you could have ended this long ago and saved all of us a great deal of time. Sleibhin, your actions breached the laws of kinship, and you will pay the price. I offer you a choice. Do battle with this man and face the judgment of the Stone Cauldron or leave this place forthwith, and let me not see you or yours again."

"But, my lord—"

"Would you challenge my decision?" Mac Dara's voice was a blade at the throat, pressing with gentle insistence. His expression was quite calm as he sat there in his chair of stone. The two men were kneeling before him, their heads bowed. "So, Sleibhin, what's it to be? Stand and fight, or flee like a mangy cur?"

"My lord"—Sleibhin's voice was unsteady—"I will take my family and leave this place."

"You disappoint me. Labhraidh, this presents us with a problem. You're left with no opponent. We can't have that." Mac Dara paused for a heartbeat. "I'm sure I can find someone for you to fight. Any volunteers?"

A silence, then a great intake of breath, as of many folk both horrified and somewhat excited. It seemed this was the way the Lord of the Oak kept his people entertained. From the crowd a man stepped forward; or perhaps not so much a man as a giant, for he stood head and shoulders above the tallest fey warrior present.

"I'll fight, my lord prince."

"Ah, Mochta," said Mac Dara, "I knew we could rely on you."

I could not understand why Labhraidh should be required to fight anyone. He had not committed any offense; it was the other man who had smirched his brother's reputation and lost him his livelihood. This made no sense.

"Drop your weapons and go, Sleibhin," Mac Dara said. "There is no place for your kind here."

Sleibhin put down his sword and knife, rose to his feet, then offered a bow that was a great deal more respectful than I thought was appropriate under the circumstances. He took three steps away before one of Mac Dara's guards, swift as a striking snake, lifted a club and delivered a hideous blow to his head. Sleibhin went down like a felled tree.

I tried to block Finbar's view, but I was too slow. We had both seen it: the head staved in, the body lying there with arms outstretched as if in prayer. The crowd roared approval.

"They killed him," Finbar said, his tone flat with disbelief.

"Shh," hissed Dioman.

What was this? Had we wandered into a realm where right and wrong no longer had any meaning? This was impossible. We couldn't be here; we couldn't do this. Home, I must get Finbar home before worse happened. "Finbar," I whispered urgently. "Luachan. We can't go through with this. It's wrong; everything's wrong. Did you hear those people cheering? We have to go home."

"It's too late for that." Luachan had been very quiet, heeding Dioman's warnings. Now he spoke in a murmur. "Outside this veil of protection we'd be clearly visible. We couldn't get home safely with Mac Dara's folk everywhere. The only way out is to do what Caisin has asked us to do."

"But—"

"Maeve," whispered Finbar, "we have to stay. You know what Mac Dara did."

My boys. My dear, brave boys. I could not speak of that dark thing lest it bring me entirely undone.

Down at the stone basin, the hapless Labhraidh was battling Mochta. The bout seemed unlikely to last long.

"Don't look," I told Finbar, turning my own eyes away.

"I don't need to look," Finbar said. "The big man will knock the other man into the fire."

I drew in a long breath, hearing sounds of scuffling and grunting, along with gasps and exclamations from the appreciative onlookers. "What fire?" I made myself ask. "There is no fire."

"There is now," said Finbar.

CHAPTER 14

For a heartbeat I allowed myself to pretend that Finbar was wrong and that the fire was all in his imagination. Then I smelled it, the unmistakable, sharp tang of smoke. Old memories flickered, caught, roared through me. I looked down at the basin. Mochta stood alone on the stone projection. He was sheathing a knife. Below him the basin was full of flame; this was indeed the great fire of Finbar's story. My heart performed a leaping dance of sheer terror. My breath left my body before I could form the words, *I can't do this.*

"Maeve." I felt my brother's hand fasten around my wrist as he spoke. "Remember the story Uncle Ciarán told? *If you are brave, good and wise you can face any challenge.* You're as brave as a"—he hunted for the right comparison—"as brave as a dragon."

"You're the bravest woman I ever met," said Luachan, fixing me with his startling blue eyes. "You can do this. *We* can do it."

And when I made no response, Finbar said, "Mac Dara had a man killed just now, for no reason. He tortured Cruinn's warriors. You know what he did to Bear and Badger. You can't let him get away with that."

I drew a ragged breath. "Of course not," I muttered, reminding myself that I had been warned there might be a ritual flame, and that I had been working on my fear of fire for ten years now and could sit reasonably close to a hearth without letting anyone see how much it disturbed me. Never mind that this blaze was a hundred times bigger than any hearth fire. Bear. Badger. My lovely boys. Whatever had to be done today, I would find the courage for it.

"The challenges will begin now," said Dioman in an undertone. "The time is drawing closer."

I made myself breathe slowly, using a technique Bran had taught me in the time when I was learning to control my fear. My heart's wild drumming became a steady march.

The challenges began. There was a pattern to this part of the proceedings. A dark-robed man of imposing bearing—Mac Dara's councilor, I guessed—unfurled a scroll and read out a list of positions of responsibility that were to be filled. I would have thought Mac Dara would simply appoint his favored candidate to each post; he did not seem the kind of person who would care about due process. But perhaps it entertained him to make folk do battle for such responsibilities as Keeper of Lore or Overseer of Margins. Or perhaps even the Lord of the Oak could not disregard the ancient laws that governed the Grand Conclave.

In a human court, such as that of the High King, rivals for a position would set out their credentials, speak of their experience and, prior to the decision, maybe work on garnering support from influential nobles. This was quite different. For each position there were only two candidates, and in each case those candidates demonstrated their qualifications by means of magic.

The councilor read out the rules before the contests began. The rivals must both stand on the tongue of stone. If one of them was the current holder of the position, that person would perform second. The horn would be sounded to indicate the start of each claimant's allotted time; it would be sounded again after a count of one hundred, at which point all magical activity must cease. The demonstration must not constitute an attack on the rival claimant, nor do unreasonable injury to any of those present. I wondered what a reasonable injury was—a cut, a bruise? Or might these folk consider anything less than a deadly wound acceptable? Ciarán had said the Fair Folk did not die, but faded and lost their power. But he'd also said they could be snuffed out by the clever use of magic. It made me think again about what we had just seen. A club to the head, a knife in the chest—there must have been more to those deaths than met the eye.

Of course, the councilor went on, almost as if he knew my train of thought, if both parties agreed to a magical combat in place of the usual display of skill, that was also acceptable. In that case the rule about reasonable injury did not apply. There must be no intervention in any challenge by any member of the conclave. Winners of each challenge would be chosen by popular acclaim.

It could be a fight to the death, then, all for the right to spend the next three years as Master of Portals, which sounded like a glorified name for a household steward. I knew the Fair Folk did not see things the same way we did; I was beginning to understand just how vast that gap was. There was a feeling like a cold stone in my chest. If this was so hard now, how could I walk out in the open and confront Mac Dara? My mind refused to show me that scene; I simply could not imagine it.

"Maeve," Luachan murmured, "are you all right?"

I said nothing, but when he met my eye I managed a smile. There had been times when Luachan had irritated me; times, such as that wet, cold sojourn in the woods, when he had disappointed me. But he had a strong arm and a good heart, and I was deeply grateful that he was here with us.

A spectacular series of magical displays followed. Overseer of Margins evidently required the ability to change the natural shape of things, or at least to give the illusion of doing so. The first contender conjured a bridge across the stone basin, along which he moved with confidence above what had become a bowl of glowing embers ten strides across. The red-gold light played on the faces of the crowd. Mac Dara on his throne was a creature of flame and shadow, watching as the man on the bridge stirred up an eerie wind that whipped the fire into swirling circles around him. The smell of smoke filled my nostrils. Under it was another odor, like charring meat.

A thought was in my mind, a hideous thought, but I would not draw my brother's attention to it. Besides, this was a festival; perhaps they had killed a sheep or a pig and were making use of this fire to roast it for later. Perhaps . . . No, I would not let my mind go down that path.

The horn sounded. As the man returned to the tongue of stone, the bridge he had made vanished behind him. An illusion. Yet I had seen him standing on it, surrounded by flame. His opponent stepped out a few paces, turned to face Mac Dara's throne, and gave a courtly bow. He straightened, turned back toward the basin, then made a rippling movement with his hands.

There was an explosive hissing sound, as of a large quantity of water suddenly released. A vast cloud of steam arose from the stone basin, sending those close to the rim reeling back. *Reasonable injury.*

A sudden breeze passed across the open area, dispersing the steam. Now the stone basin was full of water. Objects floated here and there on the surface.

"The giant knocked that man into the fire," Finbar said. "And that woman fell in, too, the one who was first to fight. You shouldn't look, Maeve."

But I had looked already and had seen what was left of her in the water.

Luachan put an arm around each of us.

"If this disturbs you," Dioman murmured, "look away."

But I could not look away. Soon we would be out there, in front of that crowd, in full sight of Mac Dara. Soon we must perform as these folk were doing. We must stand a step away from death. *Let this be a bad dream*, I prayed. *Let me wake up now.*

The Lord of the Oak had risen to his feet. His voice was crystal clear. Based on the crowd's applause, he said, the position went to the fellow who had created the bridge and conjured with fire. Both claimants had done well, but the display with water had been . . . Mac Dara searched for the right word . . . untidy. And with a snap of the fingers, he rendered the scene more acceptable. The water drained out, to where I did not know. The floating corpses descended and were lost from view. And a little later, a fiery glow once more arose from the stone cauldron. This prince, it seemed, had no problem at all in making wet wood burn.

Stay calm, Maeve, I ordered myself. *Since you must do this, make sure you do it well.* It didn't help much. We were about to play a game that could end up with all of us—me, my brother, Luachan—tossed into the flames as carelessly as one might discard a dead twig. Yes, the geis said only that Finbar must watch the proceedings; it said only that I must calm the horse without using my hands. That sounded reasonable; it sounded straightforward. But Mac Dara did not think the way a human leader would. His games were cruel and heartless. A life meant nothing to him. That woman who had fought earlier in a breathtaking display of skill and grace had not even been contending for a position; she and her opponent had merely been entertaining the crowd. Why had she been consigned to the pit?

The challenges continued their pattern: the sounding of the horn, the two contenders showing what they could do, the horn again and the decision. Keeper of Lore: a pattern of fiery runes blazoned in the air; a magic garment fashioned of tiny bright images, showing the tale of Cú Chulainn in all its grandeur and pathos. Dream-worker: a flock of butterflies, wings so bright they seemed like flying flames; a crystal sphere hanging in space, with a music ringing from it that set a look of utter wonder on every face there, save one. I had not thought to see the folk of the Tuatha De so enraptured that they forgot everything around them. That was truly a feat.

Master of Portals: a stunning display in which a woman in red simply spread her arms wide and turned her gaze toward a dark area of forest. Before the eyes of the assembled folk, an opening appeared, a rent in the fabric of things. On this side were oaks, shadowy depths, mossy stones and the cool air of autumn. On the other side, a harsh dry land, spiky plants, bright sunlight. Then, through the gap came a monstrous creature, a great, scaly, staring thing, and many of the Fair Folk put up their hands in signs of ward, perhaps thinking it might attack them. But the woman spoke and pointed, and the animal gazed at her, then turned and lumbered away, back to the strange place through the portal. Another world? Another time? A place of story, or only an illusion?

"Morrigan's britches," muttered Luachan, giving voice perfectly to my own feelings.

The fey woman moved her hands with elegant flair, and where the strange portal had been, the forest lay dark and quiet. The horn sounded. Her opponent stepped forward, an oak staff in one hand. He offered a wry smile. "I doubt I can improve on that," he said with good humor. He raised the staff up over his head and whirled around, and in an instant his adversary was gone. Not vanished in a puff of smoke, the way folk do in wonder tales. Not knocked from her feet by the swinging staff, for I could swear it had not touched her. The stone had swallowed her. A pit had opened beneath her feet, just wide enough; I could still see it. Before I had time to suck in a shocked breath the stone healed itself and the opening was no more.

The crowd gasped, muttered, craned their necks to see. Mac Dara lifted his dark brows, eyeing the man who stood quiet before him. "I hope you have not broken any rules," the Lord of the Oak said calmly. "The penalty hardly bears thinking about."

The contender, a green-clad man with gleaming corn-gold hair, smiled again. He laid the staff across his outstretched hands, made a twisting movement, spoke words I did not understand. There was a disturbance behind him and there, suddenly, was the woman who had opposed him, her eyes dark holes of shock in a face the color of fresh cheese, her crimson gown ripped and scorched. She gathered herself visibly, straightening her shoulders and lifting her chin, then took three steps away from the edge before she buckled at the knees and collapsed on the ground.

"There's no lasting damage, my lord," said the contender, not sparing her a look. "Save maybe to her pride."

The crowd erupted in applause. There was no doubting that this unpleasant piece of showmanship had won the man his position. It was clear Master of Portals meant something quite different from what I had imagined, and I wondered how many portals existed that humankind knew nothing of. Portals between our world and Mac Dara's, for instance. Now that I thought of it, Clodagh's story had contained a trip through a mysterious tunnel, accompanied by the Old Ones; that was how she had managed to return to the Otherworld to rescue Cathal. So there was indeed more than one way across. I wondered which Swift would find more unsettling, a narrow bridge of withies or a dark underground passage. Poor Swift . . . I hoped he was not too unsettled. It would be cruel to lead him out there and subject him to the crowd, the fire, the noise. Let this be over soon, and let me get him home to his quiet field and the simple companionship of Pearl.

More appointments were decided: Overseer of Border Magic, Guardian of the Prince's Treasure, Controller of Others.

"What are Others?" I whispered to Dioman.

"Lesser races. Those that dwell here and those that wander in."

"Oh." I exchanged a glance with Finbar. Dioman meant the Old Ones; he meant the tree people Finbar had seen earlier. *Lesser* covered, most likely, anyone who was not of the Fair Folk, including us.

"It can't be much longer." Something in Luachan's voice caught my attention, and when I turned to look at him, it was to see his lips pressed into a tight line. He was so pale he looked ill. "They are almost at the end of their list."

Perhaps I, too, looked as if fear was gnawing at my vitals. "Dioman—" I began, wanting to ask how long we must wait.

"Caisin Silverhair!" Mac Dara's voice came clearly from down at the basin, and I fell silent. Without rising, he turned his head to gaze at Caisin where she stood with her sister on one side and Breasal the councilor on the other. "Your clan has shown a remarkable lack of ambition today. Not one of your kinsfolk contesting a position? Not a single member of your family dazzling us with displays of brilliance? What's come over you? In all the conclaves I've had the dubious privilege to preside over, this is the first at which none of your people has stepped up to the challenges."

Caisin bent her knee in a courtly gesture that was not quite a curtsy. "True, my lord." Her tone was sweet and confident; she spoke in apparent amity.

"What have we left, Fraochan?" Mac Dara made show of turning to his councilor, who still had the scroll in his hands. "Surely we can find something to offer Caisin's folk." Fraochan opened his mouth to answer, but Mac Dara spoke over him. "I see your sister here today, Caisin, but not your brother. Surely Dioman would not absent himself from a Grand Conclave. The rules are quite plain. For a nobleman of your brother's status, the penalty for nonattendance is—"

"Severe, yes, we are aware of that, my lord, as is our brother." Caisin spoke courteously, as before. "He is not far off and will be with us soon. As for positions of office, we—"

"Ah," said the Lord of the Oak as his councilor showed him something on the scroll. "Keeper of the Hounds. How about that? Vacant, since the previous keeper suffered an unfortunate accident yesterday; someone could step right in. Isn't your brother supposed to have a way with animals?"

My flesh crawled, remembering. How dared he? How dared a man like that keep hounds of his own? How could he even dream of it?

"Fey hounds," whispered Finbar. "Not . . ." His voice faltered.

Now Mac Dara was saying something about it needing to be a test, not a challenge, and calling for Dioman to step forward or pay the penalty for disobedience. In the moment before Dioman himself spoke, I noticed something interesting: the members of Caisin's household were no longer standing together in a group, but had spread themselves out amongst the crowd. The blue and silver could be seen all around the stone basin.

"I must leave you." Dioman did not sound troubled by his prince's summons. He looked perfectly calm, as if there were nothing to fear.

"Tell us first," I said, "how much longer must we wait? Will it be time soon?"

"Oh, very soon," said Dioman, his gaze moving to Luachan and then to me.

"If you are not here, how will we—"

"Prepare yourselves. When it is time, you will know." He turned on his heel and was gone.

A sudden babble of voices soon after told me that Dioman had come into view of the crowd. He walked around the basin's edge—folk made way as he passed—and halted before Mac Dara's throne, where he delivered a sketchy bow.

"We should get ready," Finbar said. "It's nearly time."

Cold fingers clawed at my belly. Mac Dara was saying he would release his hounds against a quarry, and Dioman must show his skill by calling them off at the height of the pursuit. It should be an easy quarry, since the whole performance must take place within sight of the assembled folk. The Lord of the Oak pondered awhile; he looked around the crowd, making play of searching. I wondered why he did not conjure a fat partridge or long-limbed hare for his dogs to chase. After the displays of magic we had seen, that should be simple stuff.

"Ah," he said eventually. "Ideal. Coblaith, pass down that ridiculous creature of yours."

It was the little dog I had seen on the night the Fair Folk rode past our place of hiding; the night I was shown a perfect Maeve dancing with her beloved. The tiny creature had scant hope of escaping a pack of hunting hounds in full cry, and surely none at all if those hounds were fey.

Get down there right now, whispered Wild Maeve in my ear. *Snatch up the dog and hold him safe. Tell those sycophantic courtiers it's time someone stopped Mac Dara's acts of casual cruelty.* But Sensible Maeve had a stronger voice. There was a bigger battle to fight, a battle in which this sacrifice weighed little. I bit my lip; my eyes stung with tears.

Coblaith stood holding her pet, waiting for the signal to set it down. At least this would be over quickly. My whole body was tight.

"Bring forth my hounds!" Mac Dara ordered.

In moments there was a hubbub of barking and yipping and the pack burst through the crowd to mill about before Mac Dara, awaiting the command. I heard the excitement of the impending chase in their voices. Was Mac Dara's hall just over the next hill, that they had come so quickly, or had the Lord of the Oak summoned them by magic?

"Release the— No, wait." A pause, then Mac Dara said, "I don't want you claiming your brother did not get a fair chance, Caisin. Perhaps a count of ten between the release of the quarry and the command to follow?"

A count of ten, with the creature in panic and not knowing which way to turn—it was ludicrous. The hounds would rip the little dog apart before Dioman could say a word.

"Perhaps you might clarify, my lord prince." Dioman might have been asking Mac Dara to pass the salt. "The quarry is to be released; then I'm to count to ten, give the word for the hounds to course, then recall them before they reach the prey?"

Run, little one! Run for your very life!

"Well done, Dioman." The tone oozed contempt. "Your understanding is perfectly correct. But I see a flaw in this. We must allow the hounds a little time to run, at least, or the recall is too easy. Another ten, I think. Everyone can count. Begin, will you? I'm getting bored; these games are so tedious."

Coblaith released the dog, which stood stock-still a moment, then bolted. I closed my eyes; I could not watch this. The crowd counted to ten. Dioman spoke a command and the hounds gave voice, rushing in pursuit.

"Here!" Finbar spoke in an urgent undertone, and my eyes sprang open just in time to see the little dog hurtling straight toward us, so fast it almost seemed to fly. My brother squatted and caught it as one might a ball. The impact almost toppled him, but he regained his balance, then rose to draw his cloak over the creature and hold it firmly against his chest.

In the next moment the hounds were all around us on the rise, a confused flow of brown and gray, sniffing here and there, at a loss to find the scent. I held myself still and silent, hoping that if the Fair Folk could not see us, we would also be invisible to the hounds. Finbar stood strong. His jaw was tight, his eyes fierce, his feet planted square. I feared for him. Surely the hounds must detect the little dog's presence, if not by sight, then by smell. No veil of invisibility had been thrown over the creature or the hunting pack.

"They can't see him," Finbar mouthed.

It seemed he was right. As the dogs circled and sniffed and pawed at the earth, it became obvious that they did not know where their quarry had gone. Under Finbar's cloak the little dog was no more visible to them than we were.

"Ay-oop!" Dioman's call came on a rising cadence. "To me! To me!"

The hounds turned as one, heading back down to the stone basin. Sounds of acclaim rang out; this was a triumph for Dioman. I could hear the panicky rasp of the little dog's breathing. A count of twice ten. It had felt endless.

"Is it hurt?" I whispered to my brother.

Finbar shook his head. There was something new in his eyes; something I did not want to banish with the words that must come next. Luachan spoke for me.

"It's almost time, Finbar. We must go. Put the dog down."

Finbar wrapped his arms more firmly around the creature. He pressed his lips together. My brother had the wisdom of a seer and the courage of a chieftain. He had endured his strange and testing journey with remarkable composure. Right now he was a child.

"Luachan's right," I said quietly. "The dog will be safer up here. The hunting hounds won't come back. Dioman called them off."

"No." Finbar was adamant. "Everyone would see him. And even if he escaped, how could he look after himself in the woods?"

"He's not yours to keep," said Luachan flatly. "Let him go and he'll return to whoever had him before. Mac Dara has no interest in the dog; the whole thing was a challenge to Caisin."

Finbar and I both stared at him. Did he really imagine the dog could be safe out there after what had happened to Bear and Badger? Coblaith was fair of face and remote of expression: I had seen no link of love between her and her pet. Indeed, it had seemed to me both this creature and Dioman's owl might be ensorcelled to passivity, so the folk who carried them might not be inconvenienced. I peered into the fold of Finbar's cloak, but the little dog had its face jammed in the crook of his arm and all I could see was its trembling body.

"What if we find a safe spot by the rocks and bed him down there on your cloak? If he has any sense he'll lie low long enough for us to pick him up on the way home." And when Finbar turned betrayed eyes on me, I added, "Finbar, it simply isn't safe for him down there, even if you're holding him. Anything could happen."

"All I have to do is stand and watch. I can stand and watch and hold a dog at the same time."

"We mustn't do anything to anger Mac Dara," put in Luachan. "He might believe he's been somehow tricked."

"He has," Finbar pointed out. "It was Dioman's spell of invisibility that confused the hounds." After a moment he added, "I'm not going without him."

Now came the voice of Mac Dara's councilor, Fraochan, once more. He was drawing the conclave to a close; it seemed Dioman's effort had been considered adequate, though if he had accepted the position of Master of Hounds, the interchange had passed us by.

"Since all posts are now decided, I will invite our prince to speak once more before the commencement of feasting and revels. My lord prince—"

"Wait." Caisin's voice cut through Fraochan's, clear, sweet and firmly authoritative. "Surely there is one position as yet uncontested."

"You can't be suggesting . . ." began Fraochan, then fell silent, perhaps not brave enough to say the rest aloud.

"Are you not the Keeper of the Rules, Fraochan?"

The fire was flaming higher now; here and there it licked the basin's rim in patterns of red and gold, setting my blood pulsing with fear. *You're a grown woman*, I told myself sternly. *Stand up and fight. Make an end to the bad things.*

"Let me get this clear, my lady." Fraochan had gathered himself, but his voice had an edge to it now. "You wish to challenge for leadership of the realm? You seek to replace my lord Mac Dara?"

"The rules allow it." Caisin sounded as calm as if she were discussing the best way to lay the table. So she herself would stand against Mac Dara. I had not expected this; hadn't she implied earlier that one of her allies would put himself forward? If, as ruler, Caisin demonstrated the same kindness and compassion she had shown to us, this realm would indeed change under her leadership.

"But nobody has ever done so. The ruler has always chosen the time of his departure and named the one who will succeed him. Since time before time, my lady."

"You wish me to read you the relevant passage, Fraochan? Perhaps it's never been done before, though I very much doubt that, but I believe you'll find such a challenge falls within the rules. I am sure the wording states that *every* position of authority, up to and including that of ruler, may be contested at any Grand Conclave."

It was surely almost time for us to walk out and be seen. They must bring Swift soon. "Finbar," I whispered, crouching down beside him, "you can't take the dog. We don't know what's going to happen down there."

He turned his big, solemn eyes on me. "I do know," he said. "I'm taking him."

Down at the basin, the debate continued. "My lady, it is customary for the ruler to make the choice to stand down, and for him to select—"

Mac Dara cut his councilor short. "Caisin is right, Fraochan. What she suggests is entirely within the rules of the conclave. Why has it never happened before?" He got up and strolled forward, giving the impression that he found it all somewhat ridiculous. "Because no one has ever possessed the ambition and the folly to imagine they could win such a contest. Until Caisin Silverhair and her misguided kinsfolk, that is. So here we are, my lady." Mac Dara smiled; it was not pleasant to see. "Let it never be said Mac Dara shrank from a challenge. What's it to be—a display of magic, the winner to be decided by the crowd? Or a battle to the death?"

"Ready, Maeve?" Luachan whispered in my ear, but I found I could not summon a single word. I rose to my feet and managed a nod. My insides were churning; I thought I might faint. I recalled that it was rather a long time since I had eaten.

"What about Swift?" I looked about but could see no sign of him. I could not see Dioman, either, or the man who had taken Swift away.

"They'll bring him," Luachan said. "Don't worry."

"Oh, a display, my lord," said Caisin. "In keeping with the serious nature of the challenge, perhaps your councilor should read out the rules once more before we begin. The signals, the count of one hundred, the penalty for failure. Let us be quite sure."

She was stalling for time. While she stood there before his throne, splendid in her blue and silver, working the charm of her face and voice on the enthralled crowd, I was aware of subtle but rapid activity taking place around the circle of onlookers. While Caisin held Mac Dara's attention and that of his nearby attendants and guards, other members of her household were moving within the crowd, carrying wooden poles, mallets, coils of rope.

Fraochan droned on: ". . . in instances of magical challenge the count will be to one hundred; save where the challenge is to a ruling prince or lord, in which case it is customary to extend that count to two hundred, since it is expected that the level of skill demonstrated will be superior and the display more elaborate. An agreed signal will be used to designate the start and end of each challenge. This may be the sounding of a horn or bell, or a word of command. The signal must be given by a party not allied to either claimant."

"Yes, yes," said Mac Dara. "A count of two hundred, how utterly tedious. But we must respect it, of course, if only so my lady here will not spend the next three years boring us with complaints of unfairness. Let's get this over with, shall we? My good folk have waited too long already for their feasting and merriment."

A count of two hundred! How could I keep Swift calm for so long down there in the crowd, so close to the fire? Caisin's people had gathered in two clusters, on opposite sides of the circle. They were busy with something but their bodies blocked a clear view.

"There is one further procedural point, my lord prince." Fraochan regarded his lord, somber as an owl. His voice sounded different; there was a new strength in it. The folk around the basin's rim fell quiet.

"Enlighten us, Fraochan."

"Where the ruler is challenged and a display of magic is the chosen option, the ruler takes precedence; that is, he demonstrates his abilities first. The challenger follows."

Morrigan's curse! If Mac Dara went first, what was to stop him ignoring the rules and destroying Caisin outright, along with anyone else who dared challenge his authority? Was Fraochan, standing there unarmed in his dark robe, strong enough to enforce the rules? Would a councilor stand up to the Lord of the Oak? I hoped so, or Caisin would never get her opportunity to contest the leadership. Finbar would not get home safe and sound. And Mac Dara would not pay for the deaths of my boys.

The Lord of the Oak stepped forward. He bore no staff or other implement of magical power—at least, I could see none. Nor did he have a sword, a spear, a knife. Yet a shiver seemed to pass through the crowd, as if they anticipated marvels.

"Wait a moment, my lord prince."

Mac Dara went absolutely still. His stance suggested he was within a hair's breadth of losing his patience.

The voice was that of Breasal, Caisin's councilor, who was standing perhaps six paces from the prince. In his hands was a scroll that looked twin to Fraochan's. "Before you begin," he said, "one more point that my friend here may have overlooked, easy enough to do when such a turn of events has not occurred in living—"

"What point?" Mac Dara's tone made me shiver.

"It states here, my lord prince"—Breasal sounded perfectly calm as he made play of studying the document—"that in the event of a magical contest between ruler and challenger—"

"The ruler goes first, yes—those of us who are not deaf or stupid heard that the first time." Mac Dara made no effort to hide his displeasure. The crowd was hanging on every word. Did they sense a moment of great change was upon them?

"With respect, my lord prince, there is more, as Fraochan here can tell you if he reads a little further through the document. In the event of a magical contest between ruler and challenger, the ruler performs first. However, the challenger may choose the principal matter to be used for the demonstration; for example, water, fire, or a manipulation of borders such as we saw earlier, or creatures, or—"

"You've been studying, Breasal," Mac Dara said. He did not ask to see the scroll or to check its authenticity. Perhaps this was something he already knew and had chosen not to mention. I doubted very much that Caisin's challenge had come as a surprise to him. "Learned the whole thing off by heart, did you?"

Fraochan had been checking his own scroll. "Breasal is correct, my lord prince," he said. "I had overlooked that section, and I offer a sincere apology. It is for Lady Caisin to name the principal matter to be used, then for my lord prince to proceed to the demonstration."

"One more thing."

Mac Dara turned his dark gaze on Breasal. If Caisin did not win today, I thought, the future would not look bright for her and her clan. Nobody would want the Lord of the Oak as an enemy.

"Each display lasts to a count of two hundred, as Fraochan indicated. A starting and ending signal must be agreed upon by both parties and, as mentioned earlier, that signal must be given by a person not allied to either."

Mac Dara lifted his brows; I could not tell which was uppermost in him, annoyance or simple boredom. "Who here is not allied?" he asked, spreading his hands. "Clan is linked with clan, family with family. No one stands alone."

Fraochan hesitated; I thought perhaps he had an answer but was not prepared to put it forward.

"Call out one of the Old Ones," someone in the crowd suggested. "They're allied to nobody, not even to one another."

A silence. Then Mac Dara, incredulous: "*What* did you suggest?"

"The little folk, my lord prince." It was another councilor who spoke, a woman this time, clad in a plain gray robe. "It would not be beyond their abilities to ring a bell or to whistle or to speak a designated word."

"Counting to two hundred, now, that's another matter," someone commented, and there was general laughter.

"That's immaterial," said Fraochan, "since the Old Ones have never once attended a conclave. Whether that's from fear or from some other cause doesn't matter. They won't come."

No sooner had he spoken these words than there was a gasp from those standing near Mac Dara. Their eyes were fixed on the ground at his feet, where the solid stone was bulging and swelling and lifting. In a trice, there before the fey prince stood a small personage clad in a hooded cloak of leaf green. Under the startled eyes of the crowd, the being executed a bow, then spoke in a clear, confident voice. Its face was turned away from me; was it wearing some kind of mask?

"You require my assistance," the small person stated. "A signal, yes? This should do the trick." It lifted what looked like a simple wooden pipe and a single note rang out. It was a sound of rare purity. I pictured a bird soaring in a perfect summer sky, giving voice to the joy of flight and sunlight and open air.

"Caisin," said Mac Dara, "is this your doing? Have you been spending your idle days in plotting my downfall? You are misguided, my lady. These small folk are nothing; they are of no consequence."

Caisin looked as astonished as everyone else; either she had not expected this or she was expert at feigning. "Plotting your downfall? Is not a challenge precisely that, my lord?" She cast a disparaging glance at the figure in the green cloak. "As for our little friend here, his instrument is loud enough. Let us hope he knows his numbers."

Fraochan took the green-cloaked being aside and engaged him in conversation, perhaps feeling the need to spell out the double signal and the count of two hundred.

Finbar tugged at my sleeve. Pale as a ghost, his eyes saucerlike, he was beaming. "He knew, didn't he?" he whispered. "He was all ready to appear when it was time. Sibeal said the Old Ones are everywhere, only they blend in so people can't see them."

"Shh," Luachan warned.

Down by the basin, the small being was standing by himself now. Despite the press of bodies, the Fair Folk maintained an empty space of an arm's length around the interloper.

"Well, Caisin, what's it to be?" demanded Mac Dara. "I can't think of a single branch of the magical arts in which you have any chance at all of outshining me. Even if you've been practicing every day since the last conclave. Even if you've traveled the length and breadth of Erin and studied with every ancient sage you could find. I fear this so-called challenge will be a sad disappointment to all. But now that you've spoken, we've no choice but to go through the motions. What matter have you chosen for me to work with?"

Caisin gave him a radiant smile. "Humankind," she said.

DRUID'S JOURNEY: CENTER

Under a cool autumn sky, two crows alight in the branches of an ancient tree. They settle beneath a tattered cape of red-brown leaves, their bright eyes gazing over an endless sea of oaks. They have flown far. Now they perch side by side, wild brothers nearing journey's end.

In their bird form, they cannot exchange words. There can be no questions asked, no wise answers given. But it is understood between them that this will be the briefest of respites, and that what lies ahead will test them hard.

As they rest, there comes to them on the breeze a single note: the plangent summons of a small pipe.

One bird utters a harsh call: *Kraaa!* The other makes comment in similar fashion. It may be an interchange on the likelihood of rain, or an observation that smoke is rising from a certain point within the wood. It may be a prayer, a sigh, an acknowledgment, a farewell.

For a heartbeat the two look at each other; then as one they arise, winging away to the heart of the great forest. It is time.

CHAPTER 15

My flesh crawled. What did this mean? Fraochan had spoken of fire and water, of borders, of creatures—that had filled my mind with dark possibilities—but humankind? Using men and women as the materials of a magical display? I glanced at Luachan, but he was staring down toward the stone basin, his features as grim as I had ever seen them.

"It's fair," murmured Finbar. "I mean, Caisin's going to use us, isn't she?"

"But—" I bit back my words; Finbar was right. If Mac Dara agreed to this, and under the rules he must, it provided her with the perfect opportunity to set the pieces of the geis in place when her turn came. Oh gods, a count of two hundred and then we must step out and face the Lord of the Oak. We really were going through with it.

"The rules say nobody gets hurt," my brother whispered. "So it should be all right."

In the event it was far from all right. At Mac Dara's command, they brought forward two men of humankind, both wearing black. I took that to mean they were from his own household, perhaps servants. There might be many human folk in the Otherworld; stories abounded of men and women who wandered in by chance and never returned, or came home to find a hundred years had passed. I thought of the girl who had helped me bathe and was glad she was nowhere to be seen.

The two men were obedient, moving onto the tongue of stone and facing each other as Mac Dara bid them. If they were troubled by the flames not far below, they showed no sign of it. I wondered if Mac Dara would make them fight each other. Both were clad in simple garb, with neither weaponry nor protective garments such as leather helms, gauntlets or breastpieces.

The mood of the audience had changed again. What they expected, I did not know, but the look on their faces made my belly tight. It was not only anticipatory; it was . . . avid.

I tried to distract Finbar. "How is the dog?" I whispered, bending toward him and attempting to block his view.

"All right." My brother turned his solemn gaze on me. "You won't like this, Maeve," he said soberly.

"Hush," muttered Luachan, but I did not think anyone would hear us; all were intent upon Mac Dara.

"Ready," said the Lord of the Oak, and the little pipe sounded its pure note into the silence.

"You know I can conjure with water." As he spoke, Mac Dara lifted a casual hand and rain came, a thundering downpour all around the clearing. The fire fizzed and went out; people scrambled to put cloaks over their heads or to retreat under the trees. The deluge lasted for perhaps a count of five, then abruptly ceased. Steam arose from the stone basin. The two men standing before Mac Dara had not moved.

"You know I can conjure with fire."

I made myself watch, though everything in me shrank away. Mac Dara put up a clenched fist. He opened his fingers and a ball of flame flew into the air to burst in a cascade of colored sparks, showering down into the stone basin. Within that bowl there was an answering glow, then the crackling of flames, and the fire flared up, renewed. For this, no more than another count of five.

"You know I can conjure with any material I choose," Mac Dara said. "How unfortunate that my challenger has selected something so . . . unexciting." He cast his gaze over the two men. "But I suppose humankind might be persuaded to provide some entertainment for you, lords and ladies. Conn, Fergus!"

The two men bowed their heads.

"You will always obey my orders, yes?"

"Yes, my lord," they said in unison. Both of them had the same dazed look as my bath attendant; I wondered if they understood anything of their situation.

"You will never refuse a command?"

"No, my lord."

"Let's test that obedience a little, shall we? Conn, have you family at home, back in that realm you came from?"

Conn, a tall, red-haired man, looked confused.

"Speak up! We don't have all day. Have you a wife back home? Children running about the house? A fine son maybe? A sweet little daughter? Don't keep me waiting."

"I—I don't remember, my lord."

"And you, Fergus? What dear ones did you leave behind when you wandered into a mushroom circle and out of your own realm into mine? An aged parent needing his son's support? A comely young wife your neighbor already had his eye on? Don't be shy."

"Nobody, my lord." Stocky, broad-shouldered Fergus stared straight ahead, face wooden.

"Is that so? Turn around, lads."

They turned to face the fire, and there, on the very end of the tongue of stone, was a little girl of perhaps five. She was dressed in a homespun gown and neat linen cap, and in her arms she clutched a grubby cloth doll. Her feet were a handspan from the drop; hungry flames reached up toward them. She stood frozen, her eyes wide with terror.

Outrage filled me. Forget Caisin, forget the geis; I simply could not let this happen. I was three strides down toward the basin when a hand came over my mouth, arresting both speech and movement.

"No, Maeve!" Luachan spoke in a fierce whisper.

For a moment I fought him; then I made myself be still and he took his hand away. "Sorry," I muttered, knowing I had been foolish. I could not help that child or stop what evil plan Mac Dara had in mind. I had almost jeopardized our whole mission.

"Me, too," Luachan said as we both stepped back. "I am more sorry than I can possibly tell you."

"Fergus!" Mac Dara rapped out as the child teetered above the flames. Not a single person moved to help her. "Do you know this little girl?"

"No, my lord." The response was delivered in the same flat tone as his earlier speech.

"And you, Conn?"

An infinitesimal pause; a shadow of doubt. Then, "No, my lord."

"So, if I ordered you to push her into the fire you would do so without hesitation?"

"Yes, my lord."

A shiver of shocked delight ran through the crowd; they were hungry for spectacle.

"What if I told you this was your daughter, Conn? Your only daughter? She's grown since you left, hasn't she? How long is it, two years you've been with us now?"

The hesitation again, as if awareness were not entirely lost from the fellow's mind, even after so long. "I don't recall, my lord."

"Then let me remove the charm from your thoughts, my friend, so you will remember more clearly." A pass of the hands, deft and graceful.

Conn took a staggering step; cast a panicky glance around the clearing, taking in the crowd of beautiful folk, the tall trees, the fire, the child . . .

"Saorla!" he shouted, and in the same moment she cried out, "Papa!" Conn took two strides toward the girl. Mac Dara waved a casual hand and the man froze in place, one foot off the ground, arms reaching out vainly to snatch his child from harm.

"Not so fast," said Mac Dara. "Fergus, walk forward and push the child into the fire."

Fergus walked forward.

"No!" screamed Conn, still held immobile. "Fergus! No!"

Mac Dara lifted his hand and halfway along the tongue of stone Fergus, too, froze in place. The child was weeping, shivering, her eyes fixed on her father. Her feet were on the very edge; she was too terrified to step away and save herself. From the hem of her gown, a thread of smoke arose.

"Well, now," said Mac Dara. "Let us see what Conn is prepared to do in order to save his child. What if I told you, Conn, that you must kill your friend here before your daughter can be brought to safety?"

"You godforsaken apology for a man!" Conn spat. "How dare you play these evil games? How dare you put a child's life in the balance?"

Mac Dara folded his arms. He tapped his foot. "You didn't answer the question," he said. "So let's raise the stakes a little higher." There was an implement in his hand now; it resembled a shard of bone. "You shrink from harming your friend, though he would have killed your child without hesitation. What's to stop me from letting him go right ahead and do so? Only my kind heart, Conn, only that. Take this weapon. You'll find you can move your fingers." He came forward and put the bone knife into Conn's hand. "When I remove the immobility charm, you'll have a three-way choice. Kill Fergus and you can pull her to safety. Plunge the knife in your own heart and I'll see to it that she is spared. Do neither and she falls. Ready, now?"

The crowd gave a great gasp. Luachan muttered an oath. My stomach protested; bile rose to my mouth. Inside me someone was babbling, *This isn't real; it can't be. I want to go home.*

"He's bluffing," Finbar said, his voice not quite steady. "He wouldn't break the rules. It must be an illusion."

How close were we to two hundred? I could not see the green-cloaked personage with his pipe, but others seemed to be counting now, all around the circle.

"One hundred and seventy-three," Mac Dara said. "One hundred and seventy-four. On one hundred and eighty I will release you both from the charm."

"Papa!" screamed the child as the hem of her gown caught fire. "Help!"

I could not look. I screwed my eyes shut and prayed. A sequence of sounds followed, a roar of fury, someone shouting, *No!*, a great cheer from the crowd as if they were mightily entertained by what was unfolding. When I dared look again, Fergus lay flat on the tongue of stone. Blood pooled around his still form. Conn was at the very end, arms outstretched toward the fire. Of the girl, there was no sign at all.

A moment's terrible silence. Conn turned. "Where is she?" His face was ashen. "Where's my daughter?" He took a few staggering steps toward Mac Dara. "You promised me! You gave your word! You said she would be safe!"

"Aolu!" called the Lord of the Oak, ignoring him completely. One of the fey men came forward. It was the golden-haired fellow who had won the position of Master of Portals.

"This man is no longer required in my household," Mac Dara said crisply. "Take him back where he came from."

"My daughter—" gasped Conn.

"Go home, fool. Your daughter died last winter, of an ague. Your wife has a new man and a fine baby boy. The lives of human folk are short, their memories shorter. Take him away."

Conn gave a roar of fury and hurled himself forward, though the bone weapon still lay on the stones, red with his friend's lifeblood. Aolu stepped out and arrested his wild progress, restraining him as easily as he might a wayward terrier.

"Go on, then," said Mac Dara, not sparing a glance, and Conn, fighting, weeping, raging, was led away. "Remove the debris, will you? We must leave things tidy for my challenger."

The very large man, Mochta, came forward, scooped up the limp and bloodied form of Fergus and tossed him into the fire. The flames flared up to receive the body; it would soon be consumed. Mac Dara pointed a finger toward the tongue of stone and the pool of blood lifted in a red mist, then dissipated. The voice of the crowd rose to a shout: "One hundred and ninety-nine, two hundred!"

The pipe sounded, its delicate timbre incongruous in this place of cruelty. Mac Dara's demonstration of magic was over.

I bent double, retching up a watery bile. My heart felt like a trapped creature dashing itself against the walls of its cage. My skin crawled. "He broke the rules," I whispered, wondering if Caisin's plot was over before it had begun.

Down by the basin, someone else had the same idea.

"My lord," said Breasal, "the rule on unreasonable injury—"

"The child was not harmed," Mac Dara said. "There was no child. And these men were merely the material of the spell. The references to injury surely do not apply to humankind." His tone suggested the very idea was ludicrous.

"The rules make no distinction between races." Breasal was dogged; in view of what we had just witnessed, either he was extremely brave or exceptionally foolish. "The loss of a life, no matter whose, goes beyond reasonable injury. Nobody would dispute that, my lord."

Fraochan cleared his throat. "Does Lady Caisin wish to lodge a complaint? Is this a formal request that Lord Mac Dara's display be ruled invalid? Without a precedent, it could take some time to determine—"

"Let's ask her, shall we?" Mac Dara turned a genial smile in Caisin's direction. She was looking remarkably calm. I would have thought a person of her mettle would be disturbed by the foul display we had just witnessed, even allowing for the differences between her kind and mine.

"What would happen if it were declared invalid, Fraochan?" she asked.

"Lord Mac Dara would be required to perform another demonstration of his magical craft, my lady."

Caisin rolled her eyes. "Have mercy! In that case, I will raise no objection to his shameless flouting of the rules. May I proceed to my own display now?"

"Oh, please do," drawled Mac Dara, speaking over his councilor. "This must be the most drawn-out conclave in history."

"It's time." Dioman was beside us, come from nowhere.

"What about Swift?" I asked.

"He's over there," said Luachan, pointing. "On the far side. See?"

It was so. Swift was there, looking reasonably calm, with his leading rein held by the man who had taken him away, and a small crowd of Caisin's folk close by. Now I could see what they had been setting up earlier under cover of the dispute over the rules. Two wooden poles stood on one side of the basin, one pole on the other side. Those mallets I had seen earlier must have been used to hammer them securely between the rocks. Now Caisin's people were doing something with the ropes, and . . . Surely they didn't think they could tie Swift on one side while I stood on the other, keeping him under control with the flaming bowl between us?

"That won't work," I said, appalled. "It's too far. I won't be able to do it! And he'll be too close to the fire. He'll panic. He'll hurt himself!"

Luachan said nothing. His face was chalk white, his jaw set. He looked the way I felt: as if we were heading out to certain death.

"This is how it's supposed to be." Finbar spoke with chilling certainty.

"You must come now," said Dioman.

I couldn't make myself step forward. My body was full of my beating heart.

"I'll look after you, Maeve," said Finbar, and moved down toward the basin. His back was straight, his head held high. In his encircling arms rode the little dog.

Muttering a prayer to the gods I did not believe in, I followed.

Down among the crowd of tall folk, I couldn't see far ahead. Dioman had left us, heading for the far side of the basin. I could hear Swift whinnying, and I could hear the whispers, too. On one side, "Look at her hands! How unsightly!" And on the other side, "Isn't that child Lord Sean's son? Look, Coblaith, he has your dog!" And someone else put in, "If you could call it a dog."

Finbar led Luachan and me to the place where two poles stood side by side, three arms' lengths back from the edge of the basin; he seemed sure that was where we should be. A pair of fey men clad in Caisin's colors stood there. I glanced across to see Dioman fastening Swift's leading rope around the single pole on the opposite side. Other folk in blue and silver were there, and before I had time to put together the pieces of what I saw, one of them tossed the end of a long rope from that side to this, where it was deftly caught. Now the rope spanned the breadth of the basin, a distance of at least ten strides. What in the name of the gods were they doing? Swift was restless now, turning his head, lifting his feet, twitching his tail. Dioman gestured, making the other folk step back to give him room. A second long rope followed the first.

Finbar advanced to stand beside the two poles, and now here was Caisin, lips curved in a smile, eyes bright as stars.

"We're ready," my brother said.

"My lady," I blurted out, "I can't do this at such a distance—Swift is already upset—what are you—"

"You will do it, Maeve." Her tone was calm. "You must. Finbar, give me the dog."

He stared at her, his arms tightening around the little bundle in his cloak.

"Take the dog," Caisin said, glancing at her men. "There is no time to waste."

They wrenched the creature from Finbar's arms; he stood silent with tears streaming down his cheeks.

Fury gripped me. "What are you—" I began, but the words dried up in my mouth. Caisin had moved away, and in her place was Luachan, a knife of pale bone in his hand, its point aimed straight at my chest. His face was as white as his weapon. I stared, uncomprehending.

"Move over to the pole," he said, using the knife to gesture. "Do it, Maeve—stop wasting time. And keep quiet."

"But—"

"Move!"

I obeyed, my heart hammering. This made no sense. Luachan, a druid, Finbar's tutor and protector. Luachan, our friend. Was he under some vile enchantment? *I am more sorry than I can possibly tell you.* The words took on a sinister significance. No time to consider, for now—gods, so quick!—Caisin's men were fastening one of the long ropes around my waist and one around Finbar's. I felt the pull straightaway and struggled to hold my feet.

"Hold on to the pole," Luachan said.

Mute with horror, I did my best to obey, crossing my arms around it. What was this? The geis did not demand any of this rigmarole; all it said was *held with hands that cannot hold*. Do it this way and the plan must end in complete failure.

I found my voice when I looked across the circle and saw two men tying the other ends of the ropes to Swift's halter. "No!" I croaked in utter disbelief. "Oh, no! We won't last to a count of five, let alone two hundred. Luachan, *why*?" If it weren't for Swift's leading rope, still fastened to the pole over there, we'd already be in the fire. Had Mac Dara somehow ensorcelled Luachan, that he would suddenly turn against us? "Untie the rope! Set Finbar free at least!"

No response. Signals were exchanged across the basin to indicate all was in place. Thus far, the press of folk had shielded Finbar and me from Mac Dara's view, though he must surely have seen the flurry of preparation. I looked for Caisin and found her not far away with her sister beside her. Perhaps there was still time to stop this.

"My lady!" I called, loud enough for those nearby to hear me, despite the buzz of excited voices. "My brother is only seven years old, our father's only son. If you need me for your display, I'm ready to do it, but please tell these men to let Finbar go! There's no need for this!" *And you know it*, I thought, wondering if I had imagined the compassion in her eyes and in her voice earlier. The geis specified only that Finbar watch, not that he be placed in mortal danger. This, I could not say; not with Mac Dara so close.

Caisin smiled. Oh, her look was sweet indeed, and her smile was sunlight and flowers. "You can do this, Maeve," she said. "This is destiny; it is meant to be." She scrutinized me a moment longer, then said, "Moderate your rage, my dear. It won't help you."

Anger boiled in me, along with the knowledge that I might possibly have managed to hold Swift still, even at such a distance, had it not been for the fact that my whole body was quivering with fury and terror. It was too late to stop this. It was too late to do anything.

"Don't be afraid," said Finbar indistinctly. "This is what's supposed to happen."

"You could have warned me," I muttered as Caisin walked over to stand at the tongue of stone, a regal figure in her sky-blue gown, with her hair shimmering across her shoulders and a perfect pearl in each ear.

"You might not have done it if I'd told you," he said simply.

Gods! Could he have known all along that Luachan was . . . what? An enemy? A spy? What child could keep something like that to himself? What seven-year-old could see a violent death coming and walk calmly to meet it?

The crowd hushed. All eyes were on Caisin Silverhair. Mac Dara's throne was hidden from me by a group of Caisin's people standing on the basin's rim.

"We're ready," said Caisin. "I ask for total silence; this demonstration requires it."

I looked across the basin toward Swift. I had a choice: submit to the sheer terror that was knotting my insides and turning my mind blank, or give this the best effort I could. Perish as a helpless child or as a true daughter of Sevenwaters. No choice, when it came to it. I had to believe I could do this. And that meant getting Swift under my control right now.

"Swift, my lovely boy." I made my voice loud enough to carry across the basin, gentle enough to reassure him. "Fresh water; green fields; calm hands and quiet."

As I spoke, the pipe sounded its single note, high and sweet. The count had begun.

There was no looking at Finbar; no looking over toward Mac Dara; no way to know if Luachan had his knife poised at my back. No looking anywhere but at Swift, who stood trembling and wide-eyed across the fiery cauldron. I pressed my body against the pole, hoping I could keep my position for long enough. Finbar could use his hands for a better grip, at least. But his strength would ebb more quickly. Oh gods, what had I done?

"Good boy, Swift. Calm boy. Quiet now . . . peaceful thoughts . . . slow, slow . . . my boy, my lovely boy . . ."

Swift was listening; I saw it in his stance. He had heard the familiar voice, the voice that always calmed and steadied him. The voice of a trusted friend. He stood still, looking across the fiery pit, and I worked on my breathing. "Calm boy. Lovely boy. Green fields. Cool water . . ." Perhaps I could do it; perhaps I really could. Provided I could keep him still, provided he did not pull against the leading rope and dislodge the pole where it was tied, we might have a chance of keeping hold of our own anchors for long enough. "Hold on tight, Finbar," I muttered, then returned to my litany. "Kind hands and quiet . . ."

Mac Dara's voice broke the stillness, the hard tone making Swift start and pull. I clenched my teeth, willing strength to my arms. "What is this, Caisin? Using cripples and children to make a point? Where is the magic in that?"

"Kind hands and quiet . . ." Swift was unsettled now, shifting his feet. I felt the pull on my waist as his movement tightened the rope. "Quiet, my lovely boy, calm and quiet . . ."

"Ah," came Caisin's voice. It was sweetly musical as ever, but now there was a new note in it. If Mac Dara was iron, she was flint. "That remains to be seen. Dioman, untie the horse!"

"Maeve," said Finbar, "slide down to sit. Put your legs around the pole."

What? She hadn't really meant that, had she? Why would they— Dioman was untying the rope. I caught a glimpse of Finbar following his own advice, locking legs and arms tight around the support, his face a white mask. For me it was too late. Swift was untied, save for the double rope linking him to my brother and me. If I could not keep him standing still, he'd pull us straight into the fire.

"Sweet . . . water," I gasped, then forced my voice calm. My skin was all cold sweat. Spots danced before my eyes. "Green fields, Swift. Calm boy. My lovely boy . . ." I sucked in a sobbing breath. "Kind . . . hands . . ." My feet were sliding. Swift tossed his head one way, the other way. My arms ached; my stomach was a hard knot.

"Caisin," said Mac Dara, "this is ridiculous. What are you doing?"

"I heard tell of a charm," Caisin said. "A rhyme concerning yourself, my lord. It was revealed to me by one of the little folk. Another of the same kind as our piper here."

"Sweet water, Swift . . . green fields . . ." I was running with sweat. Swift danced from side to side, confused by the other voices. "Swift, be calm. Hold still, sweet boy."

"The rhyme may be familiar to you," Caisin went on. "It goes like this:

> *Held by hands that cannot hold*
> *Stands the steed so proud and bold*
> *Chieftain's son with seer's eyes*
> *Observes the Lord of Oak's demise."*

"What?" roared Mac Dara.

Across the stone basin, Swift shied. I bit back a scream as my arms left the pole and both Finbar and I were swept toward the edge. I crouched, hooking an arm awkwardly around the rope, leaning back with my full weight. The yearling had not bolted; not yet. He stood there trembling, looking across at us with wild eyes. No wonder he was terrified; it must feel to him as if I were trying to drag him into the fire. How long until the count reached two hundred?

"Hold still, Swift, lovely boy. Hold still for me, dear one." *Breathe, Maeve.* "Be calm, be still. All will be well."

"Be silent, save for the girl." The calm voice was Fraochan's, reminding those assembled that Caisin had asked for quiet.

"You're fools," Mac Dara spat. "There's far more to the rhyme than those few lines. Besides, there's no way the cripple can hold that creature for the full count. She'll be over the edge in a heartbeat, and the lad with her . . . Is that Lord Sean's son?" Something had entered his voice: the merest thread of unease.

A pox on you. This cripple will hold on as long as she needs to. "Be strong, Finbar," I muttered. "We can do this." Then, in the soft, confident voice Swift knew, "Calm, dear one. Green field. Sweet water."

"Over the edge in a heartbeat?" Caisin gave a musical chuckle. "We can't have that. Let's even the balance a little, shall we? In the rhyme, I believe the next lines are these: *Sever now the ties that bind,*

Brothers in purpose and in kind. You did not think, when you amused yourself playing tricks with a chieftain's sons, that your transformations would suit my purpose so very well, did you? Those brothers are fiercely loyal to the cripple, and she to them. I wonder if they would die for her? Let's find out."

My lips continued their soothing flow of words. My gaze stayed on Swift as he stepped to and fro, every move another tug on the ropes, another inch closer to the flames. But I heard her and began to understand. Caisin had lied to me. She had held back part of the geis. Something about chieftains' sons, a pair of brothers—Cruinn's boys? What had they to do with this?

Caisin gave a crisp order: "Bring them forth!"

A stifled exclamation from Finbar. A scuffling disturbance on his other side, as if someone were forcing a way through the crowd.

"*Maeve!*" my brother whispered, his tone so urgent that I turned my head for a moment.

My boys. My lovely boys, their eyes wild, their mouths muzzled, their pelts a mess of bloody wounds. My boys straining against chains held by leather-gauntleted guards. Alive. They were alive.

"*Bear!*" The name burst out of me in a great sob. "*Badger!*"

The rope tightened as Swift reacted to my cry, jerking me forward; Finbar slid alongside me, scrabbling for purchase.

"Remove the muzzles and release them!" ordered Caisin. "Quickly!"

"Hold still, Swift," I called with tears coursing down my cheeks. "Home soon. Kind hands and quiet." I could not look at Bear; I could not command his obedience, for my voice must be for Swift alone. Dear gods, if the dogs jumped up to greet me we'd all go straight over the edge.

They ran toward us, whimpering their love and confusion. My rope juddered and grew taut. Beside me Finbar copied my stance, his small body leaning back hard.

"Bear! Badger!" My brother spoke crisply, in creditable imitation of my own style. "Bite!"

We had trained them well when we taught them to chew

through bonds. Badger set his teeth to Finbar's rope and Bear attacked mine. They gnawed steadily, as if there were no fire, no crowd, no dear friend sliding inch by inch toward death.

"The count of two hundred must have been up long ago." Mac Dara spoke into the tense silence.

"I make it one hundred and sixty-seven," came Caisin's voice. "Of course, this valiant effort is doomed to failure. Is not the next part of the geis, *Evil's defeat demands the price of a brother's sacrifice?* You know, I believe this is the very first time I've managed to shock you, my lord. It's true; I do indeed have the whole geis. Very soon all the pieces will be in place. Best bid your friend there make haste, Maeve. You're perilously near the edge."

Two crows flew low over the stone basin as she spoke, startling Swift. The ropes tightened again, and this time I could not stand against the pull. As the rope holding Finbar frayed and parted under Badger's assault, my brother collapsed on the stones and in one heart-stopping slide I was on my knees, an arm's length from the edge. The flames crackled. Smoke filled my lungs, robbing me of breath. I could not speak.

A confusion, then: Finbar grabbing my arm, trying to pull me back; Luachan hauling him off. Finbar shouting, "Badger, run!" Bear's amber eyes, his bloodied pelt, his jaws still chewing on the rope; a smell of singeing hair; Caisin's laugh like a peal of little bells. The rope taut as a bowstring as Swift panicked, pulling me to the fire. The flames, oh gods, the hot flames on my face . . . Bear between me and the fire, right on the edge, still working steadily on the rope. The clearing suddenly dark, as if Morrigan herself hovered over this field of sacrifice . . . A brother's sacrifice . . .

"Bear, stop!" I gasped. "Run!" And when he would not, "Bear, please!"

The pipe sounded. The rope parted. Across the basin, Swift was a blur of white, fleeing through the crowd and away. Bear slipped over the edge and was gone.

CHAPTER 16

Facedown on the stones, I wept. I could feel Finbar's hand on my back, patting me, but I could not make myself rise.

"It's over, Caisin," said Mac Dara. It sounded as if he was smiling. "The count is up; the signal has sounded; the display is finished. You're out of time, and look! I'm still here, alive and well. What a dismal effort that was." A pause. "Fraochan," he went on, "in view of the complete lack of response from our audience, I think we can assume Lady Caisin has failed in her attempt to usurp my position. Can we make an end of this farce?"

There was a silence. Finbar's patting ceased; I thought perhaps he was rising to his feet. Despite everything, I lifted my head and looked.

Mac Dara stood on the tongue of stone. His arms were folded and his lean features wore a look of wry amusement. Close by was Caisin Silverhair, gazing at him as if she could not believe he was still there. Her serene demeanor was gone; her lovely features were distorted with angry frustration. "This can't be," she muttered. "All the pieces are there, every last one. The cripple, the boy seer, the brothers, severing the bonds; we had everything—"

"Give it up, Caisin," said the Lord of the Oak. "I've won; you've lost. What is that rhyme but a childish nonsense, spoken by a babbling old woman half out of her wits? I've never believed in it, and you're wasting your time if you imagine . . ."

I stopped listening, for close at hand there was a wheezing, rasping, desperate sound, a sound that went straight to my heart. "Finbar," I whispered, not daring to believe it. "Look."

A pair of black paws, on the edge. A whimper. *Help me.* I crawled to the rim, heedless of the burning heat. "Bear," I breathed. "Come, Bear."

He had landed on a ledge, only an arm's length down. On his own, he could not climb up, and the fire was testing him hard. If he tried to jump up he would likely fall into the basin and be lost.

"I'll do it."

Finbar was beside me, reaching down without hesitation, as if there were no fire at all. He grabbed Bear's collar and hauled, adding his small strength to the dog's. With a desperate, scrabbling effort, Bear pulled himself up over the edge to collapse, shuddering, beside me on the rocks. His breathing was like the crackle of burning pine wood; his flanks heaved. I bent over him, the world vanishing in the joy and sorrow of the moment. Oh, so many hurts. The bloody wounds, the singed patches, the sheer exhaustion of his long journey. I bathed his face with my tears. Weakly, Bear lifted his head and licked my cheek.

"Finbar," I said, "you're—"

Caisin's voice cut across mine, knife-sharp. "No wonder it didn't work. That creature is still alive! Luachan, finish him."

It happened in a flash, Luachan seizing a fist-sized stone and striding toward us, Finbar shouting, *"No!"* I threw myself over Bear. An instant later came the smashing blow as Luachan brought the stone down.

I felt the force of it first. A heartbeat later came the fearful pain. I'd flung myself down wildly, my body across Bear's, my hand over his head. The death blow had come down on that hand. All in vain, for Bear lay limp and motionless under me, his blood and mine flowing together.

A brother's sacrifice. A brother had to die for the geis to be fulfilled. And when he refused to die, when he battled his way back against all odds, she snuffed him out without a second thought, so she could get what she wanted. Not a wiser, better world. Not peace and justice for her people. Power. It was all power. Caisin was no better than Mac Dara. It was she who had stolen my dogs, she who had had them beaten and chained. When I'd refused to bend to her will, she had manipulated me with a cruel lie. If she became ruler, things would go on just the same as before. What were we in the long and devious schemes of the Fair Folk? Nothing. Nothing at all. They took us and used us and threw us away the moment they grew bored.

Finbar was crying, a child again. I lay there with Bear in my arms, my cheek against his neck. He was still warm. My boy, my dear one, my lost and found. He who never judged; who loved without reservation; who understood what happiness was. He was gone.

"It's over, Caisin," Mac Dara said. "The challenge is finished; the conclave draws to a close. And you have made me very angry. So angry, my lady, that I do not believe I can allow you to depart in peace to spend three years plotting how best you may trick me next time. There is ill work here, spying out of secrets best left untouched, meddling with matters that should be kept under lock and key. Come out and stand before me, Caisin Silverhair. Or are you afraid to face me on the tongue of stone, outside the protection of a formal challenge?"

A crow cawed, the harsh sound jolting me. I heard a murmuring from the gathered folk, a whispering, a rustling. I did not lift my head; did not dare. For as I lay prostrate with my face against the neck of my fallen warrior, I felt beneath my cheek a faint throbbing, the weak but unmistakable pulsing of blood through his veins.

I lay still, hardly daring to breathe. Caisin had been quick to order his death before; she would do it again without hesitation. *A brother's sacrifice.* Eyes squeezed shut, jaw clenched tight, injured hand screaming with pain, I made myself as still as stone.

The pipe sounded again, and this time its music was a march of celebration, a fanfare of welcome, a melody that set joy in the heart and made the blood sing with new life. I lay immobile while the wondrous tune swelled and dipped and soared through the clearing.

When the music ceased, something had changed. The silence was profound; it felt as if, in all that great crowd of folk, not one dared draw a breath.

"Maeve," whispered Finbar urgently. "Look up."

I lifted my head. The clearing was utterly still. Clouds had covered the sun and the place lay in shadow; the red-gold light from the fire played upon the lovely features of the Fair Folk and touched their rich garments with points of glittering brightness. It illuminated my brother's small face, his mouth slightly open, his eyes full of wonder. It spread deceptive warmth over the handsome countenance of Luachan, who stood close by us with his knife in his hand and eyes like death. And it lit up the two figures on the tongue of stone, each bound from shoulders to knees. The ropes that wrapped them were fibrous and leafy; they looked like vines. Mac Dara and Caisin. Caught in an enchantment; paralyzed; helpless. Who in all Erin had the power to do such a thing?

"Your reign is over, Mac Dara. Your time here is at an end." The voice rang out, deep and strong, making me tremble. A familiar voice. I struggled to sit, my injured hand against my chest, my good hand resting on Bear's neck, where the pulse still beat with steadfast will. I looked across the basin to the place opposite the tongue of stone. There stood two men. One was tall and pale, his hair dark flame, his eyes a curious shade something akin to mulberry. He was clad in the white robe of a senior druid, and around his neck he wore a golden torc. Ciarán. Ciarán here at the very heart of the Otherworld. His right arm was raised, the hand held flat, palm down, fingers pointing toward the tongue of stone.

The man beside him was in the same pose; it was plain the two of them were casting a powerful magic. This man . . . gods, it was Mac Dara! How could that be, for he was on the other side, bound and immobile . . . I looked from one to the other and back again.

"Cathal," whispered Finbar.

Cathal. My sister's husband. Mac Dara's son. There he stood, a tall young warrior dressed in black, his face as grave and solemn as Ciarán's. He spoke.

"The reign of darkness draws to a close. Would that this transition had come about in another way. But you gave us no choice."

Mac Dara's face was suddenly transformed. Boredom and malice vanished away. His narrow features were, quite simply, suffused with joy.

"My son! You've come home!" he cried out, and I shivered to hear it, for if I had thought him a person without a heart, now I knew I had been wrong. "It is true; my time here will soon be over. Thanks to this meddler who thought to challenge me, its end is upon us as I speak. But I can go gladly now. You are here, my boy—the only one worthy to take my place; the one destined to rule this realm as prince and lord. This is your home and your inheritance. Step up, take it. No need for these bonds. What is yours by blood, I give to you freely and with goodwill."

Caisin spat on the rocks by Mac Dara's feet. "This is absurd!" she snarled. "How dare you bind us, upstart! How dare you confine us? You stand in company with a druid, a man who walks the path of light—how can such as he form any part of this? He is of humankind; he is of as little consequence as the cripple there and her scrawny wretch of a brother. You, druid!" She glared at Ciarán. "What authority can you have here, when you cannot even keep your own kind in check?" Her glance moved to Luachan, then back again. "So clever, so wise, yet you never knew there was a spy in your midst! You never knew you sheltered and taught and nurtured my secret weapon among your own brethren. You were blind to him as he worked on the child, and on the cripple, so they would come to us exactly when we needed them. What kind of druid are you?"

Ciarán regarded her as a wise teacher might gaze on a disruptive student. "I am a druid whose mother was of the Tuatha De," he said mildly. "This charm of binding I learned from her, and much else besides. It seems you, too, may have overlooked something, Lady Caisin."

"You cannot pass the princedom over to Mac Dara's son," Caisin said, her tone dangerous. "A blood claim on its own cannot stand up! This should be mine! I was the one who found the geis. I was the one who set it in place! I am the challenger, not this—this half-breed! Look at him! He's his father all over again! Is that what you want? Folk of the Otherworld, you must support my claim!" She was shouting now. "My clan deserves this—it is our time! You know this! Breasal, tell them!" But her councilor bowed his head and spoke not a word.

"Enough of this!" Cathal's voice rang out, confident and clear. His expression belied it; he was pale, drawn, suddenly old beyond his years. "My lady, if you believe all the pieces of the geis are in place, you are mistaken. The verse speaks of a brother's sacrifice. The hound that lies there is indeed a brother; but I think he is not dead." He looked all around the clearing, as if assessing the hushed crowd. "This conclave marks the end of Mac Dara's rule," he said. "The time of fear and malice is over and a new age dawns. For that new age there must be a new leader, or all will quickly turn to chaos. My lords and ladies, you need a leader not only for your own kind, but for every race that dwells here—the great, the small, the powerful and the oft-overlooked. I am—"

"No, Cathal." Ciarán spoke with quiet authority. "You are a young man with a young wife. Your children need their father to guard and nurture them while they grow. I will take this burden for you. It is my destiny and my sacrifice." What I saw on his face made my heart still. It was as if a fire burned there, lighting him from within; a flame of goodness so bright that it must draw the great and the small, the weak and the strong, the privileged and the outcast to follow him.

"What of the geis?" spluttered Caisin as all around the stone basin there broke out a murmuring chorus of astonishment. "You speak of sacrifice, druid. But you and he are not brothers. There is a tie of kinship through marriage, I believe, but that is tenuous. The terms of the verse have not been met. I see no brother's sacrifice in this, if the dog lives."

Under my hand, Bear stirred, straining to lift his head. His dark hair was thick with blood.

"The geis speaks of brothers severing ties," said Ciarán calmly, "and we saw the brave hounds do just that. But do not forget the line, *brothers in purpose and in kind.* Whether or not Cathal and I share the same parents is immaterial. We are brothers in purpose, united in our will to see the end of Mac Dara's rule. We are brothers in kind, for each of us is of both fey and human parentage. I claim the leadership of this realm today, and with this promise I complete the terms of the geis. I swear by all that is good that I will rule this realm with justice and fairness. My father was chieftain of Sevenwaters. My mother was of the Tuatha De. She used dark powers; she twisted the fates of many in her time. But I have turned to the light, and while I rule here, the light will prevail."

Cathal's face was ghost-white, but he kept his composure. "Councilor!" he said, looking at Fraochan. "Will you recite the full verse for us, so there is absolutely no confusion?"

Fraochan cleared his throat; glanced somewhat nervously at the two bound figures on the stone; turned to face the druid and the warrior once more. His eyes widened. Ciarán and Cathal were no longer alone. A crowd of little figures stood around them, some resembling small human folk, some more like animals, some closer to the form of drifting smoke or cascading water or fronded plants. Above them in the trees there was movement now as beings crept out along the branches, creatures that seemed made all of leaf and bark and vine, of creeper and moss and stone. As I stared, I saw one of them raise a twiggy hand in a tentative greeting, and beside me my brother lifted his hand in response. This was wondrous indeed.

Fraochan recited the verse:

> "*Held by hands that cannot hold*
> *Stands the steed so proud and bold*
> *Chieftain's son with seer's eyes*
> *Observes the Lord of Oak's demise*
> *Overcome the fear of flame*
> *Bid the wildest beast be tame*
> *Sever now the ties that bind*

Brothers in purpose and in kind
Evil's defeat demands the price
Of a brother's sacrifice
As the age begins to turn
That is when the oak will burn."

"Thank you," said Ciarán, nodding to the councilor. "I would welcome your expert services in my household, as I would welcome the goodwill of any person here. We will all work together to restore this realm to the place of peace it once was. In expectation of that, I will call a council very soon, to which representatives of each clan and each race dwelling in this realm will be invited." There was a murmuring among the crowd at this, but nobody spoke out.

"I extend the hand of friendship to all save these two," Ciarán went on. "Yes, even to the kinsfolk of Caisin Silverhair, who has so ruthlessly exploited my own family in her quest for power." He allowed his gaze to rest on Finbar and me for a moment, and his eyes were full of love and respect. "But for the courage of these children of Sevenwaters, we would not have reached this point." He drew a long breath and squared his shoulders. "It is time. I sacrifice my life among humankind; my place as chief druid in waiting; my bonds of human kinship; my ties of human friendship."

Bear was struggling to get up, writhing, moaning. I set my hand on his collar and it fell apart under my touch. His body was stretching, changing . . .

"My first act as your ruler will be one of mercy," said Ciarán. "Mac Dara. Caisin. The two of you will leave this place in exile and never return, on pain of death. I release you from your bonds."

Sever now the ties that bind. The vinelike ropes fell away, leaving the two of them exposed on the tongue of stone. Caisin wrapped her arms around herself, her lovely face stricken, her assurance gone. She looked like an ordinary woman, too stunned by this turn of events to move. And something had happened to Mac Dara. Instead of the tall, hale prince we had seen before, a ruler in his prime, there stood before us an old, old creature, shrunken and bowed. The geis had robbed him of his glamour. It had stolen his magic.

Bear scrabbled at me with his paws . . . clutched at me with his hands . . . whimpered . . . whispered . . . *"Maeve . . ."*

"Exile?" spat the ancient that was Mac Dara. *"Exile? A pox on you, druid!"* And faster than any old man had the right to move, he hurled himself at Caisin, seized her by the hair and toppled the two of them into the fire. The flames rose to take them, devouring all.

"Maeve," whispered Bear.

And there he was, his dark hair under my crippled hand, his body prone on the rocks, his face bloodied and bruised, his tattered clothing scorched and stained. A man. A man who, with a little cleaning up, would be a younger version of that fine chieftain, Cruinn of Tirconnell.

"Bear," I said, looking into his lovely amber eyes and failing utterly to hold back my tears. "Oh, Bear."

All around us was a babble of high, overwrought voices. Folk were milling around as if they had forgotten how to go about their ordinary business. I was aware of Finbar getting up and going over to Ciarán; of both Ciarán and Cathal moving into the crowd, where they stopped to speak to one group of folk after another. A retinue of strange small personages followed the two of them wherever they went, bright-eyed and watchful. Ciarán was calm and composed; Cathal looked shattered. Amidst the upheaval, Bear and I were a small island of stillness. I gazed at him and he gazed back at me.

There were many questions yet to be answered; many things still to be explained. But in this moment, our world was all here between us. I should have been startled, perhaps. Frightened; confused. Instead, my heart was flooded with delight, for in the eyes of the man who had been Bear I saw that, to him, I was the most perfect woman in all Erin. I saw that the love of the man was as deep and steadfast as that of the dog, and a great deal more besides. There was no place here for doubt, no place for uncertainty, no room for the misgivings I had long believed would rob me of any chance to love a man and be loved in return. I hoped he could read in my own eyes that he was my beloved, my dearest boy, my one and only. I hoped he saw my longing to dance with him as a bride and as a young mother, as a wife of middle years and as an old, old woman.

"Maeve," he said again, sounding somewhat unsure, as well he might since, as far as I knew, he had not used his human voice since the day of the Disappearance. So long ago; before ever I left Harrowfield and found myself on this strange adventure. "Love . . ."

"I know," I said quietly. "It's the same for me."

"Wife . . ." he managed. "Husband . . . wife?"

I felt a grin spread across my features, incongruous in this place of blood, fire and death. If this was a proposal of marriage, it must be one of the strangest ever spoken.

"You're smiling . . ." He propped himself up on his elbow, wincing. "Is that . . . a yes?"

"I'm smiling at how quick that was."

"Had to ask . . . before he did. My brother." He was looking over my shoulder now, to the trees beyond the stone basin; Finbar was up there with Ciarán, talking to a pair of men who stood half in shadow.

I remembered, then, that before the Disappearance one of the brothers had been riding to meet his betrothed. "It's a yes," I said before he could change his mind. "Which brother are you, Bear?"

He attempted a smile. "Artagan, son of Cruinn, my lady. You chose . . . apt name for me. Yes? Really?"

I put my arms around him, trying to be gentle and wondering at how natural it felt, since, in a way, I had only just met him. Gods, my hand hurt! "Yes, dear one. I see your brother coming; can you stand up?" I remembered, then, that it was Tiernan who was to wed the daughter of an Uí Néill chieftain. Just as well. Bear was mine, and I was not giving him up for anyone.

They came down to us: my brother, his brother, Ciarán and another man, a man of slight build and wry, humorous features, clad in filthy, tattered garments like those the brothers wore. Clothing that had once been of good quality, suitable for a chieftain's sons to wear on a journey of celebration. So many lost. So many fallen. Did they know?

The man who had been Badger knelt before me, putting his arms around my waist, laying his head on my breast as a child might. I stroked his dark hair, wishing there were two of me. Tiernan drew in a long, uneven breath and released it. Then he took his arms away and rose to his feet. His features were Bear's, though he was less tall, less robust. Both resembled their father. But in Tiernan the face had an edge, a restless quality. I felt, as I had long ago, that he was searching for something yet unfound; that he had still a journey ahead of him.

"Badger," I said through tears. "You're safe, thank all the gods."

"I should have stayed by you," he said. "Stood up to them. I cannot forgive myself for that."

"You obeyed a command," said Finbar. "That's what a dog is supposed to do. If you hadn't run away when I told you to, Caisin would have killed you. It didn't matter to her which brother was sacrificed. It's just as well you were obedient or we might all be dead. My lord," he added belatedly.

"You showed remarkable presence of mind, Finbar," Ciarán said. "In every respect you surpassed what I would expect of you. And my expectations are high indeed."

I had never seen my brother blush before, but now he did. His silence spoke much.

"Daigh!" exclaimed Artagan, moving to throw his arms around the slightly built man. "You're here . . . You're safe! I cannot believe . . . What happened to you?"

Someone must tell them about the others. But not now, not in this moment of joyful reunion. How much had they taken in while they were dogs? It seemed Artagan, at least, had some memory that went beyond a creature's, or he would not have been so quick to ask me that question; he would likely not have known my name.

"It seems we were all changed," said Daigh. "There was a woman . . . I rode on her saddle . . . a soft bed and tasty food . . . harsh words and sudden beatings. Then, suddenly, I was running before the hounds and this young man saved me. A great debt to repay . . . In time, I hope I can do so."

"It was nothing much," Finbar said. "I caught you, that was all. How was it the three of you were turned into dogs, when—"

"Artagan is hurt," I said. "He needs the attention of healers."

"You as well, Maeve," Ciarán said, looking from Artagan to me. "Cathal, please do me the service of seeking out that councilor who spoke earlier. Ask him if there is a place close by where our wounded can rest and be tended to. Not in Mac Dara's hall, and not, I think, in Caisin's. My friends, go with him." He was addressing the group of small folk who had remained close by all through this encounter as if to see off anyone who might seek to harm their new prince. "Mac Dara's people must learn tolerance. We are all kinds; we must learn to live together."

Folk were leaving the stone basin now, perhaps in search of the festivities that had been mentioned earlier, but more likely to retreat to their homes and ponder a future very different from the one they had expected. I saw Cathal engage both Breasal and Fraochan in earnest conversation. I did not think Ciarán would be without allies here. Fear could be a powerful tool for holding good folk quiet when they should speak out; but the time of fear was over. I wished my uncle well.

"There's one matter that needs immediate attention," Ciarán said, and his gaze moved a little beyond our group, to the man standing all alone a few paces from us. "Luachan, come forward."

I wondered why Luachan had not taken the opportunity to slip away quietly while folk's attention was elsewhere. How could anyone make amends for the betrayal of a child?

Luachan walked up to Ciarán. He was a ghost of the handsome druid we had known. His face was a mask of sharp bones and shadowy hollows; he looked ten years older. He waited, silent, his hands loosely clasped before him.

"In the spirit of fairness and justice, Luachan," Ciarán said, "I offer you the opportunity to account for your actions. Keep it brief; we have injured folk here."

"I . . ."

"Speak plainly; a man trained in the nemetons should not lack self-control."

"They threatened my family." Luachan's head was bowed; he addressed the ground at his feet. "Caisin and her kin. Said they would harm my sisters, do unspeakable things. They gave me no choice, Master Ciarán." He looked up, his blue eyes brimming with tears. "I am sorry. More sorry than I can possibly tell you. If I can make amends—I will work in the nemetons in a menial capacity, tending to stock, scrubbing floors—or I can go home and never return here again; you need never see me—"

Ciarán held up a hand and Luachan fell silent. "Work within the sacred grove? Go back home to your comfortable life as a chieftain's son? I think not. Luachan, even in the most testing of situations, even in the direst danger, we always have a choice. Courage or cowardice; right or wrong. To stand up to evil or to bow down before it. I do not think you are wholly a bad man. But you are easily turned to wrong paths."

"Master Ciarán, I—"

"It is not for you to determine your own punishment. That falls to me and to me only. You betrayed the child whose safety was in your keeping. You deceived Maeve and placed her in deadly danger. You pretended to be other than you were. To preserve your family's safety by serving the interests of evil is the choice of a weak man."

"Master Ciarán, I love my family." Luachan's voice was shaking; I could almost feel sorry for him. "I do not understand what other choice I could have made."

Ciarán smiled thinly. "Then you have much to learn. And you will be given the opportunity to do so." Luachan made to say something, perhaps words of thanks, but Ciarán silenced him with a gesture. "You will not return to the nemetons; you have proven yourself unworthy of your place among the brethren. Instead you will remain here to assist and support me. You will learn how to tread the paths of light. Only when you can prove to me that you are a changed man, and I mean truly changed in your heart, will I release you from the Otherworld. Should you lie, should you attempt acts of trickery and deception again, the penalty will be far more severe. I advise you not to put that to the test. Go now and make yourself known to the councilors; I expect they may find a use for you."

From the shelter of an airy pavilion I watched my brother climb a tree. Two small, well-armed personages had stationed themselves at the foot of the oak. It was clear to me that their purpose was to protect him, if not from falling, then most certainly from anyone who might wish to do him harm. At the foot of the three steps leading to my place of shelter another guard was standing with spear in hand. Nothing was being left to chance, even in this hall where we had been made welcome and provided with the opportunity to bathe, rest, eat and receive the attentions of healers. Word had been sent to my father that we were safe and would be returning home tomorrow.

Finbar had reached a massive bough and seated himself, legs dangling. Beside him perched another boy. Perhaps "boy" was not quite the right term; my brother's companion was the child of sticks and leaves, of earth and bark and clay, whom I had glimpsed among the tree people watching as Ciarán claimed leadership in Mac Dara's place. They were conducting an interchange in gestures, rapid and confident; I heard Finbar laugh.

He and I had wandered into this tranquil garden after bathing. While Finbar had been eager to explore, I was content to rest in this open shelter, looking out between gossamer-fine draperies that stirred in a slight breeze. The dwelling where we were lodged resembled Caisin's in that it seemed to grow up out of the forest. It lay in a long curve like a natural mound or hillock; its many round doors and windows opened to the circle of green sward where this pavilion stood. Flowering plants, red and yellow, bordered the patch of grass. Beyond the grass, beyond the house, the trees formed another great circle, as if to close off the household from the world outside. It might have been oppressive save for the birds chirping in the branches all around. I wondered if they were exchanging tales of this strangest of days, or merely warning each other off the choicest insect or last remaining berry.

Never in my life had I felt so tired. It was as if I had been part of the most fantastic tale ever told by a wandering bard, a story of cruelty and peril, lies and trickery, visions and transformations; a story that ended, triumphantly, with courage, sacrifice and true love. Folk would applaud the tale as good entertainment, but I doubted they would believe it. Even I was finding it hard to believe.

Footsteps sounded on the gravel pathway. I was expecting Ciarán, who had said he wanted to examine my injured hand before it was bandaged. Perhaps he might have news of Swift. He had promised to send out a search party. Our lovely, long-suffering creature had not been sighted since he fled the terror of the conclave. I had been somewhat reassured when I heard that Dioman, now also vanished, had been seen to cut the burning ropes from the horse's halter before he bolted. Still, I feared for Swift.

I turned and found the footsteps were not Ciarán's. I felt my face grow rosy with happiness. "Bear!" I said, taking in the transformation. My ragged, bloodied man now wore a resplendent outfit in the red and gold of this hall's clan. He was scrubbed clean, and the cuts and bruises on his face had been salved. His unkempt beard was gone and his dark hair was trimmed. A neat bandage encircled his head. He looked beautiful. Amid the fey enchantment of this place, he looked entirely real. "Have you seen the healers?" I asked as he came up to stand beside the padded bench where I sat. "What about your burns—what did they say?"

"Your hand," Artagan said, eyeing the sling. "Shouldn't that be bound up properly?"

Then we fell silent, looking at each other. This was new, for as man and woman we were strangers; and yet it was familiar and comfortable, for at its heart our bond was unchanged. "We sound like an old married couple," I said. "Come, sit down by me awhile. I'm keeping an eye on Finbar. I think that odd creature he's talking to is the changeling child who was put in his place as a baby."

Artagan sat down beside me and took my good hand in both of his. He lifted it and touched his lips to the soft skin on the back. "Did I mention that I love you?" he murmured.

"Once or twice," I said. "But I'm always happy to hear it again."

He turned my hand over and kissed the palm. "I love you, Maeve," he said. "I did from the first moment. But you knew that, I think."

"From the first moment? As I remember it, you were quite frightened of me back then." I recalled the two of them running wild out in the forest, and the long, slow process of earning their trust.

"Frightened, yes. But fascinated, too."

"It was Rhian's cooking that fascinated you, be honest."

Artagan smiled. "You drew me to you," he said. "The scared dog, yes, but also the troubled man within the dog. Both parts of me loved you. Your courage; your kindness; your generosity; your sheer stubbornness. Your sweet words and gentle touch."

"I can't believe you saw all those things as a dog. You just knew I was the one who set down bowls of food and let you sleep on the bed."

"I see them now, Maeve, and that helps me remember how it was then; remember it with a man's understanding. I hope very much that your father will agree to our marriage. I do not like to be away from you, even for as long as it takes to bathe and change my clothing."

I kissed his temple, wondering again at how easy this was, how lacking in either pretense or awkwardness. "I feel the same," I said. "When you went away just now I felt as I did the first night I took you up to the Sevenwaters keep and my mother tried to banish you to the kennels. Bereft."

"Will Lord Sean need a great deal of persuasion? Will require incentives? A long period of waiting? I do not think I would cope well with that."

An offer from the son of an Uí Néill chieftain? For the daughter everyone thought doomed to be forever unwed? As a strategic alliance, this marriage would be even more significant than Deirdre's. "I imagine he'll want to get to know you a little, as a man rather than a dog," I said, repressing a grin. "He may be quite stern and he's sure to submit you to an interrogation. But I believe he will eventually warm to the prospect." Seeing his expression, I added, "On the matter of waiting, we must work on both of them, my father and yours. My mother won't need much convincing. I hope Lord Cruinn—" I stopped myself.

As a dog, Bear had always seemed to understand what I could not put into words. "Maeve," he said, "my father respects and honors you. He admires you. This news can only delight him. Believe me, dear heart."

Admiring someone was all very well. It did not follow that a man would want that someone as his son's wife, especially if her disability might make her an embarrassment in his household. Artagan and I would wed anyway; there woud be no keeping us apart. I knew that as I knew moon followed sun across the sky. But this might be a cloud over the future. I did not want to set son against father. "You say he admires me," I said as I realized the implication of his words, "but how can you know that?"

He looked down at his hands, a frown creasing his brow. "I talked about this with Tiernan and Daigh while we were bathing. Our perceptions, during that time, were somewhat mixed. My instincts were those of a dog, most certainly. To hunt, to eat, to provide for those under my care . . ." He glanced up, a little smile on his lips.

"I eat raw meat only in dire emergencies," I said. "And I would be glad if that part of our journey was kept between you, me and your brother."

"As for my father, I did not know who he was when I saw him that day at your father's keep, and neither did Tiernan. Only that he was important to us, someone we knew, someone dear and familiar. When I watched you and my father together tending to Swift, I saw that you were safe with him. I knew I could relax my guard. A dog's judgment. But I was not entirely lost within my animal form. I can look back on that time now and remember it as a man remembers. For Tiernan it is much the same."

"What about Daigh?"

"I do not think he was treated well; he bears the marks of old beatings all down his back. But Daigh was always able to dismiss the bad things with a joke, a song, a tale; in that he has not changed. Maeve, I know about the others. I suspected they were all gone. Finding Niall that day in the forest . . . it tested me hard. Something in me knew that if I had been a man I might have saved him. I spoke to Ciarán before, privately, and he told me how the others died. I have told Tiernan and Daigh."

"I would have done it, dear heart."

"Shh," Artagan said. "That, at least, I could spare you. I am restless to return to Sevenwaters, Maeve, to bring my father some good news at last. But the healers insist that we sleep before we consider moving on." He smiled. "I have become accustomed to sharing your bed. I suppose I must forgo the delight of that until we are husband and wife."

"Another reason to ask our respective fathers if the wedding can be soon," I said, reaching up to brush his cheek with the back of my hand. "I will be cold at night without my Bear. Lonely. Perhaps I need another dog." To conduct this kind of interchange felt remarkable; it was not something I had imagined I would ever do. I could not stop smiling.

"Not yet, please. Let me reclaim the space that is rightfully mine before I am asked to share it." His fingers moved to my temple, where the mark of my burn disfigured the skin. "I imagine," he said, "that at any moment we will have company here; I believe Ciarán wishes to examine your hand. So I should kiss you now, while there is still time." As he leaned in to do so, Finbar swung down out of the tree and pelted over to the pavilion.

"Maeve! I met that boy! I talked to him!"

Artagan and I exchanged a rueful smile. "Later," he said as Finbar ran up the steps.

"Did you see?" My brother's face was flushed with happiness.

"I did. In this place, I'm seeing something remarkable every time I turn my head. Finbar, how wonderful that you spoke to him! I know how much you wanted to."

"He tried to warn us earlier—his people suspected Caisin was up to no good; they even knew about Luachan—but he didn't have time to explain. He can't talk the way we do—it's all signs and little sounds, sort of chirrups and creaks. But it didn't matter. Everything worked out the way it was meant to."

I was struggling with this statement when Ciarán came across the sward, carrying a willow basket packed with little stone jars and rolls of cloth.

"I cannot say that you look well," my uncle said, coming up the steps and setting down his supplies, "but undoubtedly you look happy, the three of you. This has been a difficult time; a testing time for all." He seated himself on a stool beside me, turning his mulberry eyes on me in close scrutiny. Finbar settled himself cross-legged on the floor. "Maeve, I want to see that hand," Ciarán went on. "I suspect you have broken bones."

"Artagan was far more seriously hurt than I was. He took the blow on his head. And he was burned. You should—"

"I have examined Artagan's burns," said Ciarán. "They are not severe. He's been very lucky. As for his head, it did sustain some damage, yes, but the Old Ones have a powerful gift. They have sewn him up and spoken charms over the wound; it will heal. Now show me this hand."

Artagan untied my sling. I could hardly bear to move my arm; the pain was intense. His strong hands came out to support the injured limb while Ciarán performed a thorough examination. Although he was both deft and gentle, it hurt enough to bring tears to my eyes.

"There's at least one bone broken, perhaps two," my uncle said eventually. "An honorable wound, as your others were." He looked at Artagan. "You know, of course, that this hand cushioned you from a blow that would otherwise have killed you."

"I do, and it humbles me."

"Maeve," said Ciarán, "your courage defies comprehension. Now I must bind this up. Finbar, be ready to pass me what I need. As for you, Maeve, no working with horses until the bones are mended, you understand? Indeed, no strenuous activity of any kind at all." He cast another glance Artagan's way.

"I'll do my best to keep Maeve quiet," Artagan said, "as will her maidservant, I'm sure, but she is her own woman."

Rhian. I found myself smiling again. She would be fascinated by this tale of magical happenings and strange creatures. I would not tell her all of it; I had no wish to darken her dreams.

"It occurred to me," observed Ciarán as he went about wrapping my hand—Finbar passed him in turn a pungent green salve, a moss-like padding and a broad strip of linen, "that the two of you might be planning to ride to Tirconnell in the near future. Any such journey should wait until you are both recovered. Maeve, you should not subject this hand to the jolting movement of a horse. Not to speak of the fact that Sean and Aisling will want you home awhile before . . . Well, perhaps I am a little ahead of myself."

"Why would they—oh." Finbar's face fell.

"Artagan asked me to marry him, Finbar," I said gently, "and I said yes. But I don't expect Father to give his permission immediately. That's not what fathers do."

"But you'll be going away."

There was no way to soften the truth. "Yes, we will. And I will miss you very much. You're the most remarkable of brothers. One of a kind."

"There will always be a welcome for you in my father's house, Finbar." Artagan's deep voice was full of respect. "I hope Lord Sean will be amenable to your spending some time with us in Tirconnell. The place is full of dogs and horses; there is also an extensive collection of manuscripts. My brother is something of a scholar. I believe you would enjoy it there."

"And there's a precedent," I said. "Aunt Liadan and Uncle Bran fostered me for ten years; their youngest son, Coll, spent two years at Sevenwaters. There's no reason why we shouldn't do something similar with you, Finbar, if you'd like it. I can't suggest it to Mother and Father immediately, but in time I should think they'd consider letting you come." They would not want to send their only son away, but there was the alliance with Cruinn. My marriage to Artagan would set it in place; a fostering arrangement could only strengthen it.

The bandage was almost done. As Ciarán completed the binding, a small being came up the steps carrying a tiny green cup shaped like a flower. The being seemed something between a dwarf and a hedgehog. Its eyes were deep-set and distinctly non-human.

"Thank you, friend," Ciarán said, taking the cup. "Maeve, drink this and don't ask questions. Be assured that everything that passes your lips while you are in this hall is quite safe. The same goes for you, Finbar, and for all of your party. It was one of the first requirements I set out in my new role here."

I drank; the draught tasted of grass. The bandage was done. Artagan helped me get my arm back into the sling. My hand throbbed a little less. I became aware of how tired I was, oh so tired, as if the events of the last few days had finally sunk into my bones and my blood, now there was no need to be constantly ready for trouble.

"I spoke further to Luachan while you were bathing," Ciarán said. "He told me Caisin offered you a significant reward for your cooperation and you refused it. This before you understood she was not a friend."

"I was offended that she thought I might accept a bribe." A shiver ran through me. "And when I refused, when she thought I would not help her, she told me a cruel lie. She said Bear and Badger were dead. She told me Mac Dara had killed them, that he had . . ." I stopped myself; the most hideous part must not be spoken with Finbar present. "She knew that would set me in a black fury. She knew that lie would turn me to her purpose."

"A wicked deception," said Ciarán. "She must have been astonished when you refused her bribe. That was a powerful gift to offer."

"This is the way I am now." I lifted my free hand. "My honorable wounds are part of me. If salves or stretching or onion-skin poultices could have regained me the use of my hands, I would have been blissfully happy. Aunt Liadan tried all those things and many more, to little effect. Caisin's suggestion of a magical cure seemed . . . too easy. It felt wrong. It felt like something I would spend the rest of my life regretting." When nobody made comment, I added, "I know it is a decision most folk would find hard to understand. I'm not sure I understand it myself. But if she asked me again now, I'd give the same answer."

"It makes perfect sense to me," Artagan said, moving his fingers gently against my temple. "Such a choice is all Maeve."

The hedgehog-dwarf was still standing quietly beside us, the empty cup in its three-fingered hands. Now it performed a grave little bow and addressed me. "Your courage is equal to your sister's, Lady Maeve. The folk of this realm owe you a greater debt than they realize. I have with me a healer from my own people. We have not seen the marks of burns such as these before; would you allow us to look more closely?" From nowhere, another of the Old Ones appeared. It wore a hooded cloak of brindled fur. A golden mask covered its face. The mask was a cat's; eyes of gleaming green peered out through the holes.

There seemed no harm in the request, and I was well beyond feeling embarrassed. I held out my good hand, if such a misshapen thing could be called good, and the two beings peered at it. Cat Mask touched it with a furred finger, turned it over to compare the soft skin of the back to the ugly scarring of the palm. The creature wrapped its hand around each of my fingers in turn, humming a vague little tune to itself as if deep in thought. It reached out to lay its palm against my other hand in its enveloping bandage.

"If you had perished in that long-ago fire," the hedgehog-dwarf said gravely, watching as its companion performed its strange ritual, "who would have come with your brother to turn darkness to light? We might have waited a hundred years more, two hundred, to see Mac Dara meet his destined fate."

It was true, I supposed. Maybe this had been the only chance in a lifetime, or several lifetimes, for the elements of the geis to come together in one place. Caisin had planned it, of course; she had used Luachan and she had used us. Used us sorely and lied to us grievously, for of course it was not Mac Dara's people who had taken the dogs by force, but those of Caisin herself. Why coax Finbar to a place of refuge high in a tree, if not so I must leave the dogs behind while I fetched him down? But . . .

"What about the Disappearance?" I asked. "Why would Mac Dara turn three men into dogs, but condemn the others to their bizarre deaths? Or was it Caisin who changed them? How could she know I would become so close to the brothers?"

"Visions." It was Finbar who spoke. "She may not have seen everything, but if she was looking for hands that cannot hold, or brothers in purpose and in kind, or a proud, bold steed, she might have seen them in her scrying vessel. She could have seen you in the fire, long ago, the way I did. She might have seen you training Swift or coaxing the dogs out of the forest. Probably she can conjure up whatever she wants, like Cathal. Past, present or future. Real, unreal, possible, impossible."

"But how did she know the words of the geis in the first place? How did she know what to look for?"

"Ah," said the hedgehog-dwarf, and there was a world of sadness in that sound. "She learned it from one of our kind. One who was unfortunate enough to be present, long years ago, when the charm was spoken over Mac Dara's cradle. Caisin got word of this and sought her out. She obtained what she needed by the cruelest of means. That was a day of darkness; a day of great sorrow for our people. And of shame." He bowed his head for a moment, and nobody spoke. Then he said, looking up, "Today is brighter. A new dawn. We will be sad to bid farewell to Mac Dara's son; he is a staunch friend of our people. But we are content."

I could not imagine, now, that I had ever thought Caisin might be a good person. I shuddered at the risk I had taken, for myself and for Finbar. "Where is Cathal now, Uncle Ciarán?" I asked.

"Down by the stone basin. He is much troubled by what has unfolded today; he needs time alone."

Remembering the look on Mac Dara's face when he saw that his son had come home, that moment of utter transformation, I understood how hard this must be for Cathal. The Lord of the Oak had been evil. He had been cruel. He had killed without mercy and had caused untold misery. But he had still been a father, and in his own way he had loved his son. It might be a long time before Cathal came to terms with this.

"You asked what happened that day in the forest," said the hedgehog-dwarf. "I can tell you. Mac Dara's folk attacked the riders. There was a skirmish and the riders scattered under the trees. Three moved more swiftly and escaped their assailants' reach. The others fell victim to the enchantment ordered by the Lord of the Oak. It was long and cruel, a spell that twisted their minds. We would not meddle with such a potent charm; we could not help them. He prolonged their lives until it suited him to make an end of them, each in turn."

"I have a recollection of fighting an enemy that was no human warrior," Artagan said. "Our horses bolted. I was thrown, alongside my brother. And we were changed. That is the sum of it."

"A spell was cast over the two of you and over your friend," the hedgehog-dwarf said. "Not by Mac Dara. Not by Caisin Silverhair. Not by any lord or lady of the Tuatha De Danann. By my people. We did what we could to keep you from the same fate as your companions. Your friend fled in panic; he wandered long in the woods before he fell into the clutches of the Fair Folk, who kept him as a plaything. You and your brother reached kinder hands."

I laid my head on Artagan's shoulder. Warmth spread through me, tugging me toward sleep. "Then I owe your people a debt," I told the little being. "Your foresight has given me the greatest gift of all my life, and I honor you."

"Weary." Cat Mask spoke for the first time, its tone suggestive of the creature whose face it wore, for it was rich and soft, cream and sunshine. "Rest soon." It lifted one of its odd little hands and made a kneading motion, flexing the fingers. "Later, bend. Like this. Stretch. Work."

"Me? There would be no point in that; I can't move my fingers at all. I haven't been able to since I was burned as a child. They are quite stiff; look—" I held out my free hand again, wondering that the creature's close examination had not made this obvious.

"Like this," said Cat Mask, demonstrating again. "Bend. Stretch. Work. Every day." The creature turned its odd eyes on Artagan. "Salve," it added. "Song. Love. Every day."

"But I—" I fell silent. "For how long?"

"How long is hope?" purred the creature. "Weary. Rest now."

The two small beings inclined their heads to Ciarán and departed from the pavilion. The long coarse spines of the hedgehog-dwarf rattled faintly as it passed; Cat Mask padded behind on silent feet.

I worked hard not to disgrace myself by weeping. This particular hope, I had long ago set aside; I knew it could never be fulfilled. And I had made it quite plain I would not accept a magical cure.

"Would you not attempt what they suggest?" asked Ciarán, evidently reading my distress in my face.

"I told you, I've already done all of it, poultices, stretching, salves, leeches, a hundred things, every one of them useless. There was no lack of love or of knowledge. Aunt Liadan is the most expert of healers. We tried for two years. When she told me I would not regain the use of my hands, she told me the truth. I could spend the rest of my life trying to move just one finger. I could be eaten up by forlorn hope. Isn't it better to get on with things the way I am?" A pox on it, now I really was crying. I was too tired for this.

Artagan wiped away my tears with his fingers; his lips brushed my temple.

Finbar regarded me with troubled eyes, and I regretted speaking out. Ciarán appeared to be deep in thought.

"I have no doubt Liadan is the most expert of human healers," he said eventually. "I'm certain she applied all her knowledge and skill, and I'm sure you did everything she asked of you. But there are branches of healing unknown to humankind, Maeve. I do not imagine that during those ten years in Britain you consulted the healers of the Fomhóire, the Old Ones."

"Of course not." I sniffed back more tears. Finbar took a piece of cloth from Ciarán's basket and hooked it between the fingers of my good hand. I dried my eyes and wiped my nose. "But I can't accept a magical cure from them, Uncle Ciarán, any more than I could have from Caisin. It's . . . it's not right. It's too much; it's too easy."

All three of my companions studied me in silence. Then Ciarán said, "It is possible the Old Ones could use their earth magic to restore your hands instantly. Possible, but unlikely. I doubt they have such power over humankind, and I doubt they would choose to use it thus if they did. Indeed, I do not believe Caisin Silverhair had the skill to do for you what she implied she could. The illusion, she might have created; but not the reality. What you have been offered now is the expertise of a different kind of healer. A salve to which Liadan would not have access; a regimen of exercises that requires you to love and to hope. You have not been promised a complete cure. Indeed, they promised nothing, but these are good folk, and if they suggest you may gain some benefit by taking their advice, I believe you should at least consider acting as they recommend."

"But I can't move my fingers at all! How can I—"

"I would help you." Artagan spoke against my hair; he had wrapped his arms around me, careful not to jolt my damaged hand. "I have hope enough for two."

"This time it's not a bribe," said Finbar. "It's a gift of thanks. You did just save them from Mac Dara. You changed all their lives for the better. That's not a little thing. And all they've said is that you could try the salve and the stretching, so it would be you doing this yourself, not someone doing it for you."

Ciarán's somber features were transformed by a sudden smile.

"You understand your sister well, Finbar," observed Artagan.

"It's a conspiracy," I said, looking from one to another. "Do I really seem so set on doing everything myself?" A yawn overtook me.

"No more for now," Ciarán said. "All of you must rest."

"I don't feel tired at all." Finbar did indeed look rosy-cheeked and alert; he seemed a different child. "Can I go out and talk to that boy again, Uncle Ciarán? Will I be able to come back here and see him, and the other folk?"

Unusually, it seemed Ciarán was lost for words. The silence was full of things unsaid.

"You're going to lie down for a while, at least," I told my

brother. "That's what Mother would expect under the circum-stances. Come on, we'll walk over to the sleeping quarters to-gether." With Artagan's assistance, I rose to my feet. My hand hurt less than before. Something was working: the salve, the draught, the warmth of Artagan's arm around me, sheer relief that this was almost over. "Thank you, Uncle Ciarán," I said, and I saw in his eyes that he knew I was not only referring to the salving and ban-daging, or indeed to his kindness and care for us.

"We'll talk more in the morning," he said. "I hope by then we will have news of the horse. Now go to your rest, all of you. This has been a long journey. A long test. Sleep well."

We left him standing in the pavilion, gazing out toward the darkness of the oak forest. Shadows gathered in the garden, turn-ing verdant green to gray and violet and brown. Had the after-noon vanished already? Ciarán's face was that of a statue in pale stone, high-boned, authoritative, deeply sad. And yet, within, the flame burned bright. *I sacrifice my life among humankind*, he had said. *My bonds of human kinship; my ties of human friendship.*

I wanted to run back, to throw my arms around him and say how sorry we were, to tell him we understood what this must be costing him, to thank him again. But I did not. How could I begin to understand the depth of such a loss? Tomorrow I would talk to him. Right now, the most I could manage would be to stay awake long enough to reach a bed.

"Wonder what was in that draught . . ." I murmured. I felt my-self lifted up in Artagan's arms. Then I was in a lamp-lit chamber and a woman in a red robe was easing my arm out of the sling, helping me undress, slipping a night robe over my head. She tucked me into a soft bed. I sank into sleep.

CHAPTER 17

Waking, I thought myself still meshed in dreams, for around the bed hung filmy curtains, too fine to be of human make. Within the gossamer fabric, jewel-bright spots glowed, perhaps insects, perhaps only an illusion. The vine-wreathed walls of the chamber and the soft cushioning of the bed made me feel as if I were in a nest. I lay still awhile as it all came back to me. My arm was resting on a pillow; the hand Luachan had smashed with his stone lay there in its neat bandage, and I could feel every bit of damage he had inflicted. The draught had given me long and peaceful sleep, but morning had brought back the pain.

Today we would be going home. Somehow that felt the oddest thing of all. It came to me, as I maneuvered myself to an upright position, that it was not only Tiernan, Artagan and Daigh who had been changed, but all of us. Ciarán's life had turned upside down. Cathal had watched his father die; he had seen Ciarán take the burden Mac Dara had intended for his son. Luachan had earned a long penance. He had told bare-faced lies to me and to my family. His betrayal of Finbar had been unforgivable. And yet

I had some sympathy for the man. With his sisters under threat, he had faced a terrible choice.

As for me, I had found love, and that was a gift worth suffering for. Whether I could learn to bend was still to be determined; but I could try.

And Finbar . . . I had seen a new light in his eyes, and I prayed that it would keep shining. How much had he known? What terrifying secrets had he hugged to himself, lest he reveal his knowledge to Luachan or to Caisin? How could a child so young be so unutterably brave?

Without a helper I could not wash or dress. There was a fine shawl by the bedside, a swathe of delicate gray, soft as swansdown. I managed to get it around my shoulders, though the awkward movement made my hand throb anew. I felt a sharp pang of longing for Rhian, with her capable hands and droll humor. Perhaps she would not want to come to Tirconnell. Harrowfield was home for her, close to her mother and brothers. Perhaps I should let her go.

I needed the privy; I hoped I could find it on my own. I walked to the doorway, parted the curtain of dangling fronds that covered it and almost fell over the man who lay across the threshold, fast asleep. He was wrapped in a cloak, apple red with an ornate border worked in gold thread—toadstools, acorns, tiny birds complete in every detail. The bright color made Artagan's cheeks look wan; he had bruise-like shadows under his eyes. A lock of dark hair had fallen across his face. His head was pillowed on his hands. My faithful Bear.

"Sleep softly, dear one," I whispered, then stepped over him and left him to his rest.

There was a woman in the bathing chamber to help me wash and dress. She offered me an elaborate red and gold gown with trailing sleeves and rich embroidery. When I suggested it was not suitable for a journey through the forest, she brought out a skirt and tunic that were very slightly plainer in style, but still somewhat grand, with decorative borders that were small, strange forests in themselves, all curly trees and big-eyed, peering creatures. I half-expected to see the owls and badgers and not-quite-squirrels moving about. Under this, a shirt of fine linen, and for my hair a cloth of the same stuff with lacy edging. Good stockings and pretty shoes of red felt that seemed unlikely to last as far as the bottom of the garden, let alone all the way home.

When I was dressed to the woman's satisfaction, she combed and braided my hair, then tied on the head cloth. Lastly, she did a creditable job of securing my arm in the sling. I thanked her and headed out into the garden. If everyone else was still abed, I would sit quietly in the pavilion awhile and make a start on coming to terms with it all.

Someone was there before me. Ciarán stood gazing out across the grass as the first rays of dawn began to filter through the trees. A bird sounded a tentative note; another answered. *Time! Time! Awake!* Another voice joined them, then another. The garden filled up with song.

"I don't want to disturb you—" I said, halting at the foot of the steps.

"Not at all, Maeve. I wanted to see you. I have something to ask you."

I came to stand beside him. Behind us in the house there were sounds of folk stirring now.

"I'm afraid there is no news of Swift as yet," Ciarán said. "We will continue to search."

"Thank you, Uncle Ciarán." My heart sank. Swift would have been beside himself after that ordeal. Likely he had plunged over a drop or into a mire and done himself damage there was no repairing. That lay squarely on my shoulders.

"Maeve, Luachan has asked to speak to you."

I said nothing. I was not sure how I felt about this.

"It is your decision, yes or no. If you agree to see him, I will ensure someone else is present—Cathal, or Artagan if you prefer, or a guard. But I will understand if you do not wish to allow Luachan this opportunity. He asked to speak to Finbar, too. I said no to that."

"Uncle Ciarán . . ."

"What is it?"

"Finbar . . . How much do you think he knew of what was to happen? He often seemed aware of things he could not have seen, except in visions. And when I asked, he would say, *I'm not supposed to tell.* And sometimes he'd say, *This is the way it's supposed to be,* even when we were making a choice that seemed unwise. I know a seer's visions don't show exactly what will happen. I understand that they can be symbolic, or that they might show past, present and future mixed up together. And when it's the future, it's only a possible future. Sibeal explained it to me long ago. More than once, Luachan said Finbar was too young to interpret his visions correctly, so it was better for him to keep them to himself. But maybe he said that to stop Finbar from talking too much. Maybe he was becoming aware that Finbar suspected him." That made me cold to the core. How the knowledge must have weighed on my brother.

"I believe Finbar knew, in essence, that Mac Dara would not be defeated unless you and he were both present," Ciarán said. "I have spoken to him a little, not much, for he needs time to come back to himself. He may seem well and happy, but this has tested him severely. I doubt if his visions would have shown him clearly what Luachan was, or that Caisin was as ruthless as Mac Dara. But Finbar knew enough to be wary of Luachan. Until the truth came out, I had wondered why they were not better friends." His lips twisted. "It is hard to believe I missed this. Even a day ago, I still thought Luachan trustworthy. He is an expert dissembler. What shall I tell him, Maeve?"

"I'll listen to him," I said. "But not for long."

They were in a chamber with a long table of polished oak and benches to either side. A curious lamp stood in the table's center, fashioned in the shape of two birds with necks intertwined, their heads supporting the light. One was of silver and one of gold; their eyes were fashioned of gleaming gems. A fine oak chair stood at the head of the table, but nobody was seated there. Cathal stood by the far doorway, arms folded, jaw tight, dark eyes baleful, as if he would snap the head off anyone who dared to speak.

Luachan was seated at the table, staring down at his hands. When I came in, he jumped up. "Maeve!"

"Be silent," said Cathal. He spoke quietly, but it was nonetheless an order. "It's for Maeve to speak and for you to answer. If she wants to hear your excuses, she'll let you know." He looked at me. "You may wish to be seated," he said. "Tell me when you've had enough and I'll take him away."

I reminded myself that this intimidating person was my sister's husband, and that his hostility was not meant for me. I sat down opposite Luachan and made myself look him in the eye.

"Sit down," I said. "I don't want an apology. No apology would be adequate for your betrayal of my brother, or your complicity in a plot that could have seen both me and Finbar dead. If you want to set the facts before me, this is your chance. I don't imagine I will see you again after today."

At first he found it hard to get the words out. I did not help him, simply waited. Then, once he began, the story tumbled from him, an outpouring of fear, guilt and shame. How he had been in the habit of wandering into the forest when the intensity of his druidic training became too overwhelming; how one day Caisin's people had found him when he strayed beyond the protection of the nemetons. How they had threatened his family if he did not comply with Caisin's plans. He had been newly appointed as Finbar's tutor then; Caisin had seen how useful it would be to have a willing agent in the heart of my father's household. She knew that if the geis were to be used, Finbar must be part of it, and she learned soon enough how difficult it would be to get him away. Luachan would be the key to that. My arrival with Swift, so near to the next Grand Conclave, had excited her greatly, for now she could see it all falling into place: the two dogs, the brothers of the geis, or so Caisin believed; the matchless steed; the girl with claws for hands, who happened to have one rare talent. For Luachan, the pressure became more intense, the threats more dire as the conclave approached.

"You encouraged me to move down to the cottage," I said, remembering how it had been. "Just me and Rhian, without a guard. And later, it was you who suggested Finbar come to the nemetons as well. You manipulated all of us." I could not believe I had been taken in by him. I had even been somewhat flattered by his interest, since the attention of a young man, druid or no druid, was rare for me. How gullible. What a fool. I should have seen through it instantly.

"That day, Caisin's people lured Swift away with the scent of a mare in season," he said. "The moment was chosen with care, so that Finbar must follow or lose the trail; we knew you would go after him. And where you went, the dogs would follow. Caisin's people captured them later, to be sure they were ready at the conclave."

"You came searching for us. But you weren't searching; you were trying to keep us from reaching home. No wonder you were so inept at finding shelter. No wonder you couldn't locate the way back." Oh, this was a bitter draught to swallow.

"That night, after you refused to help Caisin, she asked me what incentive she could offer that would possibly weigh more than a promise to restore you to health and beauty."

"And you told her not to offer me a bribe, but to tell me a hideous falsehood . . . You knew that would make me so angry I would do what she wanted right then and there, no need to consult Father, no need to wait as any sensible person would have done . . . That was cruel, Luachan. If it were not for the fact that I know you acted out of love for your sisters, I woud think you did not understand love at all."

He looked down at his hands. "I know no apology can be adequate," he said. "I do not ask you to forgive me, Maeve; I do not deserve that. Only that you listen for a little longer."

I waited.

"I know I've done wrong. I know only a lengthy period of service here can win me back my life in the human world. I know I will never be more to you than the man who betrayed your trust and almost got you and your brother killed. If I must live with that burden, then so be it. But . . ." He drew a ragged breath. "If you could find it in yourself to . . . perhaps to understand, just a little . . . My youngest sister is only twelve years old, Maeve."

"Look at me, Luachan," I said. He turned his beautiful blue

eyes on me, eyes that had lied over and over again. "I cannot bring myself to say I forgive you. But I have sisters and a brother of my own, and I think I understand."

He bowed his head.

"I'm ready to go now," I said to Cathal. "If we're to ride back to the keep, we should probably be leaving soon."

Cathal motioned to someone beyond the entry, and a pair of fey guards in red and gold came to take Luachan away.

"That was . . . difficult," I said. "I wonder how long it will be before Ciarán lets him come back."

"You were remarkably understanding," Cathal said. "Generosity must run in the family."

"I haven't really introduced myself." Cathal and I were virtual strangers; it felt odd to be here with him, speaking of such matters. "I was too tired last night to talk to anyone."

"You're so like Clodagh," Cathal said, his thin lips quirking into a half-smile. "I'll be privileged to escort you home, Maeve. You've been forged in the fire, tested and tempered, and I see you're made of the same rare metal as my wife is. As for the journey, you will find the way out of this realm is far shorter than the way in. We won't set off before you and your companions have broken your fast. Luachan's horse must be brought over from Caisin's hall, and Finbar has some farewells to make."

"Cathal . . ." I hesitated, reluctant to bring that haunted look back to his face, for as he'd spoken of Clodagh it had faded.

"Ask me what you wish."

"This will mean Ciarán can't come back, won't it? I know Mac Dara was seen from time to time in our world, and so was the Lady of the Forest, long ago. But . . . it would be different for him, wouldn't it? He is half-human and has human ties. Ruling in the Otherworld would take all his energy, all his dedication. So when he made his speech about the sacrifice, he meant . . ."

"Nobody can be sure what will come." Cathal's tone was grave. "I had thought to take on the burden myself. I came here expecting to do so. I said good-bye to Clodagh knowing Mac Dara's defeat would likely cost me my future by her side. I embraced my children for what I thought would be the last time. What Ciarán did . . . his choice . . . When our time becomes the ancient past, when bards sing of it, that act of selflessness should be woven into their grandest tales."

We stood there awhile in silence, until Finbar appeared in the doorway, clad like me in resplendent red and gold.

"Maeve, are you hungry? It's time for breakfast."

The meal was quiet. Artagan sat beside me, helping me eat. Tiernan was opposite, watching us, not saying a word. Daigh engaged Finbar in desultory conversation. At the head of the table sat Cathal, the dark clouds back on his face. I did not see him eat a single bite. I was relieved when Ciarán came into the chamber and announced that Blaze was here and our escort was ready.

Outside on the sward that escort waited. They were many, and not one of them higher than my waist. Cat Mask was there, and the hedgehog-dwarf with a pale knife at its belt, and beings of myriad kinds, some leafy, some vaporous, some resembling nothing so much as chunks of rock with holes for eyes, some almost like ordinary men and women, save for their diminutive size. Many were creatures, or variations of creatures: a great lizard with a fox's brush, a being with bird legs and the face of a rat, another that seemed part dog, part pony.

"I will walk with you to the portal," Ciarán said.

Cathal turned to address the rest of us. "My friends here will lead us; it is thanks to them that we need not take the longer way. Maeve, can you manage this on foot?"

"Of course." Since I had been ordered not to ride until my hand was mended, there was really no choice. I wondered what had happened to my bag with my spare clothing and waterskin. Was it still in Caisin's hall? Would there be folk there now, cursing me and Finbar, plotting Ciarán's downfall? He had not banished Dioman or Fiamain; he had not laid any punishment on Caisin's kin. They could make his way forward difficult if they chose.

Nobody was carrying much by way of provisions or equipment. Even Blaze was without the saddlebags she had borne when Luachan brought her here. Cathal had a small pack and his not inconsiderable weaponry; the rest of us had nothing except our unsuitable clothing. We looked as if we were heading for a court entertainment, not a long hard walk through the forest.

"Er . . . won't we need food and water, and perhaps some means of making shelter on the way if it rains?" I did not like to appear critical of Cathal, especially with that look on his face.

"All that you need, we will provide." That came from a creature wearing a mask, this one the face of a dog wrought in silver. It was standing beside Cathal. Perhaps these small folk were already familiar to him, since he had been to this realm before. He had stayed a long time as his father's captive. Seasons had passed, years maybe, while he waited for Clodagh's return. Yet for her that absence had been only a matter of a day or two. A shiver ran through me, imagining how it would be if we stepped through this portal, wherever it was, and found our loved ones long dead and buried. In the old tales, time was often cruel to travelers between worlds.

Dog Mask was watching me closely, almost as if seeing into my thoughts. "No cause for worry," it said. "The way is not long."

In all the time we had spent as guests in this hospitable house, I had not seen any of the Fair Folk, save the woman who had helped me bathe and dress and a silent man who had brought us food. Now an imposing bearded man in a red robe came out of the house, and after him a tall woman whose gown was all of scarlet feathers. Both were pale and handsome in the manner of the Fair Folk, their eyes coolly grave.

"We wish you a safe journey," said the man.

"You are always welcome in our hall," the woman added. "But I think you will not come again." The two of them were looking at Cathal, and I wondered if they were seeing his father, whose reign of fear and cruelty had stamped a heavy mark on their fair realm. There was no telling what they thought of Mac Dara's demise and that of his rival. That they had housed us willingly and treated us with courtesy seemed to bode well for Ciarán. But this was only one household out of many.

"Who knows?" Cathal said, attempting a light touch and failing completely. "We thank you for your hospitality. Now we'd best be off."

I wondered, later, whether that walk had been designed to give us all thinking time; time to prepare for the step back into our own world. The way out was indeed different from the way in. The forest still stretched far on every side, but now it was more open, the sunlight filtering down through the half-bare branches to lighten the path. The leaf carpet, waterlogged only a day ago, was soft and dry beneath our feet. The way was broad enough for two to walk comfortably abreast. The terrain was level; no awkward stones or gnarled tree roots, no slippery rises or sudden depressions to trip unwary feet. Birds sang above. From time to time we heard a swift rustling as a forest creature passed on its business.

I walked with my arm in Artagan's, though I hardly needed his support: this was an easy path. Daigh and Finbar were some way behind us, surrounded by an enthusiastic clutch of Old Ones. Daigh was attempting to put his adventures into verse and making such a lamentable job of it that his audience was in stitches with laughter.

"In fact, Daigh has some talent in the bardic arts," Artagan told me, smiling. "But he does enjoy a joke."

At the head of the long procession walked Tiernan and Cathal, conducting an earnest conversation of which we could hear nothing. Behind them, one of the taller beings led Blaze.

"Will he be all right?" I murmured. "Tiernan, I mean. He looks so troubled."

"You're more concerned with my brother's welfare than mine, then?"

A swift glance told me he was teasing. "You are the stronger of the two," I said quite seriously, remembering how long it had taken to coax them down to the cottage, and how it had always been Bear who took the lead. "Besides, as your intended wife I'll be in a position to keep a close eye on you. I've hardly spoken to Tiernan since he became a man again, and I . . . Well, I am concerned for him, yes. Perhaps without good cause. I don't know."

We walked on in silence for a while.

"You and I are both the strong ones," Artagan said eventually. "I am happy to hear Finbar's laughter. He is young; that may help him mend more quickly. There is much I still need to learn about your family, Maeve. How many sisters did you say?"

"Apart from me, five. But there's only one living close by. You won't have to cope with a bevy of sisters-in-law."

"If they are all like you, dear heart, I have no objection at all. This Cathal . . . I can hardly imagine such a man wed to your sister. To look at him is to see Mac Dara's son; and yet, he belongs to a chieftain's war band, or so I hear."

"Not exactly. It's complicated. Cathal usually lives in the north, training elite fighters; he works with our cousin. But now . . ." I had not thought this through. With Mac Dara gone, there was no longer any need for Clodagh and her children to remain on Inis Eala, home to Johnny's school of war craft. If they wanted to, they could all come home to Sevenwaters. It made me cold to imagine how Clodagh must have felt, letting her husband go, knowing she would probably never see him again. I understood her pain in a way I could not have done before this journey, before Bear.

"All right?" he queried, slowing his pace.

"I will be glad to reach home. Though *home*, now, means something different; I'll need to get used to that."

We walked on without speaking as, behind us, Daigh and Finbar and their companions tried out one tune after another, arguing amicably as to which best suited the verses Daigh had invented.

"No matter what happens," Artagan said, "no matter where our journey takes us, my home is where you are, Maeve. Always."

"Not so long ago, I thought I might look for home all my life and never find it." I cleared my throat, knowing I did not want to shed tears at such a moment, even happy ones. "But I did find it. You're my home and my shelter. I can't tell you . . ." There was no way to describe how remarkable that moment had been when we'd first looked at each other as man and woman; when I'd realized he loved me without reservation. I'd understood in that moment that what the world saw as my handicaps and flaws were to

Bear simply part of the woman he cherished above all others. I could not explain what a profound difference that made. "There are no words," I said. "All that hope of yours—some of it must have brushed off on me."

"Good," Artagan said, reaching up his free hand to wipe his eyes. "That means we'll do as the healer recommended, yes? The salve, the exercise—I'll help with those. I'm not sure about the singing. It's not one of my strong points. I'll try."

"I look forward to hearing you."

We had walked perhaps five miles when the path began to rise, curving up under a stand of elders beside which a stream gurgled quietly to itself. As we climbed, a rock formation came into view ahead of us, the stone moss-coated and seamed with deep cracks. By the time we reached its base my legs were aching. The line came to a halt; the Old Ones moved in so we stood in one group.

"This is the place," said Dog Mask. "We will not all come with you; two to go before, two to come behind. That is all you need."

Four of the Old Ones stepped forward. The hedgehog-dwarf; two small, cloaked, manlike beings; a beady-eyed creature in a green hat. "We're ready," said the hedgehog-dwarf.

"A moment." Cat Mask was there, a little stone jar in its hands. "For you."

"Thank you," I said, since the creature was clearly addressing me. Cat Mask proffered the jar; Artagan took it. "What is this?" I asked.

"Salve. Love. Hope."

"I am grateful." Perhaps there was a question in my voice. It was a very small jar.

"All you need," said the creature in its drowsy purr, then turned its masked face toward Artagan. "Every morning. Every night. And do not neglect the song."

"I'll do my best. If nothing else it will keep the two of us smiling."

"Smiling is good." Cat Mask bowed and moved back.

There was a silence, save for the trickling music of the stream, the rustle of the breeze through the trees, the chirp of a bird.

"I must bid you farewell," Ciarán said. I thought he was going to speak further, but he fell silent. He had spoken with calm composure, but his eyes told a different story. I wanted to tell him that he would be sorely missed, that we needed his wisdom back home, that what he was doing was the bravest thing I had ever seen . . . but here, before so many eyes, I hesitated, wondering if he was holding himself together by a thread so fragile it might snap at the least touch.

"Uncle Ciarán?" Finbar moved away from his newfound friends, stepping forward to take Ciarán's hands in his, in the manner of a man greeting an equal. "You're not coming back, are you? Not ever." Perhaps only I heard the slight quaver in his voice.

"That I cannot tell you, Finbar. The future holds many possibilities. For now, it's best that I remain here and do my work of mending. My people thank you for your courage and your tenacity, son of Sevenwaters. We will be forever in your debt."

Finbar bowed his head. He had no more to say. I walked up and put my arm around his shoulders. "And we in yours," I said, making myself meet Ciarán's eye, though the sadness there was hard to look upon. "This is the stuff of future tales; we will ensure it is not forgotten, Uncle."

He smiled at that. "Be happy in your choice, Maeve. And you, Artagan. Tiernan, Daigh, you have a second chance at life; use it well."

Lastly he looked at Cathal, and something passed between them without the need for words. An acknowledgment of brotherhood; a salute to courage; a recognition of momentous change. "Safe journey, son of Firinne," Ciarán said. "Greet your family from me, and walk forward with them into the light."

"Safe journey, son of Sevenwaters." Cathal choked on the words. "Your courage is a flame in our hearts."

"Come," said the hedgehog-dwarf. Turning, I saw that between the rocks was the opening to a narrow passageway, a dark slit that looked barely sufficient for the Old Ones to enter in single file, let alone a big man like Artagan or a horse. But as we followed our leader into the unpromising entry, it proved adequate to admit us all. I glanced back over my shoulder, not sure what I might see on

Ciarán's face. But he was not looking at us. Dog Mask had engaged him in earnest conversation, and a bevy of Old Ones surrounded them. Already, he had stepped into his new world.

Good-bye, brave soul, I thought, linking my arm with Artagan's, for the underground way was full of shadows. *We'll miss your stories; we'll miss your wisdom. If there is a remedy for your sorrow, I hope you find it in that strange realm.*

It was an uncomfortable passage, but not a long one. The place was not in total darkness, for here and there tiny lights glowed on the rock walls, perhaps insects, perhaps something else. In places Artagan had to stoop; once or twice Blaze balked at going forward, and it became necessary for me to murmur in her ear, to stroke her nose, to tell her we would soon be home. *Clear water. Green field. Kind hands and quiet.* She was quickly soothed.

For a while, then, I walked with Tiernan, who was leading Blaze. His silence was a wall between us, shutting off words. I thought of Badger, his wary eyes, his slowly building confidence, his tentative steps toward trust. How much had been destroyed in this time of capture and beating, of binding and release, of fire and fear and enchantment? The astonishing part of all this was not that Badger had fled on Finbar's command, but that Bear had been so brave.

"You were riding to visit your betrothed when it happened, weren't you?" I ventured. "She will be happy to see you safe home." Why was this so awkward, when talking to Artagan was like talking to my best friend?

"I hardly know her," came Tiernan's muttered response in the semi-dark of the underground way. "It is a marriage of strategic alliance. She will be pleased, I suppose, that I have survived, since that means her prospects are unchanged. But then, had I succumbed, my brother would be the heir, and she could have wed him instead. So you, too, should be glad I lived."

I attempted to absorb this speech in all its misdirected bitterness. "I am glad, Badger," I said quietly. "I'm glad because you are dear to me, as Bear is, and after all you have endured I want to see you safe and happy. More than that, I want to see you make something good of your life now that you have this second chance." When he made no answer, I said, "We should all do that. We owe it to those men who rode out with you, and who will never come home."

"It's easy for you to say." Tiernan sounded furious, though he too was keeping his voice down, mindful of the others walking before and behind us. If not for Blaze's bulk, both Artagan and Finbar would have been within earshot. "You and he—one look tells me you have something I will never have. Something that comes only once, and even then only to the luckiest, the bravest, the best. You say I should make something good of my life. But how can I, when—" He stopped himself. "Forget I spoke. I would not spoil your happiness, Maeve. Do not be concerned; I will hide these feelings away."

I could just imagine how that would be over the years, driving a wedge between brothers, setting the women of the household at constant prickly odds.

"Tiernan," I said, "I need better from you. I need a promise."

"What promise?" The tone was less than encouraging.

"Understand that I'll be honored and delighted to have you as a brother, should your father agree to my marrying Artagan. If I come to Tirconnell I'll miss my family badly. I hope that when you are wed, your wife will become a sister to me. Ciarán spoke about his work of mending. I believe we have mending to do as well. We must forge new bonds. Mend shattered families. Make better pathways for ourselves. Support and love one another. I would consider myself rich indeed if I came out of this with both a husband and a fine new brother."

"Maeve . . ."

"What?"

"Don't you ever weep, rage, curse the gods? Don't you ever feel anger or jealousy or resentment?"

"I'm no paragon. I've done my share of weeping and raging over the years. Of course I get angry." I recalled the cold fury that had possessed me when Caisin told me Mac Dara had killed my boys. "But I've learned not to devote too much time to it, since it achieves nothing."

I heard him draw a deep, shaky breath. "What would you have me promise?"

"To accept this the way it is, without bitterness. To be a good brother to both Artagan and me. And when you are married, to do your best to love and honor your wife. A strategic marriage can be happy and successful; when you meet my sister Deirdre and her husband, you will see that."

"You ask much."

"You have much to offer."

There was a long silence, during which I realized I could see a lightening of the tunnel walls ahead of us; somewhere up there, the subterranean way opened to the outside.

"Please," I said.

"Look!" exclaimed Finbar from up in front, where he was now walking beside Cathal. "We're nearly home!"

Tiernan muttered something.

"I didn't hear you," I said.

"I'm not the man you believe me to be," he said. "I am far less than my brother. But I'll try."

We emerged from the rocks to find ourselves on a rise. At the top grew a stand of young oaks; at the foot lay a round pool. Flat stones beside the water seemed to invite a weary traveler to stop and rest awhile before journeying on. Indeed, it was clear that not so long ago someone had made a fire here among the stones. I looked about me, trying to get a sense of direction.

"We're at the nemetons," said Finbar in wonder. "See those oaks? If we climb up there we'll be able to see your cottage, Maeve, and Pearl and the cows."

I opened my mouth to tell him it was not possible; we had not walked nearly far enough, even allowing for a touch of ancient magic. But I held back the words. My brother was seldom wrong. And now that I thought about it, this place did look familiar.

"You are indeed close to home," said the hedgehog-dwarf. "Here we bid you farewell. My respects to you, Mac Dara's son. We had hoped that you would stay among us. But we honor the one who offered himself in your place." The creature turned toward me. "You have brought about great change," it said, "and we will be forever grateful, daughter of Sevenwaters."

The little being in the green hat had come up to Finbar. "A gift awaits you," it said. "It is a token of our deepest respect."

"Thank you," said Finbar politely, though there was no gift in sight. "For bringing us safely home. And . . . for letting us come into your world." I heard the regret in his voice.

"Farewell, bravest of the brave," the two wee men said together. "You will see us again."

"Sons of the North," said the hedgehog-dwarf, "we are glad our transformation saved your lives; we regret the fate that overtook your companions. Learn from this journey; carry your newfound knowledge into your lives as men, for it is given to few of your kind to enter the Otherworld. Even fewer return safely. We will watch over you. Oh yes, even in Tirconnell. We are everywhere."

Cathal spoke grave words of thanks; Artagan added his own.

"I will make a song of this," Daigh told the Old Ones. "Should our paths ever cross again, I hope I may sing it by your hearth fire. Sixteen verses in perfect rhyme, and a refrain to set every foot tapping."

"That I would like to hear," said the hedgehog-dwarf. "But think twice before you seek this realm again, young man. You've been lucky. Luckier than you can imagine."

"Perhaps, under Ciarán's leadership, our realm and yours can live in amity." Tiernan surprised me; I had not thought him yet ready to speak thus.

Four sets of strange eyes regarded him. "Time will tell," said the hedgehog-dwarf. "Go now; there are many who anxiously await your return."

Finbar set off straight up the hill, perhaps eager to prove to us that home was only a hop and a step away. "Wait, Finbar!" I called, finding myself reluctant to let him out of my sight before we were safely there. Fleet-footed Daigh went after him, catching up quickly. The two of them climbed together.

I turned to bid the Old Ones farewell.

"They're gone," said Artagan, sounding bewildered.

They had vanished from one breath to the next. Even as we

stared, the entry to the underground way blurred, as if it were a dream or vision, then disappeared. Now the hillside bore no chink or crack big enough to admit more than a beetle. The little pool lay tranquil; the trees stirred gently in the breeze.

"Maeve!" shouted Finbar from the top of the rise. "Come quick!"

Speed was impossible; the hill was too steep for Blaze, and I could not climb with my arm in the sling. With Artagan's help I made my way around the rise; Tiernan led Blaze, with Cathal coming behind. We emerged from cover to find that Finbar had indeed been right, for we were looking down on the familiar cottage, the chicken coop, the dry stone walls and green fields, the—

"Swift," I breathed. "Oh, gods, Swift! He's home!"

For there he was, white as snow, lovely as moonlight, with not a scratch on him, cropping the grass alongside Pearl the goat and looking as if he'd done nothing but rest and fatten since the day we ran off through the forest and into another world. Someone had helped him; no horse could have made such a journey on his own. Someone had healed his wounds and seen him safely home.

"No tears," Artagan said. "Best put on a brave face; I see a significant welcoming party."

Until then, I'd had eyes only for my beautiful Swift. His survival was a gift beyond any I had hoped for. But now I looked past him and saw familiar figures waiting down by the cottage steps. There was Rhian, beaming. Beside her stood a young red-haired woman who might be Deirdre, but possibly wasn't, and a pair of tiny children. There were my mother and father, and there was Cruinn with tears streaming down his broad cheeks.

"Go to him," I said. "I'll wait for Finbar and Daigh."

"Are you sure—"

"Just go."

But it was Cathal who ran. His long legs carried him swiftly across the sward and along the path. The young woman—not Deirdre—sprinted toward him and flung herself into his arms. They held on as if drowning; as well they might, for Clodagh had taken an astonishing risk to come here to Sevenwaters with him.

Those tiny children, a flame-haired girl, a dark-haired wisp of a boy, must be their twins. Indeed, now Cathal was lifting the boy onto his shoulders, while Clodagh held her daughter up so her father could kiss her cheek. *Welcome home,* I thought, shivering. *So nearly, for you, there was no homecoming at all.*

Tiernan and Artagan did not run, but they strode down the hill to their father, and he came up to meet them. Cruinn tried to gather both his sons into his embrace at once, and it looked as if tears were being shed all around. I wiped my own eyes.

Daigh and Finbar were taking a long time. I glanced up the rise toward the young oaks and saw the two of them crouched down by some bushes.

"Finbar!" I called. "Come on!"

"Not yet! We haven't got him yet!"

A scuffling up there, a few words, a squeak. The two of them rose. Finbar had something in his arms. His face was ablaze with excitement.

"Maeve, look!" He came down the hill one careful step at a time, as if he were carrying new-laid eggs. Daigh walked behind. When they reached me Finbar said, "He was hiding up there; we heard him crying! He was all alone." From his cradling arms a strange little face peered up at me. The creature was as tiny as a newborn pup, but well formed; I guessed it would be small even when fully grown. It had something of the look of a fox, though no fox ever had such ears—they looked borrowed from a much larger animal. Its coat was russet, its muzzle pointed, its eyes a deep and startling blue. The tail was a neat brush.

"It's all right; you're safe now," Finbar murmured, then looked up at me, eyes shining. "Isn't he the best dog ever?"

As if in agreement, the little creature opened its mouth and gave a minuscule bark.

"That title is already taken," I said. "But yes, he has a certain something. Just the right size to smuggle into your bed, I should think." In fact, I suspected Mother would let her only son do what he wanted for a while, now that he was safely home again.

"This is the Old Ones' gift, isn't it?"

"I think so. And wisely chosen. Finbar, we'd best go; I see Mother and Father waiting."

Daigh offered his arm and we headed down. All of a sudden I was possessed by a longing to lie down on my little bed in the cottage and sleep. Greeting everyone, explaining everything, felt like more than I could manage. I, who had faced Mac Dara. I, who had faced the fire.

"Maeve!" Clodagh was here, her green eyes bright, though it was plain she had been crying. "How wonderful! You look beautiful, just as I imagined. But exhausted. And what happened to your arm? Come, let's get you inside. All of this can wait; you're putting your feet up right now." Then Rhian was on my other side, and in a twinkling of an eye I was sitting by my own hearth fire, and Rhian was boiling the kettle, and my mother and father, after embracing me and Finbar in turn, were sitting down at the table as if they were not lord and lady of Sevenwaters but any parents welcoming lost children home. On the floor at my feet was Finbar with his new treasure on his lap, and little Firinne and Ronan on either side of him, reaching with tentative baby fingers to stroke the dog's soft hair and touch its extraordinary ears.

From outside came the voices of Cruinn and his sons, approaching.

"Maeve," said Clodagh, "did I hear one of those young men say . . ."

"Lord Sean." Artagan stood in the doorway. I heard the nervous note in his voice and willed him courage. My father must see, surely, what a fine figure of a man he was, clear-eyed and strong-featured. Not to speak of his pedigree. "I am Artagan, younger son of Cruinn of Tirconnell, and I have something to ask you."

The tale was too long to be told all at once. Nor was it a story for the whole household, for some matters are not for open airing, even in a place like Sevenwaters where one learns to expect the unexpected. So it came out in bits and pieces, the most pressing first, the more difficult and disturbing later, in private. Some of it we never told. Some of it we never spoke of, save to one another.

Mother would not hear of letting me stay at the cottage, and although I would have loved its peace and quiet for a while, the presence of Artagan made returning to the keep a more welcome prospect than it might have been. I had a home; I had a place with him. It felt as if I had set down a burden and could walk forward with light feet. Maybe that was what folk meant by hope.

Father had been chieftain for a long time, since he was only sixteen, and he was practiced at making it clear he was in charge. But when he spoke to Artagan on the matter of our betrothal, I saw a crack in that mask of authority; simply, Father was so over-joyed to see Finbar and me back home safe and well, not to speak of learning that Mac Dara's reign was over, that he could not deny us. The immense strategic advantage offered by an alliance of kin-ship with Cruinn may also have played a part, of course, not to speak of a happy ending for the daughter whose plight had wracked him with unwarranted guilt for ten years. It helped that Cruinn had said yes straightaway, without reservation. After hear-ing Artagan out, Father told us he was favorably disposed to the idea and would give it due consideration. That was as good as we would get immediately, though Artagan looked a little disap-pointed. He did not know my father as I did.

While the others were preparing to return to the keep, Cruinn asked to speak with me alone. We walked down to the wall of Swift's field and stood there feeding handfuls of grass to Pearl.

"There is no way to thank you," Cruinn said. "My boys . . ."

"No need," I said. "I'm glad mine was the hearth they found. But sad so many perished; Mac Dara cast a long shadow."

"Tiernan has said his first duty, when we return to Tirconnell, will be to seek out the kinsfolk of those who died; to offer an ex-planation, as far as he can."

That would be a heavy task. It seemed Tiernan had been serious in his promise to try. "He'll need your support," I said, wondering if it were acceptable to speak to the chieftain of Tirconnell as if I were already his daughter-in-law. "He's been much hurt by this."

"I see it," Cruinn said. "As I see the strength in my younger son, and the newfound happiness."

"We've been lucky," I said, watching Swift take a graceful turn around the field. "Despite all, so lucky."

Cruinn cleared his throat. "Maeve, there's a young mare in my stable I'm sure you'd like. A gray; sweet-tempered, biddable, clever. I believe I could design a saddle that might allow you to ride alone. I'm sure it wouldn't be beyond your skills to train the mare to carry you safely. Provided the saddle allowed you to balance, you could use your legs and your voice to guide her. Unconventional, of course. But I doubt that will bother you."

"I'll certainly try," I said, thinking ahead to the time when Swift might be put to a mare, and wondering if this sweet-tempered gray might be the one. It was widely known that Cruinn had the best stables in the north. I could be supervising the birth of Swift's first offspring; I might train that foal myself. "And Swift will come with us, of course," I said, realizing my thoughts had run far ahead of themselves. For Swift had never been formally offered to Cruinn: circumstances had prevented that. "You might suggest him as a dowry."

Cruinn grinned. "I would not be so presumptuous, though Sean knows I want the creature in my stables. But *you* might; if your father is feeling the way I am today, there's nothing in all Erin he will refuse you."

Later, after we had returned to the keep, and after I had changed from my red and gold into a comfortable gown of Clodagh's, we gathered in my father's small council chamber. Between us we told the story, including the news of Ciarán's remarkable and selfless choice. Cathal spoke briefly of Ciarán's journey to seek out the daughters of Mac Dara and the way they had revealed the geis to him, one part at a time.

"How much did you know?" I asked Finbar, who was sitting between Mother and Father with the tiny dog on his knee. The wolfhounds had given the creature a cursory sniff, then decided to ignore it. "Did you know Luachan was not what he seemed? Did you know the terms of the geis and what a risk we'd have to take, all of us? What about the Disappearance?"

"Enough for now," Father said. "This will come out in time."

"It's all right." Finbar stroked the dog's sail-like ears with gentle fingers. "I don't mind saying *now*. There were lots of things I didn't know. About Bear and Badger and the little dog being men. About it being the Old Ones who changed them. And other things. When I see visions they're mixed up, like a story that has true parts and made-up parts. Like a dream, almost. I knew we'd need to be there at the end, you and me, Swift and the dogs, and Luachan, too. I saw him in a vision, pointing a knife at you and making you stand by the pole while they tied you up. I saw the fire, how close it was; I did try to warn you about that."

"I know."

"Finbar, if you suspected Luachan all along, why didn't you come straight to me, or to your mother?" Father's brow was furrowed; he looked old.

"Or, if you felt you could not confide in us, you might have spoken to Ciarán," Mother said.

Finbar glanced up at me.

"He's seven," I said. "Luachan was his tutor, and a druid; Ciarán was Luachan's superior and had recommended him for the post. Speaking out about a matter like this would be hard even for a grown man."

"I wouldn't have said anyway." Finbar spoke firmly. "Luachan was there in the vision, at the end. If I'd told, he might have been sent away, and things might not have come out the way they did. Mac Dara might still be prince of the Otherworld."

"Finbar, did you just say you knew the dogs would be there at the end?" I knew I should not ask this, not when he'd shown such remarkable courage. But I had to ask.

"I had seen them in my vision, at the stone basin. But when Caisin told me Mac Dara had killed them, I thought I might have got it wrong. And . . . it would have been worse to tell you they might not be dead, and then for it to turn out that Caisin was telling the truth all along."

I was silenced. Such self-control would be remarkable even in a druid. In a child of seven, it was astounding. I wondered what kind of man Finbar would grow up to be.

"We should take time to think on this before we speak of it again," said my father, glancing at Finbar, then at me. "You'll be weary. Cruinn, you and I have matters to discuss. We might remain here awhile, if that suits you, and join the family later for supper."

"Of course." Cruinn's eyes went to his sons, as if he could not bear to let them out of his sight. "And there's another challenge to face: getting a small army back to Tirconnell. We should depart as soon as they can be ready. We've trespassed on Lady Aisling's hospitality long enough."

Artagan and I looked at each other. The notion that one of us might go to Tirconnell while the other remained at Sevenwaters was simply unthinkable.

"What is it, Maeve?" My mother had seen the look and perhaps guessed what it meant.

I cleared my throat, not sure if I should speak up or not. After all, Father had not yet given us permission to wed. "This may seem odd to you," I said, "but while we were in the Otherworld I was tended to by a healer of the Old Ones. He—or maybe it was she—gave Artagan and me some very strict instructions, not only about my broken hand, but . . ." With the concerned eyes of my parents and sister fixed on me, I found myself unable to go on.

"The healer believed Maeve might be able to regain some movement in her fingers, with a special salve and certain exercises carried out twice a day." Artagan spoke with quiet confidence.

I expected Mother or maybe Clodagh to say what I had said, that this was impossible, that it was too late, that Liadan had already tried everything. But nobody said a word.

"We were told quite plainly that it must be Artagan who salves my hands and helps me with the exercises," I said, giving my man a smile. "Odd as that sounds, I believe it's important. Finbar was there at the time and he'll vouch for the accuracy of what I say. He'll also tell you how vital it is that this kind of thing is done in the correct way."

Finbar nodded sagely. "Bear has to do it," he said. "So he can't go back to Tirconnell. Not yet."

I was becoming disconcerted by my parents' silence. "I'm sorry to be so blunt," I went on. "I do understand why Lord Cruinn needs to head home as soon as he can. Tiernan as well. But . . ."

"I see there's much for us to discuss, Cruinn." My father rose to his feet, an indication that our council was over, and everyone else stood as well. "The rest of you had best leave us to it, or supper may be very late indeed." He sounded stern, and I wondered if I had misread his earlier mood. But as I made to leave the chamber, Artagan coming behind me, Father spoke again.

"Maeve. Artagan. Stay."

The door closed behind the others, leaving the two of us facing our fathers across the council chamber.

"Sit down," Father said, motioning us back to the bench. "You look exhausted, the pair of you. Cruinn and I still have much to talk about, details to be hammer out, formal agreements to sign and so forth. This alliance is going to change the balance in the north considerably, and not all my neighboring chieftains will like it. But that's for us to deal with. The two of you have been through an ordeal that would have turned most folk's hair white overnight. You've saved Sevenwaters. You've banished Mac Dara. I'm sure Cruinn agrees that we shouldn't keep you waiting while we argue about dowries."

"Indeed not," Cruinn said.

"Artagan," said my father, fixing his prospective son-in-law with his steady gaze, "set out for me your solution to the difficulty you spoke of earlier."

Artagan rose to his feet as if presenting a formal petition. "I understand the need for us to return home. There's nothing to stop most of the men-at-arms from heading off as soon as their equipment is packed and ready. But, Father, I respectfully suggest that you and Tiernan might consider a ride south before you head homeward."

"Go on," said Cruinn, who had clearly not been expecting this.

"You could complete the journey we were undertaking when Mac Dara's people ambushed our party. A difficult journey for Tiernan, and for Daigh, who will want to go with you."

"But important," Cruinn said slowly, "to reassure the family of Tiernan's betrothed that this catastrophe has not changed our plans. Yes, that is well considered. They would understand, I am sure, why our visit must be brief."

It would be good for Tiernan to do it, I thought; to ride that path again, and to become better acquainted with the stranger who was his future wife.

"You are not, I take it, suggesting that you lead the men-at-arms home while we ride south?" Now Cruinn looked as if he were trying not to smile.

"No, Father," Artagan said. "As we explained, it's necessary for me to tend to Maeve's hands twice a day. Should Lord Sean—should you—even if you refuse—"

"You're offering to stay on and play healer for my daughter even if I forbid the two of you to marry?" I could hear suppressed laughter in my father's voice.

Artagan stood silent for a long moment. My heart bled for him.

"I would do that, of course. But, Lord Sean, Father, I hope you will agree to our marriage. I hope I may stay here until Maeve's broken hand is healed, and we can ride to Tirconnell together as husband and wife."

"Robbing me of the daughter I have only just welcomed home after ten long years." The light tone was suddenly gone.

"It is not so far, Father," I said. "Closer than Harrowfield."

"Finbar will miss you. First he lost Sibeal, then Eilis. And this business with Luachan . . . It will have disturbed him."

"I am sad about that, too," I told him. "But . . . Clodagh is here. Might not she and Cathal stay awhile?"

"That is possible," said Father. "And we should not forget that Finbar seems to have acquired a dog. If I've learned anything from this, it is that one should never underestimate the influence of a dog." After a moment he added, "Cruinn, anything further to ask before we send this pair away?"

"You've covered it well, Sean." Cruinn favored me with a broad smile. "If uncanny healing can gain you the ability to hang on to a horse's mane, it'll be easier for you to train the mare. Good luck with it. I have to say, if my own sons hadn't told me part of the story I heard earlier, I'd have thought it pure fantasy, the product of a bard's wild imaginings. No wonder folk think this place odd. Odd doesn't begin to describe it."

"What mare?" asked Artagan.

"I'll tell you later. Father, thank you. And you, Lord Cruinn."

"Off you go," Father said. "You'd best leave us to our negotiations. Though I have to say, Cruinn, all I really want at this stage is to sit by the fire with a jug of good mead and talk about our fine children. What do you say?"

"There," said Artagan. "A pity I can't do this with the other hand until the bone is healed, but never mind that. Now I want you to try bending this finger. Just this one."

I had swallowed the draught he had prepared for me. The salving was done, the ritual of wrapping his hand around each finger in turn and singing was over. Artagan had not attempted to copy Cat Mask's humming chant. Instead, as he worked on my fingers he sang a song about an enormous trout and the ingenious ways in which local folk tried to catch the wily creature. In my opinion, his voice was quite good; I would enjoy listening each morning and evening as he tended to my hands. This did seem like touching a tree that had been burned to charcoal and willing it to run with sap and sprout fresh green leaves. But I had said I would try, and try I would.

We worked at it for some time and my mind began to wander. Artagan's touch was both strong and gentle. I thought I would enjoy his hands on other parts of my body when the time came. I imagined ways I might please him in my turn.

"That is a mysterious smile," he said. "What are you thinking?"

"Best not say. I would surely make you blush. And I hear Rhian coming back."

Rhian had been with us, since my mother had decreed Artagan could not tend to me without a chaperone present. However, my maid had tactfully absented herself to fetch us all some mead.

"Quick, then," Artagan said, bending to kiss me on the lips. I felt the touch in my whole body; it startled me so much that when he drew back, I had not a word to say.

"Now *you* are blushing," he said. "I like it; the effect with that green gown is quite fetching."

I was surprised when Clodagh appeared at the door, carrying the tray Rhian had borne off to the kitchen. "I sent your maid away for a while," she said, coming in and setting her burden down on the little table. "I wanted to talk to you."

The tray held three cups and a jug, but Artagan rose to his feet, saying, "I might see if my father has emerged from his meeting with Lord Sean." He lifted my hand and turned his lips to my palm, where the scars were. "Until later," he said, and was gone.

"A fine man," observed my sister, pouring mead for the two of us. "Well trained."

"That's a joke, I hope," I said, though it was true that Artagan, as a man, retained the good qualities he had shown as a dog, among them a quickness to learn and a finely tuned understanding of others' needs.

Clodagh came to sit beside me, smiling. "I can't believe I'm seeing you again after so long," she said. "Ten years! And yet I feel as close to you as I did then, as if we're picking up just where we left off. I wonder if it's always like that with sisters. Oh, Maeve, don't cry!"

"Stupid," I mumbled, reaching up my good hand to scrub away the sudden tears. Her ready smile, the look in her eyes, her kind words had enveloped me with warmth; they had done everything Mother's awkward overtures had failed to do when I first arrived here. "I would give you a big hug, but I can't without hurting my hand, and I'm under orders to look after it so I recover quickly. Clodagh, it is so wonderful to see you; I can't put it into words as well as you do, but it's like coming home again, only in a good way this time."

A little frown creased her brow. "It must have been hard for you. I imagine this place is full of painful memories. You were brave to come back."

"I didn't want to; I only came because of Swift. But don't tell Mother that. I've already upset her enough. I'm certain she didn't expect me to be the way I am. I'm too forthright. Too argumentative. Too ready to break rules. And I hate people being sorry for me. I couldn't pretend for her."

"She loves you," Clodagh said. "She loves all of us; we're her world. She wants to make our lives perfect, and when she can't, she feels as if she's failed as a mother. Especially so with you. I know it doesn't make much sense, since the fire was not her fault, and afterward the wise choice was to send you away where you'd get the best care. But having children is like that. Mother is good at the clear-cut things, running the household, being an example to the serving people, standing at Father's side as a chieftain's wife should. Bringing up children isn't neat and tidy. It's all feelings: love and doubt, joy and heartbreak. When you have little ones of your own you'll understand how hard it's been for her. She's doing her best."

Now felt like the time for a drink of mead. But there would be new difficulties until my broken hand had mended. "Could you lift up my goblet for me?" I asked.

My sister tilted it so I could take a mouthful.

"Thank you. Clodagh, may I ask you something?"

"Go ahead."

"You chose to come here with Cathal. To bring your children with you. Wasn't that a huge risk?"

She took her time in answering, turning her goblet between her hands. "We argued about it," she said eventually, and now her voice was constrained, as if the memory was painful. "You know, maybe, that Ciarán asked Deirdre to speak to me through our mind link. The message he wanted her to pass on was that he believed there might be a way to challenge Mac Dara. He didn't ask Cathal to come to Sevenwaters, not in so many words. But Cathal knew already that such a challenge was more likely to be successful if both he and Ciarán were present. Mac Dara's magic was powerful; too powerful for either Cathal or Ciarán alone to be sure of overcoming him. The two of them together had a good chance of doing it. Ciarán let us know he was setting out on a journey to speak to Mac Dara's daughters and that he believed he'd need Cathal's assistance quite soon."

"I understand that part," I said. "But why would you and the children need to come with him, outside the safe borders of Inis Eala?"

"Ah," said Clodagh. "That's the part you'll find easier to understand when you and Artagan have a child. I lost my temper with Deirdre, you know, when she said Cathal should come back and I shouldn't, because of the risk to my children. That wasn't a message from Ciarán; it was her own opinion. I raged at her, then broke the link. I was almost tempted to keep the whole thing from Cathal. But I told him, of course. It was his destiny to face his father. Cathal and I both believed, in our hearts, that he must eventually return to the Otherworld, defeat Mac Dara and take his place as prince there." She set down her goblet, lifting mine to let me drink again. Her gaze was very direct. "Imagine yourself in my situation," she said. "If you knew Artagan was setting out on a journey that would test him to the limit of his courage, and if you knew he was unlikely ever to return, wouldn't you want to be by his side for as long as you possibly could, helping him be brave, warming him with your body at night, letting him hold his children by the campfire and tell them stories to remember him by?"

"You have the gift for making me cry."

"Good tears," Clodagh said. "Firinne and Ronan are protected from dark magic by a pair of amulets given to Cathal at the time of their birth. I wear the ring that was his mother's. I placed trust in those things, perhaps more trust than he did. He wanted us to stay on the island. I insisted on traveling with him. Maeve, that was the best moment of my life today, when he came running down the hill, safe and sound. We owe Ciarán such a debt."

I nodded, incapable of speech.

"Finbar told me he spoke to Becan," Clodagh said. "That made me so happy."

"Becan?"

"The changeling child, the twig and leaf baby. Finbar says he's grown into a fine boy of around his own size." She paused. "As for Finbar himself, it seems he's been well and truly tested. I'm hoping you'll tell me the whole story in time, including the parts you left out of the official account."

"Like eating a freshly killed rabbit raw, with the fur still on?" I found, to my surprise, that I could share this detail with my sister quite readily.

Clodagh grimaced. "Anything you want to tell me. And I'll give you my own Otherworld story. We sisters surely lead strange lives. But you'll be forgiven now you're marrying Artagan. No parent could object to that." A pause. "Maeve?"

"Mmm? Pass me that mead again, will you?"

She held the cup for me. "Cathal and I thought we might stay here awhile. There's no reason we shouldn't divide our time between Sevenwaters and Inis Eala, as Johnny does. It would be good for Finbar." After a moment she added, "I spoke to him earlier. Finbar, I mean. He was happy with his new dog and pleased to be home, but he's been through a difficult time. And he's never going to be an ordinary child. His gift makes that impossible. Without careful watching, his abilities could set him too much apart. I think it would be good for him if one of us was here, and it plainly isn't going to be you."

"No," I said, feeling a rush of gratitude that she understood so well, "though we're hoping Mother and Father will let him stay with us at some point. Dogs, horses and rare manuscripts, I think that was what Artagan offered. We have some interesting years ahead."

"Mm-hm," said Clodagh. "No doubt of that."

We sat enjoying our mead for a while, talking of one thing or another, and I was beginning to wonder where Rhian had gotten to when she came rushing in the door, then stopped in her tracks. Clearly she'd thought Clodagh would be gone by now. Her cheeks were flushed. Quite plainly she was bursting to tell me something.

"You can talk in front of Clodagh," I said.

But Rhian remained silent. Whatever it was, it was for my ears only.

"I must go," Clodagh said, getting up. "I promised to sing a bedtime song." With that, she was gone.

"Pour yourself some mead," I said. "And tell me whatever it is. I may have been to the Otherworld, but I'm still the same person I was before. I'm still your friend."

"It's just that . . ." Rhian sat down abruptly. "I couldn't tell you this before, with other people around. While you were gone, Emrys asked me to marry him." As I opened my mouth to congratulate her, she added, "I said no."

"Oh. But I thought—"

"Lord Cruinn offered him a position at Tirconnell. Head groom, with the chance of becoming stable master in a few years if he does well. Cruinn saw Emrys working with Swift and the other horses here, and he was impressed. But I said I wouldn't go, because I needed to stay with you. And now . . ."

She really was distressed. It didn't make sense. "But, Rhian, I'll be going to Tirconnell. You were there when Artagan spoke to Father about it."

"So you really are marrying him?"

"Don't sound so surprised. This is Bear we're talking about."

"Your father said yes?"

"He did, more or less. I am most certainly going there, and I'm hoping you'll come with me. I don't see how I can manage without you. I was working up to asking, but I was afraid you'd say no. I thought you might want to go back to Harrowfield. Especially if Emrys was going, too."

"He doesn't want to, but . . ."

"Don't you *want* to marry him?"

"It's just that—well, we argued about it, and he hasn't spoken to me since, and I don't know how to put it right. What if I tell him I've changed my mind and he says it's too late?"

"He won't," I told her with perfect confidence. Nobody who had seen the way Emrys looked at Rhian could possibly believe he would turn down a second chance. But it seemed, remarkably, that she believed exactly that. "Of course he won't. Go and talk to him right now. If he sulks, tell him you're sorry and that you'll find a way to make it up to him."

She lifted her brows at me. "Oh, so you're an authority on men now?"

"Go on!" I said. "Find him and put him out of his misery. If I'm getting a happy ending, it's only fair that you have one, too."

DRUID'S JOURNEY: FULL CIRCLE

He stands within a ring of oaks. His feet touch stone; before him lies a pool of clear water, fern-fringed. His arms are stretched wide, palms up; his gaze is skyward. He makes of himself an empty vessel. He awaits the quickening flame of the spirit. He opens himself to the whispering voices of the gods.

There is no need to make vows; no need to bind himself to this long task with formal words, though the words he spoke at the basin of stone were in themselves a promise. It seems to him, now, that he has been walking toward this all his life. Yet at the same time he walks away: from the brethren who honor and respect him, from the family that, despite all, appears to love him; from memory, sweetest and cruelest of all.

He sees them in the clouds. His daughter, creature of fire and magic, difficult, angry, clever; his mother the sorceress, despised nemesis from whom he learned so much. How she would laugh if she could see him now. What would this be to her, triumph or bitter blow? Her son, a prince of the Otherworld. Her son, a druid dedicated to the path of light. Well, she is gone, and the question remains unanswered.

Niamh. The thought of her is an ache in the heart, an emptiness never to be filled. His lovely Niamh, who danced by firelight and stole his heart forever and a day. Niamh, who gave him his child. Niamh, whom his mother killed. They are woven together, the three of them, the bright and the dark. He wears them like a garment of flowering thorn.

Others have opened cracks in his long-closed heart: that remarkable child Finbar, with his wide-open eyes and soaring courage; the sisters, Clodagh, Sibeal, Maeve, each of them more extraordinary than she can ever know. Cathal, whom he has spared to live and love, to have for a lifetime what he was granted for a scant three years. It was the right choice. It was the only choice. This duty is his and his alone.

The clouds drift before the wind and the faces are gone. The druid lowers his arms; crosses his hands at his breast. He closes his eyes. Around him the circle stills. He breathes in a slow pattern. There will be challenges; there will be dissent. There will be sharp knives and sharper words. Let them come. The flame burns in his spirit and he is not afraid.